UNSUNG HEROES

UNSUNG HEROES

Elizabeth Darrell

This first world edition published in Great Britain 2001 by
SEVERN HOUSE PUBLISHERS LTD of
9–15 High Street, Sutton, Surrey SM1 1DF.
This first world edition published in the USA 2001 by
SEVERN HOUSE PUBLISHERS INC., of
595 Madison Avenue, New York, NY 10022.

British Library Cataloguing in Publication Data

Darrell, Elizabeth, 1931–
  Unsung heroes
  1. Love stories
  I. Title
  823.9'14 [F]

ISBN 0–7278–5658–8

1/09 GiFt

Typeset by Palimpsest Book Production Limited,
Polmont, Stirlingshire, Scotland.
Printed and bound in Great Britain by
MPG Books Ltd, Bodmin, Cornwall.

Acknowledgements

M y thanks are due to the Station Commander and personnel of Operations Wing, RAF Odiham, who gave me their generous and friendly assistance in researching this novel. I am especially indebted to Squadron Leader Bob Parratt MBE, Community Relations Officer, who arranged meetings, interviews, permission for me to witness aircrew in action, and who generally smoothed the way for me; and to Flight Lieutenant Paul Smyth, the station's Test Pilot, who tirelessly advised and informed me on all aspects of flying a Chinook. If any errors remain, they are mine not his. The fictional station of RAF Hampton is not RAF Odiham in disguise; neither are the characters portrayed in these pages copies of particular people I met there. However, the aerial operations are fully descriptive of the skilled and valuable work undertaken by helicopter crews in a normal year of their professional lives.

Christmas

The lush winter grass on the village green at Hampton Heyhoe was flattened by the vicious downdraught from the helicopter's twin rotors as it hovered. The entire population appeared to have turned out for the occasion. Overexcited children were restrained by mothers and teachers as a gigantic snowball was slowly winched downwards. The young ones jumped about and clapped their hands; the women holding them wore reluctant smiles as the snowball swung only feet from the ground, sparkling in pale December sunshine which shafted between the white walls of the Bird in Hand and the solid red brick offices of James and Son, solicitors. The senior villagers were ranged on the periphery, many with their hands over their ears, and all in thick coats, woollen scarves and gloves. It was bitterly cold.

The snowball came to rest. As the waiting handler unhooked it, the outer casing fell open in six segments to reveal packages wrapped in bright paper. The children shrieked in delight as they broke from hands that held them and rushed forward. Adults ran after them protectively, almost flooring the Reverend John Barstow who planned to lead them to the church hall for cocoa, biscuits and carol singing; back to more traditional Christmas activities. He did not approve of this, but the noisy aggressive military machines had become a part of local life and one had to resign oneself to putting up with them.

"Danged row!" grumbled the village misery to his neighbour. "What were the use of putting my sigature on that there pahtition Ned Stokes got up lahst June? Didern get they things sent away."

"I likes 'em," replied the nonagenarian beside him, his faded eyes brightening as they watched the Chinook gain height and angle away to the amber distance. "If I had my time agin I'd go up in one of they things. Like great big dynosores, they are."

1

"Dynosores was animals," came the contemptuous comment. "They was birds, too. Big 'uns . . . like that there Shinoo."

The teachers began handing out presents hoping there would be a gift for every child on the list they had submitted at the request of the Community Relations Officer. The RAF was trying to soothe ruffled feathers. They had laid on a festive tea and old-time dancing for the senior citizens last week and a group of volunteers had helped to collect greenery to decorate the village church. It was inevitable that a few feathers would determinedly remain ruffled.

Back at the Station two fitters setting off on leave watched the Chinook approach and were surprised to see it slow to hover above the Officers' Mess.

"What the 'ell . . ." murmured one, studying the aircraft he knew like the back of his hand.

Both men then began to laugh as from the body of the helicopter there emerged a full-sized blow-up of a naked woman with enormous attributes. This plastic beauty was lowered until she sat astride the gable over the front entrance to the Mess.

"They must've weighted her tootsies to make her sit there like that," one chuckled.

"Never mind 'er feet, get an eyeful of those Dolly Parton boobs. That's what I call real Christmas cheer."

Still laughing they settled in a muddy saloon and drove to the main gates. "Reckon he'll get a bollocking for it, Jim?" asked the driver of his mate.

"Nah, it's Christmas."

"He'll tread on official thin ice once too often."

"Not him! He was shot at in central Africa and managed to fly safely through a blizzard in Bosnia. Then there was that business in the Gulf he got a medal for. He leads a charmed life."

Flight Lieutenant Randal Ivan Price, known as "Rip" to all at Hampton, did not think his life very charmed as he looked around the tidy silent furnished house that had once been full of clutter and babies, and a wild, chaotic relationship. Picking up his bag, he turned his back on three cardboard boxes containing his personal possessions and left the home he had rented for the last four years, slamming the door with some force. Then he attacked the road in his scarlet Porsche in much the same manner.

Roaring past houses with holly wreaths on their front doors, he knew his wife would be disparaging about the inflatable sex toy he had just perched on the Officers' Mess. The Station Commander was giving a cocktail party for local dignitaries this evening but someone would pull her down before the guests arrived. The lads on duty over the holiday would have some fun with her. "So it was another of my 'bloody juvenile antics'," he growled at his absent wife, "but it's Christmas, for God's sake! Last year I was flying medicines and mealies to starving Africans and the year before I was in a snowbound tent in Bosnia, when I wasn't out flying patrols."

As he drove fast along the winding country roads of Dorset, the familiar sense of anticlimax crept through him. At thirty-three he should be able to handle with equal competence the two worlds he lived in. Yet he was a different person away from the service environment; away from those who shared it. Fiona never had. She had never even tried. Oh, she had been dewy-eyed at the start, caught up in the excitement and danger of what he was doing when Bosnia was a war zone. An extrovert, earthy pilot three days back from helping to evacuate a doomed blazing town had been a hero to a nineteen-year-old whose parents owned racehorses and a prestigious stud.

The slender blonde with big eyes and long sexy legs had been standing beside a cream MG gazing helplessly at a very flat tyre when Randal rounded a bend and swerved into a hedge to avoid a collision. She had been flatteringly concerned for his safety; he had changed the tyre, bought her a drink in the next pub then asked for a date, all in quick succession. They had married six months later when Randal returned from a NATO exercise in Norway. Her parents had not approved: his had said all the right things and carried on with their busy lives.

Neil had been born nine months after their showy society wedding. Lydia had entered the world prematurely eighteen months later while her father was flying home from Egypt, but Randal's delight on seeing his tiny daughter had been ruined by his wife's overwrought charge that he was never there when she most needed him.

Fiona's discontent had increased and, several months after Lydia's first birthday, she had taken the children to the stud while she "thought things over". When she returned alone saying that she and her parents felt the children needed a period of stability, Randal's anger had driven him to fetch Neil and Lydia that same evening. What he said to his parents-in-law had alienated him from them completely. Fiona had cried a lot during the following weeks and Randal had had no idea what to do to mend the situation.

He was still grappling with the problem when he departed for another stint in Northern Ireland. All that had awaited him six weeks later was a letter saying Fiona had taken the children and all her things to Marylands. She begged him to see that their marriage could no longer continue under such pressure. The children needed the assurance and protection of a normal family life, which they would get with their grandparents. They all needed time to readjust, but he was free to visit whenever he wished as long as he behaved in a reasonable manner. The children had been upset enough.

Amazingly, he had not gone on a pub crawl. Stunned and sober, he had sat throughout the evening and half the night staring into space unable to believe what had happened. After little more than four years his beautiful sexy wife had given up on him; she had thrown in the towel at the end of the first round. Where did he go from here?

Raised to wealth, mixing with the cream of the racing set, Fiona had hated service life. She did not generally find it hard to make friends, nor had she a difficult personality: she was a warm wonderful girl full of fun. With her horsey friends she shone brightly, but the glow died whenever she met up with Randal's boisterous crowd.

All these thoughts churned around in his head as he drove to Marylands on the afternoon of Christmas Eve. Frost was already glistening on the road when he passed through the last village, and the moon was so huge it appeared to be just over the next rise. The sky was incredibly clear with the stars at their brightest. He suddenly longed to be up there seeing the moon-washed earth gliding past his feet. He had never been able to explain to Fiona his exultation when flying; probably because he was not good at voicing his deeper feelings.

Sighing, he turned the Porsche on to the long tree-lined drive leading to the home of his in-laws, Gerald and Mary Holland. Tonight how was he going to express adequately all he wanted to say? Reaching the house, he swore at the sight of a line of cars already parked there. Lights shone from the numerous long windows; dinner-jacketed men, and women in party glitter crowded the two large front-facing rooms. A horsey mob high on cocktails! Why the hell had he not guessed there would be festive high jinks here tonight?

The housekeeper let him in without a smile. "I'll tell Miss Fiona you're here."

"It's *Mrs* Fiona," he said to the woman's back. "And I'll wait in the breakfast room."

He crossed the hall to a spacious room seldom used by just the family. Whenever he had stayed overnight there were house guests – owners or trainers having breakfast – and talk was all of horses. It was inevitable in such a house. Tonight he had the room to himself. To pass the time he glanced at some of the Christmas cards arranged in decorative strips down the walls and was surprised to see one announcing seasons greetings from Hartley and Rhona Price. His parents could not know the present situation – he certainly had not told them – but it would have made little difference, he realised. The secretary responsible for sending out Christmas cards had a list of names which she continued to use until told to strike one off. The Hollands almost certainly used the same system. Whatever their offspring did, parents would observe the formalities.

The door opened and Randal turned swiftly. Fiona looked sensational in a black spangled dress reaching to mid thigh. Her hair had been cut very short so that it hung in an oblique fringe half-covering one eye. Her summer tan had faded during the time they had been apart and her eyes looked sharply blue against her pale skin. The children stood each side of her in fluffy dressing gowns. They gazed at him wide-eyed. His wife did the same.

"Hi," he said, filled with the pain of missing them.

"It's past their bedtime, Randal. I expected you earlier than this," Fiona said curtly. Uncertainty always made her sharp.

"You know me. Totally unreliable." It was not at all what he wanted to say to her.

She looked down at the children. "Say hallo to Daddy."

They remained silent. Feeling his way, Randal indicated the two gift-wrapped parcels he had put on the table. "Father Christmas thought you were living at home and brought presents. I promised him I'd bring them to you."

"He doesn't come until after midnight," said the pedantic Neil, nevertheless eyeing the parcels with interest.

"Fa Kissmuss," chanted Lydia, toddling forward with hands eagerly outstretched.

Randal squatted to take her in his arms. She smelled of baby powder and the sweet warmth of children recently bathed. He swallowed the lump in his throat as he kissed her chubby cheek and stood up holding her close. "Hallo, sweetheart, how's my little princess? Shall we see what's in the parcel?" He sat her on the polished table and gave her the long box wrapped in bright pink tissue. They tore the paper off together. He could not wait for her expression when she saw the doll he had bought in Germany. Only when she dragged it from the box did he realise it was almost as big as Lydia, but his daughter's round-eyed wonder was all he had hoped it would be and he laughed with pleasure.

Fiona moved up to him, Neil still close beside her. "It's beautiful, Randal, but she's far too young to appreciate it. I'll put it away for a year or so. She'll pull off its hair and poke out the eyes. And that pretty dirndl wouldn't last five minutes in her hands."

Randal's merriment died. "All right; I didn't think. But try taking it away and you'll get tantrums."

"She doesn't have them any more." It was said quietly enough, but he got the message loud and clear. "Aren't you going to open your parcel, Neil?" she added.

"I suppose so." The boy took the box covered in red with galactic symbols. He unwrapped it with great care so that he would not tear the paper. He had always been amazingly tidy. There was a moment of silence when he saw the large, sleek, radio-controlled space car with flashing lights and recorded messages from crew to base.

"I've already got one. Grandpa bought it for me when we went to Hamleys last week."

"Well, whacko for Grandpa!" Randal said harshly.

Fiona frowned at him. "Daddy wasn't to know you'd . . ."

"No, there's not much about me he does know, except what he chooses to think. I'll swap the damn thing for something Grandpa *hasn't* bought my son."

"Randal . . . please!"

"Please nothing!" It was all going wrong, as usual. "I didn't come here simply to give my children unsuitable presents, I came to talk to you about this stupid situation."

"It's taken you long enough! We've been here almost three months."

"I was in Northern Ireland for the first six weeks. You left a letter to welcome me back, remember?" When she failed to rise to that, he added, "You said you needed time. I gave you some. Then the Flight was away until last Sunday, when I left that message on your answer machine."

Her mouth twisted. "I might have guessed you'd been off again, having fun while I've been dealing with all this."

"It's not all fun," he countered, trying in vain to keep the heat from his voice. "We've been helping out in Poland. There were old people and women with young children clinging to rooftops in bitter temperatures. They had nothing to keep them warm. Nothing to eat or drink. Everything they owned was under the flood water. Over thirty people drowned and the livestock were just carcases floating past. No one was having a hell of a good time there, I promise you."

Fiona gazed at him for a moment or two, her expression unfathomable. "I'll take the children up to the au pair," she said quietly. "Then we'll talk, if you think it'll do any good." She squeezed Neil's shoulder. "Say goodnight to Daddy."

"Are you staying here with us now?" the boy asked hopefully.

Randal squatted again and took his son's arms in a gentle grip. "Mummy and I are going to talk about that. I've missed you, Superman . . . and so have your mates at Hampton."

The square face very much like his own regarded Randal solemnly. "Grandpa is teaching me to ride a horse. I like them better than Superman." Screwing his forehead into a frown he blurted out, "Dad, I like it here better than the other house. Mummy laughs now."

Randal broke contact and stood up, unable to deal with that. "I'll get Father Christmas to change the car for something else."

"It doesn't matter," said the boy whose grandparents gave him anything he asked for.

Lydia was happy to be kissed goodnight by the father she knew less well than she knew Grandpa, but this "Daddy" man had given her a lovely dolly and she already knew that kisses and cuddles often got her more presents. However, when she was taken from his arms and the dolly was taken from hers she registered her protest.

"I thought you said she didn't have tantrums," said Randal as Lydia was carried off.

Fiona threw him a look over her shoulder. "You're here!"

Oh, God, nothing's changed, he thought as he gazed at the closed door. While Lydia's screams grew fainter, he took a bottle of Chablis from several cases on the floor and opened it to pour himself a glass. The Hollands did not have beer at Marylands but right now Randal needed alcoholic stimulus of some kind before the next round. Was that what their marriage had come to: a sparring match without actual physical blows?

Fiona returned in red velvet that left her shoulders bare. "She was sick over me. She always gets so worked up." She poured herself some wine. "That black dress cost a fortune."

"I know. I bought it."

She paused momentarily, her glass halfway to her lips. "So you did. I'd forgotten."

"You seem to have forgotten rather a lot."

She ignored that. "Sorry about the presents."

"I brought one for you, too," he said, reaching into his pocket for a small box. "I hope it's more successful than the others."

Taking no notice of the gift he held out, her expression was full of distress. "It's no use pretending nothing's happened. I meant what I said in my letter."

"I know. Come back to Hampton and we'll sort it out."

"We tried three times and couldn't," she cried.

He tossed the jeweller's box on the table angrily. "So we just go our separate ways? It was fun for a while but it's time to send in the clowns? Oh no, I'm not letting your bloody parents take over my kids . . . or my wife!"

She put her glass down beside the velvet box with some force. "You're always the same. We can't discuss things calmly. Whenever we argued at Hampton you began shouting. The children were starting to be afraid of you. That's why I brought them here."

"Afraid of me?" he demanded, shaken. "I *love* them, for God's sake. I've never done anything to frighten them. What the hell have you told everyone here? That I'm a monster?"

"Of course not," she cried defensively. "It's just that . . . oh, what's the use? You'd never understand."

"Not that corny line again!" he exploded. "I've tried my damnedest to understand for four years." He drained his glass and refilled it while he tried to keep control of his temper. Then he swung back to face her. "I tried to understand why you wouldn't mix with other aircrew wives and why you refused to take part in station activities. I tried to understand your indifference when I talked about the job." He took a gulp from his glass then waved it wildly in her direction. "I tried even harder to understand why every time I went away you came here until I got back. I suppose you were rehearsing for this," he finished heatedly.

"This is exactly why the children were getting nervy when you were with us. You're so damned aggressive when we argue," she cried, turning away from him.

"I'm aggressive when we make love. You never complain then." He put down his glass and went to her, sliding his arms round her waist and saying against her hair, "That house is so bloody silent without you three. For God's sake come back. We'll work it out, I promise. Other people do."

She turned slowly, not attempting to break free but resistant to him. "We're not other people, we're us . . . and we can't seem to work it out however much we talk about it."

"Then let's not talk," he said, pushing her expensive haircut free of the eye it almost covered and kissing her hard.

She pulled away. "That's never solved the problem, only made it worse."

Wanting her badly, longing to talk her into accepting a compromise, he perched on the edge of the table with a sigh. "I thought the trouble was that I'm away too often. How does my being close to you make things worse?"

"You know damn well."

"Because that's how you want it to be all the time? I gave you a rundown of what your life would be like married to me. Why did you accept it?"

"You know damn well," she said again.

"But you no longer lust after me?"

She was angry. "Why do you have to make a joke of everything?"

"That wasn't a joke. If you felt anything deeper than lust we wouldn't be having this discussion. We'd be at Hampton decorating a tree and playing games with the kids."

"I'd be doing that. *You'd* be in the bar with the boys."

He gave her a straight look. "That's always been a problem with you, hasn't it?"

9

"And with you it's been my closeness to Mummy and Daddy."

"Well, you're here with them and I'm not in a bar with the boys. Doesn't that tell you something?"

"They're all on Christmas leave."

"Oh, for God's sake!" he exclaimed, getting to his feet. "You don't give an inch, do you? Look, are you coming back to Hampton?"

"No . . . I don't know," she said wretchedly.

"I'm not messing around like this indefinitely. You're my wife and those two upstairs are *my* kids." His voice rose again. "I was at home and far enough from a bar to father them, wasn't I?"

"Don't shout," she begged. "They'll hear you in the next room."

"Ha!" he said derisively. "They're all having too much of a bloody good time to hear anything but their own egos talking."

He was wrong. The door opened and Gerald Holland stood there. "Are you all right, Fiona?"

"No, she's been dragged away from her husband and home by her self-righteous parents," Randal snapped. "I told you last time to stop interfering in our marriage."

"Do you want me to make him leave, my dear?" her father asked Fiona in coldly furious tones.

"No, Daddy, it's OK. I'll join you all shortly."

He was not happy. "You don't have to put up with bullying. You have right on your side."

"Please, Daddy, I'll come soon," she repeated.

With great reluctance the owner of the house withdrew with a final word. "I'm just across the hall if you need me."

Fiona's bully of a husband took her in his arms. "Sorry, Fee. I didn't want a confrontation. He bloody created one."

"He's upset over all this."

"You think I'm not? I went through hell the night I got back and found your letter." He held her tighter. "Running from me isn't the answer and you know it."

"What is?" she asked in despair, drawing back to plead with him.

He brushed her forehead with his lips. "Come down to the pub with me now and we'll talk it over – away from that mob across the hall." Sensing surrender as she began to respond to his persuasion with a touch of her former passion, he murmured, "Better get a coat. It's cold outside and your sexy shoulders are bare."

He had her halfway to the door when she drew up and shook her head miserably. "It's no use. If I went off without a word they'd think . . ." She turned her troubled eyes up to his. "It would just create a scene when I got back."

Randal's anger returned in a rush. He released her and moved away. "Let's have a scene now, then, if you're so damned scared of them you won't make any effort to put things right between us. There's no way I'll leave the RAF."

"I don't want you to leave," she countered with the weariness of constant repetition. "I want you to transfer to a job that won't mean you're away more often than you're at home. The children hardly know you're their father."

"That's because they're whisked off to Gran and Grandpa the minute I take off. If you'd only stay at Hampton in my absence and talk to them about me, and if you'd let them mix with the other kids whose fathers come and go they'd get the hang of life and accept it. You want me to transfer to a job behind a desk. Yes, that's what it would amount to if I'm to stay put somewhere. I'll have to face that sooner or later, but if I did it now you wouldn't be happy because I'd be resentful. Like hell I'd be resentful! I won't give up flying until I'm forced to. I'm bloody good at it and I love it."

"More than you love me and the children!"

He gave her a long look. "That's unfair."

"Yes, but you'll never see it," she cried passionately.

He walked out. There was no point in staying. The party clamour was growing even louder, so no one would have heard the door slam or the engine roar as he drove away. He had been an almighty fool to have gone there.

When he had calmed down a little he began to notice his surroundings, and he drew up outside a pub called The Crooked Sixpence. It was just the place. Everything looked crooked to him right now. There was a jolly crowd in the bar, mostly farming folk and a group of the younger green-wellie brigade, and there were twinkling lights on a Christmas tree beside a roaring log fire.

The landlord and two women behind the bar wore Santa headgear. The extrovert regulars sported paper hats and Father

11

Christmas ties or socks. The young girls defied the chill and wore very little, which Randal appreciated along with the other men. A sprig of mistletoe was centrally hung and, after a few beers, Randal managed to kiss more than a few willing girls. He was having a good time. He *was* having a good time, dammit!

The party continued until the landlord rang a large brass bell. The clang reverberated in Randal's head like a complete carillon, and it was then he realised he had nowhere to go; no home and family waiting to welcome him. He had not seen his parents since his wedding; he had no wish to see them now. Baby Price had been reared by a nursery nurse; Price junior had been a boarder at a preparatory school; Price senior had been a boarder at college and then university. When mature Price had turned his back on the family business and joined the RAF, the frailest of bonds had dropped away unremarked by parents or son. No, there was no home to go to and, in any case, he would far rather stay in this present cosy place where everyone was his friend.

Crossing with exaggerated care to the plump landlord whose nose was now as red as his Santa hat, Randal said he wanted a room for the night.

"Lord, sir, it's Christmas Eve! My rooms were all booked weeks ago," he said jovially. "You won't get one for love nor money anywhere at this late stage."

No bloody room at the inn? Randal thought about that for a moment and then leaned confidentially across the bar. "Have you a stable, by any chance? Big enough for three kings, three wise men and a . . . and a flock of shepherds?" He grinned broadly. "I think I'm about to give birth."

The jolly fat man thought it very funny, too. Then a firm voice said, "He can't drive anywhere in that state, especially in a red danger machine like that one outside. I'll take him back with me, Jim. That'll be best. Can't leave the poor devil wandering about on Christmas Eve with nowhere to go."

The landlord laughed. "He'll have a shock when he sobers up."

"I dare say. Well, Merry Christmas, Jim."

"And you, George. Don't let the little 'uns get you up too early."

Randal appeared to have found a friend and a room for the night. He went cheerfully arm in arm with the man along a dark narrow street to a cottage with a holly wreath on the door and a lamp above it. The room was small and held nothing but a bed. He was given a pillow and some blankets after being shown a basic toilet and was soon asleep.

Bright light woke him. He stretched his stiff limbs and tried to work out where he was. The open door was thick with a grille at eye level. There were bars over the window where daylight was streaming in. How the hell had he landed in a cell? Well, he had slept in worse places. He got to his feet and looked from the window. It was snowing hard and the sky looked full of it.

"Bloody Christmas!" he breathed.

"It's snowing and he's been! Wake up, Auntie, he's *been!*"

Maggie Spencer reluctantly came from sleep as young voices chorused in her ears. Small knees and elbows were only prevented from inflicting pain by the thickness of her quilt tucked tightly around her body. She groaned softly. Christmas morning, and excited nieces and nephews! Gone was her hope of a luxurious wallow knowing duty did not call; no sleeping in until hunger drove her downstairs for breakfast.

"All right, all *right*," she muttered sleepily. "I'll come, but you'd better get beside the tree before someone else opens your presents."

They all rushed away at that prospect, but Maggie knew it was pointless to succumb to the warm lure of her bed. They would be back if she failed to appear. Five minutes later she joined her three brothers, their wives, Granny and Grandpa, every one of them yawning and dressing-gowned as she was.

Flopping in a chair, she complained, "They're not my children. I don't see why I should get up in the middle of the night to watch them open their presents."

"It's good practice for when you abandon that flying nonsense and settle for being a mum instead," said her twin brother Phil, with a sly grin.

"Get stuffed," she said, snuggling against a cushion in the hope of drifting back to sleep.

Granny, overpoweringly feminine in a pink velvet gown and fluffy mules, said, "Why you want to turn your back on your natural role and pretend to be a man by flying one of those great noisy filthy things I'll never understand."

"You've been trying to for five years, Mum. Give up the unequal struggle," said Phil, throwing Maggie an apologetic look for starting their mother on her hobby horse. "Let's open the parcels, then we can all fight for the bathrooms and decide what we'll have for breakfast. Come on, Dad, muster the kids into an orderly platoon and hand out the presents."

Amid the usual family chaffing and exaggerated oohs and ahs, the gifts stacked beneath the tree were distributed and opened. Maggie had been given silk undies, compact discs, perfume, books, chocolates and various indeterminate objects made by the children, but her best present that Christmas was promotion to Flight Lieutenant and a posting to an operational squadron based near the quaintly named Dorset village of Hampton Heyhoe.

It had taken her almost six years of intense study, fear of failure and fierce competition to reach her goal. There had been setbacks, disappointments and a certain amount of resistance from the male majority, many of whom shared her mother's view that she was pretending to be one of them. Maggie had no desire to be a man – by pretence or by any other means – but she had a burning ambition to be a pilot and the RAF had made her into one at the taxpayers' expense.

Breakfast at the Spencer home was a do-it-yourself affair. It had to be with nine adults and five children around the table. Maggie was given the job of making toast by the rackful until she eventually protested above the din, "Hey, when's someone else taking this on? At this rate I'll never get around to eating any."

"Phone!" announced one of her sisters-in-law busily feeding a toddler in a high chair.

"I'll go," offered Maggie's oldest brother, but he was soon back. "Don't think you're going to eat that slice of toast, Mags. Your boyfriend Jumbo is on the line."

"Don't call him that," she said, taking the toast with her because it would surely have disappeared the minute her back was turned.

"What can he expect with a name like Ellevan?"

"I bet they called him Jumbo at school," shouted Robin, her middle brother.

In the hall Maggie picked up the receiver. "Merry Christmas, Craig. There's nothing wrong, is there?"

"Sorry, honey, I won't be able to get to you today after all."

14

"Is the snow that bad?" she asked in surprise. "Whereabouts are you?"

"Kai Tak airport."

"You're in *Hong Kong*?"

"There was an emergency conference here. P.J. had already flown to Detroit and Eriksonn was in the hospital with a bust appendix. I had to come. But I should have flown back last night. Would you believe there's a goddam strike that grounded everything here? Apologise to your folks for me. I'm really sorry."

Maggie leaned back against the wall and watched the snow drifting down outside. "I'm sorry, too. What rotten luck. Anyway, it's pretty chaotic here. I'm not sure you'd have enjoyed your introduction to a real English family Christmas."

"I'd have *loved* it. Why don't we get together for New Year instead?"

"I won't be here. I've got a squadron at last," she said, unable to keep the excitement from her voice. "I'm joining it down on the Dorset coast on the twenty-ninth."

"Hell!" There was a pause. "I guess I could get there. After this, PJ should give me a decent break. I'll book a hotel room and we'll celebrate."

"Celebrate what?" she asked cautiously.

"Anything you like. Anything I like. Who knows after a few glasses of champagne?"

"Craig, I'll probably be on duty. Flying. I won't be able to spend time with you, and your hotel is more likely to be a slightly twee pub in the middle of nowhere. Dorset is glorious in the summer but I wouldn't recommend it in winter to someone used to five-star comfort and every luxury."

There was a brief silence. "I can take a knock or two – broke a leg on the downhill at Val d'Isère two years ago, if you recall."

"Oops, I stand rebuked. But honestly, I don't think it's worth the risk of getting snowed in at Hampton Heyhoe."

"*Where*?"

"It's one of those funny English names you like so much."

"And you're one of those funny English *girls* I like so much."

Her smile vanished. "Why don't we wait until I get leave? We could meet in London and do a show or two."

There was a longer pause before he said," This isn't working out, is it?"

"Not the way you want it to," she told him quietly. "I did warn you at the start."

"The start was in Germany six months ago. After our week in Salzburg I thought we'd crossed that bridge." At her silence he asked, "Have you met someone else?"

She stalled. "I've met a lot of people."

"Then it's your goddam career."

"Or *your* goddam career! You're in Hong Kong when you should be here."

"OK, OK," he said testily. "I'll call you when I get back."

"Yes, do. I'm really sorry you're stuck out there."

"Yeah! Merry Christmas." The line went dead.

After breakfast the fathers took their children to play snowballs in the garden while the women set about preparing the large meal to be served when the overtired overexcited youngsters had been put to bed. With three sisters-in-law and a mother all talking recipes in the kitchen Maggie opted to set on the table the best silver, crystal glasses, festive place mats, gold-trimmed crackers and a centrepiece of red ribbons and gilded fir cones. What would Craig have thought of all this? He had grown up in the super ski resort of Aspen, in Colorado.

Finishing her task, Maggie went to the patio doors to watch the antics in the garden. Grandpa was now being pelted with handfuls of snow by the children; her brothers were conducting icy warfare against each other. She smiled. It was good to belong to a large family. Her father, a country solicitor, had won an MC in the desert campaign against Rommel and, on being demobbed, had been a star in a water-polo team as well as a champion swimmer for the county. He always joked that the desert had made him over fond of water.

Of her brothers, Charles, an accountant, got his thrills from potholing. Robin, a doctor, climbed mountains; when he was not scrambling up the peaks in Cumbria he was in Tibet, South America or the Alps. Philip ran a boatyard building racing craft. He was happiest hanging over the side of a yacht in a stiff breeze, fighting the elements. The Spencers were an outgoing physical breed. Why did people raise their eyebrows because Maggie was the same?

Putting on her padded anorak she joined the snowball battle

and was soon shrieking with laughter and as wet as the others. The fun ended when one child grew too boisterous. There were tumbles and tears before Grandpa and the two dads chivvied their offspring indoors to play a quieter game, leaving Maggie and Phil alone. They had not met up for some time but their bond of twinship overrode absences, and they telephoned each other every week from wherever they happened to be. Phil's wife, Fay, still resented it after twelve months of marriage.

"They'll never last the day out if Charles and Rob get them so wound up," Maggie said, watching the last child being divested of his red wellingtons. "Dad's just as bad."

"We're all still little boys at heart. The kids are just an excuse," Phil said, turning a laughing face towards her. "It's great."

In that moment, Maggie sensed his secret and blurted it out. "You're having a baby – you and Fay!"

He nodded happily. "I should have guessed you'd know before we announced it."

"You didn't wait long." Maggie turned away, deeply upset. It had been difficult enough to accept a third person entering their special world. A fourth would take her twin even further from her.

He moved round to look at her. "It won't change *us*, Mags. You're my other half and always will be. That's different from any other relationship. Be happy for me."

"I am," she said to the snow-laden shrubs.

"Liar!"

"When are you going to tell the others?"

"Not just yet. Fay wants it to be our secret for a while."

Maggie looked back at him. "She won't like me knowing."

"We'll keep quiet, then. I'm as pleased as punch. When she told me the doc's verdict I wanted to shout it from the rooftops."

"Did you?" She knew it sounded bleak, but that was how she felt about it.

Philip put his hands on her shoulders. "Come on, cheer up. You'll be his favourite aunt because there'll be something of us both in his character, as well as something of Fay."

"How do you know it'll be a boy?"

He grinned. "It might be twins."

"Two more little monsters around the table next Christmas? Mum'll be thrilled."

"I was hoping you'd be," he said quietly.

"I am, Phil. If you are, then of course I am. That goes without saying." Slipping her arm through his, she said, "Let's walk. I'm getting chilly."

It was a long garden with an orchard and several large greenhouses. They strolled in silence, making footprints in the virgin snow, until Phil said, "Pity about poor old Craig: stuck in Hong Kong when he could be here."

"He'll have a good time. An American executive with an unrestricted expense account and all those almond-eyed girls in tight-fitting dresses."

Her brother glanced at her. "He's like that, is he?"

"No. I was just being flippant. He's nice. But he's getting too serious."

They walked on through the orchard where snow lay along the dark branches of the fruit trees. "He's not the man for you, Mags," Philip said with complete conviction. "I'll tell you when the right bloke crosses your horizon."

She laughed. "Thanks, but I'm not looking for anyone to cross my horizon at the moment."

"I know. You're dead set on making Air Vice-Marshal."

"Idiot!"

"Keep me updated."

"Haven't I always? This'll be my first real test, because I'm joining an operational squadron available for any emergency anywhere in the world." She glanced at him knowing he would understand as no one else in her family did. "Flying's like a drug. I can't get enough of it. You know that sense of elation when you're out on a rising sea with a storm threatening, and you outwit the elements with knowledge and experience to bring your boat safely back to the marina? That's how I feel at the controls of a helicopter."

She halted to study the brother whose narrow features and long-lashed green eyes so closely resembled her own and words poured from her. "It feels so *right* the moment I enter the cockpit. There's this large complicated machine sitting there waiting for me to make it come alive. When it does, so do I, Phil. *So do I.*"

"I wondered where you two had got to," said a sharp voice, breaking into Maggie's enthusiastic thoughts of her professional world. "Talking secrets again!"

Phil turned immediately. Fay's dark sultry attraction was marred by a scowl and eyes full of suspicion. "Come and share them," he invited lightly. "Maggie's telling me what it's like to climb into a helicopter and make it do whatever she wants. It's fascinating."

His wife was not appeased. "I suppose *you'll* be learning to fly now!"

"No fear." He laughed. "On the water you can always swim for it but they don't even wear parachutes in helicopters."

Fay studied Maggie intently for a few moments then rounded on Phil. "You told her, didn't you?"

"She guessed," he said, knowing lying would be useless.

Fay was livid. "We can't share one bloody thing without *her* being part of it! I suppose you'll want her beside you when I'm giving birth. After this, I'm not sure I want *you* there." She was overwrought in her jealous anger. "I'm not even sure I want this damned kid!" Turning on her heel Fay began to run towards the house. When she neared it she cried out, "Listen everyone, I'm pregnant. I'm *pregnant!*"

Maggie saw her twin's expression. "You'd better go to her. I'm sorry, Phil."

He hesitated, still watching his wife vanishing from sight. "She finds it hard to understand our mental telepathy. It isn't something I can explain to her – to anyone who isn't like us." He looked back at Maggie. "Come to that, you don't really understand that I can share with her things you have no part in. I'm between the devil and the deep blue sea with you two." He walked away moodily. "Bloody Christmas! Something invariably happens to cause friction."

Maggie watched him until he, too, went indoors. In twenty-five years there had never before been friction between herself and the person she was closest to in all the world. Standing ankle-deep in snow with more falling from a leaden sky, she felt unbearably bereft.

Dave Ashmore skied down the last stretch towards the house thanking God Christmas was almost over. Tomorrow he would head south and slowly work his way towards Hampton Heyhoe where he would join 646 Squadron two days before Hogmanay. There remained only today to get through. He would bloody well show them he could take anything life threw at him.

Fresh snow had fallen during the night. The dawn sky was clear and beautiful. Perfect weather for a Boxing Day wedding in the private chapel of a sixteenth-century castle in the Highlands. It would be, he thought bitterly. The whole affair would be perfect; his great-uncle would see to that. Major General Sir Hector Rowan would be resplendent in his kilted uniform hung with medals. The bridegroom, grandson Dougal, would also wear the kilt; although his military tunic had yet to gain medals, it was a foregone conclusion that they would soon appear. The best man and half the congregation would be in uniforms bearing pips, crowns or laurel wreaths on their epaulettes; officers and gentlemen, the whole stiff-necked lot. As for the bride, she would look stunningly gorgeous, docile and serene; not in the least like a dedicated social climber who had rejected her lover the moment the going got rough.

Dave left his skis in the rack and entered the kitchen. He hoped to reach his room via the servants' stairs, with a mug of tea and a hot bannock. Mrs McRitchie had always had a soft spot for him and she understood more than she let on. Not that he wanted any sympathy from her.

Up in his room Dave drank the welcome tea and munched the bannock he had scrounged from the maid, Ethel, as he gazed from his mullioned window. He had been delivered to the castle at the age of four. The offspring of an unequal union, he was taken in and reared with the heir and his two sisters. There had been no hint of charity. Sir Hector had dutifully welcomed the child, and so had widowed Aunt Mairie. Dave's cousins had initially been friendly enough, but Dougal soon began treating him with contempt. The girls had pitied him. It had bred in him a fierce desire to achieve.

Over the years he had studied and played hard to fulfil that desire. The row of sporting trophies in this room bore witness to the fact that he had played harder than he studied, but he had still gained a place at a redbrick university. Dougal went up to Cambridge, and Sir Hector had made rather a point of the difference to Dave.

While Dougal diligently worked his way to a first class honours degree in modern languages, Dave had struggled towards engineering qualifications while devoting a lot of time to rugby, wind surfing, squash, mountaineering and rifle shooting. It was when he was persuaded by a friend to try hang gliding that Dave knew he did not want a career in the family regiment. He wanted to fly.

Between leaving university and taking up the place at Cranwell offered by an RAF selection board, Dave indulged himself in the sporting pastimes he loved. It seemed particularly ironic, therefore, that it should be a traffic accident rather than sport that finally caused an injury.

He had travelled to Lincoln on the day before he was due to report to Cranwell and booked a room for the night in a guest house. He was shopping for toothpaste and torch batteries when a motor cyclist raced round a corner, swerved to miss an old man crossing the street and mounted the pavement. Dave twisted violently to avoid being hit but lost his balance and fell. From the pain shooting through him when he moved, he knew he had pulled more than one muscle. An ambulance took him and the injured rider to a nearby casualty department. Two hours later, Dave was sent along to the X-ray department where a girl in a white coat told him to take off his shirt. An overwhelming urge to take off *all* his clothes for her rushed through him, leaving him unnerved. She was red-haired, green-eyed, about his own age and, the moment her hands touched his bare skin, all remaining rational thought fled.

Girls had not featured strongly in Dave's life. There had been one-night stands after rugby matches, but sport left little time or inclination for ongoing relationships. Overpowering sexual attraction hit Dave for the first time, and hit hard. Desire for Leanne became a fever. He skipped private study periods in order to meet her; during lectures and outdoor training his concentration wandered to thoughts of their next meeting. He bought a second-hand motorbike so that he could rocket to Lincoln and back to spend even an hour with her.

The fever had not abated when the cadets were given leave halfway through their course, and Leanne persuaded Dave to take her to Scotland to see his castle home which had so caught her imagination. Dougal was on leave from Sandhurst and his reaction to Leanne told Dave he had finally gone one up on his cousin.

After the visit, Leanne had coaxed an engagement ring from her lover. Dave was then twenty-two and until then marriage had not been even a distant consideration, but he was so dazzled he agreed to all Leanne wanted. Yet he was subconsciously deeply

21

unsettled over the commitment he had made and how it would affect his career as a pilot.

Three weeks later, he had been called for interview and asked why his work and attitude had dramatically deteriorated. He was so shaken by the warning that unless he pulled himself together he would be considered unfit to remain at Cranwell that he swore to improve immediately and applied himself to work while trying to douse the fire within. The fact that Leanne seemed content with fewer meetings caused him some pain but his dedication to study paid off. He was commissioned as a pilot officer and received muted congratulations from Sir Hector.

The sting in the tail came immediately: he was not listed for flying training but instead posted to the personnel department of a transport squadron. A desk job! It was a terrible blow. He had missed his opportunity; thrown away what surely should have been within his grasp. He must have been crazy to think he could walk through a demanding course without working as hard as everyone else. It was the first time that something he badly wanted had not come easily to him.

Pilot Officer Ashmore had served behind his desk for almost a year, eating his heart out while watching young men like himself taking off and landing daily. He heard them talking in the Mess and was caught up in their enthusiasm for flying but he was on the outside looking in. His unhappiness was deepened by being stationed so far from his fiancée and by Leanne's cool response when they did meet.

When his depression reached its lowest ebb, a chance remark presented to him a possible solution. Round the bar one evening he heard a traffic controller say to a man generally disliked for his arrogance, "Pilots aren't God Almighty! You're no more than jumped-up bloody bus drivers. You could sit in your cockpit till kingdom come, but without engineers, fitters, mechanics, us controllers and a whole lot of other clever sods you'd never get off the effing ground. There's more to flying than sitting on your arse up front."

Dave had lain awake that night with his thoughts in turmoil as he considered a plan that might not come off and would need immense determination to set in motion. He would be courting personal and professional suicide if it failed, and certain hard knocks if it worked out right, yet his resolution was firm when morning came.

Standing in his room on the morning of Leanne's marriage to Lieutenant Dougal Rowan, Dave recalled the decision taken just over a year ago and the succession of interviews and meetings, some very hostile, which had eventually led to his resigning his commission and immediately re-enlisting in the RAF as an aircrew cadet with the basic rank of aircraftman grade one. His action had earned the united disgust of his family and the return of his engagement ring.

Throughout that difficult year, Dave's determination had not flagged. He had gone right through the initial training again with raw recruits and had not complained. He had resolutely shrugged off snide comments from a few of his fellows and the sadistic attitude of some instructors. He had worked hard and succeeded. At noon today he would stand in the family chapel to damn the eyes of anyone who looked sideways at him, as those who knew his history surely would.

Edwina Rowan had eloped with jazz pianist "Fingers" Ashmore. Her stunned family had managed to survive the shock because the couple went to live in Paris, where Edwina died soon after giving birth to a son. In some ways her death was regarded by the Rowans with relief; an unsavoury episode irrevocably closed. Yet it was not. David Oliver Ashmore had turned up on the castle doorstep one day in the charge of a somewhat dubious Frenchwoman, who claimed Monsieur Ashmore could no longer manage the boy. She demanded money for her return fare to Paris and left Dave with people he did not know in a huge intimidating castle. Sir Hector, in whom blood ties were strong, accepted the grandson of his brother – who had been murdered along with his wife in an African riot while a diplomat – and did his best to instil Rowan qualities in the child of a nightclub performer. When newspapers later reported the alcoholic decline and death of one of jazz music's most innovative exponents, the family drew a veil over the unfortunate affair and never again spoke of young David's parents. To all intents and purposes, he could have been found beneath the proverbial gooseberry bush.

Dave had traced and once visited his mother's grave during his university years. She had not voluntarily deserted him; Fingers Ashmore had, so Dave had no interest in his father's resting place. When asked about his parents he merely said he had been orphaned when he was four and left it at that, but he had sometimes wondered what kind of woman his mother had been. Visiting her grave and saying hallo and goodbye to her had put an end to his speculation and he no longer thought about his background although his family had clearly never truly forgotten it.

Dave's mouth twisted as he gazed from his window at the snowy heights. Sir Hector had been a dutiful and generous guardian. He was a fine man, a respected and courageous soldier, a gentleman in the grand tradition. God, the regiment and the family; to all three he was true. It had been a severe blow to him when Dave chose the RAF in preference to the Highland regiment revered by the family, but he had eventually appeared to accept this unpalatable fact. What he could not accept, or forgive, was a man with Rowan blood somewhere in his veins resigning his commission to become a sergeant – an RAF sergeant, at that! Despite the excellence of every aspect of today's marriage of the Rowan heir to the most ravishing girl ever to grace the castle, the occasion would be unforgivably marred by a man wearing three stripes on the sleeve of a blue uniform among so many insignia of high army rank.

Sergeant D.O. Ashmore, fully qualified Air Loadmaster about to join 646 Squadron, should have spent Christmas anywhere but at his childhood home where he was no longer welcome. He ought to slip away this morning and miss the wedding or wear a morning suit like the civilian guests, but he was determined to display those hard-earned stripes with a small eagle above them. Sir Hector and Aunt Mairie were deeply affronted by what they saw as his insensitivity; Dougal was vitriolically furious. It was sad that they had so little understanding but Dave intended to show everyone an Ashmore was not easily defeated; that he was proud of what he had achieved and would soon be doing. Most of all, he needed to prove to himself that watching Leanne pledge her future and her body to another man had no effect on him. Absolutely no effect whatever.

He got drunk that night. Paralytic. While the family and distinguished guests were dancing reels, Dave sat alone drinking steadily and telling himself he was a masochist to put himself through this. Yet he stayed to the bitter end. At least, he guessed he did. In the morning he could not remember the final part of his self-torture. Beneath the duvet he was wearing socks, shirt and underpants: his uniform adorned a suit of armour which had been set up near the window. On the sleeve beneath the stripes someone had pinned the red L normally tied to the bumper of a car. He stared at it with an echo of yesterday's pain. Some young regimental rips had left their jeering message. Time to leave.

His head thudded painfully as he took a quick shower, dressed in a tracksuit and an anorak, then took up the large backpack into which he had folded his uniform, and left by the back stairs. Clipping on his skis, he glided over the snow-covered grounds leading to the grand entrance gates reputed to have held back invaders over several centuries. In fact, the old gates had fallen apart soon after Hamish Rowan, Dave's grandfather, had been killed, and a new pair, professionally "antiquated", had been erected.

Dave stopped beside them and looked back at the impregnable stone walls of the home his mother had deserted never to see again. She had run to her lover. Dave was leaving his within the castle and he would not be coming back. He had packed all he prized into two holdalls which he had put in the left luggage hall of the railway station on Christmas Eve, to be collected today. The silver sports trophies remained in his room. They were symbols of the past. He was about to start his new life.

His head continued to thud while the branch-line train snaked its way to the airport, and the hangover plagued him for the first half of the fast flight southward. He then fell asleep and was shaken awake to find he was at Heathrow.

A good night's sleep in a London hotel, followed by a hearty hot breakfast, put Dave back on his feet and ready to move on. First, he had an exciting new possession to collect, a Christmas present to the new Dave Ashmore from the old one, which he had ordered on completing his air crew training. When he arrived at the showrooms of the motorcycle supplier, he took one look at the glittering magnificence of the black Harley Davidson and decided to take it and himself by train to Dorchester. The snow was negotiable around the capital but the salesman said he had heard it was bad in the West Country and Dorset. Knowing he must treat his new possession like a mule to get to Hampton Heyhoe, Dave wanted to limit the sacrilege.

By the time he reached Dorchester, the painful vision of Leanne in bridal finery was almost bearable. He booked into a small bed-and-breakfast farmhouse, then went skiing on a nearby hill.

Out in the clear cold air, he gave himself a lecture. He was superbly fit, he was a first-class athlete, he was about to embark on his flying career. So what if there were no pilot's wings on his breast? He would be in the air, going places, part of the action. So what if Leanne was not yet out of his system? She had taught him never again to allow a woman to dominate his life. He was about to start a new phase, a new direction. With the new year would come a new man determined to live by his own standards, not those of the Rowan family.

On the following day Dave made fairly good progress until he reached a minor road that climbed towards the coastal cliffs. There was only one route to Hampton Heyhoe and very few vehicles appeared to have used it. There were rutted tractor tracks wide enough to take the wheels of his bike but the depressed surface had frozen to icy smoothness which had not been gritted. It proved impossible to drive uphill and he was eventually forced to get off and push the laden vehicle up a one in eight ascent winding through a copse.

Breathing heavily, Dave rounded a corner to see a blue saloon abandoned and half-blocking the road. He grunted. Some fool had tried to drive home after a boozy night! He trudged onward and upward, his ridged boots slipping every now and then on the ice. Turning what he hoped was the final bend before the summit, he saw someone ahead carrying a large grip that looked heavy. He was slight, of medium height and walking aimlessly as if deep in thought. Out on a snow-covered plateau it was a surprise to find someone else venturing across it on a day like this.

Once on the level, Dave got astride the saddle and kicked the engine into life. The figure turned in alarm at the resultant roar, and he was further surprised to see it was a girl. He moved forward, balancing with his legs. "Can I give you a lift?"

"I think I'm safer walking, thanks," she said. "I wasn't expecting it to be this bad. The main road was fine. That's my car back there."

"I thought some drunk had piled it up last night. Bit crazy to attempt the hill, weren't you?"

Her green eyes glittered. "I had chains on the wheels, which is more than you have."

She walked on. Dave stayed alongside, scooting with his feet. "*I'm* still on the move."

"Then why don't you get moving?"

Her accent was middle class; her grey jog-suit and scarlet

anorak were designer sports clothes. Despite her attitude he felt he could not leave her in the middle of nowhere with a freezing wind whistling in from the sea and a skyful of snow gathering for the next fall.

"I'll get moving if you ride pillion," he offered.

She stopped again. "Aren't you being rather over-optimistic? That heavyweight machine of yours is loaded to the limit already. Do you honestly believe you could handle it on these icy tracks if I climbed on with my bag?"

He shrugged. "If you won't risk it I'll ride to the first village and get someone to send out a tractor to haul in your car. Where are you heading?"

"Hampton Heyhoe. There's an RAF station just beyond. I'm joining a squadron there."

He gave an astonished laugh. "So am I."

When she smiled it signified a total change of approach. "I should have known. Why else would anyone be going along this road two days before New Year in this weather? OK, I'll give it a go on the pillion but at the first tumble I'll walk. All right by you?"

"Aye. Hop on, I've a spare bone dome." He pulled the helmet from the rear clip. "You're my first passenger."

When she had removed her woolly hat and fastened the helmet securely, Dave revved up and carefully edged forward, conscious of the extra weight. It could not be called a triumphant ride, more a cautious chug and an affront to the superb machine but it was better than trudging. The girl was silent, leaving him to concentrate until they reached the outskirts of a hamlet marked on the map as four miles from Hampton Heyhoe. It boasted a single petrol pump with a tiny workshop behind it. Dave stopped and turned to his passenger.

"I'll ask if there's anyone who'll fetch your car."

She was off the pillion before he could move and walking over to the workshop asking loudly if anyone was about.

"Please yourself," he muttered, cutting the engine, climbing off and tugging the bike on to its stand. An elderly man in boots was walking gingerly along the narrow main road, but apart from him the population could have been in hibernation for all that could be seen of them. Dave swung his arms vigorously to help his circulation. It had been a strain on his limbs but he had proved the girl wrong. She had not tumbled once. Hampton Heyhoe was four miles on, and the station three more beyond it. He would be glad to arrive.

The girl came back smiling. "The proprietor looks at least ninety, but he assures me 'young Alf' will take his tractor out right away. And he's offered us a mug of tea. Come on! God knows what it'll taste of but it'll be hot, I hope."

It was very good tea, in fact, even if it was drunk standing in a tiny storeroom filled with tins of paint, drums of lubricating oil, cylinders of calor gas and head-high stacks of boxes containing screws, nails, rivets, washers and everything else a man needs to maintain machinery.

The girl warmed her hands around the mug and smiled at Dave. "What a day to report for duty! Thanks for the lift. You're pretty hot stuff on that bike. I'm Maggie Spencer, by the way."

"Dave Ashmore," he said, returning her smile. "I only picked up the bike two days ago. Can't wait for all this to clear and really burn rubber." He gulped more tea. "So what do you do in the RAF?"

"I'm a pilot. What about you?"

He let out his breath on a cloud of vapour. "I'm not." He walked back towards his motorcycle. "Let's get going."

When Maggie had reported her arrival and been allocated a room in the Officers' Mess, she rang her twin on his office number. "Hi Phil, thought you'd be glad to know I arrived safely."

"Oh, good."

She chuckled. "I skidded on ice trying to go uphill, and the back wheels got stuck in a ditch. I had to hoof it for a while. Then, by amazing good fortune, someone appeared out of the snow on a truly splendiferous motorbike and offered me a lift. I didn't think he'd be able to stay upright with me as well as his copious luggage – including some designer skis, would you believe – but he clearly has the physique of a Hercules because we made it without once falling off. He was joining the squadron too, but clammed up when I said I was a pilot. Think I trod on a corn in some way, and he went to the Sergeants' Mess after dropping me here. Anyway, I was grateful for his help." She glanced from her window. "I don't think there'll be much flying going on. We're pretty well snowed-in here. What's it like your way?"

"About the same."

Maggie then noticed his unusual lack of response. "What's up?" After the barest pause she asked, "How's Fay now?"

"Still upset, I'm afraid. Rob said I must expect her to have mood swings and to fly off the handle over the strangest things. It's all part of being pregnant."

"As a doctor he would say that, Phil, but we both know it had nothing to do with pregnancy."

"You've had no experience of it so you shouldn't be dismissive," came his unusually curt response. "Look, I've been thinking, Mags. Perhaps it'd be best if we didn't ring each other like we've been doing. I mean, we'd soon know if the other was in trouble and get in touch immediately." He paused long enough for her to say something, then continued more hesitantly. "It's just during this awkward period. In any case, you're going to be up to your eyes in flying and squadron duties and I've an order list as long as my arm. Everyone wants his boat by spring, of course." He gave a nervous laugh. "It's always frantic after Christmas."

She heard herself say with forced lightness, "You'd better get back to work, then. And I must unpack the only bag I rescued from the car, then go downstairs to meet my new colleagues. Cheers, Phil, and take care."

"And you," he replied unhappily before she hung up.

It took very little time to put away the few essential items and the working uniform she had dragged from another bag when locking her car, then she stood gazing at a framed photograph of herself and Phil taken at their twenty-first birthday celebration. The pair in the picture looked full of life and laughter, and *so* alike.

From the moment of birth they had been classed as one entity. Everyone referred to the Spencer children as Charles, Robin and the twins. In childhood it had been usual to have chores allocated thus: "Charles, take the rods; Rob will carry the creel and the twins can bring the bait." Being of different sexes they had not been dressed alike nor had they ever been mistaken for each other, but their one-ness had never been questioned. The two older boys had naturally paired off leaving the infant twins to play together. As time passed and the age differences mattered less, the instinctive pairing had remained; Phil and Maggie happiest when sharing.

In adolescence, brother and sister had taken the inevitable step towards schoolfellows of the same sex but no other friendship had equalled what they felt for each other. A twin was utterly reliable. Help would unhesitatingly be offered; secrets would never be betrayed. At university they had both had the normal brief involvements and had confided their uncertainties and heartaches to each other when the affairs ended.

During those subsequent years when they had spent longer periods apart, they discovered the curious yet exciting mental telepathy they shared. Commonly experienced by identical twins, it was rarer in boy/girl single births. They had initially thought it fun and deliberately tried to send each other messages, but it did not work to order. Only at times of elation or distress could one sense the need to contact the other. Face to face it was stronger. They frequently read each other's minds, as Maggie had on Christmas Day.

That thought brought her back to the present as she continued to gaze at the photograph in her hand. Phil had always been there for her. He had protected her from bullies when she was young; he had championed her career decision. He had countered their mother's constant complaint that her only daughter had abandoned her natural female role in order to ape men. Phil understood that becoming a military pilot did not make her less of a woman and he had never ridiculed her achievement. Even when Fay first came upon the scene, Phil had remained Maggie's port in a storm.

He had now hurt her unbearably. He would certainly have known that yet he had gone ahead. Fay had finally succeeded in dividing them where all else had failed and Margaret Ellen Spencer was suddenly frighteningly alone. Putting the photograph face-down in a drawer, she realised all her joy in this momentous day had vanished. Phil no longer cared how she felt.

The main body of the Mess was a large Edwardian manor house commandeered in 1940 and retained at the end of the war. Quarters had been added at the rear, but the elegance of the house had survived three generations of boisterous young men and a few young women. Originally known as RAF Hampton Heyhoe, the second half of the village name was dropped after the servicemen and women had changed it to Hampton Hoo-ha, Hampton Ha Ha, Hampton Hi Ho, Hampton Ho Ho and even Hampton What-ho!

Crossing from the modern annexe, Maggie entered the main part of the Mess still feeling a sense of severance from the brother who had shared twenty-five years with her. From the ground floor a wide curving staircase led up to the quarters of the senior officers and to several conference rooms. Maggie was never likely to go up there. She looked in at the formal dining room, oak panelled and heavy with atmosphere. Three generations had left their spiritual mark.

Crossing the impressive hallway, also oak panelled, she decided to avoid the ante-room where silence appeared to be the order of the day and open newspapers obscured faces. She headed for the sound of voices and laughter in the hope of smothering the incredible chill of her twin's rebuff. The younger members of the Mess were around the bar. Never ill at ease in company, Maggie nevertheless hesitated just inside the square room. A man would walk in, introduce himself and become one of the boys right away. While she was deciding how best to play it, one of a noisy group spotted her and beckoned. She went across, the focus of assessing male eyes.

"You're our new pilot, I take it. Welcome to six four six," he said with a hint of a northern accent. Tall and lean with mid-brown hair, a craggy face and warm amber eyes, he oozed self-assurance, but there was no smile to accompany his words as he offered his hand. "I'm Randal Price."

"Randy by name; randy by nature," chorused several of his companions.

She withdrew her crushed fingers. "Margaret Spencer. Maggie by name; most particular by nature."

"And also bloody keen," he responded crisply. "Most of us would've called in and said we were stuck in a snowdrift, then had a few days of extra carousing."

"You seem to be doing all right here," she murmured.

Ignoring that he said, "Meet the team," and pointed to each man in turn, quoting names so fast no newcomer would be able to remember them. They were clearly on their third or fourth round. All had over-bright eyes and know-it-all grins as they acknowledged her. "I'll get you a drink," the man added.

"Gin and tonic, please."

This was greeted by a high-pitched "oooh" from "the team", and one said, "If you're joining our squadron you'll have to start drinking beer."

Still upset by Phil's call, Maggie replied tartly, "Will I also have to pee standing up?"

Randal's eyes narrowed. "In some places we go to you'll have no choice." He twisted to attract a steward. "Large gin and tonic for Flight Lieutenant Spencer."

"Did you come far today?" asked a very young blond man with a navigator's single wing emblem on his pullover.

"Not as far as I'd hoped. My car's stuck in a drift about ten miles back."

"You mean you walked here? You *are* bloody keen."

"I got a lift on a motorbike, but I would've walked," Maggie said coolly. "The prospect of staying in my car until the thaw didn't appeal to me."

"Who was the madman on the bike?" asked Rusty Locke, whose name Maggie remembered because of his very red hair.

"Dave Ashmore. He's also joining six four six today."

"He's Johnny Johnson's replacement, and he's a bloody sight keener than Maggie," said Randal. "He resigned his commission and went back to basics so he could become aircrew."

Maggie instantly understood the man's abrupt reaction to her mention of being a pilot. Had he once had such aspirations?

"That's not keenness, it's insanity," someone said.

"I don't know; it's a determined guy who'd push ahead with something like that," another reasoned. "Whose round is it?"

While they argued over that, Randal said, "Bottoms up, Maggie! Squadron custom for everyone to buy new members a drink on joining."

Maggie drained her glass and fixed him with a level gaze. "They tried that one on all the women at Cranwell, and again at every place I've been stationed since. You should know by now we don't fall for juvenile tricks to give the lads a laugh. I'll have one more, then you can have the rest sent up to room eighty-four."

His aggressive reaction stunned her. "Our tricks aren't always juvenile. You're joining us because one of our most experienced pilots crashed trying to deliver vital food and water during a Bosnian blizzard. He's in hospital with a broken back, lucky to be alive. Although that's debatable, because his life's going to be hell from now on. You're his replacement, and what sex you are doesn't matter to us . . . neither does how you pee."

Maggie stiffened. "Right, point taken. Now I'll make mine.

Too much alcohol gives me migraine, so I'd appreciate it if you'd space your welcoming drinks over the next few evenings."

"I'll have all mine tonight," put in a deep voice behind her. Maggie turned to see a sturdy man in his late thirties, with silvering hair at his temples and vivid blue eyes in a scarred face. "Hello, Rip. So they haven't killed you off yet, you canny bugger."

Everyone in the group straightened and fell silent, but Randal shook the man's hand heartily, a smile changing his dark expression to show he had a warmer side. "My God, I thought you were in Bahrain making earth-shattering pronouncements, sir."

"I made 'em, then got out before the earth did shatter." He had a loud baritone laugh. "I was on my way home when the bloody weather closed in, so I decided to drop down here for the night. Knew I'd find you in the bar. What're you up to these days?"

During the crossfire of conversation Maggie edged away to where two women were sitting at a small table. One smiled and invited her to join them. "Time to let boys be boys?"

Maggie sat beside her. "A few at a time are bearable, but when a gang gets around a bar . . ."

"Why do you think we're over here? I'm Jill Ross in traffic control and this is Dandy Cummings, our dentist."

The dentist smiled. "The macho dears lose all their bravado when they sit in my chair and I get out my instruments."

"I'm Maggie Spencer, six four six's neuter replacement pilot," she said, still shaken by the animosity she had aroused. "Who's that group captain? Everyone seems to know him, especially that Price character."

"Mark Grainger. I talked him down just under an hour ago," said Jill. "He and Rip flew together on undercover missions in the Gulf. Rumour has it they were on the ground picking up SAS guys when a Scud exploded near enough to injure six, including Mark. Rip took over and brought them all out safely. It was his first operational flight. He got a medal out of it."

With her gaze on the lively group who had not noticed her departure, Maggie asked, "Why do you call him Rip?"

"Everyone does," said Dandy, glancing across to the bar. "We'll never attract a steward with that rumpus going on. Ah well, gin's not good for the teeth."

"Randal Ivan Price," supplied Jill in answer to Maggie's question. "He's been known as Rip from his time at Cranwell."

"I can think of another meaning for those initials," Maggie said with feeling. "I hope I never have to fly with him."

"It's inevitable," Jill said. "Talk about mix 'n' match; those crews switch around almost every time they go up. Didn't you take to our Rip?" she asked in surprise. "Women invariably do."

"Not this one," she murmured, watching him turn into a lively laughing man before her eyes. "I found him terse and hostile. He said he didn't give a damn what sex I am, but it's obvious he does."

"You've caught him at a bad time," said Dandy, gesturing at a steward to order more drinks. "Another gin, Maggie? Good." She held up three fingers, then turned back with a smile. "I'll overlook my teeth for the moment."

"Why's it a bad time?"

"Eh? Oh, Rip, you mean. His wife's just left him."

"Sensible woman!"

"That she isn't," declared Jill. "He's dotty about her; gave her anything she wanted. You've heard of Price's Pork Pies? Rip's grandpa started the business and made a fortune. Daddy Price expanded into frozen foods and made another. Rip wanted nothing to do with the business except for the large private income it gives him."

"So what about his wife? I find it hard to believe that man could be dotty about any woman."

After watching the steward place their drinks on the table, Dandy glanced up at Maggie. "If I say to you blonde, huge blue eyes, legs up to her armpits and bra-less boobs, can you find it easier to believe? Men of his type are forever losing their cool over creatures like that. She's ten years younger; one of the point-to-point and hunt ball brigade. They don't usually mate with pork pie people. Daddy and Mummy didn't approve and Fiona ran home to them each time Rip was away. They've two adorable kids who are never allowed to play with the others at Hampton and she just can't see how lucky she is compared with some wives here. It looks as if she's gone for good this time because he's moved to a room in the Mess."

Jill nodded. "And he's been looking like a thundercloud since he got back from Christmas leave. Stupid little bitch!"

Maggie made no comment, but she privately thought bra-less Fiona might have more sense than her companions, who were clearly fans of Randal Ivan Price. For herself, she would regard him as no more than a neuter fellow pilot. After Phil's hurtful surrender to Fay's possessiveness Maggie had had enough of men for one day. Then she remembered Dave Ashmore, who had resigned his commission in his determination to fly. He promised to be someone she could identify with. No woman was undermining *his* life, that was obvious.

January

W hen Randal nicked his cheek the second time, he threw
down his shaver with a hearty expletive. Last night had
been even more alcoholic than a normal New Year's Eve. He
had been celebrating his timely promotion to squadron leader
to fill the post of commander of B Flight. Everyone in the Mess
had stood him a drink, and he had been additionally elated by the
generous congratulations of colleagues who understood what it
meant to him. The party had continued long after "Auld Lang
Syne", followed by the toast to absent friends. No one had
mentioned Randal's absent wife and children before they had
put him to bed, beyond caring.

Staring down at the shaver he recalled Fiona buying it for him
because he had left the previous one somewhere on Salisbury
Plain, after an exercise with the Army. He had left the one before
that in a gutted hotel in Bosnia. He visualised her teasing smile
as she had said, "I'd better handcuff this one to your wrist so
you can't lose it." He still had the shaver but he had lost her.

Sinking down on the bed he stared between his knees at the
uninspiring pattern on the carpet. Had he lost her? What the hell
was the true state of their marriage? The circumstances of their
last meeting had made it impossible to get an answer. With a
cocktail party under way and her father eager for any excuse
to throw him out, Fiona had been under impossible pressure.
She had almost surrendered and gone to the pub to talk, but
the prospect of her parents creating a scene on her return had
been too much for her. And for him.

He sighed. Maybe she just needed more time. Trouble was, the
longer his children remained with their grandparents the more of
a stranger their father would seem to them. Fiona reckoned they
were afraid of him. That was crazy. He loved them, for God's
sake! Lydia was an adorable little minx who aroused in him
every protective instinct; Neil was the son he could instruct

and guide through manhood. Every father wanted that unique rapport which began the moment a small head bent with his own over a model spaceship, a toy train or a junior toolbox. But Gerald Holland was enjoying that, and he was shaping Neil Edward Price's future, damn him!

Randal stood restlessly, a dull ache in his head the legacy of last night. As soon as he had a stand-off period he would book a room somewhere away from Marylands and persuade Fiona to live with him again. They had too much going for them to throw in the towel so soon. He had stopped playing around when they married, and they were wonderful together between the storms. If he could only wean her away from her parents and their extravagant way of life she would probably settle down. She condemned his frequent absences, but they were not of his own making, unlike hers. She had never accepted his obligation to follow orders – she had been allowed to do as she pleased all her life – and, in the same way, she had not been prepared to take on the RAF along with the man she wanted.

Snatching up the shaver, Randal began removing the last of his stubble with unnecessary vigour. The squadron's schedule for the coming weeks meant he would be away far longer than he would be at Hampton, so he could do nothing decisive yet. He had blown it on Christmas Eve by walking out. She had accused him of being aggressive. Not aggressive enough that night! He should have forced a decision one way or the other from her. Suspecting that he had shelved the issue for fear of precipitating a final break merely added to his present frustration. To make things worse, he had been landed with a new pilot who was blonde, shapely and carrying some kind of chip on her shoulder. What had he done to deserve Maggie Spencer at a time like this?

Within half an hour he had more immediate things to think about. An emergency situation had developed in the West Country. With temperatures still below freezing and no prospect of a thaw for at least the next three days, a blizzard had hit Cornwall and the west of Devon overnight, bringing chaos on major roads and cutting villages off from essential supplies. Power lines were down, stranded motorists were suffering from hypothermia, animals were freezing to death or going hungry. Police and rescue services were unable to cope so, as usual in these instances, the Army and the RAF were called upon.

With one Chinook undergoing repairs Randal had only five at his disposal, and just enough personnel on the station to man them. He stood in the briefing room frowning over the list of names on what was known as the wailing wall because of the moans and groans of crew members on seeing their assignments. "Why me? I did it last time." "Bloody Bosnia again!" "It's the big game at Twickenham on Saturday." "Not the Falklands! My wife'll kill me."

Randal now reviewed the tasks they had been given. Two crews would pick up troops from camps on the Devon border and take them to the worst hit areas: troops with digging equipment, food supplies, blankets and two-way radios. Two more crews would pick up fodder to drop at designated fields and farms. They would probably have to make two or three runs each unless the troop carriers finished in time to help out. The third task was more tricky so Randal decided to take that one himself.

To the south-west of St Ives a forklift truck carrying vital medical supplies was stuck in a deep drift. The squadron had been detailed to collect its load and deliver it to eight locations scattered around the area. The Met report was lousy: low cloud, a chance of further snow and a rising wind.

Randal's frown deepened as he read further details. In the truck were supplies of fluid for patients undergoing kidney dialysis in their homes. Unlike the machines which cleansed blood two or three times a week, this fluid was flushed through the abdomen four times daily. Each patient consequently needed a delivery of supermarket proportions every month, without which they would collapse and die. The fluid needed to be handled with care and, due to the size of each consignment, had to be delivered to within manual transporting distance of the patient's home.

The crews arrived promptly and Randal gave his briefing, judiciously avoiding the risk of a personality clash between Rusty Locke and a crewman who bore the red-haired Lothario an old grudge, imagined or otherwise. A wise flight commander teamed up people known to work well together whenever he could. Four crews took down details, asked questions and left fully briefed on the job ahead. Randal was left with his new pilot, the power-packed Jimmy Crowther and the equally hefty new loadmaster, Dave Ashmore.

He glanced critically at the Scot. "I hope you're not as hung over as you look. There's some heavy manual portering needed here, which is why I've chosen to take you."

The man nodded. "That's fine by me, sir."

"Only 'sir' me on formal occasions: if you want my immediate attention in the air, you call me Boss. Otherwise I answer to Rip." He gave a faint smile. "Nothing to do with van Winkle. Never get the chance to sleep like him." He spread across the table the charts on which he had marked the eight delivery points. "OK, we can't be like Santa Claus and drop things down the bloody chimney right to the hearth rug, but in this case we have to do the next best thing." He explained what they had been asked to do and the nature of the supplies they would be handling. "Three of these places are quite isolated; one on a rocky cliff reached only by a rough dirt track." He tapped the chart with his pencil to indicate one of the deeply indented fissures common along the Cornish coast. "That's it."

"So how did the truck hope to get to it?" asked Jimmy.

Randal shook his head with gentle appreciation. "This is some organisation, apparently. These guys deliver their supplies on a set day each month and at a set time. They never fail."

"Except today," put in Maggie quietly.

Randal glanced across the table at her. "No, we'll deliver for them. Can't meet their usual times, but we'll get it all there on the right day."

"So how did the truck get up to this place," insisted Jimmy, indicating the coastal fissure.

"It couldn't. The farmer drives a cart down to the road to meet it. The local bobby knows when it's due and closes the road to other traffic until the delivery is made. No need for that today, of course. The medical suppliers have given very detailed info to emphasise the importance of this operation."

"So it's the farmer's wife who needs the stuff?" asked Dave.

"Their child. A girl of five."

"Oh, gee, that's awful!" exclaimed Jimmy, a father of four. "Poor little kid."

"So how do we deliver it with the sea on one side and deep snow on the other?" asked Maggie with professional single-mindedness.

"We'll know when we've had a look-see." Randal's glance included all three. "Five patients live near enough to a village to make landings possible in a field or on a central green."

"Watch out for buried war memorials. They're usually sited near village greens," warned Dave. "I once skied into one and knocked myself out."

Randal grinned. "You must have been pissed, but it's a good point. We'll use fields as a better option where we can. The village stalwarts will be told to expect us and should be there in force to haul the stuff to its destination." He pencilled circles as he spoke. "There's one here, in the heart of Penzance. Local emergency services will collect the load from the heliport. These two are way out in the sticks. We'll overfly and make a decision on the spot. This first one's a gift. The patient lives next to a minor public school with a large playing field. OK, Dave, we'll watch out for buried rugby posts."

The Scot smiled. "If the snow's reached even halfway up *them*, the house next door is probably totally buried."

"Especially if it's a bunglow," put in Jimmy.

Maggie's cool voice cut across their amusement. "Nothing's yet been said about how we collect the boxes in the first place. This truck is on an A road bonnet-deep in a drift, in the middle of a jam of other vehicles, maybe."

Randal frowned. "We'll assess the situation when we get there. It's likely to be the most tricky aspect of the whole operation. We'll have to find somewhere close enough to the vehicle to put down and enable us to transfer the load quickly." He included the two men in his glance. "There's a lot of ground to cover here and it'll get dark early. According to these manifest details we'll need extra hands, so we'll take along half a dozen volunteers to speed things up." He nodded at the sergeants. "Go ahead and get organised. Maggie, get cracking on the navigation. I'll sort out the extra manpower and check that the other crews are ready to roll."

Although there was unbroken whiteness during the early part of the flight, traffic was moving and people were out and about. But the sky to the west was lead-grey and full of the snow forecast for the coming night. Randal sat at the controls studying the frozen landscape thoughtfully. It was never straightforward landing in snow; it could cover all manner of hazards. However, he had done it often enough to be confident. He always felt a sense of satisfaction when flying in supplies which could not be delivered any other way, but today there was an added incentive: a little girl of five on kidney dialysis! What if Lydia's life should depend on someone flying supplies to her? Would Fiona then take a different view of his job and understand its importance?

"There's a sixteenth-century church just beyond this village," said Maggie, breaking into his straying thoughts. "Two women were convicted of witchcraft by the clergy and drowned in the ducking-stool. Their ghosts are supposed to haunt the churchyard."

"Especially when there's snow on the ground," added Jimmy over the intercom. This was followed by a series of ghostly wails from the ground crew volunteers.

Randal glanced at her. "How do you know that? It's not on the nav charts, is it?"

"I read it in a book."

Jimmy was well into his stride. Gee, she doesn't like beer and she reads books. Should we have her in B Flight?"

"I'll teach all of you to read one day when you're sober enough," came her crisp retort which was treated with the usual falsetto "oooh" from the cabin.

Randal made no attempt to hide his amusement as he looked across at her, but she was gazing straight ahead so he kept silent. A few miles further on he spotted in the garden of a house on a small estate a woman in a fake fur coat and moon boots pegging washing on the line. A few shirts already hanging there had frozen to board stiffness.

"Good God, she's even more bloody keen than you, Maggie," he said with a laugh, pointing downward.

"Bully for her," she replied. "If you can tear your gaze away you'll see a power plant dead ahead. It might be as well to avoid the chimney."

"Hell, yes," he exclaimed with mock amazement. "Never spotted that, and it's much bigger than a war memorial."

"Just doing my job," she said stiffly.

"Just kidding." He veered to the left of the tall chimney then looked pointedly at her. "Who made you into such a tough cookie?"

She ignored the question, so he abandoned his attempt to make her one of the team. So often women claimed sexual discrimination but Maggie Spencer was creating it where it did not exist. Air crew were a free and easy bunch; the job made them that way. A woman on the station was either treated as one of the boys, or she was ruthlessly pursued until she surrendered or retaliated. On the whole, the girls knew how to give as good as they got and worked happily alongside the men.

Maggie puzzled Randal. How had she passed successfully through Cranwell and her subsequent pilot training? The ability to get along with others was a strong consideration when deciding who should make the grade, so she must have convinced the selectors that she was the right type. Maybe only he brought out the worst in her. He would send her with someone else next time and find out. Long flights could be boring without banter to pass the time. If she was unwilling to take part she could be a liability. He would be loath to let her fly as boss of a crew who might grow resentful to the point of hostility. Mistakes could then be made.

Crossing the Devon–Cornwall border they soon had evidence of more extreme conditions as they passed low over stationary vehicles in zigzag tailbacks caused by the icy roads. Looking past his feet Randal saw small groups where aid was being given by police and rescue teams. A medical helicopter fitted with skis sat on the snow near a pile-up of cars. Stretchers were being carried with obvious difficulty through the deep drifts.

Randal spoke his thoughts. "All those fixed-wing purists who look down their noses at anything with a rotor forget times like this. Not even a Harrier would be much use down there."

A faint cheer came from the crew and he grinned, but it was soon wiped from his face when he spotted several media helicopters buzzing around the scene. "There are the bloody vultures, guys. I swear they *smell* disasters before they happen, or how come they're on the spot so soon?"

"They're bloody keen, too," said a soft voice in his earphones, and he glanced quickly at the woman on his left. He had momentarily forgotten who was in the cockpit with him. Her gaze was steady as she asked, "Don't you approve of the media?"

"Not when they get in the way of people trying to do a job."

"They're trying to do theirs."

He glanced back at the aircraft hovering over the rescue operation. "Is it worth doing?"

"Of course! How else would we know what's going on in the world?"

Turning his attention to where the sky ahead was darker and the cloud even lower, he asked casually, "Your father's not a Rupert Murdoch type, is he?"

"No, he's the legal eagle type. I'm sure you already know that from my service record."

"I don't go around reading stuff like that. All I really know about you is that your navigation's spot on." He pointed. "There's our truck at one o'clock."

After informing the crew Randal studied the bleak scene. Whenever he flew in icy conditions it was seldom like the pictures on calendars, where the sun in a clear blue sky sparkled the snow and bathed pretty chalets with yellow light. On those occasions in Bosnia when the days had been like that, the chalets he had flown over were blackened ruins and the snow was darkened by ash. There had often been bodies scattered around to complete the harsh contrast with the beauty of the day.

The truck driver had heard their approach and was waving his arms to attract their attention. Randal circled the area. There was plenty of open country, but if the snow had been blown into very deep drifts, as it surely had, choosing where to put down was tricky. That virgin whiteness could be covering a water-trough, a piece of abandoned farm equipment, sheep pens or even dead sheep. He had twice in his career seen pilots land in thick snow then tip sideways through bad luck or bad judgement. It could happen to the best of pilots, but he would do his damnedest to ensure it did not happen to him today. He could not forget the five-year-old who, in his mind, had become Lydia.

Reasoning that water-troughs and other hazards were most likely to be situated near the gate of any field, Randal selected his spot and prayed there was not half a flock of sheep buried there. He passed the information to his crew, and they had a brief discussion on transferring the cargo.

"I can't risk going down any closer to that gate than about thirty yards, so I guess it'll be a matter of muscles and Shanks's pony." Amusement crept into his voice. "Watch that guy scramble back to his cab when he discovers what happens next." He turned to Maggie. "Ever put down on snow?"

"Twice in Germany, but never on anything like this."

"OK, I'll talk us through it. That telegraph pole will have to be our fixed point. Thank God the wires run at ninety degrees to the road. We'll aim to land roughly thirty yards from the gate, and thirty back from a probable low wall running along beneath the phone wires. Once we blow some snow away we'll get a better sight of any ground hazards. Keep your eyes peeled. We might have to take a couple of cracks at it."

Sweeping round to cross the road, Randal lined up for his approach and descended at a steady angle from a hundred feet. He used the dark pole as his marker through the blizzard created by their powerful rotors. As they closed with the ground their vision became more and more obscured, despite the wipers oscillating madly across the windscreen. As the snow was displaced it left a shallower patch where no dark shapes suddenly materialised and Randal made his decision.

"We'll go for it, Maggie, and with all we've got. No half measures."

Using the pole as his only guide through the thick white porridge outside and following the clipped instructions of his two crewmen, he made a determined landing on the belly of the aircraft as its wheels broke through the frozen crust. His tension eased as the Chinook settled steady and level.

"If I've squashed any sheep we can all have lamb chops tonight," he announced. "OK, let's get cracking!"

Dave lowered the ramp and jumped out into snow reaching to his thighs. A chorus of moans followed as the rest jumped out with shovels and surveyed the scene. Dave and Jimmy swiftly reasoned that all they needed was a trench wide enough for one man carrying a box. In addition to the natural drifting, the snow displaced by their descent had settled again to create high banks near the gate. The grunts and puffs grew louder as the crewmen tackled the drifts. The two sergeants had decided on a moving chain in which every man would cover a short distance, passing each box to the next one in line before returning for another. The system usually produced speedy results.

The energetic shovelling warmed the crewmen after the cold flight, and they soon reached the gate twenty-five yards up the road from the stranded truck. They vaulted the gate and continued digging. The driver did his best to work towards them with his own shovel.

When they met up he said, "Am I glad to see you boys! I've driven through snow lots of times before, but I'd not have set out if I'd known it was as bad as this down here." He grinned.

"You've made it worse kicking up a squall like that! Scared the bloody daylights out of me when you started coming down. That's a mammoth thing you drive."

"Here's the man who drives it," announced Jimmy.

Randal arrived beside them and offered the driver his hand. "Can we take a look at your cargo?"

Dave crunched his way with Jimmy, the pilot and the truck driver to the back of the vehicle which was ready open. They all stared.

"Christ!" exclaimed Randal. "You deliver that lot every month?"

"Every day. I cover a large area but this sector is more spread out than most." He looked at them anxiously. "Can you get it to the patients?"

"Oh sure," said Randal, still staring at the mountain of boxes. "It's just that I had no idea this sort of thing went on."

"No one does, unless they need the stuff themselves."

"It's some operation."

"So's yours, chum."

Randal smiled at him. "Wait until we get in the air again before you say that. Right, if you'll move the boxes forward as we take them, we'll get it stacked in our hold."

Dave asked, "Is every consignment the same?"

"Oh no, it depends on what each patient needs this month. The boxes are all marked up, though. Can't get it wrong."

"I see what you're driving at, Dave," put in Jimmy, glancing at Randal. "We'd better load up to fit your flight plan."

"No problem," he said, starting to walk away. "Maggie and I set it to match the driver's schedule. Come on, we've a lot of ground to cover." He stopped and said thoughtfully to the driver, "We're not supposed to take aboard anyone who's not part of the operation, but I'd like to have you along to brief me on the terrain around each of these places. OK if we put you off at Penzance?"

"Thanks, chum. Anywhere I can get some kind of transport back to my depot will be fine."

The team went into action as Dave returned with Jimmy to the hold to stow their cargo safely and securely. "He's got a job and a half hauling that load single-handed every day," Dave observed. "I'd guess he could give us ten years, too."

"When you're his age, Dave, the RAF might let you handle this job on your tod."

The boxes came in a steady flow. Dave was surprised to see their flight commander take a place in the chain, leaving Maggie keeping her eye on the cockpit. Already liking the little he had seen and heard of him, Dave felt this gesture confirmed the squadron's general opinion that Rip Price was one of the best.

Shortly afterwards, Dave had confirmation of 646 Squadron's other opinion of the man: that a trooper's blasphemies were honeyed words compared with his language when angry. The loading was well under way when the familiar sound of rotors heralded a helicopter with BBC marked on the side. It came in low, circled once or twice, then hovered over them for camera shots.

Shouting a torrent of abuse, Randal watched it fly off and vowed that if they had been armed he would have taken a pot shot at it. "They'd be more sodding use down here helping to shift some of this," he fumed.

Dave was inclined to agree with him. He still had a few yellowing newspaper cuttings concerning his mother's elopement.

When the loading was finished all their faces were flushed from the exertion and the icy wind. The driver locked his cab and climbed aboard the Chinook with his personal things in a zip bag. Dave closed the ramp with a sense of gratification. It had gone well. Now to deliver their supplies to the anxious patients. His first flight with 646 and it was a humdinger! This was what he had surrendered his commission for; why he had gone back to basics with such determination. Part of him still yearned to be in the cockpit, but he was flying and that was one hundred per cent better than sitting behind a desk.

The driver introduced himself as Ted, asking Dave with a hint of apprehension, "You'll be able to take off with this lot in here, will you?"

"Oh aye, we can support almost our own weight in cargo."

"God knows how long I'd have been stuck out there if you hadn't come along. Those trucks I drive aren't fitted out like container jobs, you know. No gas burners, no bed, no home from home. These great green things you fly are worth their weight in gold. There's no other way my people could get their stuff in these conditions. I know them all well. We always have a chat when I deliver; they tell me about their children and their hobbies. It's like losing a friend when I'm told they're no longer on the list. They either get a transplant or . . . they don't." He pointed upwards. "Think I'll get my vehicle fitted with some of those blades. Be useful in traffic jams."

Further conversation was impossible as the engine roar increased and Dave became engaged in a take-off which would have to be as finely judged as the landing. They had been sitting on the snow for almost thirty minutes and the temperature was still below zero. As Randal put on more and more power their passenger covered his ears and looked worried, but the Chinook unstuck successfully and rose through another blizzard created by the rotors.

Over the intercom Dave heard Randal questioning Maggie on navigation and a pang of regret touched him again. But for Leanne he could almost certainly have achieved his goal. How could he have been such a fool over her? Yet thinking of her in bridal finery pledging her life to his cousin, he found he was surprisingly unmoved. At this moment, caught up in something of vital immediacy, the impact of her treachery dwindled to insignificance. Optimism kicked away the last shred of his self-contempt . . . and there was more than one way to learn to fly.

Before long, Randal asked Ted to go forward to discuss their first destination, and there he stayed during the four deliveries before reaching Penzance. It was an unusual experience for Dave to bring supplies to civilians. They, in turn, found the advent of a huge military helicopter in their village very exciting. Despite the serious nature of what they were doing, Dave could not help laughing as the eager helpers scattered in all directions the minute snow began to fly and the noise grew thunderous during their descent.

Off-loading was easy. Enterprising residents brought all manner of conveyances – from handcarts to children's toboggans – on which to drag the boxes away. The crewmen gratefully accepted mugs of tea, cocoa or even soup offered to them, but Randal limited the refreshment breaks. There was a lot of ground to cover and the light would fade early in such poor conditions.

His concerns seemed justified when they approached an

isolated farm and they struck their first real problem. They had been preceded by someone else – not from 646, they knew – who had dropped fodder haphazardly over the fields leaving no area large enough to land in between munching cattle, bales of hay and thorn hedges.

Peering in dismay from the bubble window in the cabin, Dave said to Jimmy, "Did no one tell them to expect us?"

"Must've," grunted Jimmy. "If we have to land way out it'll be a hell of a business digging ourselves to that farm."

Studying the desolation below, Dave noticed at the same time as the pilots a long narrow stretch of disturbed snow on the far side of the buildings. Piled against a fence at the end of it were red and white equestrian jumps. Beside them was a tractor to which was attached a gleaner – to rake up residue after a harvester had cleared a crop. This had been used to create an easy landing pad for them.

"God bless that man. Give him a medal," called Randal.

Not a man but the patient's wife, a wiry capable woman inured to a hard life on the land. Tough, weatherbeaten and sparing of speech she became amazingly emotional when Dave carried the last box into a heated wooden outhouse which had been especially erected to store the supplies.

While Ted exchanged a cheerful goodbye with the patient, the woman confided to Dave, "He's been in a real state. Said I was wasting my time clearing the snow; said no one could land there; said you wouldn't even come." She cast a glance over her shoulder to where her sick husband was now happy. "We always keep enough to carry on for a few days beyond the month – I make sure of that – but he's always anxious on delivery day; afraid the truck won't get here. Ted never fails. But today, well, even I had my doubts. I didn't let on to him, of course. When your life depends on something . . ." She grabbed Dave's hand. "Thank you, son."

Dave was embarrassed. "No, thank *you*, ma'am. For making things easy for us . . . and for the tea and cake." On impulse he added, "I think you're doing a grand job here."

When they reached Penzance Heliport there was a signal telling them to stay overnight at St Mawgan and to stand by to give further emergency assistance. They said goodbye to Ted, who asked to go with the boxes in the hospital van to see his patient; he had some foreign stamps for the old man's collection. While tucking in to a hot Cornish pasty from the snack bar, Dave reflected on the driver's words about losing a friend when a name was deleted from his list. His spirits rose further. This was infinitely more worthwhile than a desk job sorting out personnel problems.

By mid-afternoon, Maggie's back was starting to ache from the cold. The sky looked even more forbidding as night pushed in from the east. It had been an extraordinary day; she would remember it for a long time to come. It was all for real. Nobody was watching her, checking her performance, waiting with an analysis of her strengths and weaknesses; certainly not the man beside her, who appeared to have complete faith in her ability. He had talked through the more difficult landings but had let her do the others while remaining relaxed throughout. His professional approval did not make him any more likeable, but it enabled her fully to concentrate on the job.

They were heading for the final drop: the farm on a cliff where a five-year-old was the patient. According to Ted this one would not be easy. Most of the surrounding acreage was sloping and given over to sheep and goats from which the farmer's wife and sister ran a thriving business in hand-knitted woollens, mostly exported to America. The family aimed to be self-sufficient. They kept cows for milk and butter, goats for cheese, chickens for eggs and meat. They also grew their own vegetables.

"They're a lovely group of people," Ted had said. "They can turn their hand to anything. But they can't make the little girl well," he added sadly.

As they neared their destination Maggie thought of her two brothers' children playing snowballs at Christmas. A simple pleasure any child had a right to enjoy, but probably not this little girl. Randal had said at the outset that he would handle this landing, and there had been silence in the cockpit for a while. With few landmarks to guide them Maggie kept them on a plotted course with the sea a dark mass in the distance. In the early dusk everything looked sinister and threatening. She shivered involuntarily.

Randal glanced across. "All right?"

"Fine," she replied brightly. "We should be able to see the place before long. Three or four minutes by my calculations."

He nodded ahead. "That could be it. Give or take a few

seconds you hit it on the button. Right, let's have a look at what we've got."

What they had got was an unknown quantity. As Ted had said, the ground sloped away from the cliff top in varying degrees of steepness although there was a flat area alongside the house and outbuildings.

"This one's going to be a bugger," muttered Randal, studying the ground keenly. "Any input, Maggie?"

"The only level site is right on the edge of the cliff. It's sandwiched between the house and a great gash that plunges to the sea, and there's no way of knowing how firm the ground is."

"It's hard rock all along this coastline. Sure it's bloody close to the edge, but the wind's in our favour. The real problem is the proximity to those buildings. A couple look pretty ramshackle." He sighed. "Christ, who'd choose to live in this wilderness?"

"A family wanting to escape from the rest of the world?"

"Yeah, until their poor kid gets ill and needs the rest of the world to keep her alive."

Maggie was surprised by his savage tone and said no more as they circled over the cluster of slate-roofed buildings huddled together high above the pounding sea. She looked down on the isolated homestead standing stark against the snow and felt an echo of Randal's feelings about the place.

"I'm not risking that plateau until I know what kind of damage we might do if we land there," he said firmly. "Don't ever be fooled into accepting what looks like an easier option until you've checked that it is." He banked away from the sea and took a closer look at the fields sloping down to a winding strip of snow that marked the narrow road normally closed off to allow Ted's truck free access.

"OK, guys," he announced. "I'm going down in that area roughly a hundred and fifty yards from the end building. There's a slight flattening of the ground. Got it? One of you'll have to tramp up there to inspect the stability of the slates on the roofs. Yeah, yeah, groan, groan, but I'll buy the volunteer a couple of beers at St Mawgan. So will Maggie," he added slyly.

"They'll all go," she said absently, wondering how he would approach the hillside landing. She had tackled a couple during her training, both on gentle slopes like the one they were approaching, but not in snow. She did not envy the crewman a long tramp in poor light up to a place which would amply fit the description "Bleak House".

Whatever her personal feelings for Randal Ivan Price, Maggie admired his skill. She had flown with enough pilots through her training to know he was a "natural". She envied that flair which she felt no amount of experience would ever create in her, and watched as he dropped towards the small area he had chosen as the least of the evils. They crunched firmly on to the slope and felt that the snow had hardened further in the plunging temperature. With another snowfall due it was essential that they deliver the supplies now because it might be out of the question tomorrow.

A lone figure passed the cockpit, knee-deep in snow as he made his way upward.

Jimmy said over the intercom, "We all voted Dave should do the honours. He's a Highlander used to this weather and there's no war memorial to knock him out."

"We've promised him a haggis when he gets back," said another. "We'll take a pot-shot at one as it runs past."

"Do they turn white in winter like stoats?" asked someone else. "Might be difficult to see in the snow."

While Maggie watched with a degree of sympathy as the Scot trudged on and up, his colleagues filled in the waiting time with their certain knowledge of what a haggis would do to Dave if it happened to run up his trouser leg as he passed.

Maggie liked Dave Ashmore; admired his determination. She turned to Randal. "What if he comes back with a negative report?"

It was plain his mind had been elsewhere. "Eh? Oh . . . we unload from here. What else?"

"It'll be dark before we could finish."

"Yes."

"Isn't it worth risking the plateau?"

"No."

Silence fell between them. It seemed a very long time before a dark shape appeared over the crest and retraced his footprints. When he eventually entered the aircraft, Dave came forward to the cockpit. His face was rosy from the chill but he was not in the least breathless from his efforts.

"I'd say there's no problem. It all looks solid enough. Has to be, up here in the path of Atlantic gales. They're like crofters' places, built to withstand anything. Mr Hunter, the owner, is happy for us to move up there."

"Yeah, and he'll be happy to claim compensation if anything goes wrong."

"Wind's rising and it's freezing hard. I felt ice in the air. That snow's not far off."

"OK, if you think it's sturdy enough we'll go for it. It'll make unloading a hell of a sight easier. Thanks, Dave."

Maggie felt rising excitement. This was going to be something she could learn from in case she was ever faced with a similar decision. It had all the elements found in the kind of hypothetical situation put forward by instructors during training.

Randal lost no time in taking to the air again to have a final look at what he was facing. The delay on the ground meant that it was significantly darker than when they had circled the area the first time. He asked Maggie to switch on the lights. They came on to sparkle the snow and light the limits of the space. The fissure now looked more dangerous, and dead ahead lay the pewter-coloured sea which assaulted this coastline relentlessly. Near the cliff edge a shrub provided the only fixed point available to facilitate the landing.

"Keep your eyes on those roofs. If there's any sign of the slates shifting, yell," said Randal, starting to lose height.

"Where do we go if they do?" she asked.

"Back to hunting haggis."

Maggie stared at the dark roofs with eyes that ached but risked a quick glance forward. The edge of the cliff looked far too near as Jimmy and Dave recited their guiding patter.

"Keep watching those bloody tiles," snapped Randal, and her head swung back as sharply as his words. The tiles remained where they should be. Then she could see nothing but flying snow and realised they must be almost down. The familiar crunch on contact told Maggie they had made it, and tension flowed from her tired limbs.

A faint cheer came from the crew, followed by the sound of the ramp being lowered. Maggie felt a strong urge to say, "Congratulations", but sensed that it would be superfluous and sat silently beside Randal who seemed intent on watching the activity outside. Lights blazed from the windows of the house, illuminating the crewmen working the moving chain once more. They had worked flat out throughout the day and must now be feeling very weary. Looking around the bleak scene, the elation Maggie had felt over the successful landing was suddenly replaced by a wash of loneliness. A glance at her companion's face suggested that he shared the sensation.

Jimmy eventually crossed to them carrying a tray, leaving the others to have their drinks in the lee of the house. "Cocoa and home-made gooseberry tart," he announced in a voice hoarse with tiredness. "I told the lads to make it quick, but the kiddy's mum and auntie are real crackers. I'll have to prise them away. Auntie looks set to offer Dave more than a haggis if he stays here much longer. He's certainly got something women go for."

"We've all got one of those." Randal wiped cocoa froth from his mouth with the back of his hand. "You haven't described the patient."

"Er . . . well, she's thin and pale. Great brown eyes, plaits and the happiest smile you ever saw. This is the most exciting day of her life, she said." Jimmy glanced towards the house. "My kids have everything they want but none of them looks as happy as she does."

"What's her name?" asked Maggie through a mouthful of tart.

"Eh? Oh . . . dunno. Never asked."

Randal put his empty mug on the tray and looked the sergeant in the eye. "She'd have told you. It's the first thing they do. So is it Lydia?"

Jimmy shook his head. "Fiona."

"Nice name." He reached in his pocket to bring out a small package. "Almost forgot. This is from Ted. A book he'd promised to get for her. Didn't want to disappoint her." As Jimmy walked back through the cabin with the tray, Randal added harshly, "Get those sex-starved bastards on the move or we'll be here all night."

It was a quick flight to St Mawgan. They were all cold and aching but there was a sense of satisfaction, too. Maggie made the landing at the military airport being used by aircraft from all the emergency services, and they welcomed the warmth and the hot meal provided. As they ate conversation was desultory until Dave cried, "Hey, that's us on TV. Look! Turn up the volume, someone."

An extended news item on the severe weather in the West Country featured Ted with his truck and their own transfer of the boxes to the Chinook, filmed by the men Randal had cursed.

" . . . muscular crew from Hampton Heyhoe moving stores from a stranded truck was piloted by Flight Lieutenant Margaret Spencer, who only joined the squadron three days ago." The camera zoomed in on Maggie in the cockpit. "Not a damsel in distress, but a damsel to the rescue," said the commentator with a chuckle.

As the pictures changed to snow-covered hothouses in the Scilly Isles, Maggie felt her cheeks burn with anger and dismay. A *damsel* to the rescue! What a bloody nerve! The men were all looking at her wearing fatuous grins. They were as bad! She faced up to Randal.

"Sorry about that, Boss."

His grin was more fatuous than the rest. "You're younger and prettier than I am, and damsels are more newsworthy in these situations."

"In that case, I'll look out for one for you; with endless legs and big come-hither eyes."

He was no longer amused and they all soon headed for bed. Maggie shared a room with an army pilot called Kate, who was as eager to get to sleep as she. Even so, Maggie woke at four a.m. and, after tossing restlessly for a while, got up and headed for the nearest bathroom. Walking barefoot along the dim corridor she saw someone at the far end gazing out of the window into his private world. Was he thinking of the child called Fiona or of his own daughter? Or was he sleepless over someone with endless legs and large sexy eyes? Maggie hoped it was the first. The sick girl with the happy smile was the most deserving of his concern.

They flew in to Hampton in the late afternoon two days later. A slow thaw had begun. There would be floods to deal with soon. For Randal it was the first time in four and a half years that he had returned to a single room in the Mess. No Lydia to put chubby arms around his neck and dribble chocolate on his shirt; no Neil to listen wide-eyed to accounts of Daddy's adventures. No Fiona smelling of the French perfume he always brought her from his stints overseas. She was a real woman; sophisticated, provocative and still incredibly sexy when fully dressed. Even motherhood had failed to dim her glamour; she had looked a million dollars in maternity clothes.

Randal could not stand the kind of woman who went around

resembling a plumber's mate in denim dungarees and a T-shirt bearing vulgar messages, and who slept in a baggy, saggy, off-white garment with Wallace and Grommit on the front. In the past, he had twice woken beside girls like that and wondered what on earth had got him into bed in the first place. If Fiona wore anything at all at night, it was filmy and very brief.

Throwing his bag to the floor he headed for the showers, passing the room occupied by Maggie Spencer. There was no slow thaw where she was concerned, and he would wager a month's salary she wore a baggy, saggy, off-white thing in bed. Hers would have Superwoman on the front.

Thoroughly clean and relaxed after a long hot shower, Randal dressed in fresh clothes and picked up the telephone. This was unlikely to be a cosy chat, so he remained on his feet as he dialled Marylands. Mary Holland answered.

"I'd like to speak to my wife," he said.

There was a significant pause. "I'm afraid Fiona is engaged in putting the children to bed."

"Where's the au pair?"

"Ironing their clothes."

"Then she can switch off the iron and take over while Fiona comes to the phone."

Mary gave an audible sigh. "You upset her greatly at Christmas. It entirely ruined the holiday for us all. It's not good for the children to see their mother crying."

"They don't see their father doing anything at all."

"Whose fault is that?"

"You should know. I told you when I rescued my children from your clutches last year. No, don't hang up. I have a right to speak to Fiona. If she cried all through Christmas it hardly suggests she's happy with you, as you like to believe. Please put me through to her."

"It won't do any good," came the cold retort.

"If I make her cry it'll only be what she was doing before I rang, so what's the worry?"

There was silence followed by several clicks as an upstairs extension was paged. Mary pressed the "secret" button during her exchange with her daughter, then Fiona said cautiously, "It's a bad time, Randal. The children are getting ready for bed."

"I know what time they go to bed. They're *my* children. And if you're listening in, Mary, stop! This is a private conversation."

He waited for the telltale click, then asked quickly, "You still there, Fee?"

"Yes. What did you want to say?"

He stared at the plain wall of his room. Christ, what did he want to say? I want you back? Life's hell without you? "How are the kids?" was the best he could manage.

"Enjoying their bathtime."

"We used to enjoy ours, remember?" There was silence from the girl who could do very erotic things under soapy water. "Have you been watching news reports on the emergency in Cornwall?" he asked hopefully.

"Not particularly, why?"

That was a dead duck, so he tried something else. "How was Christmas?"

"About as bad as you could make it."

"I wasn't there," he pointed out swiftly.

"The story of your life."

Oh God, he was getting nowhere. "If it's any comfort to you, my Christmas was the worst I've ever spent. I woke up in a cell."

After a pause she asked in a softer tone, "Why did you ring?"

"Why the hell do you think? I wanted to hear your voice. I want to see you. I bloody want to *touch* you."

"Don't shout!"

"I'm trying to tell you how I feel," he said desperately. "I don't know what's going on between us. We're married, for Christ's sake, but you're there with *Mummy* and *Daddy*, and I'm . . . I'm here in a single room. Lydia and Neil are mine. I fathered them and have a right to help you bring them up." Her silence fuelled his anger. "Whatever the hell you're trying to do to me, it's working. I can't sleep. I can't think straight. And when I'm flying . . ." He broke off on hearing a muffled sob. "Fee, *don't.*"

"I'm sorry, I'm sorry," she mumbled. "I can't sleep, either. I just don't know what to *do.*"

Longing to jump in his car and race through the wintry roads to collect her, Randal could only say, "We'll talk about it; sort everything out. It's the only way to end this nonsense neither of us wants. I tried on Christmas Eve, but blew it. You know me; not high on tact." Hope was starting to bubble up. "Look, we're on emergency standby due to the severe weather, but as soon as I get the chance of a couple of days away I'll book a room at the Crow and Magpie. Remember our wild night there? We'll have another just like that."

Fiona gave a wobbly laugh. "We were both high on scrumpy."

"Then we'll get even higher." His voice was hoarse with emotion. "I want you, Fee. I want you in my life again. I want my pretty little girl and that serious, spick and span kid who looks so very like me."

"We've all missed you so much," she confessed softly. "It's even worse without you than with you."

He forced a laugh. "God, what an epitaph!"

"Come soon, darling."

"I'd come tonight if I could," he vowed. "Tell me what you're wearing and I'll imagine I'm there."

They talked for half an hour with greater intimacy than they had shared for some months. When Randal finally replaced the receiver after hearing prompted goodnights from his children, he felt like a new man. Even so, thoughts of a sick little girl on a Cornish clifftop hovered at the back of his mind.

When Maggie reached her room she threw down her bag and stood gazing at one of the letters she had taken from her pigeonhole. Phil's handwriting! Still on an operational high she hesitated before opening it. She had been part of a crew for the past few days but on the ground she was alone again and vulnerable. Her twin had sent her only a brief note.

> Dear Mags,
>   Saw you on TV and knew what a kick that must have given you. Dad rang full of excitement to ask if we were watching. I won't tell you Mum's views! Rob's at a medical conference in Geneva; Chas is down a pothole OF COURSE! They'll be told when they're available, you bet. Congrats! Yours as of yore,
>   Twin bro.

Numbly, Maggie read it through again. No mention of Fay. He had written without his wife's knowledge and wanted no reply to upset her. In a burst of anger Maggie tore the note to pieces. More than anything she longed to ring and tell Phil about the past three days. There had not been time for her to make any friends at Hampton; anyone to whom she could talk freely. In any case, it was only to one's family or lover that it was acceptable to say with enthusiasm, "I did really well" . . . "I didn't make a single error" . . . "I carried it off brilliantly." Phil would once have listened eagerly to an account of her operational debut. His surreptitious letter proved he was not entirely happy about the terms he had laid down, but he had his precious Fay to console him. Maggie had been suddenly deprived of their lifetime link and had no one to compensate her for the loss.

Putting aside the garage bill for towing her car to Hampton and an invitation from her school to an old girls' reunion, Maggie gathered up her toilet bag and dressing-gown to head for the bathroom. A long hot shower would surely improve her outlook. It did not. The longing to talk to Phil remained. Was he really so completely under Fay's thumb that he could shrug off their bond so easily? Her own loyalty was unassailable; she had believed Phil's to be as strong. He should have *rung* to congratulate her – although she was still furious over the TV report. Writing a sneaky letter that Fay would not know about was the weak way out. For Maggie it would have to be all or nothing, so he would get nothing from her.

Still on the theme of weakness her thoughts drifted to Randal, who was said to be dotty about his wife who was living in the comfort of Daddy's ranch among the hunting shooting fishing brigade. How could the self-assured, skilful man she had shared the cockpit with make such a fool of himself? Then there was Pete Landis, a tough-looking navigator, maudlin on New Year's Eve because his girl had taken his Christmas presents then ditched him for a long-haired disc jockey on Boxing Day. Maggie had dropped out of the party when it grew too hectic, but not before he had unburdened his woes on her and anyone else who would listen. Add Rusty Locke, the squadron womaniser, who was trying to wriggle out of marrying the woman he was currently living with, and Maggie felt the male sex did not show up in too good a light. Turning off the shower and wrapping herself in a large towel, she wondered why on earth she had chosen a profession overwhelmingly dominated by them.

Returning to her room she felt disinclined to eat downstairs, but she had seen enough ice and snow recently not to wish to face more merely to eat in the village. It would have to be dinner in the Mess, then straight to bed with a book that would take her to an imaginary world. Pausing in the act of applying lipstick, she muttered, "What the hell's wrong with me? In the air I felt great. Now I'm just the reverse."

The telephone rang making her jump so much the lipstick jerked across her cheek. Her spirits magically lifted; Phil must have sensed her longing and defied Fay! Snatching up the receiver, she said unsteadily, "I should have guessed you'd know, and call."

The voice was not Phil's. "Ma'am, this is Lance Corporal Phipps in the Guard Room. There's a Mr Craig Ellevan here. An American. Says he's a friend of yours. OK to send him across to the Mess?"

Disappointment and astonishment vied with each other to arrest clear thought. "He's *there* . . . in person?"

"Er . . . well, yes. He's standing in front of me."

"Good God!" Maggie tried to marshal her wits.

"Should I put him on the line?" suggested Phipps, getting nowhere and growing impatient.

"Oh . . . well, I suppose so," she said without enthusiasm.

"Hi, Maggie. Happy New Year!" Craig's accented baritone was warm and friendly in her ear.

"How did you know where I was?" It sounded ungracious but she was still struggling with disappointment.

"Hampton Heyhoe. One of those funny English names I like so much. Remember? I got down here yesterday. Booked a room in the Bird in Hand. Correction, booked *the* room. The inn's small and quaint, and I want you to come and have dinner with me."

"Oh . . . I can't, Craig."

"Why not? We had this arrangement, didn't we? No Christmas, so New Year instead." He paused briefly. "You're surely not flying tonight? I was told you've just got in after three days on the job."

Maggie scrubbed at the lipstick smudge with a tissue. "That's right. I'm exhausted."

"All the more reason to come out and relax." He added in an undertone, "I only want to talk, nothing more. You owe me that."

It was too great an effort to resist further. "All right. I'll be ready in fifteen minutes. Let me have another word with Corporal Whatsit."

After vouching for Craig she replaced the receiver with a sigh. If he was set on forcing a commitment from her tonight he would not get it. They had not made contact since his call from Hong Kong. She had forgotten his plan to come to rural Dorset. They had been eager lovers and warm friends for six months; she had gone as far as to invite him to meet her family at Christmas. How could she have forgotten him so easily? Because joining 646 Squadron had been more important to her than anything else. Yet she had not forgotten Phil.

Getting listlessly to her feet she took off her silk blouse and replaced it with a red and black sweatshirt with a fancy embroidered logo. Then she freed her hair from the twist she wore during working hours and brushed it so that it hung loose to her shoulders. The lipstick smudge was still evident so she had to wash her face and make up again from scratch.

It was a good twenty minutes later when she reached the hall, carrying a suede jacket over her arm. Craig was nowhere in view but she heard an American voice in the bar. Why, oh why had he gone in there? She did not want the guzzle and guffaw element learning about her private life. Craig was standing with some of B Flight, including their commander who appeared to be well under the influence already and in remarkable form. Craig was a whisky drinker, a connoisseur of wine; he hated English beer. Yet he held a pint half drunk.

Catching sight of Maggie he raised a hand in farewell to his companions, put the glass on the bar, then crossed to kiss her. The usual "oooh" rose from the drinkers, and there were a few lewd comments about damsels which brought laughter.

Maggie said fiercely, "You promised *me* dinner, not the other way round. You can see what that lot are like."

Craig nodded. "That's why I did it . . . in case they had ideas about you."

"Huh, they've plenty of those, but not the kind you mean. Come on, let's get out of here."

It was going to be another cold night. As they went down the steps, Craig said, "My rental car's quaint enough to match the name of the village but it's all they had. The heater has only one setting, so I brought a blanket from my bedroom to tuck around you. And that's not a sly way of getting you up there to put it back."

The car was a roomy saloon acceptable to most people other than an American. Maggie let him settle her in the passenger seat, still amazed that he had chosen to isolate himself in Hampton Heyhoe for the chance of seeing her. She would not stay late. A night spent in her warm comfortable bed was too great a lure.

The Bird in Hand was a long low building with stone walls and new thatch on the roof. Festive lights edged the windows and a Christmas tree still stood at the far end of the room. A huge fire of blazing logs added to the charm of the two-hundred-year-old hostelry and threw out welcome warmth to Maggie who still felt internally chilled. Business was quiet, which enabled them to get a table in the inglenook.

Craig went to the bar and returned with his whisky and a gin and tonic for Maggie. He held up his glass and quoted his favourite toast. "Here's looking at you, kid."

"Happy New Year, Craig," she responded quietly.

After a moment or two he said, "I caught the TV report. You really did that?"

"That ghastly waffle about damsels! They checked out my name, but not what we were doing. It was medical supplies we picked up, not *stores*. And we delivered them to eight patients, some living in remote areas. Why didn't they feature that instead of having a giggle at my expense? I wasn't in charge, either. Randal was the boss and he handled a few very tricky landings. He's some pilot!"

"And a nice guy. He invited me in and bought me a beer."

"He would! You don't like beer."

"No . . . and I guess you don't like him. Why?"

"Can we order? I'm ravenous."

"OK, sore subject," he said, holding up his hands. "The landlord says there's only two meals tonight because it's never busy after New Year. Plaice and chips or something called shepherd's pie. You'll know what that is."

She gave a faint smile. "Let's have that. You'll like it."

"If I don't you'll have to eat mine." He returned with more drinks after ordering their dinner. "You look ready for another."

She relaxed against the high-backed seat. "When did you get back from Hong Kong?"

"Two days after Christmas. Sorry I missed your family party."

"The kids got overexcited and so did their fathers. We all ate too much and Mum constantly moaned that her only daughter was pretending to be a man. Dad provided his usual sanity in the midst of bedlam!"

"You didn't mention Phil. How is he?"

"Fine."

"Still building boats?"

"Yep."

"And guessing your thoughts?"

"I can't guess yours," she countered adroitly. "What made you snow-plough down here without ringing me first? I was sent to Cornwall at a moment's notice. That's what happens when there's an emergency."

"My emergency is the need to know where we stand. If I'd called you'd have told me not to come."

She sighed. "Craig, I don't know what you want when you ask where we stand. I have an absorbing career in the RAF; you're an ambitious company man with the American drive for success. That was where we stood six months ago. Nothing's changed."

"Oh, but it has. I had to promise not to lure you into bed before you'd agree to come here."

Before Maggie could evaluate that, a girl arrived with their food. She smiled shyly at Craig. "Dad says there's plenty more if you want it. He don't expect many in."

"OK, thanks."

Neither of them paid any attention to the steaming pile of potato-topped mince, with carrots and sprouts alongside. Maggie's appetite had vanished; Craig looked intense.

"Is there someone else?"

"Someone else I'm sleeping with? No." She sighed again. "That's why I'd have stopped you coming to Hampton. Questions like that are irrelevant. We're both free agents."

"Sure we are, so why can't we go on that way? It worked before. I'd like to know why it isn't working now. Give me a good reason and I'll go find myself another free agent to enjoy life with. Maybe my American drive for success won't let me ditch a deal until I know it's good and lost."

Taking a long drink from the second gin and tonic, Maggie had no idea what to tell him. He had the healthy good looks of a man reared in an exclusive mountain resort where children learned to excel at outdoor activities from an early age. Yet he had chosen a career spent mainly in boardrooms, hotels and planes. The mix made him very appealing. A sophisticated, well travelled, sexy athlete; what more could she want from a free agent?

She said frankly, "There's no reason why you shouldn't find someone else but this deal isn't exactly good and lost. You've just caught me at a bad time."

"OK." He picked up his fork. "Let's eat this cowpoke's pie before it freezes up like everything else around here."

"That should make you happy," she said, glad he had dropped the searching questions. "Have you brought your skis?"

"Sure. If there's snow around I make use of it. Hey, this tastes better than it looks."

She started her own meal. "Are you competing at Val d'Isère this year?"

"Uh-uh. I got promotion for how I handled the crisis in Hong Kong. Can't take time out from this new job."

"So the obnoxious P.J. finally recognised your worth! Congratulations! Pity about the skiing, though," Maggie added, half her attention taken by the man in black leather who had entered along with a blast of cold air.

Craig was philosophical. "I had my day of glory. At thirty-two I'm too old to compete against teenagers who can practise every day."

She turned to him and smiled. "Poor old man! I should introduce you to Sergeant Ashmore, who's just come in. He once skied into a war memorial buried beneath snow and knocked himself out." Her smile broadened. "That's the kind of thing you might do if you whizz around these quaint villages."

Craig glanced across the bar. "He one of your guys?"

"Mmm, he flew with us for the last few days."

"Then you don't want his company tonight. I'm aiming to make you relax, ma'am."

"No ulterior motive?"

"No ulterior motive."

"You're very nice."

"I keep telling you."

That exchange prompted a speculative silence as they ate and wondered how the evening would end. Then the girl arrived to ask if they wanted seconds, and Craig said yes so long as it was as good as the firsts. Maggie declined, raising a hand in greeting to Dave sitting at a table with a pint and a plate of plaice and chips. She wondered why he was eating here after three days of snack meals. Surely the Sergeants' Mess would be a better choice.

"If you and the pilot you don't like did the flying, how come your knock-out skier was with you?" asked Craig, following her gaze.

"He handles the cargo."

"That figures. He looks tough, especially in that leather gear. I'd think twice about meeting him in a dark alley."

"He's not a thug," she protested with a chuckle. "He rides a splendiferous motorbike with the skill of a speedway rider. He gave me a lift in appallingly icy conditions when I ditched my car on the day I joined the squadron. I was very impressed."

"By his driving or his good looks?"

Maggie replied, as the girl came with Craig's second helping, "I don't go for the dark stormy type."

"That leaves me out on a limb. Thanks," he added to the girl, whose colour rose before she turned away.

"You're not stormy; you're so sweet tempered you give me a guilt complex." She lightly touched his fingers in apology. "Sorry I've been bitchy this evening."

"Maybe *I* like the stormy type . . . and maybe a bit too much. But that's my choice." He attacked the shepherd's pie with his fork for some seconds, then his dark eyes challenged her. "So now you feel guilty and a whole lot friendlier, care to tell me why this is a bad time? Could be I can help."

The gin, his persuasive charm and the warm intimacy of their corner by the fire melted the chill that had come over her since Phil's ultimatum on the telephone. A sudden reversal of mood had her longing for sympathy and physical closeness. She now wanted to go to bed with him.

"You know how much flying means to me, Craig," she began, gently staying his hand as he made to eat another forkful of mince. "We've discussed our careers enough times."

"We're both ambitious, you mean."

"I was determined to make the journey here on the twenty-ninth, but I came to grief on a steep hill and started walking. That's when Dave miraculously appeared and offered his pillion.

The road conditions were atrocious. Without his offer it would have been a long slog across lonely countryside, the last part in darkness."

"This is no place to walk around at night, especially for a woman. Oh sure, I know how well you can defend yourself, but it's crazy to face situations like that if they can be avoided."

"But I was *determined* to report on time." She found herself rushing to tell him the rest. "As soon as I could I rang Phil, knowing he would sense I'd had problems and be concerned." She frowned. "I wish I hadn't. He said . . . well, he said we should stop calling to have endless chats and only make contact if we know the other is in serious trouble. It's Fay! *She* told him to say that. She's jealous. Always has been," she added heatedly. "You can guess how desperately hurt I was. Still am. How can Phil be so weak? And how could he say that when I'd just joined my squadron? He knew it was a big day for me. *He knew that!*

"As a result, I met my new colleagues feeling as low as a worm in the grass, and that man you think is such a nice guy bawled me out over nothing in front of everyone; his wife's just left him, so he's got it in for women. To make things worse, he was promoted the very next day and became my flight commander. He may be a brilliant pilot but he can't resist getting at me. They all do. You heard them."

Craig said nothing for a moment while he studied her flushed face. "You *are* all screwed up, aren't you! You've always gotten along with people, made friends, given as good as you got." He made a wry face. "I should know. One of the things I admire in you is that you've made it in a man's world. But your Mom's got it all wrong; you're still very much a woman, Maggie." He pushed aside his plate and and took her hand. "It's not like you to have a hang-up like this. When that guy bawled you out, the girl I know would have fixed him with a few sassy words. Why didn't you? He wasn't your commander then. And why the hell are you letting them all get at you? If they see you can't take it, they'll keep on. Honey, you've been around men long enough to know that."

Maggie needed sympathy, not reason. When she said nothing, he looked at her through narrowed eyes. "Oh – oh! It's not them, it's that goddam brother who's thrown you off keel so badly. Is it because he told you not to call him, or because you think he's dancing on Fay's string?"

"Both," said Maggie savagely. "He's weak."

"He's *in love*. It makes men – and women – behave differently. I guess you've never been there or you'd understand."

"I understand that Fay's always disliked and resented me. At Christmas I guessed she was pregnant. It was obvious to me from Phil's manner, although the others didn't notice. Fay said he had told me *their* secret and flew into a rage, screaming the news to anyone within earshot. Phil told me Rob says we must all make allowances for her now. Pander to her, he means."

"She's Phil's wife, honey. She's carrying his child, and that *is* something between just the two of them. It's very special."

"So is being twins."

"I guess it must be," he conceded, "but you're not joined by flesh to each other. By all means enjoy your unique bond but don't hang it around the poor guy's neck like a goddam anchor."

His words were like a bucket of cold water over the reviving warmth between them. Maggie drew in her breath at his inference; but of course he was another man, certain to take Phil's side. She had not wanted to come here tonight. Her first instinct to refuse had been the right one and she wanted to leave right now.

From the corner of her eye she saw that Dave was on his feet and shrugging on his padded leather jacket. She stood up, calling his name. He looked over in surprise as he closed the heavy zip and picked up his gloves.

"Can I have a lift back to the Station?" she asked, taking up her coat from the back of the seat.

He looked uneasily from her to Craig and back again. "Er . . . on the bike, you mean?"

"I'd be very grateful." She slipped her arms in the sleeves of her jacket, aware that Craig was coming around the table to her. "My friend has already made one round trip this evening; I'd like to save him another." She closed on Dave. "You are going straight there, aren't you?"

"Aye," he said warily. His gaze shifted to her hefty companion. "Is that all right with you?"

Maggie gave him no chance to reply. "Thanks for dinner, Craig. Good luck with the new job . . . and I think perhaps you

66

should ditch the deals that are good and lost." She went out to the chilly night leaving Dave to follow.

He covered the distance at madness speed, hoping she was not only scared but very cold in her thin clothes. He was dearly tempted to go straight to the Sergeants' Mess and leave her to walk halfway round the perimeter to her own quarters but Rowan courtesy would not let him do that. He vented his feelings instead when she climbed from the pillion and held out the crash helmet.

"Don't ever do that to me again," he warned over the engine noise, glad to see she was shivering. "Because I picked you up on that first day it doesn't make me your chauffeur. I don't know what went wrong back there – he seemed perfectly sober and reasonable to me – but if you get yourself into situations that turn sour, get yourself out of them. Don't expect me to do it for you. He could have turned nasty and I wouldn't have blamed him. Not fifteen minutes earlier you'd been holding his hand and coming on to him. Whatever game you were playing was between you and him." He revved up with an impressive roar, then decided he had more to say to the girl standing with an astonished look on her flushed face. Their breath was clouding in the coldness, and the motorcycle exhaust added further haziness to the clear night illuminated by lights from the Officers' Mess windows.

"Let's get this straight," Dave said. "I won't have you using me."

"You were coming here anyway. I didn't *use* you," she protested in surprisingly mild tones.

"Oh aye, you did. And you used him, too, by my judgement of it. He took it lying down, but I'll not. I'm not a man to be ordered around by you or by any other woman. Keep that in your mind."

He was totally disconcerted when his remarks were greeted by a broad smile. "Thank God there's one man around here who has a mind and will of his own! Thanks for the lift. Goodnight."

He watched her climb the steps and go in, still thrown by her reaction. He could not have put it plainer, yet she had made something of a joke of what he had said. After putting his motorbike away he went to his room convinced that Maggie Spencer's skin was so thick nothing would get through to her. Of course she had used him! Presumably to make her boyfriend jealous. He had been put in a difficult position; he could hardly have refused her open request for a lift. She had definitely been leading the man on before that and Dave had seen nothing to explain her sudden desire to leave. He told himself he should have been quicker off the mark and lied about coming straight back, but he was tired and unprepared for her move. She would not try that trick on him again. His reaction next time would be impossible to treat as a joke!

Dave got into bed, switched the CD player on low and began to pore over some brochures that had arrived. His interest mounted as he found exactly what he had hoped to see. He enjoyed group activities, revelled in the company of other men engaged in hearty sports, but he was not one to sit around in bars yarning. He was reserved over his private life and happy enough roaming around alone.

His fellow sergeants were bluff uncomplicated men who liked to enjoy themselves in any manner open to them: New Year's Eve had provided a perfect excuse for booze and high jinks. The other Scottish mess member was still on leave, so Dave had been targeted to celebrate Hogmanay. They had almost certainly spiked his drinks. He had a hazy memory of being lifted up to perform a Highland reel on a table, which had come to an abrupt end when his feet encountered thin air. His last very faint recollection was of someone deciding it was time they discovered whether or not Scotsmen wore underpants.

He had awoken in the morning in much the same state as after the dread wedding; as hung over as they had guessed at the briefing. Action had thankfully cleared Dave's head quite quickly, but he had been paralytic twice in less than a week and enough was enough. Which was why he had slipped down to the Bird in Hand tonight. His alcohol intake had always been reasonably low due to his dedication to fitness. It would now return to that level.

Sliding beneath the bedclothes after reading the brochures through again, a wave of contentment flowed over him. He had thoroughly enjoyed the past few days. There was more flying to come; more challenges to meet. When the snow fully cleared he could race his motorbike along the scenic coast road. He would join the hang-gliding club which had sent him a brochure and he would take his surfboard down the three miles to the beach. On the Station were tennis and squash courts, and a good swimming pool. Best of all, he would go along to the local flying club and continue the lessons he had embarked on before he surrendered his commission. He would be a pilot yet.

He smiled in the darkness. Thank God Leanne had ditched him! He might now be shackled to her, worrying over bills and having to account for every hour spent away from some rented house furnished with basics. Oh no, life was far, far better without women. He would stay well clear of them from now on . . . and that included Maggie Spencer.

February

Bosnia was not Randal's favourite area of operations. Although the risk of being caught in crossfire had been virtually eliminated and the brutal war had subsided into an uneasy peace, there was still enough devastation, personal misery and smouldering hatred to make it a difficult place in which to work. Snow and bitter temperatures made it worse, and when a man was desperate to sort out his rocky marriage a six-week stint there amounted to a penal sentence. He had known it was scheduled when he had promised Fiona an early meeting, but he had fallen victim to a flu epidemic soon after the new emergency caused by floods in the West Country, and that was that. Fiona had frozen again after her sudden thaw, reiterating her protest against his constant absences. This time he had added a protest of his own and left Hampton for Bosnia filled with resentment and frustration. Now there was only a week left before they returned, and there would probably be a few days' stand-down. He could achieve a lot in that time if he played it right.

The past five weeks had contained the usual ingredients. There had been a tricky incident when someone on the ground whose brains must have been numbed by the cold failed to stack a load properly and a box fell crushing his leg. There had been a hilarious episode when a billy goat had invaded a cabin during loading and resisted all attempts to get him out. Jimmy had been butted in an area his fellow crewman claimed would ensure he never had a fifth child. The tale was circulated and exaggerated to provide light relief from the dreariness of winter in a country ravaged by its own people.

Randal was pleased with the way the two additions to the Flight had settled in. Maggie was a capable pilot and took the rough with the smooth like the rest. She had dismounted from her high horse somewhat and her quick wit brought some devastating replies to ribbing. Yet there was a bitter edge to her responses. Maggie Spencer very clearly did not like men, in particular her flight commander. Randal admitted that their initial meeting had been thorny – she had tried to be too clever when he was going through a bad time, but then when wasn't he these days?

In the cockpit Maggie was on the ball and fizzing with life. She was animated when talking about the job, but once the conversation turned to other things she flickered out like a candle flame. It was not that she was uninformed – odd comments had betrayed a mind packed with knowledge – she was simply disinclined to contribute in anything other than professional areas. She refused to drink beer; she claimed to hate the taste and had no intention of cultivating it, yet she happily stood a round when it was her turn. She participated in sports with energy. Life with three brothers had made her highly competitive.

One of the Navy Sea King pilots based with them had inadvisedly tried his luck with her one boozy evening and, when he would not take no for an answer, he discovered she knew some moves he had not encountered. Maggie had a black belt in *Goju ryu*. This news prompted a challenge from another Navy pilot who had a black belt in *Taekwon do*. The RAF contingent roared approval when she ended an entertaining and hard fought contest with a throw her opponent was unfamiliar with. After the ritual of expressing mutual honour, the loser was thoroughly tormented by his friends over the blow to his macho pride. Maggie was proclaimed the hero of the evening by her high-spirited fellows, but Randal was sure she was privately chalking up a victory against the entire male sex. He once more wondered who was responsible for her attitude. It must make life difficult for her but that was her problem, and as long as it did not affect general morale Randal left her to deal with it. He had enough problems of his own.

Dave Ashmore, on the other hand, was an easy member of the Flight. Apart from a certain reserve about his private life he mixed well with everyone. They all knew his family were officers in a famous Highland regiment and he had resigned his commission to fly, but he never talked about it. He was a superb athlete, and they were popular in any male group. He invented a form of curling which the crewmen indulged in on a stretch of ice they created behind their quarters. Dave was happier in

71

the extreme cold than most of them, and he had somehow laid hands on a pair of snowshoes as issued to Norwegian troops. Despite all attempts to prise from him the means by which he had got them, he kept his secret. There had been many bids to relieve him of them, but his canny Scottish ability to guard his possessions ensured that no one ever managed to filch them. It was apparent that he cared more for sport than for women and he made little secret of his dislike of Maggie. Ironically, Dave seemed to be the only man in B Flight she halfway respected. That was life, Randal mused.

The rest were their normal selves. Rusty was in hot pursuit of a Croatian interpreter with whom Randal had had a brief affair before he met Fiona. She was aiming for a British name and passport. Pete was still making a meal of being dumped in favour of a disc jockey and Jimmy could not get to the bottom of why his children did not seem as happy as the Cornish Fiona on dialysis. Their commander was afraid of losing the Berkshire Fiona – and Lydia and Neil. Situation normal!

Against the background of these personal ups and downs they airlifted supplies to troops manning outposts, flew with armoured cars or light guns slung beneath them and transported water, food, medical supplies, mail, warm clothing and fuel in all weathers. They took VIPs to emergency meetings and they sometimes acted as an air ambulance in remote areas. There was also still a demand for patrols whenever it was suspected trouble might flare again between people whose hatred went so deep it would outlast their lifetimes.

As he flew back to the airfield through fine sleet five days before their scheduled return to Hampton, Randal was depressed. They had delivered fuel to a base which had been cut off by an avalanche blocking the only access road. He never liked carrying volatile loads – none of them did – and the smell was still strong although there were only sacks of mail in the cabin now. As the airfield came in sight, with the stormy sea beyond, he said to Pete beside him, "I'm not sure I fancy whatever they're going to dish up to tempt us with this evening. That stuff has penetrated to my lungs."

"I'm not hungry, anyway," Pete grunted.

"For God's sake, snap out of it," he said, thinking nothing of pots who call kettles black. "It's two months since Moira went off with that weirdo. No woman is worth pining over."

"It's not her, Rip."

"Then what the hell is it?"

"She took my bloody presents. I spent a fortune on her and she should have returned them."

Randal grinned. "What would you do with satin knickers and a bottle of 'orgasm in Paris' perfume?"

"It's the principle of it."

"The principle of it is not to be such a bloody fool over a bimbo. Find a rich widow who'll spend a fortune on you instead."

Making his approach, Randal did not notice the jeep set out from the main building until Pete said, "Someone's after us."

The vehicle was approaching at speed. Randal's heart sank. "Don't say we've been nailed to take someone to HQ in a hurry."

"Nah, they wouldn't wait for us to come in when there are other cabs sitting here doing nothing. What've you done wrong, Rip?"

"Nothing you wouldn't do." He was puzzled by the sight of their immediate boss in the passenger seat. "That's Haslett making speed-it-up signals. What the hell's going on?"

"Aliens from space have landed?" suggested Pete.

They came to rest and the jeep halted just beyond the range of the downdraught. "Better make this fast," said Randal. "There's obviously some kind of emergency."

They made it fast, then he jumped to the ground and crossed to the jeep, leaving Pete to collect their gear. "What's wrong, sir?"

Haslett opened the door. "Get in. Your crew can follow when they're ready."

Certain that hostilities had broken out and they were on an emergency footing Randal sat beside him, his mind racing as the driver swung the jeep around and drove, not for the Ops Room but the living quarters. He turned to Haslett with a question but was forestalled.

"I'm afraid I've some bad news, Rip. Your son has had an accident. He's in intensive care at Swindon hospital. The signal says his condition is stable but is causing some concern." He glanced at his watch. "There's a VC10 leaving in thirty minutes. You've been cleared to fly home." He sighed. "I'm very sorry. These things always seem to happen when we're miles away."

*　　*　　*

73

At RAF Brize Norton a hired car was waiting. Randal was given priority clearance; he had planned his route during the flight so he was on his way very quickly, the car's headlights penetrating a light swirling mist. His mind was as numb as it had been from the moment he had been given the news. The signal had mentioned a serious accident. No details. Stable but causing concern. What the hell did that mean? He yearned for his Porsche which ate the miles. Yet he must drive carefully. Earlier today he had carried out a lengthy flight in grim conditions and he had been too tense to sleep in the VC10. That meant he had been on the go for more than twelve hours during which he had eaten nothing but a sandwich since breakfast. There was an ache behind his eyes and an unfamiliar fearfulness in the pit of his stomach. He glanced at the dashboard clock. Twenty-two thirty. Neil would be in bed and asleep when he reached the hospital. Oh God, was he crazy? The poor kid was probably unconscious. In a coma, even.

The hospital corridors were hushed and empty, his heavy footsteps sounding hollow against the rubberised flooring. The absence of other people increased his fearfulness. The walk seemed endless but he stifled the urge to run. You did not do that in a place full of sick people.

He knew when he was near because Mary and Gerald Holland were sitting on chairs against the wall, holding cups of tea. He passed them without speaking and pushed open the double doors. A middle-aged fair woman in dark blue came forward to block his path. "Can I help you?"

"I'm Randal Price. You have my son here," he said in a voice husky with weariness.

She smiled. "You've had a long journey, I'm afraid, but your wife will be very relieved to see you."

"How's Neil? I've been told very little."

"When you've had a chance to speak to your wife I'll come and explain any queries you may have. Neil's in a side room."

He followed her through the dim ward hung about with drips and tubes, where electrocardiographs bleeped and blood pressure monitors buzzed, and bodies lay cocooned in plastic tubes. Fear rose to fill Randal's throat. His son was part of *this*?

Fiona spotted him through the glass and rose to cling to him the moment he opened the door of the room. Her body shook with silent sobs which frightened him further. Holding her tightly he pivoted to get a clear view of the bed. Neil looked too tiny for the weight of apparatus around him. Bleeps and buzzes signified that he was alive, but he was so white and still he could well not have been.

"Shhh," he murmured as he stroked Fiona's back. "This won't help anything."

She looked up with red-rimmed eyes. "You're never here, are you?"

He tried to stay calm. "I'm here now and I'll stay until he's better."

"He's so *small*," she whispered tearfully. "How can he survive all this?"

"He's tough. He'll survive." He wished he believed that. "How long has he been here?"

She put her face against his chest. "Since mid-morning. They've offered me a room overnight."

"We'll both stay." He could hold off no longer. "What happened, Fee? The signal said only that he'd had a serious accident."

The question set her sobbing again, and she clung to him like a drowning woman to a rock. He gazed at the little body almost smothered by bedclothes and wondered why the sister was taking so long to come and put him out of his misery. By the time she appeared, Fiona was so quiet Randal wondered if she could possibly have fallen asleep.

The sister smiled. "I've asked a nurse to bring you both a cup of tea. Perhaps you and Mrs Price would like to sit down while we talk." She waited while he coaxed Fiona into a chair, but he was too restless to sit. "Is there anything you'd like to ask?"

"Damn right I would," he said with feeling. "No one has yet told me the nature of this accident, how it happened and if he's going to recover. That'll do to start with."

She raised her eyebrows. "I imagined your wife would tell you those details."

"She's very upset."

That apparently warranted no comment. "Your son was thrown from a horse, Squadron Leader. He sustained some injury to his neck and spine, but there is no way yet of telling the extent of this. We are presently more concerned with the effects of trauma. That is why Neil is here where we can keep an eye on him. When he recovers consciousness we shall know more about his physical condition."

Randal stared at the woman's pleasant face without seeing it. Now he knew why Fiona was so distraught; why she had avoided telling him the facts. Rage began to boil up in him. His son, not yet four years old, had been put on a capricious horse by grandparents who had claimed he would have a better life with them. They could have killed him!

"I can see it's come as a shock, although you must have been prepared to a certain extent by the fact that we suggested you should come home." She spoke gently and calmly, used to dealing with distressed relatives. "Neil is reasonably stable. There's nothing you can do for him right now. You must be hungry after your journey, and your wife refused the meal we offered her earlier. If you could persuade her to go with you to the staff canteen I'll give you a note allowing you to buy something." Seeing his hesitation, she added, "It would do her good to have a break for a short while. Someone will fetch you if anything changes, and the night duty doctor won't be doing his rounds for another hour. He'll talk to you then." She turned to go. "I'll write that note for you."

Fiona sat gazing at him with eyes darkened by an emotion he had never seen in them before. Her guilty apprehension added to his anger. He strode down the ward past the sister writing at her desk and punched open the doors leading to the corridor. Mary and Gerald Holland appeared to have aged ten years. Both were grey-faced, red-eyed and silent. They were holding hands so tightly their knuckles were white. As he confronted them a flash of intuition told Randal it was impossible to punish them more than they were punishing themselves. He stood breathing heavily, trying to master his need to hit out at someone.

"We love that boy so very much," whispered Mary, her eyes filling with tears.

"*So do I*. But the worst thing I've ever done to him is go away on the job," Randal replied in a voice that shook. "If he comes through this you'll never put my son on a horse again. Is that understood?"

Gerald said huskily, "A *pony*. A sweet-tempered gentle beast. We bought it for him. Something startled . . . oh God, I never thought it—"

"*Is that understood?*" Randal repeated, still fighting for control.

They nodded.

"Where's Lydia?"

"With the au pair. She's completely reliable."

"Like the pony?" He looked from one to the other. "Go home. Sitting there like a pair of wraiths helps no one, least of all Neil, and Lydia will be less upset if you're there when she wakes." Suddenly aware of immense weariness he turned away. "You'll be notified of any change." With his hand on the swing doors, he added, "As soon as I can arrange some quarters, my wife and children will come back where they belong."

"We're *so* sorry," cried Mary miserably.

He pushed through the doors without a word.

It was one of the longest nights Randal had ever spent. The doctor said the next twelve hours or so would be critical. He suggested they get some sleep and assured them they would be told if there was any change in Neil's condition. Fiona refused to take off her outer clothes and get beneath the bedclothes. She needed to be held and comforted, so Randal propped himself against banked pillows and she curled up close against him beneath a blanket. She soon fell into an exhausted sleep but he was too tense to relax. He longed for a shower. There had been time only to throw a few things into a bag before he caught the VC10. During the flight he had changed from his flying suit into trousers and pullover and before settling for the night he washed in the hospital cloakroom, but he felt tired and dirty. He had left his shaver with the rest of his gear. Someone would bring it over when the flight returned. Meanwhile he would have to make do with a plastic razor from the shop at the hospital entrance. The rest of his clothes and possessions were at Hampton. So was his Porsche.

He pushed these inconsequential facts around his mind during the dragging hours to stop himself thinking of the possibility of losing his son. He had to face the prospect sooner or later, and did so at four a.m. when a nurse crept in with a cup of tea. Many people relinquished their lives in the early hours of the day, and stark truths also refused to be ignored in those witching hours. Randal shouldered the blame for what had occurred. He should have accepted that Fiona would never settle to the kind of life he could offer. Her parents doted on her; had surrounded her with luxury and companionship, shielded her from knocks. Yet he had expected her to adjust to his way of life and bring up two children during his absences. They had both wanted children; the pregnancies had been planned, but marriage and those two small lives to cope with within four years was too drastic a change for Gerald Holland's daughter. Randal now told himself he should have been more aware of her struggle to cope.

Half an hour later he was telling himself she had known well enough what she was taking on by marrying him and agreeing to have children so soon. He could not bear all the blame but he should have fetched her back from Marylands right away. If she could run home when things got tough she would never settle. Right now she needed him badly because she felt that her parents had failed her. Whenever he went away she saw it in reverse.

Looking down on her blonde shining hair he knew his life was brighter and more satisfying when she was with him; knew he was still crazy about her. She was vivid and irresistible. He had to find a way to make her happier, their marriage stronger and yet continue to fly. He would not pack that in until he must. Resting his cheek against his wife's head he sensed that he held all the aces at the moment. Somehow he must play a winning hand that would keep her content until age or promotion put him behind a desk where she wanted him.

Then Randal faced the prospect of losing their child. At Christmas, Neil had admitted that his grandfather was teaching him to ride a horse, yet Randal's need to win Fiona back had overshadowed all else. If only he had listened to the boy, if he had settled the issue instead of storming out in a temper, Neil would not now be fighting for his life. He suddenly thought of the parents of a little girl on a Cornish cliff. They were living with this same prospect day after day, knowing that unless a suitable kidney became available Ted would one day be told to cross from his list the name of the Fiona with a happy smile. He tightened his hold around his sleeping wife and suffered with all parents of sick children.

Neil recovered consciousness at eight a.m. and listlessly acknowledged his mother and father. By mid-afternoon the results of initial tests suggested that the boy would not suffer permanent disabling mental or physical damage. He would need to wear spinal supports and a collar around his neck for a short time, but physiotherapy and massage would eventually alleviate all effects of the fall. The remnants of concussion were affecting his sight, but they would diminish within a day or two when he would be moved to a normal children's ward. The crisis was over.

Randal rang the Hollands, told them the news and said he would bring Fiona to Marylands after Neil had settled for that night. His call was short and brusque. Mary merely said, "Thank God!"

The house was unusually quiet when Randal parked the hired car and took Fiona inside. There were no rowdy guests; no cocktail party was under way. It seemed like a real home for once. The Hollands still looked haggard and were visibly upset when their daughter made no attempt to kiss them.

"Thank you for ringing us," Gerald said quietly. "We're sure you'd like to see Lydia. She's asleep. She has coped very well without Neil." He managed a faint smile. "The extra attention suited her. You both look stressed and tired. Do have a bath and change your clothes. Randal, I've put a few of my things in Fiona's room. When you're both ready Mary has prepared a meal that can be served very quickly."

Mary added, "You'll need to be near the hospital for a while. We hope you'll accept our hospitality until you find alternative accommodation."

Bathed, shaved and wearing his father-in-law's trousers and a roll-neck sweater, Randal ate grilled chops, potatoes and *mange toute* reflecting that it had taken a near-tragedy to make him accepted at Marylands for the first time. They were all suffering from nervous exhaustion and lack of sleep, so it was a quiet meal. When Gerald went out to make his usual last rounds of the stables, Randal took his wife upstairs.

Her room was huge, airy and furnished in white and apple-green. Randal undressed and tossed aside the pyjamas Gerald had left for him. "Your father can't be that old-fashioned," he murmured, getting beneath the duvet to watch Fiona take off her clothes. She had a superb body which he had not seen naked for six months, yet he had urgent things to say to her tonight before they succumbed to the sleep they really needed. In the morning he would be raring to go.

She slid in beside him and, for a while, they explored each other with the delight of rediscovery. Then Randal lay back drawing her against his chest, and she snuggled there, her soft sigh warm against his skin.

"I've done a lot of thinking, Fee," he said quietly. "I'm going to get us a house; not a rented job, one of our own with enough space for a playroom and a bedroom each for the kids. We'll get a decorator in to do it up the way we want. You can choose all the furniture. Take as long as you like over it, so long as we have beds and a table with chairs while you're sorting it all out. We'll have a large garden where they can play with their friends. We'll get them a puppy; maybe one each," he added with a smile. "Neil can start prep school after the summer and there's bound to be a nursery for Lydia near the house. You'll have a lot of free time. You could get a part-time job or meet your horsey friends for lunch at some halfway hotel whenever you feel like it. When I'm away you could even invite them to stay with you. Get in a supply of fodder and horse nuts and they'll be happy. Ahhh," he protested with a laugh as she squeezed him provocatively. "That's below the belt."

"Exactly. Any more comments like that and you'll be begging for mercy," she warned.

"No, I'll be begging for more." He sighed and kissed her forehead. "It's been hell without you."

"It was starting to be hell *with* you."

He let that ride while he stroked her back and hips with remembered pleasure, but the future had not yet been settled. "Fee, you know there's no way I'll give up flying, but it needn't go back to the way it was. I've tried to resist the temptation of letting Price's Pork Pies subsidise everything, but my grandfather willed the damn money to me, so I might as well use it to buy us a country house far enough from Hampton to isolate you from the RAF, but within easy driving distance for me. You won't have to do more than attend the occasional Mess dinner or cocktail party. You can live among the kind of people you're used to, make your own friends, send the kids to schools you choose for them. In return I want you to make that house your permanent home – *our* home – and live there even when I'm away. I want us to spend the rest of our lives together." After a few moments of silence, he asked, "Well, what about it?"

When she moved her face against his chest he felt the dampness of tears. She shifted to lie half across him and kiss his mouth with lingering pressure. "It sounds wonderful . . . if you really mean it."

"Of course I mean it."

"Then yes, yes and *yes*, darling." She climbed further across him to demonstrate her appreciation and several seconds later whispered, "Are you *sure* you're too tired?"

"Christ, we'd better find out," he said, rolling her over with renewed energy.

As senior flight lieutenant, Rusty became acting commander in Randal's place. He had a more prosaic approach but they were all happy enough with his decisions. Two days before their scheduled return to Hampton, B Flight was given a task they had hoped would not come their way. Earlier in the week, Rusty's drinking and whoring partner, Jeff Daniels, had flown out with Maggie to pick up food supplies from a truck which had slipped fifty feet from a crumbling track leading through mountains. Two vehicles in the convoy had already passed the danger spot, but the remainder had had to back carefully to the main road and return to base, from where the entire consignment had been airlifted. The stranded truck had now been listed as worth recovering.

"Guess who's been told to go and fetch it," said Rusty as they gathered in the briefing room.

"And aren't you the lucky one," called Pete. "As it's a job for two pilots that lets me out."

"I've a nice one here for a navigator. I want Jeff with me on this. He's already seen the terrain and the position of the truck."

"So have I," Maggie pointed out aggressively.

Rusty responded with a slightly malicious grin. "I've put you down to fly Pete out to evacuate the patients of a maternity hospital in the hills. Their water pipes have frozen solid and the heating system has packed up. Not that it was up to much, anyway. The building was heavily shelled during the fighting."

Pete scowled. "Just so long as no one decides to give birth in mid-air."

"Jimmy's going with you. He's got four kids so he'll know what to do."

"Easy." Jimmy nodded. "When the head appears grab it and pull. It flops out like a calf from a cow."

"That's disgusting," said the disgruntled Maggie. "Why send me on that job? It doesn't matter who's at the controls."

The irrepressible Jimmy stirred things further. "Expectant mothers will feel happier with a damsel in command."

Rusty intervened. "Rip would shut you all up with some of his ripe language, so consider it said and shut up."

Dave was pleased to learn that he was to go out to pick up the truck with a crewman called Sandy with whom he had struck up a friendship. In training he had lifted all manner of loads but this would be a real challenge. The crewmen who had fetched the cargo gave a graphic description of the snow-swept area and the precise manoeuvring necessary. Jeff and Maggie also said it was a pig of a spot to work in.

A couple of experienced army ground handlers were to go with them. They soon arrived, introduced themselves as Dick and Harry and offered to break the arm of anyone who asked where Tom was. No one did, so they began an in-depth discussion on the best way to deal with the problem, with Jeff and Maggie giving the benefit of their earlier visit to the truck.

"It's pretty tight in there," warned Jeff. "They must value that vehicle pretty highly."

"Ours is not to reason why, mate." Rusty focused on the soldiers. "Any problems?"

"Won't know until we're on the ground with it," said Harry, blond, freckled and muscular. "That report you have says it's in a stable position resting on a ridge of rock. Should be OK."

Rusty enlightened him. "That report was made by Norwegian engineers and translated into English by a Croat."

The experts exchanged glances. "Point taken. We'll make our own assessment when we see it," said Dick. "There's very little we can't do."

"How about crawling through a small hole with that big head?" asked Jeff.

He grinned. "Takes a bit longer."

They left half an hour later and flew towards the hills. The cloud was high, the wind light: favourable conditions. They were relaxed, and chatted amiably about ice hockey which Harry had played during his teens in Canada and Dave had slight knowledge of. His yearning to be in the cockpit was easing and he was happier than he had been for some while. Each time they lifted something from the ground and he lay beside the hatch in the floor to guide the pilots who could not see the load from their forward position, he realised he was a vital member of a close-knit team.

After an hour and twenty minutes they were among mountains and Rusty announced that they were approaching the location. Dave watched from the front door as they flew over an isolated valley where shrubs and rocks showed dark against the snow. The coldness bit into his cheeks as he searched for a sign of the truck. Then Jeff spotted it, thinly coated with fresh snow. The vehicle lay on its off side some fifty feet down from the track. From the air it looked well enough supported by a substantial ridge crossing a steep slope dropping to a snow-filled gully where maps showed a narrow tributary running through to join a river to the east.

It was easy to see why Jeff and Maggie had found it tricky. The track hugged the side of a steep ascent which had given them a problem with space when hovering. There was plenty of room in the valley itself, but the real test would come when they attempted to lift the truck.

Rusty spoke to Dave, who was acting as winchman. "Get the guys ready to go down. I'm going straight in."

With Harry standing harnessed beside him, Dave slowly talked the pilots forward until they were over the location. "Twenty, fifteen, ten . . . four, three, two, one. Steady! Height is good. Winching first man down. He's going down. He's there. The first man is on the ground. He's away and clear. Winching in. The second man is ready. Steady! Height is still good. Winching second man down."

Talking constantly to inform the pilots of activity they could not see, Dave knew Jeff in the left-hand seat would be closely watching the steep wall as they hovered in its shadow. When the ground handlers had been supplied with their gear, they were left to get on with the job while Rusty flew off to find an area of flat ground. He landed in a truly bleak spot so that Dave and Sandy could climb out and link together lengths of strop to which the truck would be hooked. On the ground Dave felt the full bite of the wind. It reminded him of climbing expeditions in his youth.

"God, it's bloody perishing," exclaimed Sandy, who had grown up in the Far East and had thin blood. "It's all right for hairy Scots weaned on porridge and haggis, but we normal guys feel the cold."

Dave grinned across at him. "Hothouse plant, you. This'll toughen you up."

When the extended strop had been laid out flat across the snow, Dave straightened up and looked around: frozen peaks, row upon row, darkened here and there by outcrops of rock, battered by the wind, inhospitable and challenging. The awesome stillness was broken only by the throbbing of their rotors. The Chinook sat in surreal contrast to primeval nature, like something from another planet. Dave's spirits exalted in the knowledge that they could alight here then depart, like the huge birds of prey which inhabited the Highlands. Many people might fly over this area and look down, but how splendid to perch for a while in the heart of the wilderness! He had sacrificed nothing to gain this.

Sandy poked him, shouting above the noise, "Stop looking like the Cock of the North and get moving. You're on the job, not communing with your ancestors."

They flew back with a hundred feet of strop dangling. True to their boast, Dick and Harry had attached chains to the truck at the vital points. They signalled their readiness. Dave knew the next minutes would take concentrated judgement by the whole team as, once the load had been secured to the strop, the pilots would have to manoeuvre in towards the mountainside until the vehicle had been gently righted. He hung out through the door, held by his harness, once more talking them forward until Sandy, lying flat beside the open hatch, took over the patter for the final link-up.

As they made their careful approach, one of the soldiers climbed on the truck ready to catch the end of the strop. He straightened up and signalled with his arms, but his boots slipped on the ice-coated metal and he plunged over the rocky ledge.

"He's gone!" yelled Dave. "One of them has fallen."

"Fallen where? Can you see him?" demanded Rusty, ceasing forward motion and hovering.

"Negative. He's fallen further into the valley."

"OK, we'll jettison the strop and bin this. Dave, you're experienced in mountain rescue. Prepare to go down after him. Sandy, man the winch and stand by to receive the casualty."

The man left on the ground was leaning perilously over the rocks to look for his companion, but he soon signalled negatively with his arms and returned to a more secure position. As Dave stood ready to be lowered he was worried. The man had fallen outward and could have dropped a considerable distance. If he had come to rest somewhere inaccessible by the winch it would be a while before he received aid. In these temperatures he could soon die.

Rusty swung the aircraft out over the valley and dropped into it, hovering to allow them all a visual search for a body. It was never easy to see a tiny figure lying on uneven terrain but they had a fair idea of where to look and Jeff soon spotted him.

"There he is; two hundred or more feet below the truck and slightly to the right of it."

"Got him," said Rusty calmly. "Dave, I'll turn and come back in as close to him as possible. That buttress is going to bugger things up. There's no way we can get right over the spot with that jutting out so far."

Dave prepared for the rescue with all his daydreams banished by the emergency. He stood in the icy blast beside the door while Rusty turned and headed back so that the winch was on the right side for the job in hand. Dave saw the buttress first and knew it would present a considerable problem for the pilots. Rip might have had the nerve and experience to overcome it but in this situation it was wiser to play safe.

The soldier lay on a very narrow ledge close to the buttress. Rusty took time to assess the best way to recover him, in consultation with Dave who had once been a member of a Highland mountain rescue team. It was impossible to hover directly above the ledge so it was agreed that Dave would be lowered about a hundred and twenty feet from it, attached to a hi-line that would secure him to the winch throughout. When the casualty was strapped to the stretcher he, too, would be secured.

Once on the ground with the rolled stretcher and the first aid kit, Dave clipped on the hi-line and began laboriously to kick footholds as he edged across the slope towards the body. His breath clouded swiftly in the chill air and the frozen snow squeaked beneath his boots as he drew nearer to the looming buttress. The Chinook hovered high enough above him to avoid setting off an avalanche with the downdraught. Dave hoped the man was alive. He knew from experience that the human body could survive the most appalling climbing accidents, yet just as often perish as the result of a minor fall.

Breathing heavily, he reached the ledge which was wide

enough to allow him only restricted movement. Glancing around he saw a scene that might have daunted many a man. To his right rose the wall of jutting rock; no more than two feet from his heels was a formidable drop to a frozen cleft; and ahead the mountain rose sharply to where he could see the roof of the truck they had come to recover. As a Highlander, this was something Dave understood; as a trained rescuer he was glad there was no need for an arduous descent with the casualty. Help hovered overhead.

Harry, the ice hockey player, was breathing but shallowly; his right arm and leg were lying at abnormal angles yet the injuries could be worse. His back could be broken. The first step was to inject morphine, not easy squatting on a small ledge in a biting wind with a patient dressed in several layers of clothing. The clumsy business brought Harry to semi-consciousness and he gazed at Dave in bewilderment.

"You slipped. Nothing much to worry about." Dave forced a smile. "You've a broken arm and leg, but that big head of yours is only dented."

"Bloody stupid of me," Harry mumbled.

"Try moving these fingers." Dave touched the man's unbroken arm. "Good. Now the toes on this foot. Yes? Great! Hey, hey, don't go to sleep yet. Very gently move your head right and left. *Slowly!* That's fine. As I said, nothing much to worry about."

Dave was greatly relieved. The spine would surely be bruised but almost certainly not broken. The effects of shock were the big problem. It was essential to get Harry to hospital swiftly. Looking up at the Chinook Dave signalled by touching his arm and leg, then made a snapping motion with his hands. Sandy waved acknowledgement. Dave bent to his task.

Thankful for his experience as he straightened the broken limbs, Dave carefully bound Harry's legs together then strapped his right arm to his body before embarking on the difficult task of shifting the heavy man onto the stretcher, keeping in mind the sharp drop immediately behind him. Harry passed out again during this agonising operation.

Signalling his intentions to Sandy, Dave prepared to return to his set-down point using the footholds he had made and dragging the casualty with him. Although the stretcher slid easily across the icy surface, it was very laborious work. His boots several times slipped from the foothold, racing Dave's heartbeat as he dangled at the end of the hi-line clinging to the heavy stretcher until he recovered his balance. Even so, he was quietly exhilarated as he crossed the mountainside, breathing clear frosty air, until he was directly beneath the aircraft. Looking up, he gave his friend a grinning thumbs-up.

Sandy brought them both up and hauled in the casualty. Harry was covered in blankets to combat hypothermia and Dave removed his harness while giving Rusty an account of the man's probable injuries. Stopping just long enough to winch up Dick still beside the truck, they headed for the nearest hospital.

"Thanks, Dave, you did a great job," said Rusty. "Beers all round for you tonight . . . but anyone else stupid enough to want a truck picked up from some God-forsaken spot can do it themselves."

"Or send in the Navy," suggested Sandy.

Dave drank cocoa from a flask as he gazed through the door at mountains now gentling into softer hills. He did not need praise and beer, just this sense of fulfilment those bars on his shoulder had never produced.

They relaxed that evening with English newspapers which all bore much the same headline.

POLLY RECEIVES
HERO'S WELCOME

England's ace footballer returned to the game yesterday after being acquitted of a date-rape charge due to unsound evidence offered by the prosecution. Marianna Blaise, the model who alleged Pollinger drugged her drink then raped her in his hotel room, said on hearing the verdict: "I'd like to amputate his legs. That would be worse punishment than cutting off his penis." When Polly ran on the pitch for Chelsea's game against United, thousands of fans wearing T-shirts bearing the parrot's head logo chanted POLL-EE continuously, delaying the start of the match while he acknowledged their adulation. It was fully justified. Pollinger appeared to have wings on his feet and scored a sizzling winning goal just thirty seconds before the final whistle. A jubilant crowd invaded the pitch to surround their hero, who had to be protected by a cordon of police.

Into the silence Sandy made an expression of disgust. "These guys earn fantastic money for kicking a ball into a net, apart from what they get for advertising anything from underwear to toothpaste. It's a doddle! Girls all over them and thousands cheering every time they put on a pair of shorts. I'd like to see them have to go at something like we did today."

"And for the money we get," added Jeff.

"Yeah, we're in the wrong job," muttered Rusty.

But Dave knew he was in exactly the right job. He did not yearn to have mass adulation, and he certainly did not want to entertain models in hotel rooms. Tonight, he felt he had everything he could desire even if his flying suit lacked a pair of wings.

March

They were flying over fields bathed in welcome sunshine, Maggie and Rusty in total accord, for once. They were almost home and five days' leave beckoned. England looked wonderfully green. After the January emergency and Bosnia, they were sick of snow and bitter winds. Spring had arrived and they all needed a rest. In the cabin, Nobby and Ray were playing a duet on second-hand banjos they had bought to liven up the boring hours on standby. They had improved so much lately, the rest of the team no longer threatened to stamp on the instruments.

From another aircraft Jeff was quizzing Rusty over the radio about Marsha, the girl who expected a wedding this year. "Tell her the truth on day one, then join me at my folks' cottage outside Plymouth. There's good drinking down there and plenty of farmers' daughters eager to oblige. Don't be a mug, man."

"Yeah, I'll tell her," Rusty said heavily. "It works great the way it is. Why the hell does she want veils, bouquets and giggling bridesmaids?"

"Can't imagine," put in Maggie. "Any woman craving legal ties to you is in need of medical advice."

"So you're the expert," Jeff chipped in. "Now you've chewed up and spat out the macho Yank, who's next?"

"None of you lot, that's for sure. I . . ." She broke off as a wave of deep distress washed over her, overwhelming where she was and what she was doing. She knew as certainly as if the news had been read out over the radio that Phil was in trouble.

"Maggie, are you all right?"

She looked at the helmeted man beside her without really seeing him. She felt sick and her skin was clammy.

"*Maggie*, what's wrong?"

She heard herself say. "I have to get to a phone."

89

"Nobby, I think she might faint," Rusty said over the intercom. "Can you bring something for her to drink?"

A plastic cup soon appeared near her hand and an arm reached across to open the window beside her. A welcome rush of air cooled her skin. As she drank the lukewarm mineral water the sickness slowly passed but the sensation of anxiety did not.

"Twenty minutes to go. Can you make it OK?"

Maggie nodded. Twenty minutes before she could get to a phone.

"I'll radio for the blood wagon to meet us."

"You're joking, of course," she said quickly. "I can fly us back. It's the heat, that's all." Maggie forced herself to concentrate on being in a familiar cockpit doing familiar things, but the knowledge that her twin was suffering in some way was strong enough to keep her in a state of apprehension.

"You said something about getting to a phone. What was that about?" asked Rusty, who was the non-handling pilot.

The real concern in his light-brown eyes surprised her. "I was just speaking my thoughts."

"I'll speak mine. You look God-awful. You should see the Doc."

She glanced away towards the distant coast and hazy sea beyond. "If I said that to you, you'd all start clucking over the airwaves like mother hens. Give it a rest, Rusty."

"Rip wouldn't."

"He's not here."

"Wonder how his boy is," said Ray, and talk then centred around the signal that had been sent to notify them the crisis was over. Maggie gazed at the sea and thought of Phil, who loved it in all weathers and who was going through his own crisis at the moment. In the short while before they landed she tried to transmit her supportive love to him. Surely Fay could not entirely have killed their unique link.

Maggie rang the boatyard from the Briefing Room. A machine invited her to leave her name and number. Her twin's cheery voice plus the fact that his secretary was not there increased her fears. She dialled his home number. Another machine! When there was no reply from her parents, real panic gripped her by the throat. Was it that serious?

Reaching her room, Maggie tried her parents' number once more. No reply. They hated answering machines and refused to

90

have one. She rang Charles. His secretary announced precisely that Mr Spencer was on holiday in the Caribbean and would be back on Monday week. Would she care to leave a message? Maggie replaced the receiver with a shaking hand before lifting it again to punch out the number of Rob's surgery. His antiseptic receptionist was highly efficient but treated every caller like a child or a simple-minded geriatric.

"Very sorry, dear. Doctor has a patient with him. He can't possibly take a call at the moment. Try again after six."

"Damn the patient," said Maggie explosively. "There's a family crisis. Put me through to him at once, Brenda."

"It's most unprofessional, Margaret, I . . ."

"Do it!"

Her brother sounded tetchy. "I have a patient here, Maggie."

He surely could not know anything. "Rob, something's happened to Phil. You know how he and I can tell these things. Mum and Dad aren't at home and I'm scared. I thought you'd have been able to put me out of my misery."

There was a brief pause. "It's not Phil, it's Fay. I'll ring when I've dealt with my patient. What's your number?"

Her legs were shaking so much she sat on the bed feeling cold and shivery. So Phil's distress was for his wife, not himself. It must be very deep to reach across to her as it had.

Rob rang within minutes. He was more himself. "Sorry, Mags, I'd just told a woman she had inoperable cancer. It wasn't the right time to speak to you. Fay's miscarried. She began haemorrhaging during the night. They did what they could but Phil rang just before surgery to say it was all over. He's taken it hard. Chas and I had no problems with our kids and he wanted this child so much. I don't know all the medical details. It could have been caused by any one of many conditions . . . and Fay finds it impossible to relax. You know how highly strung she is. If she was told to rest, I doubt if she did. It's upsetting for them but she'll probably be fine with the next pregnancy. Your much vaunted ESP got it wrong this time. I thought you were in Bosnia, anyway. Mum was cracking on about how unsuitable she thought it was when she rang last week."

"I came back today. Rob, is Fay in the cottage hospital?"

"Yes."

"I'll drive along there. I've five days' leave and you're too far away to do anything to help Phil."

"*No!* I . . . er, I don't think that's a good idea. They have to see this through together. Leave them alone, Mags."

Shaken by his tone, she said, "They're family, Rob. They need our support. Someone's support. Of course I must go."

"For once in your life listen to advice and use the intelligence you've been blessed with. You're the last person Fay wants to see."

"Why, for God's sake? I didn't cause her miscarriage."

"Look, I have patients waiting. Write to Phil; ring him if you must but don't go. I know what I'm talking about. Take care, Mags."

It was a two-hour drive from Hampton Heyhoe to the New Forest village where Spencer's Boatyard lay on the shore of a quiet inlet. Maggie made it in an hour and forty minutes, then drove on past to Phil's house with its fine view of The Needles. It was in darkness, so she left her car in the drive and stepped out towards the Cottage Hospital a short distance away. Now she knew what had happened, now she was doing something positive, her energy had returned. What a blessing that she had flown in today. She would not have been granted compassionate leave, as Randal had, to come home to a distressed twin. No one fully understood that bond. It was nevertheless very powerful.

She enjoyed the walk. The evening air still held the perfume of early flowers and the sea added its salty tang. A full moon hung low over the white-walled hotel where yachtsmen and anyone who messed about in boats gathered to drink and exaggerate their expertise. It was good to be back in England.

It was a great pity about the baby but, as Rob had said, the next one would probably be all right.

There was a silver-haired woman at the reception desk. Nothing antiseptic about her and her manner was not in the least patronising. Yes, Mrs Spencer was in a small room at the end of the corridor. Her husband was with her. Goodness, what a strong family likeness! Twins? She had always thought that must be very special. Yes, go on down. There was still half an hour of visiting time.

Clutching the flowers she had bought along the way, Maggie entered the room where Phil was sitting beside the bed on a hard hospital chair. She had not seen him since Christmas and was excited by this reunion that would end the hurtful hiatus between them. Her brother turned to see who had come in

92

and got to his feet wearing an expression remarkably akin to shock.

"*Maggie!* What are you doing here?"

She crossed to hug him and kiss his cheek. Studying his drawn face she said fondly, "I *knew*, of course. When we were twenty minutes from landing I had such a sensation of distress I was certain something had happened to you. I rang your office, then the house. Mum and Dad weren't at home, Chas is on holiday and I had to shout down that simpering receptionist of Rob's to get the news from him. Phil, I'm *so* sorry. It must be a dreadful disappointment to you both. I felt your pain so strongly." She turned, putting the flowers on the table across the bed. "We *all* sympathise, Fay, the whole family. I have five days' leave so I can keep Phil company, see that he eats and so on while you're in here. So you mustn't worry about him."

The ashen red-eyed woman in the bed was staring as if at a ghost and Maggie then noticed the blood slowly dripping into her vein.

"Get her out of here. Get her out of here. *Get her out!*" Fay's voice grew louder and louder until she was screaming the words. "Get her away from us. Oh God, take her away, someone!"

Phil grabbed Maggie's arm and almost dragged her through the door as a frowning nurse appeared from the next room. "My wife's upset. Please go in," he said. "I'll be there shortly."

Thoroughly taken aback, Maggie let her brother lead her to the entrance and out into the clear evening. There he stopped, breathing heavily, and let go of her arm. His emotion was echoed in her. She was so shaken by the depth of it that she stood as silently as he for some moments.

"What was all that about?" she asked eventually in a voice hushed by shock. "What's going on?"

He gave a heavy sigh and pushed back his flopping hair. "Oh hell, what a night! Whatever made you turn up here knowing how it is? Mags, she's just lost the baby, for Christ's sake. This afternoon. *Four hours ago.* They should have stopped you coming in. She's terribly upset – we both are – and she lost so much blood they're giving her a transfusion. She's scared." He took a few agitated steps, then turned back to her. "I tried to tell you it's a difficult time. Pregnant women can be irrational. They're ultra-emotional; get upset over the strangest things, see insults and slights where there aren't any. We all have to make allowances. When they miscarry, those things are further heightened. It's a trauma that can easily lead to months of depression, loss of self-confidence, feelings of guilt, and . . . well, they can turn against anyone. Even the husband. You know what I mean."

Maggie was starting to shiver. "You sound as if you're quoting word for word. Did they give you a pamphlet to read, or did Rob reel all that off over the phone? Instead of giving me the official guff, why don't you remember who I am and tell me what you really want to say? At Christmas we were 'the twins', as usual. Now you're acting like someone who looks like Phil Spencer but has become another person. Aren't you brother enough to explain what's happened to you in the weeks since Christmas? I came here because I shared your distress. If you can't share mine over the way you're behaving, at least explain why," she begged with a touch of desperation.

He sought for words, then gave up. "Not now, Mags, please. I've been up all night and watching her agony throughout today. It was my child, too, you know. I didn't carry it in my body but I feel the loss." He drew his key ring from his pocket. "Go to the house. I'll be along later. We'll talk then."

Maggie asked painfully, "Does she really think this is *my* doing; that I somehow willed her to lose the baby?"

Misery clouded his striking features. "I told you they become highly irrational; believe anything, however absurd. I *must* go to her. See you later."

Maggie collected her car from the house, then stopped at the hospital to give the silver-haired woman the keys. "My brother dropped them. Perhaps you'd give them to him when he leaves."

In the middle of the forest her headlamps illuminated some deer. She stopped to let them cross. As they disappeared among the trees, knowing where they were heading, she stared at the narrow road stretching away beyond the light beams. Where was *she* heading? After several cars had edged past and another from the opposite direction containing two men had stopped ten yards beyond her then began to back, Maggie released the brake and drove towards the main road. When she reached it she turned west and headed back to Dorset. For now, RAF Hampton was her home and B Flight had replaced her family. She knew where she stood with them.

* * *

At eleven thirty the following morning Maggie showered and dressed, then slipped out to her car. It was another warm day, but her spirits were leaden as she drove along the coast road seeing little of the beauty around her. Faint from hunger, she eventually pulled in at a small café overlooking the sea for her first meal since landing the day before. Leaving her car there she then followed a footpath leading to the beach and walked for two hours. Anglers were out in force as well as a number of rubber-suited surfers. None took any notice of the slender girl in a scarlet tracksuit, whose long blonde hair blew across her face and hid her stricken expression.

On the return drive Maggie felt so exhausted she had to fight sleep although the lethargy softened her pain. As she parked her car outside the Mess, in a dusk filled with blackbird song, she decided the only way to get through the hours until bedtime was to get drunk. Too much alcohol always gave her migraine but a headache would give her the perfect excuse to stay in bed all day tomorrow. Yes, it was a first-class plan.

Later, when she entered the bar she was hailed by Jill and Dandy. She crossed to them forcing a bright smile on to her face. "I don't think you two do any work. You sit drinking at this same table all day long."

"B Flight are on stand-down, so what are you doing here all tarted up?" asked Jill, eying the amount of make-up Maggie had used to camouflage her pale cheeks. "Don't tell me you've relented and invited that yummy Yank here again."

"Who wants a gin?" Maggie asked. She had forgotten Craig.

"Just time for one more," said Dandy. "We're having dinner at Jim's place. He has an old college friend visiting so Jill's on a blind date."

"I don't know why I let myself in for these things," sighed the air traffic controller notorious for playing the field. "Why haven't you disappeared for a few days, Maggie?"

"Didn't seem worth going to my parents' place so I decided to laze here. *Not* get up for briefing, *not* attend a lecture, not do anything to order. It's great. I went to the beach near Bridport and walked all afternoon. Can either of you tell me how anglers and surfers get so much time off during the week? Don't they have jobs?"

"Not any lorded over by men in blue," said Dandy waspishly.

"I practically begged for a few hours off last week to hear my aunt's lunchtime recital in Salisbury Cathedral. It was for charity but that held no sway with *him*."

"I don't suppose it did." As the orderly brought the drinks Maggie ordered another for herself. "Show me the wing commander who'd believe a woman wanted time off to hear her aunt sing in a cathedral. We know what they'd all think."

"Wait till I get him in my chair again. He'll have a taste of the drill he won't quickly forget."

"And do it without anaesthetic," Maggie suggested.

"By the way, you'd have missed our drama this afternoon," said Jill. "We have a presence in our midst."

"A what?"

"A Harrier pilot. Had us all on our toes for a while. He'd hit something and wanted emergency clearance to land. It was touch and go whether he'd make it down or have to eject. The damage was incredible. He was lucky to be in one piece."

Dandy got to her feet. "Come on. Time we were moving."

Maggie looked up at Jill. "What was he doing in this part of the country?"

"Oh, he's one of those clever dicks who give solo displays at air shows and such." She gave a malicious grin. "He didn't look so clever when he climbed out covered in blood."

"Good God!"

"Not as bad as it looked, Maggie. I heard that when the Doc washed him most of the gore wasn't his own. Probably hit some birds. Well, I'm off to the slaughter. If this pal of Jim's has bad breath and a horsey laugh I'll be back for another gin with you before you go to bed. Toodle-oo."

After their departure Maggie downed two more drinks, then decided she should eat before she got too light-headed. In the absence of B Flight she chose a solitary table in the corner, wishing the girls were not dining with Dandy's fiancé. Their bubbly feminine company was just what she needed tonight. As it was, she would eat her chicken stew quickly and get back to the bar.

When he came in Maggie knew who he must be. He had borrowed some clothes from the pool and there was a large dressing below his left ear. He looked around at the tables occupied by men deep in conversation, then headed for her corner.

"You look as lonely as I feel. Mind if I join you?"

She looked him over. "I heard you're a clever dick who operates solo. You can't be lonely."

He leaned on the table to study her with amused interest. "OK, how about 'You're the most beautiful girl in the room?'"

"The most beautiful *pilot* in the room; and that line's worse than the first one."

He chuckled. "I can turn somersaults, sit up and beg and chase my tail but I don't know how to fly a Chinook." He sat facing her. "I'm Mark Hascham, *not* a very clever dick today."

Astonished by the effect the gin was having on her, Maggie smiled back and introduced herself. "It must have been an alarming experience."

"First emergency I've had. Don't want another in a hurry. I've ordered that stew, is it any good?"

"Not bad. Where are you from?"

"Wittering."

"No, that accent."

"Ah, I was born and raised in South Africa. When my mother crashed her Cessna and was killed, I was sent to my grandparents in York. A couple of years later I got hooked on the idea of flying fast jets and applied to the RAF. I never dreamed they'd grant my dearest wish."

She thought that a slightly better line than the others. "I suppose your father's a government minister in Pretoria." He looked puzzled. "A director of De Beers?"

"He's a game warden in Kruger Park," he said as his stew was brought to the table. "I was sent to England to study veterinary science but I qualified in engineering sponsored by the RAF instead. Dad isn't best pleased and my grandmother hates what I do. But it's my life." He began on his meal. "What was that about De Beers?"

"Oh, just nonsense." On impulse she added, "I'm on a binge tonight."

"Bravo. Any special reason?"

"Not one I'd discuss with a stranger, and a clever dick at that."

He smiled. "Want a boozing partner?"

It was not the gin affecting her, it was him. Crinkly light-brown hair, lean brown face, medium height; nothing very exciting apart from exceptionally clear, long-lashed green eyes. It must be his positive energy that touched a chord in her. Here was a man who knew what he wanted, went after it and probably usually got it. Like tonight.

They went to the Bird in Hand, the only pub Maggie had had time to discover. In the car park Mark took the keys from her. "I never allow a woman on a binge to drive me anywhere. You can navigate." Amazingly, she raised no objection.

The old inn was busy, but they found a table for two where it was possible to hear each other without shouting. "Beer?" he asked.

"Hate it. Gin and tonic, please." She watched him at the bar; one of those people who manage to get served instantly without being aggressive.

He returned with the drinks. "No self-respecting pilot should be seen with anything but a pint in his hand."

"It's *her* hand. Therein lies the difference."

"Mmm, it's *some* difference!"

"Mark, what'll happen about your Harrier?"

He leaned back with a frown. "They'll send a team here to decide whether or not she can be salvaged. Took a hell of a knock. Sounded like an explosion. Bloody crazy to think a tiny bird or two could have any impact on a sensational piece of engineering, much less turn her into a possible heap of scrap."

She watched him closely as he spoke. His hands moved with nervous energy and the South African inflections put unfamiliar emphasis on some of his words, but his eyes were his most expressive feature. "It's a bit early for air shows. What were you doing flying solo around here?"

His smile betrayed his joy in what he did. "I was showing off for a group of Middle Eastern gentlemen. Prospective customers. Dazzle them, I was told. So I dazzled. Threw the little darling all over the sky above Exeter, then showed her off on the ground. Black and white smiles all round. I was sent off with a pat and a bone. All was fine until . . . *wham*! Good thing I was well out of their sight when it happened." He gazed into his glass. "I hope to God they find feathers and beaks. No one saw it happen."

"Not even you?"

He glanced up quickly. "I was whooping it up a bit coming along the coast. You know how it is when it goes to your head. But I wasn't low enough to hit anything."

Maggie was surprised by his anxiety. "Jill said you were

covered in blood mostly not your own. Unless you were flying along the M4 it could only have been birds."

"Who's Jill?"

"She's in air traffic control. There's no reason to worry."

"When you're responsible for millions of pounds-worth of aeroplane you like to bring her down in one piece. If they start a bloody inquiry they never know when to stop."

"But you did bring her down, which I guess must have been no mean feat. You could have panicked and ejected, then they'd have no aeroplane at all." She smiled encouragingly. "I think you're in need of a binge tonight, too. Drink up. I'll get us another."

An hour later, Mark had forgotten about courts of inquiry and Maggie had forgotten why she had decided to get drunk. Their alcoholic intake had actually been reasonably low. They found so much to say to each other, drinking took second place. When the landlord called time they were amazed.

"Can't we go on somewhere?" asked Mark as they went out into the night.

"You're joking. Hampton Heyhoe closes down at twenty-three hundred. Any naughty boys and girls still out of bed half an hour later are rounded up by the beadle."

He trapped her against the car by resting a hand on the roof each side of her. "Then we'd better get to bed, hadn't we?"

She was quite relaxed. "You're not in a fast jet now. Slow down, boy!"

He gave a rueful smile. "It's always worth having a shot."

"Keep trying. You might get lucky some day."

He kissed her lingeringly. "This place is the Bird in Hand but you're clearly the two in the bush. I've enjoyed this evening. We'll do it again sometime." He straightened and freed her. "Now I'd better drive you back before the beadle gets you."

They set off in silence along the narrow lanes leading to the Station. Maggie was dreamy but keenly aware of Mark's proximity. He seemed happy enough to accept her rules, although she started to question that assumption when the car slowed on a lonely stretch. When Mark brought it to a halt and pulled on the handbrake, Maggie was deeply disappointed. She did not want to end the evening by kicking him where it hurt the most.

He turned to her. "You'd better take over the driving. My vision's bloody awful all of a sudden. Must be the shot the

MO gave me. Sorry." With that he slumped forward over the wheel, out cold.

"Oh *hell*! she muttered, trying to get her brain working. It would be impossible to pull him from behind the wheel across to the passenger seat, yet if she dragged him out on to the road, she would never lift him back in. While she could throw quite a large man during a karate encounter, it would be difficult to move Mark's unconscious weight. She sat for a moment or two trying to come up with some kind of plan then his words penetrated. *The shot the MO gave me.* She gazed at his neck where the plaster was visible. He had given a demanding aerobatic display then had a mid air accident leading to a tricky emergency landing. The plaster covered a minor injury which might nevertheless have bled copiously. The MO had apparently given him a sedative, usually accompanied by advice to take things easy and get to bed early. The patient had instead needed company, so he had gone to a pub with a woman he had just invited to bed. It was amazing he had lasted this long.

"Here's another fine mess you've got me in," she murmured, using a favourite quotation of Rob's who was a Laurel and Hardy enthusiast. "So how do I get out of it, Superman?"

Five minutes passed while she struggled to tug Mark towards her so that his torso was lying across the seat she had vacated. Then she walked round and opened the driver's door to unhook his legs from beneath the wheel. She would decide her next move after that. It was while she was bent inside the car, wrestling to free his right knee and foot, that Maggie heard the faint roar of an engine and craned her neck to see a distant wobbling beam piercing the darkness. Thank God! With help, she could get Mark on the back seat and drive home.

The light advanced rapidly, and the roar told her it was produced by a motorcycle. Great! The driver was more likely to be a man, with the strength she needed for this. She stood beside the open door so that he would be forced to stop or drive past on the rough ground. The beam was blinding, and she had a brief moment of alarm thinking he would hit her. He stopped a few feet away, the deep roar quietening into a softer rumble as the light dimmed. Then her dazzled eyes made out a tall figure in black coming towards her.

"What the hell are you doing here? I thought you were on leave."

She could not believe her luck. "And I thought *you* were, Dave. You're the answer to my prayer. I need your help."

He came over to her, pushing up the visor of his helmet. Then he saw Mark sprawled over the front seats. "Oh no, you're not using me again to get you out of a tricky situation. What is it with you and men? You've no sense, have you? I'm not taking you on the pillion again. You can forget it." He began walking away.

Maggie grabbed his arm. "I don't want to ride on your bloody pillion. I want your help to shift him to the rear seat so I can drive back."

"And have him throw up all over me? No thanks. If you choose to spend your evening with a drunk, part of the fun is coping with his vomit." He pushed her hand away and prepared to mount his bike, but Maggie put herself between him and the saddle, furious at his attitude.

"He's not drunk. He was given a shot by the MO and it's just caught up with him. He's passed out. Stop being such a pig and help me move him from behind the wheel. Then I can drive back to the Officers' Mess, and you can go over the edge of the cliff for all I care. *Come on!*"

She stomped over to the car and stood waiting. He eventually crossed to join her and, without a word, bent to seize hold of Mark's right arm, tug him upright, then grip him beneath both armpits and pull him free. Maggie hurriedly opened the rear door and Dave threw the unconscious man in like a sack of coal.

He pointed to the feet. "I suppose you can manage to tuck them in without my help?"

As he walked away, Maggie followed. "I don't know what you have against me, but if you'd found any other member of the team in a predicament, you'd muscle in without question. Even if they were all as pissed as newts. I'm not. Neither is he," she added, nodding at the car. "He had to make a difficult emergency landing in a Harrier this afternoon, so I took pity on him and invited him for a quiet drink. I didn't know he'd been sedated."

"How d'you know now?"

"He told me just before he passed out."

"Bright boy!" he said sarcastically.

"Get stuffed, Dave!"

He swung his leg over the saddle, pulled down his visor and opened the throttle. "Aye, and if I do it'll be with enough wits to avoid getting you out of a scrape with some other man you take pity on."

He roared off into the night leaving Maggie exasperated. He was so damn prickly with her and totally different with the men. Cramming Mark's feet in the car, she slammed the door and got behind the wheel with a sigh. Prickly or not, Dave had been her salvation tonight. Mark Hascham could easily become the reverse.

It was eleven when Maggie awoke. It was too late for breakfast downstairs, so she snuggled into the pillow letting her mind drift. It drifted to thoughts that sent her from the bed to the window. The damaged Harrier stood on the tarmac, a sobering sight to any pilot. Washing and dressing quickly, she hurried from her room unsure where she might find Mark. In the hall she encountered the catering sergeant, who stopped with a smile.

"Good morning, ma'am. Flight Lieutenant Hascham was asking for you before he left for Wittering. He wrote a note. It's in your pigeonhole."

She went swiftly to the corridor where letters and messages were put. There were four envelopes in her place, one bearing no stamp and just her name. She went back to her room and tore open the note from Mark. The thick angular writing typified his nervous energy.

I apologise profusely! Jason Doyle from Personnel told me you drove me back and persuaded him to help you smuggle me to my room. Can't imagine how you managed it but I deeply appreciate your tact. You really are some woman, Maggie Spencer.

Good news! It *was* a bird strike. Several hang gliders saw it happen. They heard a shot and a flock of gulls rose from a field on the cliff top to wheel out over the sea. It seems to have been one of those bird-scaring devices that lets off a bang at regular intervals. One of the witnesses was a guy called Dave Ashmore, a sergeant from 646 – maybe you know him – so he called Hampton to warn them. Bit of luck for me that he was gliding in the right place at the right time. Or should that be the *wrong* time?

Maggie, thanks for everything. I greatly enjoyed what

I remember of last night. We'll do it again, with a better ending. I'll call you.

Mark (or not-so-clever Dick!)

Maggie gazed out at the damaged Harrier, the letter in her hand, anger mounting. Dave had said nothing when she explained to him why Mark had been sedated, yet he had seen the disaster happen and phoned in to report it.

Her letters were from her father, Rob and Phil, all on the same theme: very stressful time, must make allowances, difficult miscarriage, Fay terribly upset, give it time, exercise tact and understanding. She put the letters aside and reread the note from Mark, glad he had had confirmation of the cause of his accident. He claimed to have been "whooping it up" along the coast. Too much, perhaps? It must be a relief for him to have a witness, and an RAF one. She scowled, her anger reviving. Dave had let her stand on a dark isolated road at midnight trying to explain to him why she needed his help, all the time knowing more about the affair than she did. Damn him!

After making a cup of coffee Maggie went out for another day in the sunshine, thinking of yesterday's dramatic chain of events. It so occupied her thoughts and spirits she felt as bright and bursting with life as the day itself.

Mark rang as she was about to take a shower before bed with a book. The South African inflections were even more pronounced over the telephone. "Ah, third time lucky! I thought you might be on another binge."

"One was enough."

"Frankly, as binges go it wasn't in the premier league."

"Just as well or we'd both have spent the night in the car."

"Thanks for the Good Samaritan bit. How ever did you get me on the back seat? That guy Doyle said I was there when you dragged him from the Mess to help."

"It's a long story. I'll tell you it one day. I'm glad you had witnesses, by the way. It'll make life easier for you."

"I'll say. Do you know that sergeant?"

"Vaguely. Are you grounded?"

"Until next week," he chuckled. "The men in flowing robes placed an immediate order for Harriers, so I'm the blue-eyed boy in spite of it all."

"A big-headed blue-eyed boy."

His chuckle continued. "Ah, ma'am, you know we don't earn our wings unless our heads are slightly bigger than normal."

They talked for nearly an hour. Then Mark asked, "Does the reason still exist, by the way?"

"What reason?"

"For the half-hearted binge."

"Oh . . . no."

"Good. I'll ring you tomorrow to make arrangements for the weekend. *Tot Siens*."

Maggie drove to Alresford on Saturday in high spirits. Mark was waiting in the specified pub, where they had lunch before taking a trip on the Watercress Line steam railway. Mark was an enthusiast. The sunny weather still held so they walked hand in hand through woods filled with bluebells while Mark told her about his childhood in and around Kruger Park. Then he asked Maggie about her family.

"Dad's a solicitor. I've three brothers. Phil builds specialist yachts, Rob's a doctor and Charles is an accountant. Home is near your grandparents', just outside York. My life is more exciting than they can even imagine. Mother thinks I'm trying to turn into a man."

"Please don't," he said with a grin.

The conversation then centred on flying, the great love of their lives, until they went to a smart country club Mark knew of for dinner followed by drinks in an intimate corner of the bar.

Just before midnight, Mark said, "I booked a room here on the off chance that you might like to escape the beadle with me."

"Make it two rooms and you're on."

He showed only the slightest hesitation before getting to his feet. "Right, I'll go to reception and see what I can do."

"On the other hand, it seems a pity to spend all that money when there'll be beds for two in the room you've booked," she murmured with a sleepy smile.

Randal arrived back on Sunday evening in the middle of a violent thunderstorm. Typical, he thought. Someone sends an e-mail to the rain gods whenever we're lined up for a spell in tents on Salisbury Plain. Yet even that prospect could not dampen his mood. Neil was doing well. He was a quiet serious boy – God knew who he got those qualities from – and was therefore a model patient likely to be released from hospital within a week or two.

Fiona was still loving and reliant on him. They had stayed at Marylands because it was convenient for visiting Neil and Lydia was familiar with the surroundings, but they had talked a great deal about the house in the country they would buy and their new life as a family. Gerald and Mary Holland had done their best to stay on the sidelines and, although there would always be tension between the horse breeders and the dedicated service pilot, there had been a temporary armistice.

Randal accepted that Fiona should remain with her parents until Neil had settled again after his spell in hospital, but she had agreed to live with him after that in a rented place near Hampton Heyhoe, leaving the children at Marylands while they looked at property. She was as excited as a child at the prospect but showed her feelings like a real woman, to Randal's great satisfaction. This was the reason why the thought of Salisbury Plain in a torrential downpour hardly bothered him.

Taking his mail up to the room he would not be occupying for much longer, he flicked through the usual bank statements and bills, then came upon a handwritten rather grubby envelope bearing a Taunton postmark. Puzzled, he slit it open and took out a short note paperclipped to some thicker paper folded twice. The note was from Ted, the truck driver, who wrote that he had been given the enclosed at his last delivery and had promised to send it on. Randal unfolded the large sheet of rough paper and read:

> Deer skadron leeder Thank you for cuming to me in the sno. It was my best day even better than farther krismus slay. I never see him wen he cums and I didert see you. I wood like to. heer is a pikchur of your playn. wood you send me one of you plees Ted can bring it nex time
> luv and kisses
> Fiona Hunter
> thank you

Beneath the laborious letter was a crayon drawing of the Chinook, remarkably accurate for a five-year-old. She had talent.

The anguish of that night when Neil lay unconscious returned in a rush as Randal gazed at the paper in his hand. His own ordeal was over; the Hunters continued to suffer. He visualised that isolated slate-roofed farm on the cliff; the deep snow, the dark ravine, the angry sea just ahead. He had taken a calculated risk with that landing. A little girl who had no notion of that risk had thought it her best day ever. He hoped desperately that Ted would only be told to take Fiona's name from his list if it meant the girl had been given a transplant.

Next morning he spent an hour in his office dealing with the paperwork he hated, before the daily briefing. He read Rusty's report on the Flight's last few days at Split. They had had plenty to do. He was impressed by Dave's mountain rescue and resolved to talk to the Squadron Commander on the subject. The Scot was a valuable member of the team, although a bit of a dark horse. The rest of the tasks had been fairly run-of-the-mill for Bosnia.

He then read Rusty's unofficial account of Maggie's fainting fit on their return flight and her curious panic to make a phone call. Randal chewed the end of his pen thoughtfully. Rusty should have sent her straight to the MO – no arguments – if she had been flying with a navigator it could have been dangerous. He would insist on an immediate medical check. A woman suddenly fainting could indicate pregnancy. He thought Maggie too sold on her career for carelessness in that direction, but that American had definitely featured in her life. Rumour had it he had been given the cold shoulder two months ago, but the timing would be about right. If she was even the slightest bit anxious on that score and was continuing to fly he would have her guts for garters. Whatever the cause, he would ground her until he was sure of her fitness. He would speak to Rusty over this, too.

When they all trooped in at eight thirty Randal cast a shrewd glance at Maggie. She looked in radiant health and so sexually beckoning he was involuntarily aroused. He swiftly attributed this unwelcome response to ten hectic nights with Fiona. His libido had not yet quietened down. But there was an invitation in Maggie's eyes that had not been there before. He had known at the outset she would be trouble. Women always were.

"Morning, everyone," he began. "I hope you enjoyed your leave. Neil is doing fine and should be out of hospital by the weekend. Thanks for your combined message of support radioed to the hospital. It was greatly appreciated." He grinned. "Thanks, also, to whoever ensured that my shaver came back with my gear. Anything special to report on the domestic front? When's the wedding to be, Rusty?"

The redhead scowled. "Very funny."

"How are the kids, Jimmy?"

"Never satisfied."

"Like Jeff," said Sandy. "I saw him last Tuesday night with *three* girls."

"That was my sister and her friends," he protested.

"Oh yeah?" they all chorused.

"OK, let's get down to business," said Randal. "You'll have seen the wailing wall. Frank, Titch, Benny and Dave are in for more snow. Sorry, guys, but there's a bid for an aircraft and crew to make up numbers in Norway for the next ten days. The Army has two helicopters out of action and several crewmen on the sick list. You'll join A Flight already on the NATO exercise and I'm confident you'll show them how much better we are in this flight. Three of you have had plenty of experience over there. Add Dave and his magic snowshoes and you'll be sitting pretty. Congratulations on that mountain rescue, Dave. Sorry I missed it. Frank, you're programmed to take off at fourteen hundred. Unless you've any problems I suggest you get together and carry on. Good luck."

The four moved to the far end of the long room with the relevant charts and, before Randal addressed the rest, he noticed an almost venomous glare given to Dave by Maggie. Surely that pair were not an item.

"We fortunate ones can look forward to five days under canvas playing at war. We've done it before, so you know what to expect, and that's more often than not the *un*expected. We take off at fifteen hundred, so we've enough time to get our gear assembled. There'll be a combined services briefing at nineteen thirty, when we'll be given the positions of the opposing armies. The PBI will take up those positions during the night. Bids for reinforcements, weapons, supplies and Casevac will come in from o-six hundred tomorrow."

They settled down to general discussion and note-taking until all their points had been thrashed out. When the briefing ended, Randal asked Maggie to stay behind. She seemed unworried at being singled out, probably thinking it was because this was her first attendance at these regular combined exercises. In fact, she was unusually receptive, almost friendly.

"I'm glad your son's on the mend. It must be a great relief."

"Yeah," he said absently. "I've arranged for you to see the MO at ten."

She looked puzzled. "I'm up to date with all my jabs."

"Rusty says you fainted half an hour before landing last week. He should have sent you to the sick bay immediately. *You* should have taken yourself there. You have a responsibility to your crew, if not to yourself. Did you intend to fly today and every day, until it happened again? What if you had no second pilot with you? What the *hell* do you think you're playing at here?"

Her face had lost some of that glow but although she was clearly thrown by his attack she came right back at him. "Rusty's wrong. I didn't faint."

"Why did he record that you did? Are you claiming he lied?"

"I'm claiming that I didn't faint, and even if there had been no second pilot the aircraft would still have been constantly under control. I intend to fly whenever I'm required to. If you're ordering me to see the MO I'll have to go but there's nothing wrong with my health and it'll be a waste of everyone's time."

Her attitude put his back up, as it usually did, and he pulled rank for once. "You're grounded until I'm satisfied of your fitness to fly. It's as simple as that." As she faced him, tight-lipped, he added, "There might be nothing wrong with your health; there are other reasons why women start fainting."

As his inference dawned on her, her eyes widened. "You think I'm *pregnant*? My God, you'll all be knitting white shawls next! That's every male's explanation, isn't it! If it's not that, it must be PMT. Doesn't it ever occur to you that women are affected by things other than their reproductive systems?"

"Such as?" That pulled her up short and while she hesitated he added, "You're grounded until you give me a satisfactory explanation of Rusty's report, or the MO clears you."

Now she looked worried. "It's personal."

"Not if it affects the rest of B Flight."

"I've already assured you my work won't be affected."

"I need the MO's assurance."

"You won't accept my word as a responsible pilot?"

"You're telling me I shouldn't accept Rusty's word as a responsible pilot. Why should I accept yours?"

They faced each other belligerently for long moments before she said, "The MO will clear me, but you insist on an explanation before you'll let me fly?"

He leaned back against the wall, arms folded. "Got it in one. Maggie, if I pass Rusty's report to the Squadron Commander he'll go out of his way to keep you on the ground permanently. We all know his views on women pilots. Much better talk to me on the quiet."

She sighed with frustration. "It's *very* personal."

"It'll stay that way," he assured her, wondering what on earth she could be about to confess. "You have my word."

His gentler tone did nothing to help and, for the first time, he had some insight into what it must be like for her in this man's world. He could have had a frank talk with any of the men without a clash of genders.

Maggie regarded him with stony hostility. "I'm one of twins. My brother was born five minutes after me."

"You've never told us that."

"Why should I? It has nothing to do with my professional ability."

"Not a deep dark secret or anything to hide, is it?"

She ignored that. "All our lives we've been exceptionally close; sharing everything. In our teens we discovered a mutual ESP, the kind that's very common in identical twins. We can sense when the other is troubled or not well."

"Good God, can you? I've read about it, but I've never met twins to find out first hand. Go on."

Her aggression returned with a vengeance just as he was starting to get some idea what this was all about. "I'm telling you this under duress. Because it's that or stay grounded."

"Yes, I'm afraid it is," he agreed, once more aware of a sexual interest he did not welcome. It was because she had changed from being one of his pilots into a lovely young woman in trouble. *A damsel in distress.* How she would hate him if she could read his thoughts!

She got to her feet, saying defiantly, "I didn't faint; I had an overwhelming sensation that took me unawares and told me Phil was in desperate trouble. I did *not* lose control. If I had had Pete with me instead of Rusty there would have been absolutely *no* danger. I was thinking about how swiftly I could get to a phone, but we've all flown with personal problems at the backs of our minds. As you must have lately. But we all keep the job in the forefront and fly safely. That's what we're trained to do." The light of battle was back in her eyes. "I'm not pregnant, I'm not suffering from PMT and I'm not an irresponsible fool. I wouldn't fly if I had any doubt about my ability. Of course I wouldn't. At least give me credit for taking my responsibilities seriously."

He levered himself away from the wall. "If you didn't you wouldn't be in my flight. I'd have booted you out pronto." He sighed. "Why didn't you tell Rusty what was wrong?"

She looked daggers at him.

"So how is your twin brother?"

"Shattered by his wife's miscarriage."

"It was *that* that caused this . . . sensation you experienced?" he ventured, feeling out of his depth.

"It won't happen again. Definitely."

He felt even further out of his depth. He was a realist, down to earth. Anything even vaguely paranormal made him uncomfortable. "How can you be sure? What if he runs into further trouble? Won't this ESP thing activate again?"

"No." She sounded coldly certain. "The link has broken. He's wired up to his wife, and I . . . I'm very close to someone I've met recently. Now, is there anything else you want to know about my private life, Boss?"

She was back to the fierce pilot in a green flying suit with a chip on her shoulder. He shook his head in exasperation. "Don't fight me, Maggie. Everyone in the team is on the same side, ready to help each other. I thought you'd finally recognised that."

He might not have spoken. "Am I grounded or not?"

"You can fly, but only with another pilot," he ruled brusquely. "You'd better get moving. We've wasted enough time already."

After she left he thumped the wall gently with his fist. What had he done to deserve "Mystic Mag" as one of his pilots? Then he gave a rueful smile. She was bloody keen, all the same.

Three days and nights of relentless rain and wind. The air crews were browned off but the ground troops were more so. The exercise was following the usual pattern, with a few of the participants treating it as no more than a lark, a jolly rollicking

110

break from dreary routine, and some regarding it as a matter of life or death. In war it could well be, but an exercise was only a rehearsal and adrenalin did not flow as swiftly as when facing an enemy out to kill. Men who had been in action kept a sense of proportion during exercises. Those who had not often regarded them as a possible path to promotion or glory.

Captain Clive Grierson, the army liaison officer for Y Sector of Red Force was one of the latter. He and Randal had met before and disliked each other intensely. Grierson in fact disliked the RAF down to the last man. He thought them undisciplined where rank was concerned – the habit of calling the captain of an aircraft "Boss" was appalling – and he considered them too full of themselves. The British Army had existed for centuries before aeroplanes were invented. What answer had the free and easy conceited fliers to that?

In Randal's opinion, Grierson was the worst kind of officer. The spit and polish, do everything by the book, steeped in tradition kind, who were a menace during real conflict. He had once pointed out to the man that the Army's history was littered with fools unable to adapt to circumstances or accept the advice of experienced but junior battlefield soldiers. As Grierson had been unable to produce a comparable example from the history of the RAF Randal had won that argument. They had not met again until now, so liaison was not the best word to describe their dealings.

Captain Grierson occupied a large tent with a big table, maps and charts covered with marking pins and highlighted in various colours indicating the positions of the opposing armies, and a battery of radio equipment linking him to air and ground forces. To assist him he had a subaltern, John Fifield, and two corporals, to whom he never spoke but barked. The only difference in treatment he afforded the second lieutenant was that he addressed him as Mister whenever he barked at him in the presence of the corporals. Grierson had a small canvas annexe containing a bed, a camp stool and a folding washbowl. He napped in his uniform, including his boots, having given his subaltern strict orders to make no decision or give no directive without waking him to handle the situation.

Squadron Leader Price, on the other hand, selected his crews, gave them details of the tasks that came in and trusted them to get on with it. He stripped to his underwear and enjoyed a good sleep whenever Rusty took command, despite the noise of simulated warfare. He was doing this on their penultimate night, having flown during the previous hours of darkness and again in late afternoon. He was dreaming that Fiona had selected a mansion large enough for royalty and committed him to paying for it, when he was shaken awake.

One of his corporals was beside him, with a torch aimed at the tent roof. "Sorry to disturb you, sir. You're wanted by Squadron Leader Collins over at Flight HQ."

"What, right now?" he asked irritably, peering at his watch through half-closed eyes. It was three thirty.

"Captain Grierson is with him and in a right state. There's some kind of emergency."

"Oh, *Christ*!" Randal rolled from the camp bed, reached for his flying suit, pulled on his boots and groped around for his thick jacket, still shaking off the nightmarish vision of his palatial future home. Snatching up his torch he left the tent to trot in drenching rain through a stretch of copse, then across several hundred yards of open muddy ground, deeply concerned there had been a crash and casualties. He had two crews out: Rusty flying with Pete, and Maggie co-piloting with Jeff. What if Maggie had had another of her curious messages from her twin and Jeff's attention had been distracted? Randal had himself flown with her for the first couple of days. Apart from the smouldering resentment towards him she had been fine, so he had sent her out tonight to deliver thirty men as reinforcements. The pair were good pilots, but ESP was an unknown hazard.

If there had been an accident he was to blame. He should have grounded her. Common sense told him to, but when he had questioned Rusty he admitted Maggie had not actually fainted or really lost control. At the back of Randal's mind had also been the question of what reason he would give to the Squadron Commander, another man with little imagination and a rule book mentality. Loath to condemn Maggie to permanent grounding Randal would compromise until he was convinced the link with her brother had been broken, as she claimed. This was quite out of his range of experience, so he did not know how seriously to treat it, but if he had misjudged the situation he had put at risk a crew and thirty soldiers.

When he pushed into the tent and saw Grierson's expression in the harsh light his worst fears seemed justified. The man was bent over a large map on the table, jabbing at marker pins and muttering angrily.

Randal looked at Micky Collins, the RAF liaison officer. "What's up?"

Grierson answered him with snapping jaws. "What's up? *What's up?* Your bloody people, that's what's up! Taking thirty troops to the Red Force dug in in this wood." He jabbed the map with a finger stained by yellow highlighter fluid, then consulted the number on the marker. "Aircraft PQ777J."

Randal said involuntarily, "Jeff and Maggie! Christ, what's happened?"

Grierson looked ready to explode. "They delivered the troops to Blue Force. *The bloody enemy!* They put thirty men down beside a wood then flew off leaving them to walk into the arms of the hostile force, who immediately made them prisoners."

Randal's relief was so great he laughed. For a moment he believed Grierson would strike him, but Micky Collins swiftly intervened.

"Rip, Blue Force has radioed in. The men were definitely dropped in the wrong place."

"And you find it amusing," Grierson said viciously.

"Only because I thought there'd been a disaster."

"There *was*. Your aircraft flown by that . . . that *female*, deposited *our* reinforcements in the heart of enemy territory."

Randal said to Micky, "There must have been a mix-up over the location. My crews are highly experienced. They wouldn't make an error of that kind; you know that." He raised his voice to combat the sudden increase in the thunder of rain on canvas, and turned on the army man. "It isn't enemy territory, Grierson. The worst the 'prisoners' will suffer is some humiliating baiting by their 'captors' before they all go back to camp on Friday night for a booze-up to celebrate the end of a bloody awful wet week playing at war."

"How typical of the RAF to see it as a game," Grierson sneered.

Micky, phlegmatic and conciliatory as always, said, "Suppose we calm down and try to find out where the error occurred."

"We know where," Grierson snapped. "The ineptitude of this crew has changed the face of the entire action in Y Sector. Our Red companies had orders to link up with those in Z Sector by noon tomorrow. That's now out of the question thanks to you,

Price. Small wonder your subordinates are so incompetent; you appear to have no personal sense of responsibility whatever."

Randal lost his temper, ignoring Micky as the other had. "We're not fighting the Third World War here, Grierson. We're simulating battle so that we'll be prepared for the real thing; and that means being prepared for mistakes, cock-ups and the unexpected. Doesn't matter how often men rehearse for war, things go wrong. They always have, they always will. That's because troops are human, from generals down to the poor bloody infantry. Sometimes signals go astray, guns jam, vehicles break down or thick fog comes down at the vital moment. We have to carry on, not kick up a sodding song and dance in the middle of the night."

Flushed and vindictive, Grierson hit back. "If it had been an army slip-up you'd be even more vulgar and unrestrained. Your answer to everything is to shout the loudest."

"I have to to get through thick skulls like yours." Randal tried unsuccessfully to hold on to his control. "In an exercise one side has to lose. This time it'll be the Reds." He thumped his fist on the table. "It won't be the end of the bloody world. Not even the end of Red Force. No one's going to shoot you at dawn, more's the pity."

"All right, this slanging match is getting us nowhere," said Micky, sick of playing pig in the middle. "The men have been taken prisoner, and that's that. Red Force commander put in a bid for air support and gave the pick-up and put-down points. Somewhere between his headquarters and your pilots' briefing an error was made. I suggest we disperse and find out where," he finished, looking pointedly at the other two.

Randal said testily, "All right, Micky, I'll question my crew when they get back. If they've been careless I'll skin 'em alive, but I've enough faith in them to be sure there's a reasonable explanation for their actions." He put on his torch ready to leave, but first shone the blinding beam on Grierson's rigid features. "Don't you *ever* refer to one of my pilots as 'that female' again. Flight Lieutenant Spencer could make mincemeat of you in any contest, and I'd enjoy watching it happen."

He was still furious as he trudged across the churned-up ground to the copse enclosing the tents occupied by B Flight. Thankfully there had been no crash, but what the blazes could have caused Jeff and Maggie to make such a monumental miscalculation? The ESP thing was still in the front of his mind. Both pilots were hot enough on navigation, but something had sent them off course. He did not care whether Red or Blue were proclaimed the winners at the end of the week, but it mattered to him that his flight carried out any task with professional diligence.

Back in his tent he removed his wet coat and cap, then sat in his flying suit to read through the note he had made of what the pair had been directed to do. The details had been sent to Flight Headquarters by Grierson, who would have got them from the commander of Y Sector. Randal had scanned the signal and given it to Jeff because he was experienced at low-level night flying; to Maggie because she was not. What the hell had happened between them?

Forty-five minutes passed before he heard the Chinook come in, by which time his temper had calmed but not his intention to wade into his pilots. When the noise of the rotors died he waited by the entrance to his tent, from where he eventually saw the dark outlines of the crew members heading for theirs.

"Jeff! Maggie! In here," he called, and waited by the map table until they entered carrying their helmets fitted with night vision goggles.

Jeff looked surprised. "We were going to report in the morning. Thought you'd be snoring the night away."

"So did I," he said tersely, watching Maggie closely. Apart from the uncommunicative expression she adopted whenever they were face to face she looked perfectly controlled.

"Has something happened?" asked Jeff. "Don't tell me we have to go out again."

"One cock-up per night is enough, thanks."

Jeff frowned but Maggie asked calmly, "Is that aimed at us?"

He enlightened them in his inimitable way, watching Maggie for a giveaway sign. She gave none, just listened until he had finished.

Jeff looked flabbergasted. "It went like clockwork. The thirty guys were waiting. Ray and Nobby got them settled in with all their gear, and we off-loaded them as instructed. Maggie's nav was spot on. There wasn't a cock-up."

"There bloody *was*!" Randal turned to Maggie. "Were you on the ball the whole time?"

Angry colour rushed to her cheeks. "Yes. If you won't accept my word, ask Jeff."

"Just checking," he said in quieter tones. "You dropped them in X Sector instead of Y. That's a fact. The Blue Force reported their capture. It's my job to find out why you were so far off course."

"We weren't," she countered with fierce confidence.

He indicated the map on his table. "OK, let's go over the details until we get to the bottom of it."

Jeff took his notes from his knee pocket, and Maggie took from hers the navigational calculations she had made. They bent over the map on which were marked the various sectors and the positions of the opposing forces. In less than five minutes Randal found something curious.

"This reference you noted for the drop-off is very clearly just inside X Sector, which is highlighted in blue. You must have seen that."

"Of course we did," Jeff countered defensively.

"Why didn't you question it?"

His blue eyes gazed back unclouded by guilt. "I thought the point of this exercise was for the Reds or Blues to overrun the other's territory and win the war. I assumed the Reds had moved forward and needed the reinforcements to press home their advantage."

"Then you thought wrong, chum. They wanted the extra men to try to halt the Blue advance. In war you never assume, Jeff. You check before delivering anything in support of an army. Maggie, didn't it occur to you to question that position?"

Her green eyes were as unclouded as Jeff's. "It was given to us by a Red commander, who should know where his men are. And in war, while you're checking everything, surely the battle could be lost because reinforcements or supplies didn't arrive in time?"

He nodded. "It's a point, but it shouldn't take long to check. Requests for our help normally aren't left until they can see the whites of the enemy's eyes. I was referring, anyway, to instances like this one, when your own troops appear to have moved to hostile territory but you have no proof of it other than a map reference passed through the chain of command." He frowned. "According to the map it should have read thirty-six not thirty-eight, Jeff. Did you copy it correctly?"

"I should have the original signal you handed to me some-where among all this." He shuffled through pieces of paper from his pocket and produced it. "There you are: thirty-eight."

While Randal stared at it thoughtfully, Maggie said, "It also mentions setting down beside a wooded area, and we did. If you take a look at the map you'll see there are two very similar areas within easy reach of each other."

He glanced at where she was pointing, then straightened. "Someone was careless and gave the reference for the wrong one. OK, I take back the initial bollocking, but not the warn-ing to confirm friendly positions behind enemy lines before playing Father Christmas to the other side." He strengthened his point. "A real enemy would have knocked you out of the sky tonight, or taken you prisoner with the rest. Dwell on that."

"Right, Boss. Sorry. All our fault. Won't happen again. Goodnight," said Jeff, bending his head beneath the tent opening and facing the rain again.

"Maggie." She turned back as Randal delayed her. "About my veiled remark. Put it down to the fact that when I was dragged from my bed and told there was an emergency with your aircraft, I imagined the worst."

"At least you'd have been rid of me."

"Along with three aircrew and thirty troops? An expensive way of doing it." He gave a faint smile. "If I ever want you out of the Flight, I'll go about it through normal channels. Goodnight . . . what's left of it."

She hesitated, seemed about to say something, then changed her mind and walked off into the night. After putting the signal safely with the mountain of paperwork he would take to the commanders' review at the conclusion of the exercise, Randal glanced at his watch. Almost five o'clock. Pointless to hope for more sleep, better to settle for thirty minutes stretched out on the bed letting his thoughts wander.

They wandered pleasantly enough until someone spoke his name, asking if he were awake. His heart sank. Rusty was still out. What had he said to Jeff about one cock-up per night being enough? "Yes, who is it?" he asked heavily.

"John Fifield."

Oh God, not another summons to Grierson. He rolled from the bed. "Come in out of the rain, man."

The subaltern wore a waterproof jacket but his cap was sodden. Runnels of water streaked his pink boyish cheeks as he gave a different smile. "Sorry to disturb you again, sir, but I saw you had a light on."

"What's the problem?" Randal asked, surmising that it was not urgent.

"Oh, no problem. I . . . well, I just felt I should have a word with you about that other business."

"About us being given the wrong map reference?"

"You've found out." He frowned. "I feel responsible."

"Why?"

"When Corporal Roach gave us the signal I queried it with Grierson and pointed out that we'd had no intelligence regarding a Red advance to that second copse. In fact, everything pointed to their having a tough time holding on to the copse they were already in."

"Grierson ignored you?"

"No, he merely asked for confirmation of the map references without giving his reasons. Well, you know how it is: the NCO manning the radio at Red Force HQ looks at the paper he's been given and simply repeats the info. So the signal was passed to Squadron Leader Collins. I should have insisted that we check the Red position first."

Randal gave a faint smile. "You'd not have got anywhere. Grierson is totally inflexible. We've met before. I know him."

"I hope you didn't give your pilots a lot of stick. They weren't to blame."

"They were as much to blame as the rest of us who didn't check the references and ask questions. If we were doing this for real it would have been a disastrous blunder. As it is, so many of us were careless it'll probably be glossed over at the summing-up. But if Grierson tries to shift all blame on my crew I'll have something to say, believe me."

"It won't come to that, sir. I intend to point out that I twice expressed my concern over a position lying in enemy territory and I was ignored. I know one shouldn't drop a fellow officer in it, but he's done it to me several times and his turn has come." He prepared to go. "I just thought I'd tell you what I'm going to do."

Randal offered his hand. "Thanks. I appreciate the gesture. Give Grierson hell, and give yourself a pat on the back. You seem to be the only one of us who didn't take things for granted."

While he washed and changed for breakfast, Randal heard Rusty's Chinook come in and breathed a sigh of relief. One more day and a night, then they could go home and take the weekend off. They deserved it after this rain, mud and inter-service wrangling. B Flight was surely due for a spell somewhere hot, but not until he had installed Fiona and the children in a country house where he knew they would always be waiting when he got home.

April

They had been in Munich three days, practising mountain flying, when Sandy discovered that it was Dave's birthday. For B Flight there was just one way to celebrate; in Munich there was just one place at which to do it in style. They set off in a fleet of taxis, the old hands promising the birthday boy a night he would never forget. Dave soon discovered they were following a ritual whenever they visited Munich, but the start of his twenty-fifth year would give the revels an added kick. Squashed into a taxi with Sandy, Jimmy, Ray and Nobby, Dave resigned himself to being put to bed paralytic again.

They rendezvoused at Spiegel's beer garden with five local girls known to crew members who had served in Germany before. The plan was to add more girls as they went along. Jeff suggested they find a man for Maggie, but she said it was more than enough for any woman to have to deal with them. She was not particularly looking forward to the evening. The emphasis would be on beer and sex. She hated the first and wanted sex only with Mark. How she wanted it!

Spiegel's was a typical Bavarian beer garden: a chalet-style restaurant with guest rooms above, a large garden hung with lights and filled with tables and long benches. In the suburbs, it commanded open views of the distant mountains, and long-term members of B Flight swore the beer was the best in Munich. Frau Spiegel loved fliers, in particular one Randal Ivan Price, whom she had hoped to make her son-in-law but who instead had introduced her to Price's Pork Pies. She now imported this British delicacy on a regular basis. In consequence, Randal was welcome to bring his friends whenever he was in Munich and was certain of a boisterous evening.

He spilled from the leading taxi feeling on top of the world. He liked Munich, he loved mountain flying, he enjoyed going on the razzle with his team. It was a fine warm evening, he felt at home at Spiegel's and all was right again with his marriage. He had left Fiona in a rented cottage at Hampton Heyhoe with a list of properties she was eager to inspect during his short absence. What more could a man want?

The garden was unusually full at this early hour, but the girls waiting for them had confiscated an entire table and they soon fully occupied it. Randal went in search of Frau Spiegel. The restaurant was empty, but each of the tables was set for a meal and adorned with a circlet of flowers as a centrepiece. At the far end of the room a long table had an additional huge wreath of flowers, fruit and ribbons hanging over the centre chairs. A wedding party was expected! No wonder the garden was full.

"Reep!" The name came out as a shriek of pleasure. Randal turned with a broad smile to see Frau Spiegel emerging from the kitchen with a trayful of glasses. Resplendent in her most ornate dirndl and jacket, she put the tray on a sideboard and advanced to enfold him and plant kisses on both his cheeks.

He swung her off her feet, making her shriek again, and asked, *"Wie gehtest ihr meine Liebe?"*

They exchanged greetings and items of gossip in rapid German until eventually Randal said, "My friends are outside waiting to greet you. We're celebrating a birthday, so set up the steins. We'll be making a night of it."

"Always you make a night of it, Reep. Always you are naughty boys," she said with a chuckle. "But so nice naughty boys. We have soon a wedding, but there is first time for beer."

On the point of following her outside Randal was aware of movement by the kitchen door, and he glanced across. She was also wearing her best dirndl, with a beribboned floral wreath over her dark hair. There had been too much between them for an exchange of smiles. Her dark eyes reflected that as he walked across and took her hands.

"It's good to see you, Anna," he said with sincerity, bending to kiss her lightly on the mouth. "How's Gerda?"

"She is already five years old." Studying him closely, she asked, "Rip, why do you never tell me you are coming?"

"I'm never sure. You know that well enough." He touched her cheek with gentle fingers. "You look beautiful. Does that mean you've finally found someone to replace Rolf?"

"How are Neil and Lydia?"

"Fine," he said, knowing she had avoided his question because he knew the answer. He wished it were otherwise.

"And your wife?"

"She's fine, too." He tried to lighten an intense situation. When a man was on top of the world he was susceptible. "Come out and meet the boys." He forced a smile. "One of them is a girl."

Grabbing her arm he led her to the garden where her mother was laughing delightedly with the British airmen while chivvying waiters to fetch beer for the *Geburtstag* celebration. Dave was introduced and kissed soundly on both cheeks, whereupon the rest demanded kisses. Waving her arms in a shooing motion, Frau Spiegel hurried off with pink cheeks, smiling with pleasure.

Those who already knew Anna greeted her in more subdued fashion. Randal introduced the rest in turn, leaving Dave until last. "Here's the birthday boy. Today he is twenty-five and finally becomes a man," he added with a grin.

To everyone's surprise Dave stood, kissed Anna's hand and spoke to her in fluent German. She responded with obvious pleasure and her grave expression finally brightened. At that point, the sound of distant cheering could be heard. Anna turned away to hurry indoors.

"Hey, Dave, didn't she give you an invitation to follow her?" Nobby called down the length of the table. "There was a definite come-hither look in her eye."

"That was aimed at someone else," put in Rusty. "Why do you think he's so welcome here?"

"Because I always stand the first round," said Randal, brushing the inference aside.

His affair with Anna had been no secret when 646 Squadron had been based in Germany but he felt such remarks were now out of place. The beer arrived, and the interest of the drinkers in the growing volume of cheering distracted them from that subject. Soon, they heard a cacophony of cowbells mingled with the shouts, and Randal told them it must be the wedding party arriving.

A few minutes later, the revellers came around the corner and burst into the car park of the inn, cowbells ringing and guests cheering enthusiastically. Young and old were dressed in elaborate national costumes adorned with ribbons and flowers. Young men, presumably the bridegroom's friends, were shaking painted bells of all sizes and pulling the newly-weds, seated on bales of hay, in a brightly painted and decorated cart. Their jollity spilled over to those at the garden tables who got to their feet, steins in hands, to cheer and drink to the happiness of the young couple.

Although the wedding party vanished into the restaurant, the small band hired for the occasion stood outside the open doors to play for the pleasure of everyone. Extra waiters had been employed to keep the beer coming, and it was inevitable that some couples began to dance to the music. Enough beer had flowed to persuade the members of B Flight to follow suit, those men without partners soon finding them. More and more people joined in until Rusty and Jeff suggested moving the tables back to the sides to make an open dance floor. There was a rush of volunteers. The old and the staid settled happily behind these barriers to watch the unexpected entertainment.

The sky darkened, the moon glowed brightly. The coloured lights looped around the trellis-work swayed in the gentle breeze and the easy comradeship to be found in beer gardens had never been warmer. Before long, the wedding guests began to come out to watch the dancing then join in. B Flight made way for them as huge helpings of veal and rice, with bowls of salad, drew them back to their table to eat and fuel their energy.

Randal was in his element. It was great to really let his hair down with men he liked and trusted and spent most days with under every kind of condition. He knew that Fiona would hate this rustic, somewhat earthy impromptu party he was enjoying with such relish but he thought of nothing but the boisterous present and, when more beer arrived and he saw Maggie wave it away, he decided that the general *bonhomie* should be enough to bring a thaw to their relationship. She had been dancing with some of the lads and with one or two local hopefuls, so it was time she stepped out with him.

When he tapped her shoulder and made a comical bow, she looked surprised. "Come on, Maggie, let's show them how it's done."

The dancing was of an improvised hoppity-skippity variety, with much clapping of hands in time with the oompah Bavarian music. No opportunity to cuddle up. To his surprise, Randal found himself regretting it. Maggie wore a dark-red top and swirling skirt with her fair hair loose to her shoulders, so it was possible to forget the efficient, aggressive, flying-suited pilot and see instead a desirable woman.

She swiftly sent desire packing. "Now I know why Pete and the others wailed about being sent to the Falklands while the rest of us came here. It wasn't the thought of missing out on mountain flying, it was the abundance of beer."

"And the prospect of facing autumn at the bottom of the world." He gripped her hand and swung her round with more than necessary vigour. "I'll be sending you there before long."

"I can take it," she said calmly. "Just as I can take being thrown around by you to prove a point."

"What point's that?" he asked, as they stamped their feet to the music.

"Oh, come on, you can't be *that* drunk!"

As she spun round again, her skirt flying up, he grabbed her arm and walked her between the merrymakers to a dim corner by the private parlour windows. "I must be *that* drunk," he said. "What point?"

"When are you going to let me fly without a pilot nursemaid?"

"Christ, you never get off the job, do you?"

"Not when I want something badly."

"Want on, chum!" The garden lights were reflected in her eyes and he was inebriated enough to connect that unnatural glow with her confession of some kind of supersensitive foresight. "How can I be sure you'll get no more magic messages in mid air?"

"Oh, for God's sake! You've no understanding of it at all. *Magic messages!* You think I'm some kind of witch or magician?"

"I don't know. I've never met anyone who can do what you say you can do."

"We don't *do* it. It happens. But it won't happen again," she added hastily.

"Convince me. Tell me about this twin business. I'm fascinated."

She was sceptical. "Oh yeah?"

"How badly do you want to lose the nursemaid?"

Some seconds passed. He was genuinely interested in the subject and this was a pleasant interlude in the midst of the hectic evening which he was in no hurry to cut short.

"Twins are born together and are brought up that way. As

124

babies they're fed at the same time, share a pram, get used to being alongside each other. Unlike others born at least ten months apart, they reach each stage of development as a pair. They share a birthday; they get cards addressed to 'the twins'. They start school on the same day, go to university on the same day, graduate together. It goes on and on," she said, waving her arms about.

"And you were happy with that?" he asked, perching on the low wall.

"I didn't know life any other way."

"But you didn't both join the RAF."

"Phil's crazy about small boats and sailing."

"So things began to change a few years ago. How come you got this . . ." He was about to say magic message again but changed it somewhat feebly to " . . . this *feeling* about him six weeks ago?"

She avoided his eyes. "You wouldn't understand."

"I don't. Enlighten me." When she appeared reluctant, he added, "You said his wife had a miscarriage. Your twin wasn't personally hurt or in trouble, so why the message?"

He must have touched a nerve. She said bitterly, "He was personally hurt, all right. I know what you men are."

"An expert on the subject, are you?"

"Growing up with three brothers gave me a pretty good insight, warts and all! Chas and Rob both have kids. Phil needed one to prove he was also a 'real man'."

"I have two. What does that make me?" he asked with amusement.

"An absent father."

He laughed. "That goes for most of us." He studied her for a moment or two then said, "It must have been tough as the only girl in the family. What on earth made you choose a career with the same uneven balance?"

"I wanted to fly. I want to go on doing it," she added pointedly.

"I'm not stopping you." His attention was drawn by a deafening salvo of cowbells in the garden. The bride and groom had emerged to dance. Everyone cleared a space for them as the band struck up a waltz, the sound of which was almost drowned by the ornate bells. Randal watched them, lost in reflection. Had they any idea of the hazards ahead?

Maggie came up beside him. "Do you now understand?"

"Why we feel driven to go through this caper?" he responded with a grin, nodding at the twirling newly-weds.

"You wanted me to explain twinship."

He patted the wall beside him. "Sit here and tell me why you reckon it's all over."

"It's not over. We'll be twins until we die," she said, staying where she was.

"This message business," he insisted, half his attention still on the activity in the garden, "I haven't got to grips with it yet."

"Must I go into that?"

"Mmm, I think so."

"We discovered it when we first lived apart," she began. "It continued when Phil married Fay. At Christmas, I sensed he was excited about something and made a guess. I was right, but Fay was furious because she swore he'd told me." She ran a hand through her long hair in a nervous gesture. "I suppose that was the turning point; when Phil transferred his . . . when he stopped sharing my reactions to things. He was astonished when I walked into the cottage hospital. He should have known I'd be aware of his distress and go there. That was absolute evidence that it's over."

"But not for you, because you *did* know and went to him," he pointed out, fully concentrating now. "You're the twin I'm concerned about."

"You don't have to be."

"So you say."

"Look, it ended for Phil when he felt more deeply committed to his wife and unborn child than to me. *I'm* now more committed to someone else. It's as simple as that."

"Anyone I know?"

"No." She made a restless movement with her feet. "Well, what about it?"

"What about what?"

"Do I lose the nursemaid?"

He got to his feet. "We all fly with another pilot most of the time. I don't know what your beef is."

"Is that a yes or no?"

"It's a not yet."

Maggie damned him with her eyes before saying, "You're a bastard, Boss."

"So I'm often told," he returned equably, "but I'm a *responsible* bastard where my team is concerned." As she turned away he caught her arm. "Maggie, thanks for telling me all that."

Jerking free, she said, "Thanks, nothing! You'd listen to anything *any* woman said tonight – just like the rest of your precious drunken team."

Randal watched her walk back to where B Flight, well tanked up, had appropriated some cowbells and were busy hanging them around Dave's neck. She had been partially right: it was a night for wine, women and song, and seeing Anna was always disturbing. He had enjoyed sitting in a quiet corner beneath the moon with Maggie while she divulged the problems of twinship and been well on the way to understanding what might have been bugging her all this time when she had changed tack and turned a pleasant interlude into an official interview. No, more an interrogation during which he had turned the thumbscrews. Last time they talked on the subject she had mentioned duress. What the hell was so sacred about it? It was not as if he had demanded details of how she preferred sex. And why make such an issue about flying with another pilot? They had four navigators in the team. Pete and Chris were in the Falklands and Tom was on convalescent leave so, unless this sudden love of her life was heavily-married Vince, why get so uptight about going out with a navigator? No one else was.

As he headed back to where the fun was taking place, he wondered what kind of man could possibly captivate Maggie Spencer. More to the point, what man would want to?

Dave was no longer certain whether it was his birthday or he had just got married. There was something heavy around his neck that clanged each time he moved and a dark-haired beauty in a bridal dress had just kissed him on both cheeks. He sat grinning at her. He certainly knew how to pick 'em. She was a real teaser. He would have one more drink with the lads then carry her upstairs and consume the marriage. No, that was not the right word. Surely it was longer than that? Anyway, what he would do upstairs would not depend on words.

Someone put another beer in his hand and urged him to drink up. They all linked arms again and swayed while they roared out the words of a song in the curious local dialect. Each line ended with *Ja, Ja, Ja* and they stamped and thumped the table in time with the words. The bride winked at him, so he winked back. They both knew what would happen upstairs before long.

The song ended, and six – he thought there were six but he could be wrong – strapping young men in leather shorts, checked shirts and green pixie hats ran in to the accompaniment of cheers and bowed to Dave's bride. She kissed each in turn. Bloody cheek! He would have a word with her about that when they went upstairs. The band struck up, and the six brawny pixies began to jump about slapping their ankles, thighs and anything else handy, including each other. It proved hugely popular, so they repeated it several times.

Then Dave gawped in astonishment. Some of the lads were propelling their flight commander towards the pixies. He was laughing and struggling, but he was seized by the biggest pixie and thrust into the place he had just vacated. The music began again, and Dave watched in alcoholic admiration as Squadron Leader R.I. Price pranced and slapped to perfection. Everyone roared encouragement as the band gradually increased the tempo, making the dancers work even harder. It appeared to be the finale. The band took a bow, the pixies took a bow, and the RAF volunteer was flat on his back on the grass, laughing uproariously.

The party started to break up; the lights began to go out. Some man was walking off with Dave's bride! He was fighting mad and got up vowing to take him apart but he was led off in the opposite direction by Sandy, Ray and Nobby, who said his birthday treat would be much better. He still clanged with every movement but he was squashed in a taxi with Rusty and Jeff so it was impossible to move much.

The lights came back on and began flashing past as they did on a runway. There was traffic noise and lots of people. The car stopped. Dave got out and collapsed on the pavement with a deafening clang. They laughed and picked him up. There were steps leading down to a door lit by a dim light. Inside, there was a woman with amazing make-up and purple hair. Rusty and Jeff appeared to know her because they had some laughs together and money changed hands. They went along a corridor covered in dark red with zodiac signs. Sandy opened a black door and pushed Dave forward.

"See you later, but not too late," he chanted with a laugh. "We've only paid for an hour."

A girl in black stockings and a brightly-striped corset was sitting beside a large bed covered in black satin. She rose and approached with a smile, but he was still encumbered by the weight around his neck.

"Hallo," he mumbled. "Can you take this off me?"

She took everything off him before leading him to the bed. What happened next was outside his previous experience but he thought he managed to "consume" the marriage very well, under the circumstances. Unfortunately, when he felt wonderfully exhausted and ready to sleep, the girl insisted that he get dressed and leave. There was no sign of the others, but she would not let him hang around to wait. Two heavyweights led him to the door and closed it behind him. Clutching his jacket and a large cowbell they insisted he take with him, Dave began walking unsteadily with the idea of looking for a taxi to drive him somewhere or the other. He could not think where at present. There were a few men about but no one he knew. He wandered around a corner, something hit the back of his head and bright stars turned to blackness.

Maggie hailed a taxi and welcomed the solitude of its musty interior. The cabaret in the club to which fellow pilots Frank and Simon and navigator Vince had taken her from the beer garden had somewhat changed after midnight. Until then, it had been purely witty innuendo. After twelve, the entertainers wore a lot less and frankly performed what had been hinted at earlier. In other words, it became a sex show. Maggie left the boys to enjoy it.

They had split into several groups after the fun at the beer garden. The randiest element had borne Dave off, still hung around with a large bell, and it was easy to guess their destination. A group had gone off with the local girls hoping to get for nothing what the others would pay for. Frank, Simon and Vince were married and somewhat quieter, but they liked watching sex given the chance. Randal had disappeared into the restaurant as they all made their onward plans and no one suggested waiting for him.

According to Jimmy, their flight commander had been deeply involved with Anna six years ago. When 646 moved to Hampton, Anna had swiftly married a local mountain guide, who was killed in a fall six months later. Rumours that the child was Randal's were not true, Jimmy claimed, but it was obvious Anna had not got over the affair. Maggie guessed Randal was taking advantage of that fact. What would Fiona think of that?

Indeed, what would she make of this entire evening? Could a bimbo wife reared in the champagne world of racing ever whoop it up in a beer garden with her extrovert husband? Watching his laughing exuberance during the *Shuhplattler* dance Maggie remembered the tense aggressive man she had encountered on that first evening at Hampton. Fiona Price must be some woman if she could take all the gaiety from him, yet have him going back for more.

He was a deeper character than Maggie had first thought. He spoke French and German fluently and held a degree in European history. He shared Prince Charles' opinion of modern architecture and was very knowledgeable on the world's most famous and lesser known buildings. A large number of subjects appealed to his quick mind, so there were lively debates in tents and other spartan quarters when they were overseas. In addition, he somehow easily managed to command while still being "one of the lads", as he had been tonight.

As far as Maggie was concerned, he had definitely been a different man since the emergency with his son had brought reconciliation with his wife. He was certainly fond of children. Evidently touched by the plight of the little girl on dialysis he had persuaded a number of them to pose for camera shots beside a Chinook, because the child had sent a letter via Ted to ask for one.

If he were not so infuriating over his refusal to let her fly with a navigator Maggie would probably grow to like him, yet she could not help despising any man who let a woman dominate him. He was breaking the rules tonight with his old love while his long-legged wife went shopping for a country mansion. She smiled cynically as she gazed from the taxi window. Was it a case of when the cat's away, or did Fiona make him buy her affection? He should get rather a lot in return for a house in the country, well away from the RAF . . . but maybe not until he had exchanged contracts. The man was an utter fool. Like Phil.

She had not replied to her twin's letter, nor Rob's. After sending a short neutral answer to her father, Maggie had dropped the subject of Fay's behaviour. What the present situation was she could only guess. That was why she was so certain the ESP link had been broken. Phil had hurt her so badly she no longer sensed his emotions and her own were too deeply engaged elsewhere.

Settling further into her seat she thought of Mark and their next meeting. He had burst into her life at exactly the right time. With him she shared a close rapport like there had once been with Phil. In addition, Mark was an energetic demanding lover able also to make sex amusing. She had never known another man who could manage that combination. Mark was like a hurricane. Before their encounters she began preparing for the onslaught; the hours with him were fast and furious, the aftermath exhausting. Mark was going places. He was young, fit and eager, using all those qualities to the limit in everything he did. He loved flying; he revelled in giving aerobatic displays. "Showing off," he had confessed with a grin. "I've always been a terror in that direction. I expect you've noticed." She had, but anyone with an outstanding talent became a show-off the minute he or she used it. Sportsmen, stage performers, preachers, after-dinner speakers; the list was long and aircrew were high on it.

They rang each other whenever possible and talked for an hour or more. They had found several country hotels conveniently placed between Wittering and Hampton, all with indoor pool, squash courts and fitness centre. And bedrooms, naturally. Apart from Mark's physical impact, Maggie was captivated by the way he handled the gender question. He treated her as a professional pilot, a serious sporting rival but a very definite woman in bed.

Maggie was presently full of life. She found mountain flying exhilarating, Munich in spring was delightful and she had now more or less integrated with the rest of the team. She was also in love. The only small cloud on her horizon was Randal's stupid restriction on who she partnered in the cockpit. When would he start to trust her again?

When the taxi stopped at traffic lights in a quiet street, Maggie glanced idly from the window then sat forward to look more intently at a man slumped in a corner on a low wall. She would have thought him a down-and-out if there had not been a large cowbell on the pavement beside him.

"Oh, Lord," she breathed. "What's he doing there? Where are the others?"

The taxi moved on. She told the driver to pull up and wait,

then got out and ran to Dave. His eyes were closed, his face ashen. Those few of his shirt buttons that were done up were in the wrong holes, his jacket was nowhere to be seen and he was no longer wearing the waterproof, shockproof, everything-proof watch he prized so highly.

"Oh, Lord," she said again. "Those tarts did a really good job on you." She slapped his face gently. "Dave, come on! Time to go home."

He appeared to be out cold, hearing and feeling nothing. She grew angry. It was typical infantile male behaviour to set up a pal for a stag-night-style antic, but they should stick around to keep him out of serious trouble. If he had been picked up by the *Polizei* it would be no joke.

She slapped him harder. "Dave, wake up! You can't stay here."

His eyes opened to slits. "Uh? Wha?"

"I've a taxi waiting. I'll take you back."

"Uh? Wha?"

He was clearly far too drunk to understand or do anything, yet she could not leave him there. Running back, she asked the taxi driver to help fetch her friend. He was adamant that he only carried respectable customers. No prostitutes, no drunks. Did she want to go on or pay him off here?

Still bending to the open window, Maggie said firmly that she wanted to go on and take her friend with her. "If you won't help me, I won't pay. Please yourself."

Her attitude brought forth a torrent of German, ending with mention of the *Polizei*. She did not think he would call them. It would be her word against his – no witnesses – but she needed his help. "I'll give you a large tip if you take us both."

"*Nein, nein!*"

"Then forget it," she cried angrily, and moved away. A few moments later she heard the car drive off. How could she possibly get Dave back to their quarters? His eyes had closed again and his pallor was worse. She looked up and down the street. There was no sign of Rusty, Jeff or the three sergeants. "Some pals!" she said emphatically. "I don't know why *I'm* doing this. If someone chooses to get plastered out of his mind he deserves the consequences. You said as much when you thought Mark was drunk in my car that night. You were very loath to help me, if you recall."

Frustrated, she slapped his face really hard. His eyes opened wide to stare vacantly. Her words fell on deaf ears and her predicament remained. She had no transport and he was far too big a man to cope with on her own. He passed out again, drooping forward against her, a dead weight. Maggie was worried. She had seen men drunk at university and elsewhere but never quite like this. Someone had either doctored his drinks or drugged him. Rusty, Jeff and Co. would not do that but where were they?

With a screech of tyres a taxi pulled up at the kerb. The same driver leaned out. "The fare will be two times if he comes."

Maggie accepted his terms. "You'll have to help me with him."

The German was little bigger than her so, with Dave out cold, they had to literally drag him to the car and drop him on the back seat. Maggie squeezed in beside him as best she could, angry and disturbed. Whatever the journey cost, it would be paid for by those irresponsible idiots who had taken him to a brothel that dealt deeper than they suspected. Were they all in a similar state somewhere? Men! Did they never grow up?

The German drove fast, muttering about her friend being sick in his clean *Auto*. Maggie was more concerned about Dave throwing up in her lap so, when he fell across her as they rounded a corner with a squeal of tyres, she attempted to angle his head away. His thick dark hair felt matted and sticky, but when she lifted her hand in disgust she smelled blood and everything began to make sense. Her instinct was to tell the driver to head for the nearest hospital, then she thought better of it. Questions would be asked; the *Polizei* would be involved.

Glancing at the dashboard clock she saw it was almost two a.m. She was reluctant to call out the Luftwaffe doctor at the airfield. Dave was very thoroughly drunk, he had been with a prostitute, and the injury to the back of his head could be the result of an inebriated fall. She had no proof that he had been mugged, as she suspected. His watch and the expensive leather jacket containing his wallet could have been lifted from him at the brothel. Whatever the truth, she was reluctant to make the situation too public or too official.

The taxi halted at the entrance to the base. Maggie fumbled in her bag for her service identification; the guard inspected it and waved them through. Feverishly seeking a solution Maggie remembered that there was a British army doctor on attachment to the station and she muttered a prayer of thanks. Unless he too had been out doing what servicemen abroad so frequently did, he could take over responsibility for Dave.

Directing the driver to where visiting personnel were accommodated, Maggie scrambled free of Dave and told the man to wait while she fetched help. He would not drive off without his fat fare. Inside the modern block, Maggie swiftly scanned the board giving the names of those occupying the rooms. Captain P. McGrath ought to be in bed asleep in Room 30. Climbing the stairs two at a time, Maggie knocked lightly on the appropriate door and entered. She sincerely hoped P. McGrath was a reasonable man.

He was certainly a champion snorer, but it was a sweet sound to her ears as she crossed to the bed and switched on the small lamp before prodding the hump beneath the bedclothes. The man had either once been in the SAS or he had read too many spy thrillers; he awoke and turned to grab at her in one swift movement. She jumped back in alarm; her nerves were not at their best.

Dark eyes gazed at her as if spellbound. "Who the hell are you, and what are you doing here, *Liebchen*?" he demanded, sitting up to reveal a bare torso.

"I'm Flight Lieutenant Spencer. One of my crewmen has been hurt. He's unconscious in a taxi."

He looked her over from head to toe, then grinned. "You don't look in the least like a flight lieutenant. Are you up to no good and having me on . . . I hope?"

Maggie had had enough of masculine one-track minds for one evening. She waved her indentification before his doubting eyes. "I'm trying to keep this low key and all British, so I need your help. As a doctor you're obliged to tend someone needing medical treatment. *Please*," she added as a sweetener.

He considered for a few moments, then said, "I'm sure you've seen worse sights but you'd better look away. I sleep in the nude."

"I'll wait outside," she said, turning.

"No, you can fill me in while I dress . . . that's if you're really on the level."

"Oh, for heaven's sake!" she exploded. "I'm not so desperate

134

I'd creep into a stranger's room at this hour with some fantasy about an injured friend. *He needs medical help.*"

"OK, keep your cool. Was there an accident? Where's he injured?" There was a rustling sound as he pulled on some clothes. "I don't understand this all-British stuff. We're no longer at war with these guys."

Maggie decided on the whole truth, "It's his birthday. His pals got him drunk and took him to the red light district. I came upon him unconscious in a dark street, minus his money and an expensive watch. The back of his head has congealed blood on it and I can't bring him round. I think he might have been mugged when he left the brothel. This was the best solution I could come up with."

He grunted. "That sounds like my future epitaph." He appeared beside her in a shirt and grey trousers, holding a medical bag. "I'm continually surprised by life. I've never been called out this way before." He had an attractive smile. "Name's Peter. What's yours?"

"Maggie." She managed a return smile. "Thanks."

"I haven't done anything yet." He pulled open the door for her to go ahead. "Have you a thing going with this guy?"

"*No!*"

"Like that, is it? So why this concern for him?" They started down the dark stairway. "Frankly, this is nothing unusual. He was probably fleeced at the brothel. Can't be proved, so they often get away with it. The head wound's most likely due to a fall. Beer and sex in hefty quantities impede controlled movement. I see cases like this all the time."

"Then you'll know exactly what to do," said Maggie crisply.

Out in the darkness the taxi's engine was running; so was the meter. Dave was as she had left him, so Peter McGrath ducked inside with his bag and took out a torch to examine the unconscious man's head. Peering through the rear window Maggie could now see that the wound had bled copiously. How fortunate that she had spotted that cowbell and stopped to check.

A couple of minutes passed, then her companion withdrew his large frame and said, "Hang on there, Maggie. I'll phone for an ambulance."

"Must you?" she cried.

"He needs to be under constant observation in the sick bay. Something gave him a hefty blow. Won't be long."

135

The driver was growing aggressively impatient. He kept up a complaining monologue while Maggie hugged herself against the night-time chill and her anxiety about Dave. She again wondered why he had been deserted by the others. It was not typical behaviour; they stuck by each other. Gazing at the stars, ultra-bright against the cold sky, Maggie also wondered why fate chose to involve her in nocturnal situations with unconscious companions. Dave had himself asked, "What is it with you and men?" She wished she knew the answer.

"It'll be here shortly," announced Peter, coming up beside her. "Are you all right? You're shivering."

"It's cold, in case you hadn't noticed."

"There's no need for you to stay. I'll see to it from here."

"I feel responsible for him."

"Which is more than his pals did."

She made no comment, agreeing with him nevertheless. Then she asked, "Will he be all right?"

"I won't know until I can examine him in the sick bay."

"Oh, *you'll* look after him?"

"Isn't that what you wanted; why you dragged me from my bed?"

She gave a faint smile. "You're very nice, Peter McGrath."

"You're nicer, Flight Lieutenant Spencer. I'll be one of your crew any day, if you care about them to this degree. Now you'd better give me a few details about him. If he's been robbed there'll be nothing on him and he's likely to be unconscious for a long time."

Maggie gave Dave's rank, age and marital status, and said he was very fit. "He's the athletic type. I often see him in the pool and on the squash courts. He goes hang gliding and he owns top-grade skis. That's really all I can tell you about him, except that he's a Scot who has little time for women."

"But he frequents brothels?"

"He doesn't make a habit of it," she protested, then realised she could not be sure of that. He rarely talked about himself other than his sporting interests and flying . . . or perhaps that was only when she was around.

"Ah, here's the ambulance! You can pay off that pain in the arse in the taxi."

Maggie took out her purse. "God knows how much he'll

expect. He initially refused to bring Dave, then demanded twice the fare."

"Here, give me that." Peter took her purse and spoke to the man in execrable German before handing him a few notes. He turned back to Maggie wearing a smug smile. "He didn't see an able and loyal RAF officer, just a pretty English girl in a predicament. He now understands the situation." He handed back the purse. "Go to bed. There's nothing more you can do."

She hesitated, glancing at Dave's sprawled body. "He looks really bad. You will let me know how ill he is, won't you?"

"Sure." His face looked demonic in the flashing light from the approaching ambulance. "I'll put a message under your door or tell you at breakfast. This may take some time."

She nodded, hugging herself tighter as the ambulance stopped and the attendants jumped down, drawing out a stretcher. "Sorry about dragging you out of bed but it couldn't have happened to a nicer person. I'll buy you a drink tomorrow."

He directed the attendants in terse German and they soon had Dave on the stretcher and covered with blankets. Peter prepared to climb in after his patient. "Go to bed," he reiterated gently. "He's a lucky guy to have had you around at the critical time. Forget the drink. Let me take you to dinner instead."

Randal tackled them when they gathered in the dining hall for breakfast. He had been given an official report fuller than the note Maggie had found beneath her door on waking.

"So what the hell happened?" he challenged, fixing Rusty with a puzzled look. "What went wrong?"

They all looked the worse for wear, although Maggie noticed they had plates piled with eggs, ham and chunks of cheese, along with several *brotchen* spread thickly with butter. How could they stomach it after last night?

Rusty was plainly concerned. "We – Jeff and I – had been to the place before. It's safe and above board. No kids, nothing kinky. We asked for a girl who knows every trick in the book and pushed Dave in the room telling him we'd see him later." He sighed. "God, he must work fast! When we emerged we were told he'd already gone. We thought he'd got a taxi back. We wouldn't have taken off without him, Rip, you know that."

"But none of you checked that he *was* back?"

137

Jeff looked uneasily at Rusty, then at Randal. "We were pretty pickled. We assumed he was tucked up in bed."

Randal poured more coffee. "I've told you before you shouldn't assume without checking, Jeff. Where were Sandy, Nobby and Ray?"

"With us. We all crammed into a taxi and called it a night."

"And they didn't check on Dave, either. I've already asked. You ought to be shot, the whole pack of you. This is exactly the kind of incident the media likes to blow up out of all proportion. *RAF lager lout arrested after leaving infamous brothel.*"

Rusty put up a defence. "It wasn't meant to go that way. Dave did take himself off, and we couldn't be expected to search the streets in case he got himself beaten up before he got back. We *all* assumed he was in bed. It wasn't just Jeff."

Maggie thought Randal was being amazingly tolerant for someone with a quick temper. She ate toast in silence while they held the post-mortem. Happily, it was not literally that. Peter McGrath had written in his note to her that splinters of wood in the head wound suggested that Dave might have been hit with something like a baseball bat. He was suffering from concussion and high levels of alcohol in the bloodstream, drifting in and out of consciousness and incapable of coherent thought. There appeared to be no serious problems and, unless anything unexpected developed, the patient should be well enough to be discharged by the following morning. The note had ended with a reminder of their dinner date.

Randal had been given by McGrath a report in purely medical terms. It was reassuringly low key, unlikely to cause a rumpus here or at Hampton. They would make no official complaint to the *Polizei*, so the whole business could be put aside. Maybe Dave would keep his birthday a secret in future, thought Maggie, and maybe he would be a little less intolerant if he came across someone in trouble on a dark road again.

She grew aware that Randal was speaking to her. "Sorry, I was miles away."

"After last night I'm not surprised. You handled it with commendable coolness but you should have come to me first. Why didn't you?"

"I thought you were sleeping . . . staying on at the beer garden."

His eyes narrowed. "You thought wrong, chum. I was back

here just after midnight. If you'd woken me I'd have dealt with it; as a flight commander should."

Maggie thought the implied reprimand a bit thick under the circumstances. Just as Rusty and Co. could not have known what Dave was up to, she could not be expected to guess the whereabouts of a man possibly visiting his former mistress whose child might or might not be his. She decided to make a point.

"Going straight to a doctor saved time. I had no way of knowing how ill Dave was. He needed urgent attention." It seemed the right moment to say something else. "If grown men stopped getting each other stoned out of their skulls to show what great pals they are, this sort of thing wouldn't happen."

Everyone concentrated on breakfast as silence reigned. Maggie drank her coffee, mentally chalking one up for the female of the species. Finishing first, she left the table and headed back to her room to prepare for briefing. Randal caught up with her on the stairs and invited her to his room, which was the first along the corridor. Bracing herself to deal with his reaction to her last comment, she stood beside the wardrobe with mutiny in the offing.

He closed the door and leaned against it, perfectly relaxed. "Six years ago, Anna Spiegel and I had a lengthy relationship. Soon after the squadron returned to England she married Rolf Müller, whom she had several times turned down because he was a mountain guide; her father had also been one before he was engulfed by an avalanche. Six months later, Rolf met a similar fate. Anna was then five months pregnant. She and her mother have had a tough time: two widows trying to keep that place going and bringing up Gerda. Spring and summer they're rushed off their feet. When winter hits them life becomes thankless and dreary. They're lovely women. Both have been kind and generous to me and my friends over the years. The little girl calls me *Onkel*. Whenever I'm over here, I visit and take Gerda a present. The women would be offended if I offered help to them so I take the team there. We spend a lot and spread some jollity around. As usual, I had a last drink with them while I caught up on all their news. Then I got a cab back."

He had taken the wind out of Maggie's sails. She had no idea how to follow that.

139

"Is there anything else you'd like to know about my private life?" he asked, a smile lighting his eyes.

"No, thank you," she murmured.

"Right." He opened the door. "Briefing in ten minutes." As she walked past, he added, "I heard a rumour you're having dinner with Doctor McGrath tonight."

How the hell had that become public knowledge? "Yes, that's right."

The smile now reached his mouth. "Double indemnity against receiving magic messages?"

She ignored that, but his voice followed her along the corridor. "I've put you down to fly with Vince. You're the only pilot fit enough to go with a navigator today."

She turned back eagerly, but he cut off anything she might have said. "I hope Dave's appropriately grateful when he hears what you did. We've ribbed you about being bloody keen. Thank God you were last night."

The remaining three days in Munich seemed jinxed. Nobby crushed his right hand so badly he could not work, Rusty had a painful abscess on a wisdom tooth and Randal's aircraft developed a malfunction in the gearbox forcing him to land in a remote valley and wait for it to be fixed.

Dave was detained in the airfield sick bay until he was fully coherent and his vision reverted to normal. Of the night his friends had promised he would never forget, he remembered nothing. He was told about it and how it ended, but apart from a recollection of piling into a taxi to head for a beer garden the rest was a blank. It was sobering to discover things could be erased so totally from his mind. Peter McGrath had treated it all lightly; had laughingly suggested that the evening was probably better forgotten.

Dave's wallet, minus money and credit cards, was handed in by a woman who found it in her front garden with his service identity intact. Details of his credit card were e-mailed to his bank, but it was goodbye to his expensive leather jacket and also the watch presented to him by the grateful family of a small boy he had brought up from a dangerous cleft during his teenage days with mountain rescue. It was a poignant loss; all the more so because it had been snatched under such circumstances. Dave dearly wanted to draw a veil over the episode but first he had to thank Maggie for her part in it. It was not something he relished particularly, because she knew exactly how he had behaved that evening and he did not. Sandy vowed he had been well and truly out of control.

They were all flying when he was discharged from sick bay, so he hung around for most of the day trying to decide how best to deal with the situation. He rehearsed a pithy speech, forgetting there would be input from Maggie. It was essential to get her on her own, he felt. He would not eat humble pie before an interested audience.

He heard them come in. Knowing how long debriefing took and how they all sat around talking it out of their systems before going off to shower and change to gather around the bar prior to dinner, Dave made a guess at when Maggie was likely to be in her room.

She came to the door in a bathrobe, with a towel wrapped turbanwise around her head. "Dave." She greeted him with a bright smile. "Are you feeling better?"

"Oh aye, I just . . ."

"Would you wait while I get some clothes on? I've just had a shower."

"It won't take long," he said quickly. "I just wanted—"

"I'll only be a few minutes." She shut the door.

He shuffled around moodily in the corridor, hoping no one would come along and see him loitering outside her room. He waited longer than a few minutes and was on the point of walking off when the door opened again. Maggie was dressed in a dark skirt and a pale-yellow blouse, stiff collar turned up at the back of her neck and the front unbuttoned to cleavage level. Her hair hung damply to her shoulders.

"You can come in now," she said in school-mistressy manner, which put his back up. "Peter told me you don't recall anything about that night."

He halted just inside the door. "I'm afraid not."

"Don't be afraid. It's probably just as well." She wore a grin like a Cheshire cat's.

"I've come to thank you for getting me back in one piece."

"Go on, then. I'm all ears."

He gritted his teeth. She was making a meal of this and enjoying every mouthful. "It was lucky you were passing."

"It certainly was, but I'd have passed by if it hadn't been

141

for that cowbell you had draped around your neck for most of the evening. You looked like a druggie or a wino. Good thing the tarts and the mugger saw the funny side and let you keep the bell."

Dave had taken enough. "OK, I've seen *this* joke. You want revenge for that night at Hampton Heyhoe. I jumped to the wrong conclusion but you seemed to be making a habit of getting into awkward situations with men."

"You put me in another two nights ago."

"And I'm doing my best to apologise."

She was still grinning. "Your best doesn't appear to be working. I'd say you're spoiling for a fight."

Too late. Dave knew he would have been wiser after all to do this at the bar surrounded by the others. A quick apology and thanks for getting him to a doctor could have been followed by an offer to buy her a drink, and that would have been that. It would be enough for a man but, however hard one tried, it was impossible to treat Maggie the same way. The scent of shampoo and talc hung in the room; a bra and knickers lay over the radiator to dry. When she was in the cockpit dressed in a flying suit and helmet it was easier. Right now, she was female to her back teeth and gleefully using the fact.

"Isn't a fight what you're after?" he challenged.

"No, Dave, I want to know why you said nothing about being a witness to Mark's bird strike once you discovered who he was that night. Why you zoomed off still muttering about getting me out of scrapes when you knew he wasn't drunk and incapable . . . like *you* were the other night. I also want to know why you resent me but not the other pilots. You once asked what it was with me and men. Have you some kind of hang-up about women who achieve?"

His back was to the wall. "I didn't come here for an inquisition. Why don't you have the decency to let me say thanks, ask how much the taxi cost you and offer you a drink downstairs?"

"Or is it a hang-up about me as a person?"

"I don't like being used by women," he snapped, turning to go.

"What was her name?"

Caught off guard, he hesitated in the doorway.

"She must have hurt you deeply, but don't hold it against me. If it had been one of the guys who'd picked you up, you'd have slapped him on the back and bought him a few pints. All a big laugh! Because it was me, you're uptight about it. I'm just another member of the team, Dave. There's no need for all this." She picked up a hairdryer. "When I've sorted out my hair, I'll be down for a gin and tonic off you. I've already collected the taxi fare from your pals who set you up that night. The big laugh that went wrong!"

He still hesitated, uncertain and uncomfortable, knowing he could have been in deeper trouble over the evening but for her timely intervention. "I came to say I'm grateful for all you did: keeping it low key, getting the doctor, and . . . well, I hope I didn't say or do anything to you while I was—"

The Cheshire cat grin was back. "Oh, you've no idea how even decent men can behave when they're drunk, fresh from a brothel and suffering from concussion. The next time you find me in a fix on a dark country road and are churlish about helping, I'll tell you the sordid details." She switched on the dryer. "Get that drink set up. I'll be down for it in five minutes."

He made his way to the bar, uttering a string of good Celtic oaths, knowing he was about to face further baiting from the rest of B Flight. He could take it from men, but he had an aversion to being made a fool of by any woman.

May

D ave flew to Scotland a week after his return from Munich to attend the funeral of Sir Hector. The news of his death from a stroke was passed to him when he arrived at Hampton after a two-day refresher course on survival at sea. His immediate telephone call to the castle confirmed what he already guessed: Dougal was there on compassionate leave to mastermind his grandfather's burial with the assistance of the regiment. Sir Hector was to have a full military service with a reception afterwards for several hundred mourners. The will would be read the following morning and McFarlane would inform Dave of any relevant matters it might contain. The Rowan family understood that Dave would probably not be granted leave to attend.

The commander of 646 Squadron, Jerard Jeffries, was known to everyone as Judge Jeffries because of his inflexible attitude and general lack of compassion. These qualities had earned him an AFC during the Falklands campaign, when exact flying skill, cold reason and fearlessness were necessary. He worked hard for promotion, trained his wife and children to work equally hard for it and knew the rule book by heart. He instinctively disliked and distrusted men who were generally popular or who bent the rules to keep things running.

Squadron Leader Price was guilty on both counts, which made for difficulties between them. However, Wing Commander Jeffries was a stickler for protocol, so when Randal took him a request from one of his crewmen for leave to attend the burial of his great-uncle and former legal guardian, it was granted. Major General Sir Hector Rowan had been a distinguished and much decorated soldier. The funeral would be attended by the famous and influential. Of course Ashmore must go. He would represent the RAF, said Jeffries.

Ashmore had no intention of representing the RAF, which

was just as well since the family had very definite ideas on the subject. When he arrived they were all gathered round the immense fireplace in what was known, for obvious reasons, as the tapestry room. The warmth from the log fire reached little further than a few yards, so Dave's relations were concentrated in a small area. Aunt Mairie came forward to mouth a kiss in the air beneath his left ear – she had always been a meek gentle soul – and his cousins Bridie and Margaret managed a vague smile apiece. Their stolid successful husbands nodded at him. Dougal glared. Leanne was not in the room. The women wore black dresses, the men dark suits with black ties. Dave had flown up in jeans, a blue shirt and a thick navy sweatshirt.

Dougal looked pointedly at the large black sports bag in Dave's hand. "We'll hold dinner until you've had time to clean up and change. Mrs McRitchie will show you where."

"With so many people coming tomorrow, we've had to set your room aside for guests," ventured Aunt Mairie, trying to soften her son's attitude. "It's only for a night or two."

Mrs McRitchie made a great fuss of someone she would forever see as the little boy dumped on the doorstep of a family who had never wholly accepted him, and she explained far too fulsomely why his things had been *temporarily* moved to the small tower room. Dave was silent; the familiar dark corridors, heavy furniture and grim battle paintings affected him more deeply than he had bargained for. Small wonder his mother had fled from such gloom. He, himself, had left only five months ago.

Sir Hector's presence was too strong for comfort. Dave knew the old warrior had done his duty to the four-year-old kinsman delivered by a surly Frenchwoman; done it without prejudice and with some affection until the man the boy became had emulated his mother's decision to break the mould. Coming to the funeral was Dave's gesture of apology for being what he was, and of thanks he might not have fully expressed during Sir Hector's lifetime.

There was a small fire in the circular tower room which was sparsely furnished and smelled of years of unoccupation. Dave had forgotten how cold it could be this far north. He hung up the formal clothes he had hired in London before catching the shuttle, then washed quickly and changed into the only suit he possessed. It was pale grey, but the best he could do. He made his way downstairs with resignation, knowing a showdown with Dougal was inevitable. Regardless of his black tie and strict adherence to convention, his cousin would not hesitate to break the family code before the old man was even laid to rest.

On the lowest landing Dave pulled up sharply at the sight of Leanne walking towards him. In a body-hugging black wool dress with her glowing hair loosely drawn back into a black velvet scrunchie, she set his pulse racing. He had forgotten her tremendous impact.

She gave a sad smile, her lovely green eyes misty. "I didn't dare hope you'd come. It's *wonderful* to see you again, David." She had always refused to shorten his name.

"I don't think anyone expected me to turn up," he said, remembering the feel of her warm skin beneath his palms and her soft cries as he took her.

She sighed. "I hate deaths. They make me so depressed. Dougal expects me to be with the family all the time, but I can't stand their talk of coffins and burial. I keep bursting into tears, then he gets angry and upsets me more." She fell in beside him with a waft of expensive perfume, and they went down to the lofty hall. "He was such a dear man, deeply fond of me. He gave me some beautiful pieces of jewellery – family heirlooms, of course. I used to sit on the window seat with him while he read Scottish poetry to me. He enjoyed doing that." Her quick smile was more like the ones that had badly affected Dave's heartbeat two years ago. "I didn't understand a word, mind you. All that wee timorous beastie stuff's not really my scene, as you well know."

"They're classics, Leanne," he said, as they entered the room to find Dougal looking expectantly at the door.

Dinner was subdued with everyone speaking in near-whispers. It surprised Dave to rediscover the family he had grown up with. Aunt Mairie had always allowed herself to be ruled by Sir Hector and her husband, then by Dougal when Rory Rowan was killed, but had Bridie and Margaret always been so staid? Their husbands were men of considerable property who, very clearly, were no longer their lovers – if they ever had been. When they exchanged looks there was no spark of intimacy; they could have been mere business associates. With a shock Dave realised the same could be said of Dougal and his sensational wife, married only five months ago. But if his

146

cousin appeared immune to his wife's sensual lure Dave was not. In the midst of that hushed group he sat with his mind full of memories of those hectic sessions with her in Lincoln when he should have been studying. He could well understand why he had been besotted. Glancing across the table at that point, he encountered more than a spark of intimacy in her eyes. She was telling him something he had never expected and it aroused conflicting emotions in him.

After dinner Dougal made his move. As if by prior arrangement everyone vanished, leaving the male cousins together in the large draughty room with mullioned windows.

True to Dave's expectations, Dougal opened the skirmish without preliminary fencing. "I don't understand why you thought you'd be welcome here after the way you behaved."

Dave moved closer to the fire. "I was pretty certain I wouldn't be."

"Then why the hell come?"

"To say goodbye to the old man."

"Because you failed to at Christmas?"

"Because he was a person I respected and did my best to please."

"Hypocrite!"

Dave studied his darkly handsome cousin and wondered just when the lukewarm tolerance of boyhood had cooled to active dislike. "What you seem unable to grasp is that there's life beyond the regiment, Dougal. Sir Hector was a man of his time; a grand old Highland warrior and gentleman. They've thrown away that mould because it's out of place in today's world."

"*Your* world, you mean."

"*Our* world." He perched on one of the padded inglenook seats. "You spent four years at Cambridge then did your officer training at Sandhurst. How did you manage to keep your ancient illusions intact?"

His cousin's scowl deepened. "You have the wrong word. *Traditions* are the very foundations of our country. Cambridge and Sandhurst are two of them. You wouldn't have appreciated that at your redbrick college aspiring to the dignity of university status."

"It was fairly evident at Cranwell."

"So evident you chucked it all up to join the ranks of the great unwashed."

147

Dave's eyes narrowed. "You're a bloody prig, Dougal. If that's how you regard the men under your command, you've let the old man down more than I have. How many times did we listen to his tales when we were boys, and how often did he refer to his men as 'the dear courageous laddies'? He would have died for them. Almost did on two occasions. If you hold them in such contempt, there'll only be a sprinkling of other prigs at your funeral. I'm guessing 'the great unwashed' will turn out in force tomorrow and even strong men will be in tears."

Dougal changed tack. "I can't allow you to add further insult by wearing your uniform tomorrow."

"I don't intend to wear it. I'll follow his coffin as his kinsman, that's all."

"I see." Momentarily thrown, Dougal rallied swiftly, walking round the large armchair where his grandfather had sat to relate stirring war stories to two impressionable boys and coming up beside Dave. "You do know that your deliberate flaunting of your rank at my wedding contributed to the deterioration of his health leading to the stroke."

"What?"

"Oh aye! He took your ingratitude to heart; your insensitivity to his feelings. To say nothing of mine and Mother's. The marriage of the heir was something he'd relished from the day my father was killed. Tradition again, you see. It was his life's blood. Even more so the regiment. He'd planned that wedding to the last detail. It had to be perfect. Although you knew he was deeply upset over your insistence on displaying to everyone your absurd shunning of officer rank, you then got so pissed at the reception I had to get Duncan and Roddy McLay to carry you upstairs out of sight." His expression grew uglier still. "For a sportsman you were a bad loser; wouldn't acknowledge that the better man won Leanne. And you didn't even have the guts to apologise to the family the next day. You simply crawled off without a word to anyone." He retraced his steps around the chair to stand, feet firmly apart, dark eyes hostile, confronting Dave. "I'm Master here now, and you no longer have a place at my hearth. Grandfather did his bounden duty when he took you in, but not all his influence or example changed you from what you are – the son of a long-haired, alcoholic *piano player.*"

Dave stood, his face flushed from more than the heat of the fire. "When I left here on the morning after your wedding I

148

took with me everything I valued. I didn't mean to return. Then I found I couldn't pass up the chance to say goodbye to the only one of you I felt any affection for. When that's been said tomorrow, I'll shake the dust of this place from my shoes for good. I have a home, Dougal. Among the ranks of the great unwashed. I'm happier there than you'll ever be in your damned ancestral castle. Get real, you smug bastard!"

They did the old general proud. The horses pulling the gun carriage wore black plumes and muffles on their hooves. A lone piper led the procession up to the kirk on the hill overlooking the castle, and many of those lining the narrow winding road were in tears. The regiment turned out in force. Homage was paid verbally by the present commanding officer, Colonel Ralph Finlayson, and the coffin was carried to the family burial plot between rows of kilted officers with downturned swords and bowed heads.

Dave was more deeply moved than he expected to be. There was something about a military ceremony that stirred his blood, and the mournful dirge on the pipes reached right into a man's soul. The son of a long-haired, alcoholic piano player felt the call of his mother's ancestry that morning more than he ever had before, and he had difficulty singing the old Celtic hymns because of a lump in his throat. Looking around at the "dear courageous laddies", now in their seventies and eighties, who had tears on their cheeks, Dave knew Dougal's sense of tradition was in his mouth not his heart. The Rowan mould had been broken on the death of Uncle Rory, Dougal's father.

The wake was expected to last for the whole afternoon. While most mourners departed, a few privileged guests would remain overnight and leave before McFarlane came to read the will at eleven the following morning. Dave stayed in the background, although he had taken his rightful place with the family for the service. It was easy enough to find a quiet corner in which to eat a little of the fine fare provided and wash it down with whisky, but his retreat was invaded several times by elderly women. They had no idea who he was but revealed that they wanted "just a wee morsel more" of whatever and could not push through the wall of brawny soldiers to get it. After he had made a third foray for them, Dave decided he had had enough and began making his escape.

At the foot of the stairs he was hailed by a man emerging from the ground-floor cloakroom. "You've not to go already, have you? I've had no chance yet to speak to the man who chose to fly rather than join us. I couldn't get to Dougal's wedding when we might have had a chat."

Ralph Finlayson was smiling as he approached. "You're Sir Hector's ward and kinsman, aren't you?"

"Aye, Colonel, and I was being very cowardly, running from hungry old ladies wanting me to fetch and carry for them."

"Ladies all do that, whatever their age," he said with a laugh. "I was caught on that game myself a short while ago." He nodded at the outer door. "Care to get some air for a minute or two?"

Surprised, Dave went to the terrace with him and found the chill welcome after the closeness inside. They exchanged comments about the fine view and how good it had been to see so many lining the road for the funeral. Then the older man asked how Dave liked being in the RAF, and he briefly described his work as an air loadmaster.

"That's quite a skill, man. As you discovered, the old gentleman deplored your decision while knowing that each of us has the right to follow his star. It's easier to do that now. My father and Sir Hector were brother officers. Their destiny was decided for them at birth and there was no escaping it." He pulled a comic face. "Poor devils! It was what happened in those days. If they broke out they were considered beyond the pale and cut off without the proverbial bob. We still get some who either haven't the guts to go against their parent or enough gumption to create a dream of their own to fulfil. Mostly, they're in the regiment because they want to be." He smiled warmly. "Better for you to branch out than join us against your will and you look a pretty determined character, David. I hope Sir Hector was reconciled to your choice before he passed on."

"He was, until I gave up being a 'gentleman' to become a sergeant. He found that impossible to accept for a family member."

"Oh aye, quite probably. His generation could not allow that a man can be a gentleman by his behaviour, not necessarily by his rank."

Dave studied the youngest colonel the regiment had ever had. Dark-haired, dark-eyed, he was a handsome man by any standards and he possessed that quality Dave liked in his flight commander. Born leaders?

"Were you press-ganged into the regiment, sir?"

That was met with a shout of laughter. "I'd have joined at the age of three if they'd have had me. Father was delighted with his bonny wee warrior, naturally." He sobered quickly. "When a man wants something so badly there's a price to pay and someone invariably gets hurt. My wife was killed in a car accident five years after our marriage. She'd been unhappy for a long time. There are no children, which is probably just as well. When a man gives himself so wholly to something there's little left over." He squared his shoulders. "Can't say that of the grand old man we buried today. He loved his family and every last one of his men. We won't see the like of him again."

"There's Dougal," Dave pointed out.

"Mmm. Don't let him take up his grandfather's cudgel with you. You're your own man, young David. Be proud of the fact." He smiled with a hint of conspiracy. "Do you think the old ladies have had enough to eat yet? Safe to go in?"

Dave shook his head. "I'm not risking it, but I think you'll probably have to. It's one of the penalties of being *your* own man, sir." He offered his hand on impulse. "I've enjoyed talking to you."

His hand was strongly gripped. "It's mutual." Finlayson turned back at the door, kilt swinging. "I knew your mother. You're very like her."

Dave stayed for a while on the terrace, gazing at the mountains. He had mentally abandoned his parents after visiting his mother's grave but this visit was calling them back. "Fingers" Ashmore he knew only from press cuttings and a fulsome obituary in *The Daily Telegraph*. Exceptional talent frequently went hand in hand with mental fragility, and his father had succumbed to alcohol. Recalling the recent night in Munich, Dave acknowledged how easily he had fallen into a situation that had got out of hand. He did not condemn his father but had he felt nothing on sending his small son away for ever? Had he ever loved the seventeen-year-old girl who had left all this to run away to Paris with him? Surely Ashmore had been a person of worth to attract Edwina Rowan so strongly.

The only visual impression of his parents he had came from the yellowed newspaper cutting Dave had torn from a back number in a public library. The Rowans had hidden or destroyed all photographs of the runaway, but the news

151

picture of her was a copy of a studio portrait painted two days before her elopement. Ashmore's picture showed a long rather mournful face and shoulder-length waving hair. Edwina had large sad eyes and a dreamy expression. Dave did not think he resembled either of them. The family had buried his parents beneath their disapproving silence all these years but now Dougal had referred to Ashmore and Colonel Finlayson owned to knowing his mother. Feelings Dave had put to rest seven years ago at his mother's graveside returned strongly. Finlayson thought Edwina's son very like her. The urge to seek the man out and question him further sent Dave back to the crowded rooms.

It was a while before he came upon the Colonel talking to a ring of silver-haired retired officers. He could not barge in on them. Getting another whisky, Dave positioned himself where he could watch his quarry and cursed the fact that he had not detained him out on the terrace. The comment had taken him by surprise and Finlayson had walked off before he had recovered.

Minutes ticked past as Dave waited. Slowly, maybe as a result of yet another whisky or maybe because of the overwhelming presence of kilts and Highland pride, the urge that had set him in pursuit of knowledge faded. Perhaps it was best to leave things as they were; better not to chase something he had managed without for most of his life. His mother had chosen to leave all this, possibly for ever. Let her rest in peace in France.

Swinging round with the intention of going to his room, he inadvertently collided with a group of elderly black-hatted ladies, knocking one off-balance and sending two glasses flying. He grabbed in vain at the toppling woman. She collapsed inelegantly on the smashed glass.

"Terribly sorry. Are you all right?" asked Dave, struggling to pick the matron up.

The attention of others was caught by the commotion and several men past their prime came up. "Can you manage, young man? Shall I lend a hand? Are you all right, Lady Marjorie?"

Between them they raised the woman, who was mostly concerned about the expanse of leg she was showing and the angle of her hat. Then their host appeared on the scene. "A simple accident, Dougal," one of the victim's companions explained while Lady Marjorie was settled in a chair and fussed over by another ageing helper. "This young man turned rather quickly, not knowing we were so close behind him. There's no harm done, except for a few broken glasses and a battered hat," she added with something of a malicious laugh.

Dougal added his fussing to those around the lady who was still worried about the angle of her expensive hat, then he straightened and signalled to a lingering steward. "Get this mess cleared up," he ordered, indicating the glass on the carpet. He next grabbed Dave's arm and thrust him back in the corner he had been occupying.

"You bastard!" he said with suppressed rage. "Can't you mix in decent company without getting pissed? I don't want you carried out like you were at the wedding. Clear off while you can still walk!"

Dave pushed his way between the noisy mourners and mounted the stairs at a run, only to be halted on the second landing by someone calling his name. A short way along the dark-carpeted corridor Leanne sat on a padded window embrasure.

"What are you doing there? Your place is beside the man you married to get your hands on all this," he said roughly. "As from now on it's his, you'd better jump to his orders."

She came after him as he turned towards the stairs leading to the tower room. "I'm so depressed. Stay and talk, David."

"We did all our talking in Lincoln, and your note when you returned the engagement ring said more than enough."

As he made to move on, she held his arm and circled to face him. "I've never forgotten Lincoln. Those were wonderful days."

He studied her flawless creamy complexion and the expressive eyes that used to excite him beyond reason. "Yeah, they were," he agreed tonelessly. "Now you've got money, jewellery and cousin Dougal to make your days even more wonderful."

"But they're not," she cried, still clasping his arm. "They're *not*. You don't know what Dougal's like."

"I grew up with him. I know."

"You're not a woman, so you can't *really* know." The magic was back in force: the misty eyes, slightly parted lips and husky voice. "Since we've been married, Dougal has treated me as no more than an accessory to his army career; an obedient service wife and a simpering hostess to important dinner guests." She put her hands on the lapels of his coat and adopted her deep wide-eyed gaze that once he could not resist. "Dougal's so *unimaginative*, even when he really gets going. It's all over in five minutes."

Dave could not help feeling smug over that, although he was not altogether surprised. Dougal was basically selfish and would treat sex as pure self-gratification. Leanne's hands slid down to unbutton his coat, then her palms closed over his nipples. He felt the warmth through his shirt and his body reacted instinctively.

"You know me, darling," she said softly. "I need a lot of satisfying. He never manages it. All he gets worked up about is the bloody regiment and this draughty heap of stone." Her palms began to circle his taut nipples. "I need a *real* man. Someone who knows just what to do to set a woman on fire. Someone like you."

Dave felt heat rush through him as he took in what she was suggesting. Then he pulled her hands from his body and held her wrists in a tight grip. "Give me ten minutes to get out of this hired suit, then come to my room. I'll give you something to set you on fire, and it won't be over in five minutes."

She laughed breathlessly. "It never was, darling. It went on and on."

"So will this," he promised, releasing her. "Ten minutes."

She must have been watching the second hand on her diamond watch. Exactly ten minutes later she walked in without knocking and went into his arms. Her ravenous kisses set his hands reacquainting themselves with her body, until he held her at arms' length.

"I thought you were going to undress," she accused, indicating his jeans and blue shirt.

"We have to make this last. Remember how we used to excite each other by stripping very slowly? I want to do that again."

She gave a delighted laugh. "You could never wait; I'll tie you to a chair next time."

"You might have to do that today if you make it too sexy." He leaned against the door. "Let's find out how long I can stand it."

Leanne Rowan could have been a professional stripper. She was unbearably sensuous as she slid down the zipper of her dress, inch by inch. Dave marvelled that any woman could take so long to wriggle from a one-piece garment. Beneath it she wore a black lace bra and wispy briefs, with a narrow suspender belt holding up her sheer black stockings. He sighed with past pain.

She giggled. "Suffering already?"

"You know I am."

"There's more to come."

"More to come off, you mean."

Putting a foot up on the bed she threw him a smouldering glance as she deliberately released one stocking and began to slide it down her leg. "Bet you'd rather be doing this."

"That would be giving in too soon."

The other stocking was removed in the same tantalising manner. Then she unfastened the frilly suspender belt to leave an expanse of smooth flesh from her bra to low on her hips where a scrap of black lace only just covered her most exciting area.

"How ya doing?" she teased, as she swung the belt from her fingers.

"Hope you've got the ropes and chair handy."

"Oh, darling! I've *missed* you," she cried softly, starting towards him,

"Stay where you are! Touching is cheating, remember."

From three feet away, she said, "I'm not sure I can wait. I want you so badly. I always did."

The knife twisted. "If I can wait, so can you. It adds to the final enjoyment."

"Then add this, *lover*." She slowly pulled her bra away from her taut breasts and tossed it to him.

The lace was warm and soft and smelled of her perfume. He grew worried about his ability to get through this. Naked except for the tiny briefs, she reached up and pulled her hair free of the restraining combs so that it tumbled to her shoulders.

"Need the ropes and chair yet?" she taunted.

"I'm desperately trying to hold out."

Her soft sexy laugh really got to him, and so did the next few moments as she paraded around proudly displaying all he had once thought of as exclusively his to enjoy. Then she suddenly stepped from the panties and threw them at him in a startling change of mood. "Here! I can't play this unbearable game any longer. For God's sake, take me!"

"Say that again," he demanded in an unsteady voice.

It aroused her further. "Take me, you gorgeous bastard! I'm on *fire*."

He gave her one last comprehensive look. "Another time, perhaps. Right now I've a train to catch." Snatching up the bag he had packed before she came, he walked out slamming the door behind him. Totally ruled by his anger, Dave saw nothing of the paintings and faded tapestries along the corridors until he came upon the suit of armour on which the McLay brothers had hung his sergeant's uniform. He kicked at it wildly causing it to collapse, clanking, to the floor. How dare she, how *dare* she try to use him yet again! After throwing him over for a bigger prize, how bloody dare she prance around naked as if he were some kind of obliging stud!

He ran down the final flight of stairs with great strides, flung his bag towards the front door, then crossed to a steward.

"Find Lieutenant Rowan and tell him his wife needs him urgently in the tower room. Interrupt, no matter who he's with. She's desperate."

"Certainly, sir." The man moved off swiftly.

As Dave left the castle through its pseudo-antique gates for the very last time, rage still possessed him. It continued until he arrived at Hampton, where his friends welcomed him and he again became part of the life he loved.

It was not until he returned from a four-day intensive course on armed defence in the air, two weeks after the funeral, that Dave received an official letter from the Rowan family solicitor. The large envelope contained a smaller sealed one addressed to "My son, David Oliver". There was also a typewritten page signed by Hamish McFarlane, which Dave read frowning.

Sir Hector had left to his great-nephew five paintings depicting the land and traditions of his forbears *in the hope that he may come to his senses and understand his heritage*. What would Mr Ashmore like McFarlane to do with the valuable paintings? Perhaps he would be good enough to write his instructions on the matter. The enclosed letter written by Edwina Moira Rowan shortly before her demise had been accompanied by instructions for said letter to be given to her son on the death of Sir Hector. McFarlane would be happy to advise on any matter arising from the letter and he remained Mr Ashmore's obedient servant.

Dave gazed at the envelope sealed by his mother twenty-five years ago and felt strongly inclined to leave it unopened. He had his life beautifully under control: he had cleansed Leanne from his system; he had evened the score with Dougal; he had made a clean break with his family. Words from the girl who had given him birth and nothing more were surely of no relevance to him. Sliding the envelope back within the larger one, he got out shorts and a cotton shirt for squash with Sandy before supper. At the weekend he would scribble a note to McFarlane telling him to leave the paintings where they were, as Sir Hector had known he would. Five huge canvasses of misty glens, stag hunts and Highland castles could not be hung in a Sergeants' Mess bedroom, and the old boy had known his great-nephew would not slip so far from being a "gentleman" as to sell the heirlooms and pocket the proceeds; he was too independent. The sly old devil had been generous to the kinsman fallen from grace without actually giving him anything. Dave could not help appreciating the move.

At two a.m. he was still awake. His body was pleasantly tired from the squash; he had then enjoyed a few pints with his fellow crewmen while arguing the relative merits of Damon Hill and Schumacher. He normally slept well but tonight, he was disturbed by a letter from the past. At three he opened it.

My darling boy,

Where in the world will you be when you read this? Will you be a boy still, or a man? What will you look like? Will you possess my wretched obstinacy or your father's strength of will? I wish I could know the answers now, before I leave you, but I loved you while you grew inside me and I've loved the little creature placed in my arms at your first cry. So much love, my wee boy, and you must understand why.

Freddie Ashmore has promised to care for you. He's a kind man, in the way people who live by unconventional rules often are. We are not married, but we have given you his name for your sake. He knows about this letter, so it won't create awkwardness between you later. He understands why it has to be written, and I hope with all my heart you'll also understand.

Your father is Lieutenant Ralph Finlayson, an officer in the family regiment. If a similar devastating thing ever happens to you, you'll know how it was for us from the first moment. Please believe it was never sordid. When I knew I was pregnant I appealed to Freddie to let me go with him to Paris. We have been happy enough, but Ralph has been my only love.

He doesn't know about you; won't ever know unless you choose to tell him. He's married and starting a career he's longed for since childhood. Uncle Hector has been good to me. Whatever distress I've caused both him and Ralph by running away, it's nothing to the pain the truth would bring them. When you receive this, Uncle will be beyond being hurt. Ralph also, perhaps; lost in some future war. Your father's knowledge or continued ignorance of your blood tie is in your hands. What a burden to give my dear wee lad, I think, as I gaze at you in the bassinet beside me. Ralph does not have to be told, but you deserve to be David Oliver Finlayson.

I pray life has been good to you. If you've grown to resemble Ralph you'll be a fine man; if you've favoured your foolish mother may fate be kinder to you. God bless you.

At third sight Randal found the house growing on him. A few pieces of furniture and a rug or two had softened the stark Scandinavian lines, and the sound of his children's voices echoing as they ran from room to room put life into the silence that had hung here on his other two visits.

Fiona's eyes were sparkling with pleasure. "I'm going to be *so* happy here. I love it more every time I come."

"I'll have to put a stop to that, or I'll be taking second place to a pile of Swedish pine and strengthened glass," he said, lightly kissing her temple. "I hope they remembered to deliver the bed yesterday."

"You have a one-track mind," she accused, linking her arms around his neck and smiling up into his eyes. "Thank you, darling, it's a fantastic house."

He pulled her close. "It's Price's Pork Pies you have to thank, but I'm happy to accept all gestures of gratitude on behalf of the company."

Fiona was showing her gratitude in unrestrained manner when they heard a splash and a scream. *"Oh Christ!"* Randal broke contact and ran fearfully across the large lofty room, through a smaller one then on to the vast conservatory around the swimming pool, the sound of Neil's shouts adding to his sense of urgency. Lydia was a pink and green shimmering shape on the bottom of the pool. Taking a running dive into the water, Randal snatched her up and brought her to the surface just as Fiona arrived beside their frightened son.

The moment Lydia's lungs were free of water, she filled the humid air with what Neil called her "first division" screams. Fiona bent to take her from Randal and tried to comfort her, but the child who revelled in being the centre of attention had never before screamed in a perfect echo chamber and enjoyed the reverberating sounds. She kept on screaming.

Randal climbed from the pool and squelched across to them knowing he had been quick enough off the mark to prevent serious upset. Neil was pale and shaken and Randal ruffled the boy's hair affectionately. "It wasn't your fault, Tiger. She was specifically told not to go near the water."

Serious brown eyes looked up at him. "I should have stopped her."

Randal squatted beside him, smiling reassuringly. "You'd better start accepting that when girls are determined there's no way of stopping them. The best thing you can do is learn to swim as soon as you can so you can fish her out, like I did."

"That was some fab dive," he said with shy admiration. "I bet Grandpa couldn't have done *that*."

"Well, he's a lot older than I am," allowed the father not renowned for modesty, bathing in the filial hero-worship he had been deprived of for so long. He took Lydia from Fiona's trembling arms and began to calm the child. "Now stop that terrible noise or we'll all be deafened." He pushed back strands of hair sticking to her face. "I'm just as wet as you, but I'm not screaming."

He walked through to the adjoining room knowing the echo would go, and his ploy worked. Lydia soon became more interested in slapping her dimpled hands against his sodden shirt to create tiny splashes, so he then set her down and held her firmly by the arms. "Young lady, you were told *not* to go near the water. Now you know why. You only go to the pool with Mummy or me, is that understood?" As her face crumpled, he added hastily, "And don't start screaming again because it's all over. I think we should ask Mummy for some dry clothes, don't you?"

159

Fiona came up with Neil. They both still looked shaken. "We'll have to do something about the pool, Randal."

He straightened. "I should have foreseen it but we've only been in the place ten minutes. Trust the little minx to go straight to the forbidden area! I'll get one of those safety nets to cover it." He squelched the few yards to the door. "Meanwhile, we'll keep this locked and the key on the lintel."

"You were amazingly quick, darling."

He grinned. "All part of my air-sea rescue training."

"Mmm." She took Lydia's hand. "Come on, poppet, I'll get you dry. She glanced up at Randal. "You'd better change, too, before the men from Lombards arrive with the furniture for the children's rooms."

Randal watched her walk off, knowing that in one area nothing had changed: she was unlikely ever to show interest in how he spent his time away from her. "Is there anything here for me to change into?"

Fiona half turned. "Only what you brought with you. I've enough to do sorting out clothes for the kids and me."

"You do a fantastic job," he murmured, running an appreciative glance over her tight fitting white trousers and burnt-orange silk shirt. "If the Lombards men are at all red-blooded, you'd better change, too. Lydia made you so wet I can clearly see my two greatest delights through that blouse."

She gave her wicked smile. "Lucky old you."

"Yeah, but I don't want the furniture men sharing my good fortune."

Her laugh hung in the air as she went to the room where they had stacked boxes and suitcases marking their occupation of their new home, but Randal's attention was drawn by a tug on his hand.

"Daddy, you're dripping water all over this little carpet . . . and when will you teach me to dive like you?"

He smiled down at his son. "I'll teach you to swim first. No use diving in and not coming up again. You're right, Tiger, I'd better get dry or Mummy will have to deal with the furniture men and I'll be in the doghouse."

As he walked towards the master bedroom, Neil asked, "Did Lydia nearly die?"

Randal turned in surprise. "Whatever put that idea in your head? She had a ducking, that's all."

"I nearly died, didn't I?"

Totally unprepared for that, Randal hesitated, and the boy said, "I heard Mummy tell Grandpa it was his fault I nearly died." He frowned. "What would have happened to me if I had?"

"We'll have a talk about that one day, but first there's a lot I must tell you about girls and ladies," said Randal, angry that the boy had been allowed to overhear something so disturbing. "They get very upset over things. Little 'uns scream and cry, like Lydia. Bigger girls and ladies still cry, but they're too grown up to scream so they often say things that aren't really true, instead. We men know that so we don't worry too much about it."

"So does Mummy tell lies?"

"Of course not," he said hastily.

"Then I *did* nearly die?"

Randal realised he had got himself into one of those tricky parental situations and took the standard way out. "I promise we'll talk about it soon, but I must change into dry things before the men arrive with your furniture. I can't wait to see what Mummy chose for you, can you?"

What Mummy had chosen pleased her children no end, but Daddy whistled in disbelief when he was handed the invoice.

"They're the first things of their own they've had," Fiona reminded him. "That grotty stuff in the rented house was useless. This is all designed with kids in mind."

"But they'll grow out of it in no time," he protested.

"It's completely adaptable. There are instructions showing how to change the layout as they need different things. Play tables turn into desks, cupboards into TV and stereo cabinets. You know." She waved her elegant hands dismissively. "That's what you pay for."

"What does our furniture turn into as we grow older: rocking chairs and walking frames?"

She put out her tongue at him. "You gave me a blank cheque. Don't start moaning at this stage. You haven't yet seen what I'm planning for the living room."

"Come over here and I'll tell you what I'm planning for the bedroom," he invited, glancing up from the sheets of instructions.

"You never give up, do you? I think you'd have it morning, noon *and* night if you could."

161

"Didn't guess you knew me so well. OK, where do you want this wardrobe that turns into a boat when Neil's ten?"

"*Very* funny!"

"Does it really turn into a boat, Daddy, and what is it you'd have morning, noon and night?" asked Neil eagerly.

Randal gave a happy laugh. "We'll have a talk about that one day, too, but for now you can give me a hand with this and hold the box of screws. I can't do it without your help."

By the time they collapsed on to piles of cushions, with glasses of champagne, to watch the sun set over the willows at the far end of the garden, Randal and Fiona were tired but wonderfully contented.

"Here's to us," he murmured, clinking his glass against hers. "I wasn't sure about this place, but I admit you picked a real winner." He drank and grimaced. "Can't say the same about this stuff. I'd rather have a beer."

"You have your sour old gut rot with the boys almost every day of the week. This is our first night in our gorgeous new home and we have to celebrate in style."

He ran his fingers lightly up her arm. "In the style to which I'm accustomed, I hope."

"After the rude things you said about the nursery furniture, I'm not so sure."

"I take it all back. Honest."

She traced his mouth with a finger until he trapped it between his lips. "When we're together like this it's so perfect. I just wish . . ."

He interrupted, rolling on to his back. "Don't spoil it, Fee. It can't get any better than this. It's further from Hampton than I expected but the kids love it and I know you'll all be here each time I come." He put an arm above his head and found her hand to hold. "It was hell without you. Don't ever do that to me again."

They missed the sunset. Later, they were so high on champagne they decided to go skinny-dipping in the pool.

In the morning, they ate breakfast in their dressing gowns in the kitchen – fitted with every conceivable device – a close happy family. The children begged to go in the pool, so it was nine thirty before Neil and Lydia were dressed and engrossed in new toys. A similar peace did not reign in the master bedroom where Randal was for the third time going through the boxes he

162

had packed in his room at Hampton the morning before, and the air was faintly blue.

Flinging socks and underwear on to the smooth woodblock floor, he muttered, "I know I brought it back from Munich. It must bloody be here."

Fiona waved something before his eyes, saying calmly, "Use this and stop being a bear with a sore head. You'd better buy one to keep here. I'll padlock it to the shelf and keep the key."

Randal looked at her pink Ladyshave with distaste. "I can't use that."

"It's that or designer stubble. Take your pick."

"*Designer stubble!*"

She giggled, picking something from the midst of his scattered clothes. "Where did this come from?"

His scowl turned into a smile. "It's a handspun jumper for Lydia's teddy bear. I forgot to give it to her yesterday, although she won't appreciate its significance."

"Neither do I."

He took from her the tiny brightly woven garment and sat on the bed, still smiling. "It was sent to me by your five-year-old namesake. Her mother made it especially for my little girl's teddy. The Hunters live in Cornwall on an isolated clifftop. They're self-sufficient and quite remarkable." He recounted how the women spun wool from their own sheep to make individual knitwear mostly exported to America. "I didn't have the chance to see any of the stuff but the lads did."

"Why was that sent to you if you didn't go there?"

"Oh, I went there. We delivered medical supplies to them during the big freeze in January. It was one hell of a tricky landing." He was mentally back to that time. "The lads had to tramp through deep snow with all the boxes and said the family was amazed we got there. The little girl, Fiona, sent me a drawing of the Chinook; said she'd been excited by our visit and asked for a picture of us all. When I sent it I mentioned that I had a little girl called Lydia. This was waiting when I got back from Munich. Perhaps you'd write a thank you from Lydia. It'd mean such a lot to the kid."

Fiona was still looking mystified, so he explained further. "She's on kidney dialysis, Fee. Unless she gets a transplant her life's going to be a short one. Jimmy said she had the happiest smile he's ever seen on a child, yet she's a virtual prisoner because of her treatment. What if that ever happened to one of our kids?" He studied the little jumper. "She thought our delivery of her medicines was more exciting than Father Christmas coming." He glanced up at his wife. "When I get another five day stand-down I thought we could drive to Cornwall and see her; take a present or something."

"You're not serious."

He was not expecting that. "Well, yes. She can't run around and enjoy life like our two. You don't know what she has to undergo each day."

"And I don't want to," she said passionately. "You've gone soft all of a sudden. If this happened in January you were missing Lydia and were drawn to any child to compensate. Now you have our two to be with and care for. That girl has a family of her own, Randal, and you should keep out of it. They would most probably resent your interference. You know how reclusive Cornish people are."

"Do you?" he challenged.

"I know I want you to concentrate on your own children, not someone else's. You've a lot of time to make up with Neil and Lydia, and you'll doubtless be going away again soon." She was surprisingly worked up. "You've always kicked up a hell of a fuss about them being *your* children, and wanting a father's rights. Now you're getting involved with some sick child who thinks you're more exciting than Father Christmas. Have your priorities gone haywire? Do you want this to work or not?"

Shaken by her outburst, he put the jumper aside and got to his feet. "Of course I want it to work. You know I do. And I'm going to make up for the lost time with the kids, although most of it wasn't of my own choosing. Fee, this has nothing to do with priorities. No one comes before you and those two along the corridor creating such a din. If I haven't made that clear enough over the past month I don't know where I went wrong," he finished aggressively.

"You didn't, darling. Let's forget it and get dressed before the Lombards van arrives with the poolside bar and loungers."

Five minutes and three nicks later, Randal threw the Ladyshave down and decided to get a more suitable model before the morning was out. Yesterday, last night, had been all any man could hope for; this morning was slowly degenerating and

164

making him bad-tempered. Maybe he should get out and calm down for a while.

Fiona came from the bathroom looking stunning in black trousers and a pale-yellow knitted silk top. She tut-tutted and began sticking scraps of tissue over his cuts. Then she stood back to survey her handiwork. "You'd have been better with designer stubble. You now look positively villainous."

"Grrr," he snarled, but it was half-hearted.

She walked away. "You don't frighten me. I've seen you when you've got a cold and think you're dying." At the door she turned back hesitantly. "It's not that I don't pity that child, darling, but I couldn't visit her. You know I can't bear sickness, invalids or anything abnormal. I've always been that way. I can't help it. Since Neil was in hospital I've been worse. I still have nightmares about it. All those machines, and bodies attached to them by tubes." She shuddered. "And that hospital smell! If you hadn't flown home I couldn't have coped with it all. Mummy and Daddy were useless. They went to pieces. Then you calmly took over and dealt with everything. You're so good at that. That's why I need you with us all the time."

Randal stared at the doorway, his anger finally kindling. Snatching up the woolly scrap which had caused the trouble, he thrust it in the briefcase he would take back to Hampton at the crack of dawn tomorrow. He had done his utmost not to rock the boat over the past few weeks, but Fiona had just shown that it was far from stable. What more could he bloody well do?

June

It was the type of confrontation Randal deplored. He had very reluctantly left a sleeping Fiona as dawn was breaking and was in no mood for one of the Squadron Commander's clampdowns on discipline. It was also a Monday morning, a bad time for Judge Jeffries to be officious, particularly since half B Flight had made the long journey back from the Falklands only two days earlier.

Jeffries flashed his cold smile. "This is necessary at intervals, man." He could never bring himself to call Randal "Rip" because it might suggest he shared the general liking for him, so he used an impersonal approach. "Over the last three months three of your aircrew have applied for compassionate leave and eight have been grounded through sickness or injury. It's not good enough!"

"Nor was it deliberate. I was called home because my son's life was at risk. Simon's wife collapsed with pneumonia, and you were dead keen on Dave representing the RAF at the Rowan funeral. He actually returned a day early and made himself useful, if you recall."

Jeffries was invariably smooth. "I was stating facts, that's all. I know why leave was granted but it nevertheless left your flight barely able to deal with the tasks coming in."

"We *did* deal with them, however."

Jeffries studied his notes as if Randal had not spoken. "These injuries: a crushed hand and a case of concussion from a mugging in Munich, a twisted ankle during the exercise on Salisbury Plain, lacerations to an arm while testing a winch . . . *a black eye?*" he queried acidly, glancing up at Randal.

"Jeff walked into a tree in the dark," he offered, straightfaced.

"More likely another man's fist! They're getting slipshod. Your ground crew are as bad: six unfit for duty during last month alone."

"Accidents are exactly that," Randal pointed out. "They happen to us all. I'm sure no one accused you of being slipshod when

166

you fell off the ladder while putting up Christmas lights for your family." Jeffries had taken five extra days' sick leave and Randal liked to remind him every now and then. He pushed on swiftly. "And illness is no one's fault but the bugs. Colds, flu, enteritis and the rest come around every year. We're not immune because we're servicemen. In fact, we're more vulnerable because we're also exposed to any epidemics in Bosnia, Ireland, Germany and any other place we have to visit. I still have mild attacks of malaria from two years ago, and so do you."

Jeffries' pale eyes narrowed. "The point is we have a duty to keep ourselves fit enough to resist infection. Under battle conditions in the jungle it was impossible to follow a normal routine but there's no excuse for slackness here. I want your men to spend at least two hours each day at some form of physical exercise, and before you claim it's impossible I suggest they head for the swimming pool instead of the bar at the end of a working day. I want to see our squash and tennis courts fully occupied and men working out in the gym before or after duty. It can be done."

"We'd all like an ideal world. The one we occupy isn't," said Randal with sarcasm. "Look at the coming week, for instance. Only four of us will be here to use the courts; the rest will be scattered. I'll have a job juggling availability with demand."

"I've already done that." Jeffries offered a sheet of paper.

Highly incensed, Randal glanced at the neat list which designated personnel for each of the tasks they had been allotted for the next seven days, or longer. It was usual to leave deployment with each flight commander, who knew more about his men than anyone on the station, so Randal took great exception to this. Jeffries must have been at his desk well before breakfast.

Pushing his chair back on two legs as he studied the details, he said, "Rusty can't go to Northern Ireland; he's booked for his annual medical check on Wednesday, and I want Maggie on this naval exercise. She's never landed on a carrier at sea and needs the experience as much as Jeff and Simon. Frank's done it. So have Vince and Pete. In any case, Frank's not yet been cleared by the Doc over that ear infection. He's effectively grounded for another two days, so I'll strike him off that detail."

Jeffries always had a comeback. "What have I just said about general unfitness? I suggest Maggie needs experience of Northern Ireland. If it should ever become necessary for her to

167

operate from a carrier she can fly with someone who's already mastered it."

"And what if there's only a navigator available? Northern Ireland is pretty routine these days. I prefer her to be given the chance of something more demanding."

"You've always been a pushover where women are concerned."

"Maggie's one of my pilots, not one of my women," Randal snapped, letting his chair fall back on four legs. "She should be trained in every aspect of what we're called upon to do under peaceful and wartime conditions. Trouble can break out anywhere at any time and I can't send an experienced pilot on this exercise when another needs the opportunity."

"And I suppose you plan personally to show her the ropes." It was super smooth.

"Along with Simon and Jeff, yes. B Flight will then be staffed by pilots who can all operate at sea." Suggesting that the matter was closed, he went on to rearrange the other names on the list. "Steve can go to Ireland instead of Maggie, and Frank will replace Steve on the small-arms course. Rusty can organise some low-level practice after his medical check and I'll swap—"

"I meant what I said about getting your men fit." Jeffries cut across Randal's deliberations with a change of emphasis that put him back in command. "Your flight hasn't pulled its weight since their return from Bosnia. It's difficult enough for me to stretch the squadron's resources to meet the demands, without crewmen getting mugged and pilots *bumping into trees*! Get that message through to them."

Randal headed for the door. "You're the Boss."

The moans at the wailing wall were nothing to those when Randal passed on the news that they were all expected to spend their evenings with some kind of racket in their hands instead of a pint glass.

"He cannot be *serious*," cried Vince *à la* John McEnroe.

Randal smiled somewhat grimly. "As only four of you will be on station this week I expect you to uphold the sporting honour of B Flight by rushing around in shorts every spare moment. Meanwhile, the rest of us will do our utmost *not* to get mugged with a cowbell strung around the neck." His gazed moved on from Dave to Jeff. "Or get socked in the eye by a girl who says no twice, then backs it up with her fist."

Maggie was delighted to be listed for the naval exercise. So far she had been lucky to avoid the dreary routine of Northern Ireland and the winter weather in the Falklands. She had taken no sick leave since joining 646 Squadron and no one could accuse her of standing around every evening with a pint in her hand. When she was not telephoning Mark she was actually using the swimming pool or squash courts. However, this did not breed respect for Jeffries. He had unquestionably served the RAF with skill and diligence but that had not made the man likeable. A few misdemeanours would have given his popularity a boost; no one warmed to a saint.

Maggie grimaced as she continued packing her bag. Had she not just branded herself one? Maybe she should "walk into a tree" like Jeff, or blot her copybook in some other way. Since airing her views on drunken masculine capers like the one in Munich, she sensed that her acceptance by the rest had taken a backward step. Her opinion of the cowbell episode would not change. Mark thought it hilarious but he was another man and would, naturally.

Dave had been quieter after the affair. There had been a death in his family which might account for some of his recent introspection, but he seemed very pensive when not actually on the job. Maybe he had girl trouble. He was such an impressive hunk of masculinity he ought to be leaving a trail of seductions wherever he went, like Jeff. Maggie had seen that Dave was listed for the naval exercise. Perhaps he would find a "Jolly Jill Tar" on the aircraft carrier and go overboard for her. Zipping her bag, she chuckled. Hardly the best metaphor in view of where they were going.

Split on the Adriatic Sea was more inviting in midsummer and the two crews settled in familiar quarters on their arrival. After dinner there was an hour-long briefing from a senior naval pilot on the art of landing on a moving deck in the middle of an ocean in all weathers.

"During the next five days you'll be expected to land and take off again on schedule, whatever the conditions. There'll be other aircraft operating from the carrier as part of the exercise, so it's important to keep the deck clear for jets coming in. You'll be guided by a marshal on deck and by radio from a controller. The schedule suggests you'll be coming in both fully loaded and empty during the five days, so you'll experience the balance of wind velocity and the weight of your aircraft. There's a probability you'll also carry armed personnel at some stage of the exercise, but if it gets rough out there that'll be scrapped as too risky. Any questions?"

After ten minutes of giving answers, he said, "I've never flown a Chinook so I'll leave your flight commander to add what I can't. When he's done that I suggest we meet in the bar and enjoy the rest of the evening."

"Sorry, we'll be playing squash instead," murmured Jeff.

"Or tiddleywinks," added Nobby.

Randal was not amused, for once. "OK, shut it and take this in. It's more important than ever for crewmen to give accurate patter. The poor bloody pilots are trying to hover alongside something moving at fifteen knots or so. And there's a humping great superstructure on the right, to say nothing of parked aircraft occupying half the deck. In a strong wind and poor visibility the pilot needs all the help he can get. On deck there's a marshal directing him where to go, and from the cabin his crew are telling him he's not getting there. It's not a time for monkeying about, guys. Good judgement and clear directions are essential. I'll fly with each pilot in turn, which means that two of you will be going in cold first time. Crew line-up for tomorrow is Jeff, Maggie, Sandy and Dave. I'll fly with Simon, Nobby and Ray. Any questions for now?"

There was a silence; everyone had taken for granted that Randal would babysit Maggie on the first day. Once she recovered from her surprise Maggie was delighted, although his decision seemed totally out of character. Simon was visibly annoyed. The rest were still amazed. They could accept that she should be watched over but not one of them. Maggie gleefully chalked up one to the female sex as the silence lengthened.

"Let's go for that beer," suggested Randal heavily and went out.

Walking alongside Jeff, Maggie asked, "What's up with the Boss? Memories of last time he was here?"

"Bosnia isn't his favourite place, but I suspect it's because of the ding-dong he had with Jeffries this morning. Started him off in a bad mood after a weekend at home. You know what that means."

"An overdose of sex?"

170

He raised his brows. "That, too, probably."

"What else, then? I thought now he's bought her a country mansion all was sweetness and light."

Jeff put his hand on the swing door as the disgruntled Simon let it go, and they went through to the noisy bar area. "Rusty says it's not. She doesn't run home to Mummy and Daddy when he's away but she invites her horsey friends to stay instead. Seems he often gets home to find the place swarming with Nigels and Debbies."

Maggie was impatient. "Why doesn't he put his foot down?"

Jeff's eyebrows rose again. "You haven't seen her, or you wouldn't ask."

"But I've seen him," she said forcefully. "What is it with you men? When you're all together you make out you're such tough sexy guys, but you can't stand up to a woman when you're on your own. My brother . . ." She changed direction. "Rusty's a fine one to spread tales. He can't pluck up the courage to tell Marsha he's no intention of going to the altar with her. How does he know about the horsey friends, anyway?"

"He and Rip have been together a long time. Before the fabulous Fiona came on the scene."

"Two fools together," said Maggie as they reached the bar. "And you're another. We all know the tree you walked into had red hair and a very short skirt." She ordered a gin and tonic.

Jeff asked for beer, then turned to her. "You don't expect me to believe you meekly obey lover boy. Knowing you, I bet you give him a bollocking when you feel like it."

To her chagrin she blushed; something she had not done for years. "We have the ratio nicely balanced."

Jeff roared with laughter, and Maggie cursed herself for being confused into such an idiotic reply. She should have ignored the jibe. The others were immediately let in on the joke, and she was the subject of prolonged taunts about her sex life with Mark until she turned the tables.

"As the ratio here is seven to one you can all pitch in and buy me another gin and tonic."

Geoff was looking over her shoulder. "Here come the Navy guys. Try them; we only buy beer."

It grew markedly noisier and Maggie decided to leave them to it. A ratio of seven to one she could take for limited periods but more than that, with beer flowing freely, was too much. She slipped away unnoticed. Ahead of her on the stairs leading to the bedrooms she saw Dave.

"Tired?" she asked, catching up with him.

He started, as if she had broken into a reverie. "Eh?"

"Need an early night?"

"Oh . . . aye."

She grinned. "That's what comes of all that swimming, squash, hang gliding and long-distance jogging. I've spotted you running around the perimeter at daybreak in all weathers. You must be Jeffries' blue-eyed boy."

They walked in silence the few yards to Maggie's door, where she stopped and tackled him. "You've been very quiet since you returned from Scotland. Were you very close to your uncle . . . guardian . . . whatever? The one who died last month."

He stopped reluctantly several feet away. "I didn't see much of him; only in school holidays and on leave from Cranwell. He was a good age, anyway."

As he turned away Maggie said impulsively, "If you ever want to talk about anything to someone who won't spread it around the whole squadron, I'm here." To combat his visible suspicion, she added, "You know what they're like: the biggest blabbermouths in town."

"And you're not?"

"Not if it's told to me in confidence. In spite of the run-ins we've had, I admire you, Dave."

His mouth twisted. "Is that another of your sick jokes?"

"No, it isn't! My God, the girl who hurt you made a thorough job of it. Don't you trust any of us? Is that why you're the only one in B Flight who hasn't a woman of some kind?"

His dark eyes narrowed. "Stick with your equal ratio, fast-jet man, Maggie, and don't meddle."

"Fair enough, Sergeant Ashmore. And you go off and get quietly and totally *stuffed*!"

In her room she told herself once again that men were impossible – all except Mark, of course. She had truly wanted to help Dave, who had been so determined to fly he resigned his commission after working to gain it. All at once, it occurred to her that a girl might have been mixed up somewhere in that decision. Had he seen her again on his sad visit home? She sat on the bed, certain she was on the right track. It must have been a severe blow. Most men went on the rampage on the rebound from a disastrous affair, and Dave would surely attract almost any girl with his looks alone. Bragging, the favourite aircrew come-on line, would then win over even those immune to black curling hair, broad shoulders and moody brown eyes. Rejection had plainly done the reverse to Dave. He wanted to punish the whole female population. Well, he could do so with her blessing; she washed her hands of him.

The day dawned clear and sunny. Everyone was at breakfast bright-eyed and bushy-tailed. Maggie always marvelled that they could get awash with beer yet surface in the morning with few apparent after-effects. The experience of sharing a tent on Salisbury Plain with three of them had shown that they staggered to their sleeping bags, fell into a deep stupor and snored heavily until someone poked them awake in the morning. Who needed sleeping pills when beer was readily available?

She had spent the night tossing and turning, thinking about deck landings. During her training she had gone to Yeovilton to learn the theory. One aspect of the course was to be strapped, in full flying kit, into a mock-up of a cockpit, which then plunged down a ramp to submerge in a tank of water. Divers had been on hand for anyone who failed to get free and surface. Although Maggie had a background of life-saving at sea from family sailing holidays, she had hated the prospect of being trapped under water. This morning the notion seemed distant, but at three a.m. all things seemed possible.

They were gathering for a final briefing when Wing Commander Haslett entered and approached Randal. "Rip, there's a top-priority emergency. I need your two aircraft. The Navy has been informed of the change of plan."

Leaving the senior man to give the new briefing, Randal took a seat beside Dave. Haslett began. "At o-five hundred a fully loaded Algerian 747 flew into a mountain in thick fog. It has not yet been established why this aircraft was so far off course and flying so low. Traffic controllers lost contact fifteen minutes before the crash." He referred to the map on the wall behind him. "The information we've been given pinpoints the wreckage here, in our least favourable operational area. You'll know the problems, especially in winter, but the situation is dire. Because of the exceptionally hot dry weather over the last six weeks all vegetation is highly inflammable. The forest on the upper reaches is alight and out of control, which suggests the 747 was on fire on impact.

Rescue services are hampered by the fog, but the Met says it'll burn off within the next two hours. Dead, injured and wreckage are scattered fairly widely through the valley. It's a major disaster. The fire is racing uphill and firefighting teams are being mustered from the multi-national forces based nearest to the scene. They will have to be flown in. Access by road is tortuous and, in thick fog, highly risky. The Americans are organising water-dropping aircraft but that's a lengthy business.

"The fire would naturally extinguish when it reached the higher altitudes of bare rock but, not only is the forest an important source of building timber, there's a village and a large former sanatorium in the path of the flames. This old building has been used as an orphanage for the past three years, and we've been told there are around two hundred babies and children, with twenty members of staff. They have to be brought out, along with the people of the village. You are programmed to effect this evacuation. Each aircraft will carry a Croatian nurse to translate and prevent panic if the fire gets too close during the operation. Once the fog lifts the wind might rise. If it does we must hope it will blow the smoke away from the area and not obscure it." He faced Randal. "Your Chinooks are fuelled and ready for the naval exercise. Get your crews airborne as soon as possible."

They speedily worked on navigation and dredged up mental reminders of the area they had flown over so often. They were still deep in discussion as they walked out to their aircraft with the two Croatian nurses.

Randal said, "Jeff, you'll fly with Simon. I'll go with Maggie's crew."

"Why?" she cried involuntarily.

"Because I say so." And that was the end of that.

They took off into the clear blue of a fine summer morning and headed for the mountains where Dave had rescued Harry, the army handler, from a frozen ledge in February. Maggie sat wordlessly beside an equally silent Randal after the initial take-off routine. Flying low over early morning meadows and sparkling streams, over villages still marked with the evidence of war, it was hard to imagine the scene awaiting them.

Maggie had encountered fog several times over marshland, and it was a hazard she dreaded. They were now flying towards fog and smoke in a mountainous area. Hazards plus! She glanced at Randal studying charts and making notes on the pad on his knee; she was, perhaps, glad to have him with her. He had experienced most things, including war, and he was calmer than Jeff when flying. Curiously, the reverse applied when they were on the ground.

"This village is right in the middle of the bloody forest," he muttered. "But there's surely a flat reasonably clear area we can use. The orphanage is apparently further down the mountain and built on a plateau. Ideal when it was a sanatorium, but a hell of a place to keep kids in. What's to stop them going over the edge?"

"Walls?" she suggested tentatively.

"Yeah, very funny!" He was still absorbed in the chart. "We'll have to size up the situation when we get there, but if they haven't used some initiative and taken them up to the village our priority will be to get *them* out, the best way we can."

"Two hundred babies and toddlers can't be moved in a hurry," she pointed out.

"When they're right in the path of a fire they'll give it a bloody good try, chum."

Maggie sensed his deep concern and the danger increased her own. Fire or no, moving two hundred children with only twenty adults to do it would not be simple. It would surely depend on the number of actual babies in the orphanage. Any child who could walk would be led to safety, but unless there was a supply of prams or other wheeled transport how would babies be carried away?

Information on the situation was being spasmodically relayed to them over the airwaves, but little of it was encouraging. The firefighting troops had been dropped some distance from the head of the flames because dense smoke had prevented aircraft from overflying the area. The American water-dropping operation had not yet got off the ground; water in rivers and reservoirs was low due to the drought. The fog was slowly clearing but thick black smoke covered a large area.

Randal discussed options with Jeff and Simon, who agreed that they would put down first on the best available site and get what information they could about the children. If they had been brought up to the village and conditions enabled Maggie to land as well, both crews would get everyone aboard, check that no one was left behind, then get away together. If it proved impossible for both Chinooks to be on the ground together, Jeff's crewmen would take on board the children first, then as many adults as necessary to leave an acceptable number for the other aircraft. When Jeff took off, Maggie would go in to pick up the remainder.

The plan would be changed if the children were not in the village and on-the-spot decisions would depend on the situation as they found it. Whatever that was, Maggie's aircraft would be responsible for the evacuation of the orphanage.

"We'll play it by ear," Randal told everyone. "The authorities are supposed to be telling the people we're coming. Hopefully, they'll already be gathered somewhere suitable."

"In the church," guessed Maggie. "That's where people tend to congregate in times of danger."

"You bet they won't be in neat rows alongside a perfect landing pad," said Simon.

Randal said, "In my experience they'll expect to bring their livestock: goats and fowls. Our brief is to get the people to safety. Animals will have to take their chances."

"I rather fancy a bit of roast goat," mused Jeff. "I've heard it gives a man extra virility."

"Forget it! You walk into enough trees as it is."

A concerted jeer greeted Randal's terse comment, then all inclination for lightness was banished by the sight of the dark pall ahead. They had flown through clear skies, so there was no doubt this was smoke, not fog. It belched upward in a broad swathe some two thousand feet from the rocky peak. It was impossible to make out the head of the fire or to deduce how far ahead of it the smoke drifted.

"I hope to God that doesn't mark the progress of the flames," said Randal. "I know fire can race through dry timber, but it spreads sideways as fast as it goes forwards and has even been known to extinguish itself by completing a circle, leaving the centre untouched."

Maggie looked at him in surprise. "Have you dealt with fire before?"

"Nope. But I made a study of natural disasters several years ago: earthquakes, tidal waves, hurricanes, landslips, fires, avalanches. Reckoned I'd have to deal with one or the other at some time in my career." He gave an unexpected grin. "You're not the only one in B Flight who reads serious books, our Maggie."

176

She made no answer to that, but several minutes later she asked quietly, "What if the fire's already reached the village?"

"What do you think?"

"We try to land further up and hope some of the people have made it that far."

"Seems like the best idea." His tone changed. "Oh Christ, look over there."

Several hundred feet above the valley floor the skeleton of the 747 was scattered over a wide area. Rescue teams swarmed across the grassy slopes, now burned and blackened, and air ambulances were flying to and fro. Silence reigned in the Chinooks as they flew past the tragedy and headed for the smoke.

"We'll need to go around this before heading back to the village," Randal said. "Too dangerous to fly through it, and getting to the rear will give us a better idea of what we're up against."

"How do we know it's drifting high enough for us to get behind it?" asked Maggie.

"We don't, and we'll try something else if that's not on. OK Jeff, let's take a wide sweep to the right into that offshoot valley and size up the situation from there. Should be possible to see the head of the fire if we can get behind that smoke curtain."

They flew with the black layer on their left until it began to thin and peter out. Now they could see tongues of flame and, as they banked, it became clear that the smoke was rising almost vertically in the still air.

"Bingo!" breathed Randal. "Unless the wind springs up we'll be all right."

There was a wide enough corridor between the billowing wall and the mountainside to fly fast and low towards their objective, one behind the other, and Maggie was glad of all the practice at mountain flying they had had. The stench of burning now filled the cockpit and her stomach muscles tensed nervously. This was the riskiest operation she had yet encountered. Landing on an aircraft carrier seemed mild in comparison; certainly not worth loss of sleep last night.

"There's the orphanage, Boss," said Dave. "Two o'clock, mile and a half ahead."

"Got it," said Randal. "God, you've got eyes like bloody Superman."

"I'm used to mountains."

"Just as well; because that place is built on an overhang. You might have to do some climbing if those kids are still there."

"Nah," put in Sandy with confidence. "They'll have a fine view of the fire from there and will have got out sharpish."

They gained height and everyone save Maggie and Jeff, who were flying the aircraft and carefully watching the mountain rising to their right, searched for signs of the village.

Dave was ahead again. "Two o'clock. Hundred and fifty feet up. Church spire."

They climbed towards the old stone spire, and as more of it came into view it was possible to see one or two rough wooden dwellings near the church. In front of the huts was an earth-floored clearing large enough for one Chinook. As they circled what was in essence not a village but a small foresters' settlement, they saw other huts but not a single person.

"It's deserted," cried Jeff. "Where the hell have they gone?"

Randal cursed loud and long. "They couldn't have been told we were coming for them. The only way they'll be safe is sitting up there on the bare peak, and the fire will overtake them long before they reach it."

"I saw a wee boy," cried Dave, lapsing into the Scottish vernacular in his excitement. "He ran out from that hut with the sagging roof then was dragged back inside. Couldn't see who got him. Too quick."

"You sure, Dave?"

"Aye, certain. It's my guess they're all there, hiding."

"We'll soon see," said Randal vigorously. "Get on the ground, Jeff, and find out what's going on."

"OK. Will do."

"Don't worry about blowing any roofs off those huts; they're going to be burnt down, anyway. Get Ray and Nobby out with the interpreter as soon as you're down. I want news of the orphanage kids, fast!"

"OK, Boss."

While Maggie hovered, Jeff landed within the clearing, scattering several flimsy lean-tos with the downdraught. Maggie was too busy with the controls to study the scene, but the comments of the others kept her informed. Dave relayed to the crewmen where he had spotted the child, and they went in search of him, taking the Croatian nurse.

Maggie had a curious sense of unreality as she held the aircraft steady high above the other on the ground. Tilting her head up to the right she saw dark green coniferous forest stretching upwards and then thinning to grey rock stark against a vivid blue sky. Looking down to her left the contrast was bizarre: black and grey obscurity shot through every so often with orange flames. The smell of burning was more intense, but the creeping fire seemed unreal to her because she could not hear the crackle and roar.

"They've brought an old man out but there's no sign of the boy," announced Sandy.

Randal was impatient. "Jeff, what's going on?"

"Simon's in the cabin finding out. They've found an old guy but he's slow giving answers. I'm signalling to speed it up."

"They'd better. This fire isn't standing still."

Seconds later Jeff's voice came over the radio. "Boss, when they were told helicopters were coming for them, they went into hiding. They've no idea what caused the fire and they think the war's on again. Aircraft and uniformed men suggested an enemy invasion. They're terrified."

"So they flaming well should be! They'll be roasted to death within the hour. Get that through to them and drag them out by the hair if you have to. How many up here?"

"Total population sixty-two. The orphanage kids aren't here. The old guy says they'll be hiding in the cellar, like they did during the war."

"Right. Load everyone and take them to the valley rendezvous. We'll pick up the rest and meet you there. Jeff, make it quick!"

"Will do. Good luck!"

Randal turned to Maggie. "Let's get down to that building and see what we've got."

Her stomach muscles had knotted further. The orphanage was nearer the advancing fire and it sat way out on a plateau above a sheer drop. There was no obvious place to land, unless they discovered another clearing. Unreality had suddenly become very real.

"War's a way of life over here. They're peasant people in settlements like this. Can't imagine any kind of disaster other than men with guns coming to take what little they own."

Maggie glanced at the man beside her. "It's a way of life in more countries than this."

"God, what a mess of a world we live in!"

They were close to the building now. It was an old stone structure with a steeply pointed roof of ancient tiles and two broad stone terraces along the sides where consumptive patients must have lain in their beds to benefit from the pure air. There was a large courtyard with a silent fountain in the centre and a high wall surrounding the whole.

"It's hopeless," said Maggie in despair. "Better look around for another clearing then send Dave and Sandy to fetch them. There must be a track of some kind leading to it."

"No time," murmured Randal. "If we don't pick them up within thirty minutes we won't do it at all."

"How can we pick them up? The only flat area is just beyond the wall and there's no way we can put down on that. The rotors would foul up on the incline."

"Yeah." He was silent as Maggie continued to hover over the building, then he said, "We'll have to go for it."

Shocked, she said, "Not while I'm at the controls. It can't be done."

"I'm at the controls too, and it can," he returned calmly "There's not enough space for an all-points landing, so we'll touch down on the rear wheels and hold the hover at the front while they lower the ramp, fetch everyone from the cellar and load them in."

"You're mad!"

"I'm prepared to take the only chance we have."

"Have you done anything like this before?" she demanded.

"Yes, although the bulk of the fuselage wasn't hanging over a raging fire. OK, guys," he said to the crewmen, "you can see what we've got here and there are no choices. We'll go in backwards and sit on our rear end. Soon as we do, get the ramp down. Sandy will take the translator and fetch the kids. Dave, we'll need you to keep us out of trouble. If things get too difficult we'll have to bin it, but I want to give it our best shot first. It's going to be tricky, so we'll need accurate and speedy instructions as we ease the tail in. Keep the blades well clear of the incline. If we foul up against it we'll burn along with the kids. We're in your hands, guys."

"OK, Boss. Understood," said Dave.

If Maggie was tense before she was doubly so now. She had practised sitting like a praying mantis, but only on straight level ground during her training. What Randal was set on needed a high level of flying skill and very steady nerves because they would have fire ahead and a mountain behind. The devil and the deep blue sea?

They took the Chinook out over the valley as far from the building as they could without drawing too near the rise of billowing smoke, then swung round for the reverse approach. Unable to see from the cockpit the small plateau with the rock face rising steeply from it, they had to put complete faith in their crewmen. Maggie appreciated Randal's quiet assurance as they slowly backed, guided by Dave and Sandy.

"Straight back one hundred . . . eighty . . . sixty . . . tail right eight degrees . . . tail steady . . . straight back forty . . . thirty . . . *Steady!* Tail clear."

In her concentration Maggie pushed to the back of her mind details of what they were about to perch on. Only when the crewmen gave directions emphasising the state of the tail did she become fully aware that beneath her seat was a long drop to the heart of the fire racing up towards them.

At that point Dave gave a sharp warning. "Hold everything! We've dislodged a tree. There are loose branches flying about. Could be a hazard. And there's a cascade of shale."

"How much?" demanded Randal tersely, as they held the aircraft steady at the hover.

"It's easing already . . . The branches have dropped over the edge." A lengthy pause. "No more shale." Another, briefer pause. "All clear again."

"Any more trees on that scarp?"

"Only one near enough to worry about," said Dave calmly. "It looks secure from here."

Maggie looked at Randal. "Too risky?"

"Not if everything stays put." He gazed downward. "We're running out of time, guys. The flames are getting too close. It's now or never. What's the verdict?"

"Everything's settled down. Should be safe enough to go for it. I'll keep you posted on that tree, and be ready to take off if things start to move again."

"OK, go ahead and take us in," said Randal decisively. "Once we're down go like hell to get those kids aboard. We can't hang around for long."

Back to the familiar patter as they carefully reversed the huge helicopter towards the plateau and then gently down to sit on two wheels, all the time ready for the unexpected hazard that would force them to abandon the rescue. Maggie was tense and perspiring as they strove to hang motionless above a band of smoke shot through by tongues of fire, with nothing to use as a fixed point to indicate their attitude as the ramp was lowered.

Dave informed them that Sandy and Irma the Croatian nurse were entering the building at a run. He then gave non-stop guidance to correct their fuselage swings and constantly reassured them that the tree was holding and there were no visible hazards.

"Right five . . . *Steady!*"

They made the correction and waited.

"Where the hell *are* they?" Randal demanded.

"No sign yet. It's a big place to search."

The first thin wisps of smoke began to drift up beneath the cockpit as Dave indicated that they were again swinging to the right. They corrected and waited . . . waited.

"Boss, they're coming! Women carrying cots filled with babies, a long crocodile of kids, men and women pushing wheelchairs. Sandy's at the rear signalling they've got them all."

"Speed them up . . . And keep watching that bloody tree!" Randal's voice betrayed his relief, and Maggie shared it as she glanced swiftly at the cabin where the orphans were being bundled aboard, then back to the thickening smoke beneath her feet.

Dave reverted to official patter while Sandy raised the ramp and announced all was secure, but leaving that dangerous perch was not as simple as it could have been. The corridor between the mountain and the curtain of smoke had narrowed and, for several short stretches, they flew through thinly drifting greyness until they had climbed above it. Their passengers were silent – even the babies packed into five cots.

Once they were well clear of the area and heading towards a small airfield, Sandy brought the pilots up to date. "Two of the doctors were standing guard at the door. Once Irma explained they led us to the cellar. They weren't sure what or who started the fire, but they had decided their best chance was to go underground and hope it would bypass them. Actually, it was all they could do. They own a clapped-out minibus-cum-ambulance-cum-stores truck, but that went down yesterday to collect supplies from the railway station and their weekly food order. The driver always stays overnight with his family, so they had no means of escaping by the track that goes over the top of the mountain. Sorry it took so long. What we weren't told was that these kids are not only orphaned, they're all disabled in some way."

"Poor little buggers! What a start in life," said Randal with feeling. "My two—" he broke off and switched to a comment on how quiet they were.

Sandy chuckled. "Yeah, I guess they think we're from outer space."

"We are," commented Maggie. "We arrive up a mountain from the heart of a fire, in a metal bird with a hollow belly. We speak in gobbledegook and wear weird clothes. They've no idea where we're taking them. For all they know we're going to eat them for dinner."

There was momentary silence, then Randal said lightly, "There's more to this girl than good looks and a doubting nature. She's deep."

With the fiery mountain well behind them Randal gave Dave a verbal pat on the back. "A brilliant piece of judgement. I'll see our revered squadron commander hears about it when we return to Hampton. Maggie and I just sat here and did as we were told. You were the one who pulled off that difficult manoeuvre. Thanks, Dave."

When they approached the airfield where they would offload their passengers, they were pleased to see the other Chinook had arrived. "If they've brought any goats or scrawny old fowl I'll skin them alive," grunted Randal.

"The animals, or our esteemed brethren?" asked Maggie. "Aren't you interested in the beneficial properties of roast goat?"

He ignored the jibe, and they were soon occupied with the landing and departure of their passengers who were met by American Red Cross women. Irma leaned into the cockpit to pass on the gratitude of the medical staff and lay helpers.

"You are very good and brave people," she added with sincere warmth. "I thank you for myself, also."

Randal watched her walk away behind the line of refugees from the fire. Sandy and Dave had rounded up some men to help them carry the laden cots to the waiting vehicles. "Several dozen babies but not a single yell from any one of them," he mused, shaking his head. "I've never known anything like it."

Following his glance, Maggie said, "After all they've been through these past few years they'll have cried themselves

183

out. It could be months, years, before they're able to shed tears."

After a moment or two, he murmured, "You *are* deep, aren't you!"

She turned back to him. "No, just a woman."

They collected all their gear and climbed to the ground. Walking towards the small offices Maggie continued the theme. "Sorry about the doubting nature." They advanced a few more steps. "If I tried to express my admiration of your judgement would you take it amiss?"

"Definitely!"

She tried again. "Will you let me buy you a beer?"

"*Very* definitely. Then I'll stand you a G and T."

"What for?"

"You were bloody cool up there." He smiled down at her. "Now you know the answer to your protest at my decision to change crews this morning."

He pushed open the door and walked inside, leaving her totally nonplussed.

A violent storm broke the heatwave and drought that night. It was still pouring next day, when the fire was little more than thin spirals of smoke from blackened skeletal trees. Both crews of B Flight made successful deck landings on the last day of the naval exercise, when the weather finally cleared enough to allow aircraft to operate from the carrier.

First reports on the 747 crash suggested that some kind of explosive device had detonated. Another act of terrorism, but which group was responsible? There were so many it was impossible to pinpoint any one until further investigations had been undertaken. Media sources hinted at the presence on board of a Middle Eastern leader travelling incognito. There was a security clampdown on details of the passenger list. More than one hundred and sixty people perished in the crash.

In the face of this mammoth disaster the rescue of the orphans and villagers passed unnoted.

July

It was a VIP occasion; their attendance was more or less obligatory. Fiona had understood and was prepared to play her part. She had been perfectly amenable while they discussed the arrangements, even asking his opinion on the dress she planned to wear. So why was he edgy as he waited for her call from the carphone to tell him she was almost at the hotel?

The dinner dance was being held to round off a visit by an American general, a French diplomat, a senior Norwegian air force officer and Air Vice-Marshal Connisby with his ADC, all of them deeply involved in NATO. As 646 Squadron was part of a special force the alliance could call upon at any time, periodic visits were made by those whose job it was to check the strength, efficiency and readiness of such units.

It so happened that half the crews of A Flight were currently at Hampton when four members of B Flight returned from a week of night flying practice over the Scottish Isles to find that the Station had been painted, polished and decked out with flowers to impress the visitors. Leave was out of the question and a three-day schedule of demonstrations and duties awaited them. There had been a scramble to catch up on a backlog of laundry and tidy bedrooms. Wing Commander Jeffries' suggestion that the tennis and squash courts should be full each evening became tantamount to an order; there had not been such devoted athleticism since the last VIP visit. Judge Jeffries himself could be seen racing about the courts in impeccable white, proving to everyone's disgust that he was a fine sportsman. Such skills could help promotion, so he had taken professional coaching early in his career.

Randal was no more than competent with a racket or a bat. He had fun playing games, and no man could be a serious contender when he laughed uproariously at his own mistakes. He was not at all bothered by the sporting binge and only mildly irritated by the unnatural spit and polish atmosphere at Hampton, but he was tense and worried about the coming evening. He had booked a room at a hotel just north of Hampton Heyhoe as their new home was too far to return to at the end of the evening, and Randal had used the hotel to change into his mess kit and wait for his wife to join him.

He moved restlessly about the tasteful room, uncomfortable in his stiff high collar, close-fitting trousers, tailored waist-length jacket and wide grey cummerbund. He supposed he looked well in it all, but he could hear old Grandfather Price saying, "All don oop like an organ grinder's moonkey, lad!"

He glanced at the digital clock once more. Where the hell was she? This was the first service demand he had made on her since she had run away from it last autumn. Surely she would not duck out? On the point of breaking his resolution not to ring her carphone to check, there was a knock on the door. Fiona stood in the corridor with a youthful porter bearing her luggage.

"Traffic on the motorway was horrendous," she said, walking in. "I'll have to change in a rush. Where's the shower?"

Randal tipped the boy then followed her to the bathroom, where she was wriggling out of her trousers having already discarded the Italian striped shirt he had brought her back from one of his trips.

"You were going to ring me, Fee."

"Sorry, darling. Forgot." Naked now, she went up on her toes to kiss him. "You look good enough to eat in that get-up. It really turns me on."

"I'll turn on the shower instead," he said with a grin, his tension melting away. "We're tight for time."

"Then go away and stop distracting me." She pulled on a shower cap. "Order some drinks to put us in the mood while I dress."

Fiona did not take hours to get ready like some women. She was extremely organised over clothes – never tried on everything in her wardrobe in last-minute uncertainty – and she applied her minimal make-up with expert swiftness. Randal took pleasure in watching her prepare for an outing. Tonight, it removed the last of his tension. Sipping her martini Fiona pencilled her brows, applied mascara and painted her lips apricot to blend with the golden tan she had acquired on one of the sun loungers Lombards had sold them. A generous squirt of perfume, a quick flick with

186

her comb to settle the expensively simple hairstyle, then she shed the bathrobe to pull on satin briefs before stepping into a dress she took from a wardrobe bag.

"That isn't the one you showed me last week!" Randal exclaimed.

She pulled up the concealed zip fastener and smiled at him as she slid her feet into matching shoes and picked up an evening purse. "I decided to buy something new for the occasion as it's so important to you. You can demonstrate how much you approve when we get back. No time now." At the door she added with an amused glance, "Stop looking at me that way or those tight trousers will show everyone where your thoughts are."

Maggie fastened her long blue skirt then put on her smart mess jacket. Apart from the skirt and a floppy bow instead of a bow tie, she was dressed like her male colleagues. She yearned for a sexy evening dress. Mark brought out the tigress in her and he would be here in a very few minutes. They had not met for five weeks, not only due to the complications of normal duty but also because summer months were always demanding on display pilots. It was sheer luck that Mark was free to partner her tonight. Hardly the ideal date, but she had booked a room in a country hotel where they could later compensate for their obligatory best behaviour in the Mess.

In the oak-panelled entrance hall now decked with flowers Maggie chatted to Jill as they waited, with a number of other officers, for their partners. Jill's blind date with Dandy's fiancé's college friend had not been a success, and her latest was a TV cameraman.

"I warned him it was a very formal do, so I hope to God he doesn't turn up in jeans and an emerald satin shirt," confessed Jill. "Maybe I should have asked dreary Tom from the bookshop. He's my normal choice for nights like this because he owns a dinner jacket."

Maggie laughed. "I hope he does turn up in emerald satin; liven the evening up."

"And shorten my career. I'm a pushover where men are concerned."

"More like the other way around. You have any number of them tucked up your sleeve to call on when needed."

Jill gave a knowing wink. "So long as it's only my sleeve

they're tucked up in." She nudged Maggie. "Here's Rusty with that girl who wants to tie him down. I'd say they've just had a row, wouldn't you?"

Maggie knew Rusty in most of his moods and he certainly looked grim. Marsha resembled a storm: grey dress and black expression. "It had to happen," observed Maggie. "Like most men he plays around like crazy whenever we're away, doing the macho male thing, then he scuttles home and hasn't the guts to tell her the truth." She caught sight of the pair behind Rusty. "There's another idiot. Pete's been griping for months because his girl ditched him the day after taking his Christmas presents. That's her he's bringing in. The disc jockey dumped her last week, so she rang Pete and he's besotted again. At least Jeff's honest," she added, nodding in the direction of the pilot she most liked to fly with. "He finds a series of good-time girls who know the score." She grinned. "That one looks equal to any score."

"Hey, there's yours," said Jill, and gave an exaggerated sigh. "Life ain't fair. I was the one who talked him safely down after that bird strike, yet you got him. I bet he'd look gorgeous in emerald satin."

Maggie thought Mark looked pretty gorgeous in mess dress as she hurried to greet him. His tanned face lit up when he spotted her, but all he said as he took her hands in his strong grip was, "Snap!"

They had not met in uniform before and she made a face, disappointed that he had not said more. "It is a bit his and hers isn't it, but at least we don't have Mickey Mouse or 'I've flown through the Grand Canyon' on the back. How was the air show yesterday?"

"Exhilarating, as always." He glanced around. "This is some place. I barely noticed it when I landed here in March. Other things on my mind."

"It's been tarted up for the VIPs, but it's quite grand and nice to come home to."

"After night flying over the Outer Isles? How did it go?"

"OK, except for the abysmal weather. Small wonder Dave's so introverted."

"How's he been since you sorted him out?"

She chuckled. "Sweetness itself."

"No, that's you, *liefling*," he murmured, "although you scare me dressed up like this."

"I'm the same girl underneath," she replied softly.

"I'll test that out tonight. I don't have to be back until late tomorrow; any chance of spending the day together?"

They moved to the crowded ante-room where stewards were offering glasses of sherry and the noise prevented intimate conversation. While they attempted to make plans for the morrow Mark's attention was caught by something behind Maggie. His eyes widened.

"Wow! Who's that?"

She followed his gaze and guessed most of the men were discreetly wowing. "As she's with my boss, who's looking fatuously smug, that must be bra-less Fiona."

"I'd say she's less everything beneath that dress. I'm not surprised he bought her a house to woo her back."

Jill was wrong, Maggie decided. Randal's wife was no bimbo, she was what Mrs Spencer called "top drawer". Everything about her was classy and she was the only woman there who could have carried off the clinging chartreuse gown which revealed most of her shapely tanned back, and a hairstyle straight from a fashion magazine. Watching her flight commander watching his wife, Maggie thought Jill was right on one score: he *was* dotty about her. But he could not keep on buying houses.

Everyone behaved with the requisite decorum during dinner and the first hour of the dancing. Randal relaxed and enjoyed himself, pleased with Fiona's generous participation. She was the sensation of the evening, something which very obviously annoyed his squadron commander. Della Jeffries was so socially correct tonight she was an embarrassment even to her husband. In black with pearls she made conversation according to books on etiquette, which soon produced bored expressions on VIP faces. Yet when B Flight commander and his wife were introduced, the ritual short polite interchange became an extended merry conversation.

Earlier enquiries of the Station Commander regarding the very beautiful young woman with the squadron leader had elicited the information that Mrs Price was the daughter of Gerald Holland, prominent horse breeder. The American general was from Kentucky where his family owned racehorses, so he was doubly eager to meet her, and the Norwegian's interest only just stopped short of lecherous. Fiona could handle it, but Randal would happily have put his fist through the man's knowing smile.

189

Very little interest was shown in him until the Kentuckian asked if Randal's people also dealt in bloodstock.

"No, sir, the Price family only breeds pork pies," he murmured which, after a pause, brought a roar of laughter to further annoy Jeffries and his wife.

"Cain't lose your shirt on *them*, Squadron Leader, and that's a fact!"

By ten thirty the main guests had departed, soon to be followed by the senior officers and those on early duty tomorrow. The lively younger couples remaining set about enjoying the final hour, among them Maggie and Mark. She had been ribbed by her friends because of her moment of distinction when Air Vice-Marshal Connisby recognised Mark as the pilot who had helped to sell the Harrier to a visiting Arab ruler earlier in the year. Sitting with Vince and his wife, Jeff and his latest good-time girl, and Jill with a suitably dressed cameraman, Maggie good naturedly bore their predictions of instant promotion and invitations to NATO Headquarters for "secret manoeuvres" now she had been noticed by top brass. She was having a good time, although Mark's normal infectious vitality was somewhat subdued. Maybe he was tired or, better, reserving his energy for later.

On her way to the ladies' Maggie noticed the Prices sitting alone. Rusty and Marsha had made a foursome for a while, but they were ignoring each other and Fiona had made no attempt to converse with either of them so they left early. Jill was probably right in saying the wives who had once tried to befriend Fiona had no time for her, and those avid for their husbands' advancement would dislike her even more after her success with the VIPs.

The married men had not dared to dance with the sexiest woman there, although they surely would have if their wives had not been watching them carefully. A few of the raunchier bachelors, including Jeff, had risked censure from their partners for the chance to charm the stunning Mrs Price but, after the departure of the senior men who could use the excuse of social duty to circle the floor with her, Randal had mostly danced with his wife.

Once, when they had passed Maggie and Mark, he had winked at her and said, "Insurance policy against magic messages, I take it."

Already irritated by the smug expression he had worn all evening, she had given him a sour smile. Now, as she powdered her nose in the ladies' room, she wondered if her expression had been similar when Mark was singled out by Connisby. Pot calling the kettle, she told herself with a grimace as she returned to where the tempo was hotting up.

Mark was a dancer with more willingness than flair, but their little group made the most of the music and the alcohol to throw themselves into the revels. Maggie was getting her breath back and relishing the coming night with Mark when the band struck up an unusual bongo beat.

Jeff said swiftly to Vince, "Come on, let's get the poor sod on the floor for this."

They crossed to Randal and, when he shook his head, grabbed his arms to haul him to his feet. Other members of B Flight skated across the polished floor to hijack their boss and pull him, laughing and protesting, to centre stage where someone put an ice-bucket upside down on his head like a fez. Maggie watched him capitulate and, with melting ice cubes wetting his cheeks and shoulders, begin a comical kind of Egypian conga with a line of his colleagues behind him. Advancing with knees bent, one arm outstretched in a pecking movement and the other arm doing the same behind their backs in time with the beat, they crossed the room and snaked around the tables behind their commander who appeared to have come vitally alive.

"Come on, Maggie," shouted Jeff as they undulated past. "It's B Flight's speciality."

Laughing, she jumped up and fell in behind him, copying the "Pharaonic" movements with gusto. The musicians were as entertained as the onlookers and emphasised the beat, while men still at the tables called out rude or encouraging comments. By the time the band reprised the number, B Flight's ground crew officers had joined the conga line, and they made very un-Egyptian threats to A Flight members who tried to trip them up or whack their behinds as they danced past. It was fun, it was crazy and it was highly entertaining for everyone.

The band began a third rendition as the line headed out to the entrance hall. When Randal re-entered there was a roar of laughter as he had now balanced on top of the "fez" a basket of flowers snatched up from a table beside the main door of the Mess. It miraculously stayed in place as he snaked around tables again, and it even remained secure when a squadron leader from A Flight placed a full glass of beer in the midst of the flowers.

The music finally ended with a roll of drums and crashing cymbals. Randal was surrounded and noisily urged to drink the beer in one draught, after which he pretended to collapse on the floor. Vince swiftly placed the flowers on Randal's chest, and the band concluded the fun by playing a few bars from the "Dead March".

Order was gradually restored as flight members picked up their boss and dusted him down before dispersing to their seats. When Maggie returned to their table she found Mark missing. Following the direction of Jill's knowing nod she felt a surprisingly sharp stab of jealousy on seeing him deep in conversation with Fiona Price. So that was why he was subdued. His "wow" had been more heartfelt than Maggie guessed.

She was halfway across the floor towards them when Randal reached his wife. Grinning and giving a comical bow, he presented the basket of flowers. "For the most beautiful woman in the room."

Fiona ignored the flowers, saying coolly, "I think it's time we left."

He put the basket on the chair beside her. "It'll wind up in thirty minutes or so. Might as well see it through."

His wife stood, her expression cold. "I've smiled and simpered at the VIPs and I've danced with a succession of old bores and young gropers. I've done my duty for your precious career, Randal, and I want to leave *now*." She glanced at the young pilot beside her who had also got to his feet. "Mark has told me he's spending the night at Farley Grange, so why doesn't he drive me there while you stay and play with the other little boys until going-home time?"

Her cultured voice carried in the comparative hush between dances, but Maggie was unaware of heads turning so heated was her anger. "Mark is my partner tonight, and I'm not ready to leave. If you really can't bear to wait another half-hour, Mrs Price, I suggest you drive yourself to the hotel and we'll give your husband a lift when this best part of the evening ends."

Randal spoke up quickly, and only then did Maggie turn to see his gaunt expression. "It's OK, Maggie. You two go off and enjoy yourselves. Goodnight," he added with a nod at Mark, then he gripped his wife's elbow and led her out.

"The bitch!" said Maggie explosively, watching Fiona's sexily swinging hips as she walked beside a man who had changed in an instant to the grim-faced person Maggie had encountered on arrival at Hampton. "How *can* he put up with that?"

"Take a good look at her," advised Mark dryly.

She rounded on him. "You certainly did."

"Your temper's showing, sweetie."

"Bra-less Fiona was showing a lot more than her temper. It drew you like a magnet."

He gently tucked a strand of hair behind her right ear. "She was sitting alone; I was sitting alone. I was merely being sociable."

"Oh yeah? You could have joined in the fun."

He shook his head. "That was a team thing, not for outsiders." He took her arm. "Let's look at the stars and calm down."

As they reached the cool darkness they saw a red Porsche roar away towards the main gate.

"I hope to God their room isn't next to ours. Whatever he gets from her tonight, it ain't goin' to be fun!" mused Mark.

Still angry, Maggie asked, "Have you brought me out here to watch her disappear into the night, or is there another reason?"

He shrugged. "After that marital venom I thought we could do with some air. Let's walk."

Maggie's jealous wrath faded to unease. He had not been himself all evening. Whatever was behind his mood she sensed that it concerned her more than Fiona Price. As they strolled in the warm midsummer night with the music only a faint sound on the still air, Maggie knew as surely as if the man beside her were her twin that there was a subtle change in their relationship. That familiar sixth sense was confused, however, by conflicting messages.

"He's done that before, I imagine?"

"Sorry?"

"Your boss; that Middle East conga."

"Oh. He also does a Bavarian dance that's a hoot to watch." Maggie kept talking to delay what she knew he would soon say. "He's a brilliant pilot and he leads the flight with energy and understanding. He can be extremely provoking, but he's also great fun when he gets going. Why on earth does he throw sanity to the four winds over that woman? He's a complete fool!"

"Women make fools of most of us sometime in our lives."

She halted, cursing the fact that she had given him the opening he needed. "Is that what you brought me out here to say?

Something's been on your mind all evening, so you'd better come out with it."

He was silent, gazing at the stars with a troubled expression until Maggie spoke his name. He looked down at her almost apologetically. "I'm getting very serious about you and I'm not sure what to do about it. It's absolutely the wrong bloody time. I'm riding the crest of a wave and want to go on doing it. In another few years . . . Hell, Maggie, you're the same. Been with your squadron only six months and loving every day of it. You've told me enough times. We're both under thirty. It's just the wrong bloody time to get serious."

Maggie's throat was dry. "You want to end it?"

"I didn't say that, did I?"

She shook her head. "I've been serious about you from the very first moment."

He managed a faint smile. "You were on a binge at the time."

"And you were on medication."

"What an introduction! I'm surprised you bothered with me after the situation I landed you in."

"Must have been because you're such a clever dick."

He hesitated for a moment then said, "I'm aiming to be even cleverer. I applied some time ago to join the Red Arrows. I didn't say anything to you because I was one of forty or more hopefuls. I heard this morning I've been shortlisted. At this stage the team members themselves decide on the lucky three, and I've several pals there who'll root for me. So, unless I do something bloody stupid and foul up, there's every chance I'll be in the team come September."

"Darling, how *marvellous*! Why didn't you tell me as soon as you got here?"

"You're really pleased?" He sounded surpised.

"Of course! It's so special; so once-in-a-lifetime." She kissed him with enthusiasm. "You love showing off and with them you can do it on a grand scale."

"It's not certain until they offer me the job. I wouldn't have told you now, except . . ."

"Except what?"

He sighed. "I've seen the other you tonight. Wearing that uniform with the wings, being introduced to the VIPs as *Flight Lieutenant* Spencer. Even that crazy Egyptian conga made me realise you're no ordinary woman. You're a career girl; part of a team doing an important job."

"You've always known that, Mark."

"I didn't really take it on board. There was no need. We had fun, shared a lot of interests, it was great in bed. What more could I want."

"Is that a question or a statement?"

He walked on a few paces, then turned to face her again. "If I get this opportunity it'll be a three-year stint. I'll be based at Cranwell, but I'll spend eighty per cent of the time chasing all over the UK and abroad. It's difficult enough trying to get together now and Cranwell's a hell of a distance from here. That's why it's the bloody wrong time to get serious."

Her spontaneous excitement was subsiding rapidly as he outlined the realities. "So you do want to end it."

"Didn't you hear me just now? Oh Christ, there's no easy way to say this. I'll be taking on a really demanding job with very little time off during the display season. The only hope for us would be if you applied for a ground posting at Cranwell, and I know that's not on." He reached out and took her hands. "The survival rate for relationships under such circumstances is low, *liefling*. I think it'd be a mistake to exchange any promises, but if you haven't found anyone you like better when the three years are up maybe we could consider something more permanent."

Daunted by his words, Maggie's initial reaction was to try to make light of everything. "Once you put on that red flying suit you'll be interviewed, photographed, hero-worshipped and propositioned by hordes of women. When your three years are up I'll be lucky to get your autograph, much less anything more permanent."

With obvious relief Mark followed her lead and said teasingly, "In that case, you'd better come to Farley Grange and get what you can while it's still available."

She gazed up at him. "If you're going to join a team of the biggest clever dicks in the world, you'd better make it impressive. Anything less will be a terrible let-down."

"Wow, what a challenge! Come on, let's see how I make out."

Randal drove at speed along the dark coast road leading to Hampton Heyhoe, tugging loose his bow tie and grappling with the stud holding together his stiff collar.

"For God's sake keep both hands on the wheel," Fiona snapped. "You're not in the air now."

He was a fast but skilled driver under normal conditions. Tonight he had been drinking and anger ruled him. After clearing the village he threw the car around twisting lanes empty of daytime tourist traffic, and did the twenty-minute journey in fifteen. He wisely shunned a space between two BMWs and parked well clear of other vehicles. Venting his feelings by slamming the car door, he ran up the steps to the busy foyer and collected the room key, ignoring the receptionist's smiling, "Goodnight, sir."

Once in the room he tore off his collar and tossed it on the bed before prowling around the restricted space until Fiona entered and closed the door behind her.

"You're still behaving like a little boy," she accused. "Flouncing up here like a bad-tempered brat in front of the other guests."

"What the hell were you playing at back there?" he exploded. "You've sneered before at what you call my juvenile antics, but I won't have you doing it in public."

Her brows rose. "Public? A young South African and his girlfriend."

"Maggie's a pilot in my flight. I'm her boss."

"Is that what she was supposed to be?"

"Not supposed: *is*. How dare you bloody put me down in front of her!"

She paled. "Do you want everyone in the hotel to hear you?"

"I don't give a piss," he countered harshly. "They're all strangers. But those people tonight are my friends and colleagues. One night, that's all I've asked of you. *One flaming night*, and you couldn't even do that without showing your contempt for what I do."

Fiona flung her jewelled purse on the bed. "My God, I gave your career a hearty upward shove by charming a beefy Yank and simpering at a Nordic lecher. I had my toes bruised by stupid old buffers and I was pawed by arrogant young bastards stinking of beer. I don't know what more I could have done to boost what you do."

"Kept your mouth shut! I know your opinion of my job – I've heard it enough times – but you shared it with everyone within earshot. It was degrading."

"More so than dancing around with a basket of flowers on your head and guzzling beer?" She kicked off her shoes, her eyes glittering coldly. "You ask me to support you at boring service dos then behave like a lager lout. How d'you think that affects *me*? Isn't that putting *me* down in public?"

The truth hit him like a flash of lightning. "No, pussycat, it's called stealing your thunder. What upset you was a shift of focus from the dazzling Mrs Price to someone else. And don't quote lager lout at me. I've been to some of your horsey parties, and baskets of flowers on heads is nothing to what they get up to when they're fully ginned-up. When someone shouts 'They're off!' they're not generally referring to horses."

"Oh, how typical," she cried. "You always hit back by ridiculing my lifestyle. It's a damn sight classier than yours. 'No, sir, the Price family only breeds pork pies,'" she mimicked derisively. "Me put you down, Randal? You put yourself down when you say things like that to men who could help you. I worked hard to impress them but I most probably wasted my time. If they're anything like you and your pals, they'll have just two interests: what moves through the air and what moves in their underpants."

He stood trying to accept that she had said that, then he swung round and charged into the bathroom where he threw things into a toilet bag. Back in the bedroom he dragged his holdall from the wardrobe and began thrusting into it spare trousers, a sports shirt, underwear and socks.

"What are you doing?" demanded Fiona in a voice high with emotion.

Randal zipped the holdall and walked to the door. "I'm about to give you a taste of what it's like when someone walks out on you."

She looked incredulous. "You can't! For God's sake grow up." As he gripped the door handle she changed tactics. "I warn you, if you go off you'll regret it."

"Don't try that line, Fiona. I may be a pushover when you come on to me full throttle, but threats release an entirely different animal."

He passed Maggie and Mark on the stairs as if they were strangers, and he saw nothing of the receptionist's surprise as he left the hotel.

197

August

D ave had never wailed at the wall as much as he did on discovering he was listed for one of the most unpopular tasks of all. His colleagues' jeers did not help, nor did their sly jibes of "Who's a pretty boy, then?" prompted by the fact that good looks were often a decisive factor. B Flight had to provide a Chinook for static display at a four-day air show, and any event which put the RAF beneath the public gaze had to show the service in the best possible light. Looks and personality were taken into account when selecting a crew to answer questions and explain all aspects of their work and aircraft.

Maggie had volunteered – unheard of before – and everyone knew why. Her lover would be giving an aerial display in his Harrier. She suffered worse tormenting than Dave but, for once, their flight commander did nothing to stop it. He had not been in a good mood lately. Again, everyone knew why. Pete had been chosen because a navigator could be more easily spared than a second pilot when other demands on the Flight were heavy. Pete was not happy, and with Rusty full of moans because Marsha had kicked him out of her cottage, there were a number of glum expressions in B Flight's crew room. Dave was suffering deep personal uncertainty, but not a soul knew about that.

Dave was promised four days of purgatory, and his friends were not far wrong. Each day between ten and six thirty there was a stream of visitors to the Chinook. There were the kind who walked up the ramp to the cabin, looked around, said, "Big, isn't it?" then left. There were World War veterans who told tales and wished they had had such versatile aircraft in their day. There were others who looked the Chinook over without a word, then grunted that it was not a *proper* aeroplane; and there were the helicopter aficionados. These stayed interminably, buttonholing a crew member, reeling off the statistics and history of any aircraft that had ever sported a rotor. When they eventually departed, clutching their notebooks lovingly filled in during long winter evenings and having had a thoroughly satisfying day, Maggie, Dave, Pete or Jimmy felt exhausted.

Worst of all were the young boys who wandered around pulling levers, pushing knobs and turning handles, saying, "What's this for?" before they could be stopped. They asked endless questions. "How many screws in this chopper?" "What happens if the rotor flies off?" "How many miles has it done?" "If you fly backwards how do you see where you're going?"

There was another aspect of this duty: giggling teenage girls wearing next to nothing in the summer heat pestered Dave and Pete with sexual innuendo and invitations to meet them when they had a tea break. Maggie had the same problem with a few men. Jimmy, four times a father, had been selected to deal with the children, but even he, surely no one's idea of a heart-throb, had his share of attention from the girls. By halfway through the first day Dave knew why B Flight dreaded this.

The weather was sunny and hot, making time spent inside the cabin something of a punishment. The only compensation came to Maggie. After Mark Hascham's spectacular display she took her long break to spend time with him before he flew back to Wittering. Dave and Jimmy, who shared a hotel room next to hers, later heard her talking endlessly to him on the telephone after dinner.

"She's got it bad," Jimmy said knowledgeably.

For the short periods during which Dave had seen them together he recognised that Mark and Maggie felt something deeper than he had known with Leanne: something akin to what Edwina Rowan had felt for Ralph Finlayson? A devotion so strong she had run from him and her family to bear his child rather than harm his future. Dave wondered whether, if Maggie became pregnant by Hascham, she would go quietly from his life rather than ruin his career with the truth. There was no real parallel; Hascham was not married, modern thinking had destroyed many former stigmas, and there was no proud Highland family involved – or proud regiment, for that matter.

Since reading Edwina's letter Dave had been tormented by uncertainty over whether or not to tell Finlayson. She had left it to him and he could not think of them as his parents. He had never known the young girl who had lied about Ashmore being her husband, and Dave had met her lover for the first time only weeks ago. The instinct for self-preservation urged him to destroy the letter and get on with his life, and yet . . .

Time and again Dave asked himself if Edwina's love would have survived if she had confronted her seducer with the result of his passion and seen his reaction. Would Finlayson have acknowledged parentage and supported her, or would he have slipped her a few hundred pounds to have it aborted? *It* being David Oliver.

Had Edwina been heroically selfless or had her youthful infatuation not survived the shock of pregnancy? Had the easy-going Ashmore been a convenient way out? If only he could understand the true nature of that relationship between a romantic seventeen-year-old and a married subaltern destined for high rank, Dave might know how to act.

On the third evening of the show he walked beside the river which ran through the town, still racked by indecision and cursing himself for being so weak. He had to make swift decisions on the job and during his sporting activities, so why was he waffling over this? Still unable to settle the matter, he returned to the stuffy hotel room where Jimmy was watching TV and drinking beer.

Jimmy switched off the set when Dave entered and let rip. "Another bloody thing with no ending! You sit for an hour or more watching a group of people tie themselves in knots, and just as you're wondering how they'll sort it out up go the credits and you realise you've been conned again. God, *I* could write a spicy play – plenty of hot stuff going on at Hampton for a start – and leave the whole thing up in the air. Any fool could." He threw Dave a can of beer and opened another for himself. "What happened to the good old-fashioned writers who gave us an exciting yarn then came up with an ingenious solution? There's no such thing these days as a whodunnit. Even the crappy writers don't know who done it. I could kick myself for sitting here watching that rubbish."

Dave sat heavily on the bed with his beer. "You should have come for a walk."

Jimmy shook his head. "I rarely get the chance to watch without the kids around."

"But if the programme has no ending . . ."

"You don't know that until the bloody credits go up, do you? Anyway, I didn't want to cramp your style with the girls down by the river. It's time you got yourself a bit of tasty, Dave.

200

You've got something under your sporran. Use it before it seizes up."

Purely to move off that subject, Dave said, "Did you ever watch that series several years back when they acted out a drama and left a panel of guests to decide how it should end?"

"I've just seen one like that," Jimmy grunted. "I'd tell them it never should have started. Christ, it's hot in here. They forecast another scorcher tomorrow. Last day, thank God."

Dave was not listening. He had been struck by a possible solution to his problem. "That series I was on about; there was one I particularly remember because the panel got quite aggressive about their opinions." He knew Jimmy had half his mind elsewhere but he persevered. "There was a young guy making a name for himself in business and set to go to the top. His parents were killed when he was a baby and he was brought up by relatives of his father. They emigrated to Australia when this guy was adult, but they kept in touch." Dave was inventing like mad but he had Jimmy's attention.

"So what was the problem?"

He had to think fast. "The old man in Australia died and his solicitor sent the guy a letter acting on instructions in the will. The letter was written by his mother twenty years earlier, telling him his real father was the son of the old man's closest friend, an up-and-coming politician married to some socialite."

"Randy devil. Typical of a politician," observed Jimmy.

Dave pushed on. "The letter said his mother and her lover had cared deeply for each other but she had never told him about his child."

"Didn't her husband have something to say about it, or did he think the kid was his?"

Dave brushed that aside. "The mother left her son to decide whether or not to contact his true father. By this time, he's chairman of his political party and well liked. He's also a widower with no children."

"Apart from the one he doesn't know about." Jimmy upended the can. "So?"

"So the panel had to decide whether the guy should spill the beans or what."

Jimmy scratched his side and frowned. "Wouldn't get far. The guy has no proof apart from his mother's letter. Could be any man's child, although there's DNA these days. Can't see the MP agreeing to be tested, can you? What did they decide?"

Caught on the hop, Dave said wildly, "They couldn't. That's why I remember it so well."

Jimmy opened another beer thoughtfully, now caught up in the problem. "If there was money involved it might influence things but the young guy would still be on shifting ground. I mean, the MP isn't going to welcome his bastard son with open arms and he'd be in a position to have it laughed out of court. These politicians all have friends who'll get them out of trouble. You scratch my back and so on. No, I think he'd be wiser to leave things as they stand. He's managed all right without his father so far, and he's doing well in business, you said?"

"Oh aye."

"Then he'd gain nothing and instead stand to lose by taking on a public figure with connections in all the right places. Interesting. Sorry I missed that series; sounds right up my street. Tell me some of the other set-ups." He settled back ready to make a session of it.

"Eh? It was some time ago. I don't remember any others." Dave headed for the bathroom. "I'm going to take a shower."

The spray cooled his body and he relaxed. Why had he not thought to ask someone's opinion of a supposedly hypothetical case before this? Jimmy had strengthened his own feeling that he should leave well alone. When he got back to Hampton he would tear up the letter and put the whole thing out of his mind. More light-hearted than he had been for weeks, Dave tucked a towel around his waist and returned to the bedroom.

"Been thinking," said Jimmy, glancing up at him. "There's another side to it. Why should the bugger get off scot-free? I have to support my four monsters on my measly salary. This MP didn't have any legit kids so why shouldn't he fork out something for the one he had on the side?" He stood and headed for the bathroom. "If I'd been on that panel I think I'd have said the son should have a word with the editor of the *Daily Mirror*. That'd fix chummy fair and square, no matter what friends he had." He went for a shower, yawning and scratching his side.

At five a.m., after very little sleep, Dave pulled on jog trousers and a shirt to go down to the hotel lounge where there was a writing desk with a supply of paper. He began his letter.

Dear Colonel Finlayson,

I enclose a copy of a letter written by Edwina Rowan and forwarded to me by the family solicitor on the death of Sir Hector. I'm sending it only because I think she would want you to know what she did for you, for my uncle and for the regiment. If you cared at all about her this news should make you feel very humble. If she meant nothing, you'll toss this in the bin. What you do isn't important to me, but after weeks of uncertainty I've decided that between the lines she is asking me to do what she wouldn't. I suppose I owe her that. I want nothing from you.

He signed and folded the sheet before sliding it inside an envelope bearing the hotel's crest. Back at Hampton, he would take a copy of Edwina's letter to send with it, and that would be the end of the business. As it had been when resigning his commission to train as a loadmaster, his mind was now made up and would not change. He was master of his own life again.

The day followed the usual pattern, although the smiles of service personnel, caterers and first-aid providers were hard to maintain as double the numbers poured through the gates, lured by the final-day appearance of the Red Arrows. David Oliver Ashmore/Finlayson was however on top form as he told small boys there were eighty thousand, four hundred and eight screws in the Chinook – it varied from hour to hour – and chatted easily to men about winches, pulleys, strops and load differentials. He happily recited how to load and offload fully equipped troops, and described how the aircraft could swiftly turn into an aerial ambulance. He did not scowl at aficionados and was even persuaded to walk to the nearest bar tent with an American brunette whose father was in the design room at Boeing. She was flying home on the morrow so he felt safe enough.

When he returned there were snide remarks from Jimmy and Pete, while Maggie had on her Cheshire cat grin. "Oh aye, you can all think your filthy thoughts," he said equably. "She'd been on a tour of Scotland and wanted to talk about it."

"And the rest," jeered Pete. "Did you show her your hairy knees?"

"Good thing she hadn't visited Munich," teased Maggie. "What would you have talked about then?"

Dave vowed he would get back at her one day over that; she never let pass an opportunity to remind him of the cowbell episode. As the stream of visitors had ceased now that the aerial displays had begun, they sat on the grass in the shade, glad of a break and seeing the end of this onerous duty in sight.

Pete glanced at his watch. "Romeo should be arriving any minute, Maggie. Better powder your nose."

Jimmy chuckled. "After raising his adrenalin in that Harrier what makes you think it's her nose he'd be interested in?"

"It's *his* nose that'll be put out of joint today," said Dave slyly. "The Red Arrows are the real Romeos."

Maggie turned to look at him, a flush of excitement on her face. "He's joining them next month. They gave him the news when he got back to Wittering and he phoned me last night. We're going out to celebrate tomorrow."

"That's great, Maggie," said Jimmy warmly. "Lucky devil."

"That's the last you'll see of him," advised Pete. "Those guys are so full of themselves one woman is nowhere near enough. I'll be happy to comfort you when he vanishes to the wilds of Lincoln."

"Thanks, but no." Maggie grinned at him. "Although I suppose I'd get *very* expensive Christmas presents."

"Oh, ha ha!" he returned sourly. "She came back for more, though."

"You're a fool, Pete. She'll go off again as soon as someone catches her eye."

"Yeah, well, we'll see how long Master Hascham stays around after September."

"There he is, right on time," murmured Dave as the Harrier swept across the airfield with a roar. In that moment he felt a surge of deep envy, and he wondered yet again if he would have made the grade as a pilot without Leanne. Would he have got to fly fast jets? Could he have emulated this man Maggie was crazy about? The yearning to be in the cockpit returned with a vengeance. He had continued taking private flying lessons but his instructor said he was wasting his money because his attendance was too irregular. He saw the sense in that. Four lessons in six months! When he did spend time at Hampton he was seldom free during the day, and when he was either the weather grounded everything or the instructors were fully booked.

Maggie had got to her feet to stand beside the cockpit and

watch her lover thrill the crowd, gazing upward as he dived and climbed against the brilliant sky. Dave was driven to her side by resurgent regret and longing. Mark Hascham was the luckiest man alive to be doing this and nursing the knowledge that he had been chosen to join the most renowned aerobatic team in the world. God, how Dave envied him.

The Harrier climbed steeply yet again; there was an explosion, a spurt of flame, and the jet slowly keeled over to fall in several pieces to the ground somewhere beyond the airfield. The plume of black smoke looked to be about two miles from where they were standing.

Randal had returned after an overnight trip to Northern Ireland and was spending the afternoon in his office catching up with the paperwork he loathed. When the telephone rang yet again he snatched up the receiver and growled, "Price."

"Boss, it's Dave. I'm glad you're there. Mark Hascham's Harrier blew up and crashed. Maggie was watching."

Randal grew cold. "Jesus Christ! Get her to a doctor."

"She won't go."

"Then get the sodding man to her," he shouted.

"It's pandemonium here: some women have fainted, kids are screaming. There's a rush for the parking areas. The ghouls are trying to reach the crash site."

"Isn't it there?" he asked sharply.

"About two miles off, I'd say."

"What state's she in?"

"Severe shock. She won't move, won't speak. When we try to touch her she fights us off. Keeps staring at the black smoke."

"Poor kid!"

"There's no hope of finding a doctor. Thousands are trying to leave – other aerial displays have been cancelled – but someone said all the roads are blocked.

"Right. You know your stuff, Dave. Give Maggie a shot to calm her down, then bin it and come back."

"Who's going to fly us?"

"Oh, Christ!" Randal thought swiftly. "I'll be there as soon as I can fix it."

"Watch it, the sky's full of media. Mainly over the crash site but they're swarming like bees. It was some explosion."

"Look after Maggie and for Christ's sake don't let on to

anyone she was Hascham's girl. The press will hound her to death."

When Squadron Leader Price was determined he mowed down all obstacles and he was soon a passenger in a Puma programmed for a navigational practice flight and now heading for the airfield. He and the crew spoke little during the forty-five-minute flight, except to comment on information coming in over the airwaves. All roads were reported blocked by stationary cars left across narrow lanes while the passengers trampled crops to get a ringside view of the funeral pyre of Flight Lieutenant Mark Hascham.

Reports continued to come in. Police helicopters were flying more men in to control the situation and air ambulances were on their way to take out people suffering from shock and the heat. Road rage was rife between motorists jamming the junctions around the airfield and a woman had given premature birth in a first-aid tent.

"She'll probably call the kid Harrier," said the pilot savagely.

Nearing the scene they were told to circle outside the immediate airspace, priority being given to police and medical aircraft.

"Come on! Come on!" Randal fumed, as the minutes ticked past. "This is an emergency too, chum."

They received permission to approach and land. The airfield had litter blowing like tumbleweed across the brown grass. A few broken canvas stools had been abandoned; beer and coke cans lay everywhere and streamers of striped boundary tape fluttered in the breeze. Stalls and tents were being dismantled; knots of people stood beside the static displays. Here and there picnics were going on as wiser spectators left others to rant and rave in overheating cars. The sun boiled down on static lines of vehicles on country roads.

"There they are." Randal pointed over the pilot's shoulder. "Put me down as close to them as you can, Jon."

The Puma hovered three feet from the ground as Randal jumped out and signalled his thanks. Then it rose and swung away well clear of the media aircraft angling for the best shots of the burning wreck. Pete hurried towards Randal. He looked strained.

"No hope of a medic, Rip. Dave's tried to give her a shot several times but she's not having any."

"She'll have to," he snapped, crossing the parched grass. "Christ, there's three of you."

"All right, you have a go," snapped Pete in reply. "Do you think we just sat back and let her suffer?"

Maggie was standing beside the cockpit, staring at what was now a thin drift of dark smoke on the horizon. Her face was ashen, her green eyes wide and staring. It was plain she was unaware of anything but the vision locked in her memory. Randal slowed, involuntarily caught up in her pain. Dave came forward. He looked deeply shaken.

"I couldn't do anything. She looks calm but fights like mad if you touch her. I've never seen anything like this before. I'm sorry."

Randal halted. He *had* seen it before, during the Gulf War as a very young pilot. This girl had seen a man she loved die publicly in a ball of flame. It was more than her mind could accept. That was what she was fighting, not her friends. She was watching for that Harrier to climb into the blue and make everything all right again.

Keeping his gaze on Maggie, he said quietly to Dave, "Have that shot ready. She's going to need it soon."

Standing three feet from her Randal made no attempt to move nearer and touch her. Instead, he began speaking in a firm authoritative voice. "Maggie, he's gone. It's all over. It's no use waiting here. He won't come. He won't come however long you stay. Mark's gone, Maggie. It's all over."

He lost track of how many minutes passed while he steadily repeated the words she would refuse to hear until she could deny them no longer. He grew oblivious of all that was going on around him as he watched her stricken face and remembered it laughing, defiant, determined or glowing with life and love. He ached for her loss but this was the easy part. Once she accepted the truth the pain would be insupportable.

He began to recognise the first signs and braced himself. Her body started to tremble, slightly at first, and then the tremble became a shake. She still stared with horror in her eyes but now saw him there. Her mouth moved, her teeth began to chatter.

"Why? Why? Why?" she whispered convulsively.

He inched nearer. "No one ever knows the answer, Maggie."

Her shakes worsened. Tears began to roll down her white cheeks. Randal moved even closer.

"He was . . . he was such a . . . such a c-clever dick." She gave a terrible moan and would have folded up if Randal had not grabbed her and held her very close as she was racked with agonised sobbing.

Over her shoulder he saw the other three watching with tense expressions. Dave held up the syringe but Randal gave a slight negative gesture. Only a strong man could prise her away from the support she needed so desperately. When the terror eased he would coax her to the cabin and let Dave give her the shot to deaden her senses. Keeping a firm grip on Maggie he indicated with head movements that they should get the Chinook ready to leave.

Speaking soft words of assurance and stroking her hair – much as he did to comfort Lydia when the child was distraught – Randal waited for the right moment. When it came, he coaxed her very slowly inside the familiar cabin. She still clung to him, shaking so badly she stumbled several times. When Dave approached she was too exhausted to care what he did, although Randal explained gently that the shot would help her. With Dave's help he got her seated and strapped in. She refused to lie down and Randal squatted before her until the drug took effect.

"We're going home, Maggie," he said. "Dave and Jimmy'll be here with you. OK?"

She nodded like a zombie, and he knew it was time to get going. Several times during the flight to Hampton, Randal looked over his shoulder to check and saw Maggie slumped against Dave, who had a supporting arm around her. The station ambulance drove out to meet them and Dave went with her to the sick bay. He had been standing beside her when the disaster had occurred so he was best able to describe the pattern of her behaviour.

Leaving Pete and Jimmy still looking shaken, Randal reported to the Station Commander, John Baldwin. After his brief report on what had taken place, Randal was given some extraordinary news.

"A few minutes after the Puma took off the switchboard put through a call from a Philip Spencer, who was extremely agitated and concerned about Maggie. He said he's her twin brother and had just received evidence that she was badly hurt." Baldwin frowned. "He knew nothing about the Harrier crash; he thought his sister had been in a smash-up of some kind. It was weird, there's no other word for it. I wasn't sure how much he knew about Maggie's relationship with Hascham so I gave him a carefully worded assurance that she was unhurt but somewhat shocked. Made no difference. He said he would drive here and arrive about . . ." he glanced at the clock on the wall, "about now. Can you make any sense of it, Rip?"

"I think so. Well, I suppose I can. Maggie said they can send each other . . ." He hesitated. The phrase "magic messages" was too flippant, he realised. Small wonder she had resented it. "They can sense when the other is in trouble, apparently. But I understood it was at an end."

"What was at an end?"

"The . . . er . . . the contact." He was thunderstruck by what he had been told. How could her brother have known?

The senior man studied him. "You look bushed. You're rather close to that girl, aren't you?"

Randal detected a note of censure and bridled. "She's in my team, sir. I'm close to them all."

"Yes, of course. This is a bad business, Rip. The media are already hinting at sabotage; terrorist activity."

"*What*?"

"We've just sold Harriers to an Arab."

"Oh, come on."

"Who could be acting as an agent for someone with powerful enemies in that part of the world."

"Yes, but—"

"Then there are the pacifist cranks who see air shows as displays of military power."

"They are."

"The press have already unearthed the fact that Hascham was South African. Good copy can be made from that."

With angry sarcasm Randal said, "Those bloodsuckers could link him with animal rights, hunt saboteurs or those nuts who sit in trees to prevent motorway construction if they put their minds to it."

"Well, the accident investigation team'll find the truth. It sure as hell can't be blamed on pilot error. Not this time," said Baldwin.

"We'll have to ensure the news-hounds don't get wind of Maggie's connection with Hascham. She'll suffer enough without them prying."

"I've seen to that. She's one of *my* team, too," came the acid reminder. "However, I'll leave you to deal with the brother as you

209

seem to be *au fait* with this strange business." The CO shook his head. "I've never before had a call from a relative telling *me* what no one here has yet told *him* about one of my aircrew. Weird. No other word for it." As Randal reached the door, he added, "When you've dealt with the brother have a stiff drink. You look as if you need one."

Reaching his office without meeting Jeffries, Randal sat reflecting on the astonishing fact that the ESP between the twins was still strong. Maggie had sworn to him it would never happen again because they had both grown too close to other people. He rose restlessly, unable to forget her agonised "Why? Why? Why?" And what the hell had John Baldwin been suggesting a moment ago? Dave, Pete and Jimmy were equally concerned. They were a team; they supported each other. There was no difference because Maggie was a woman. To hell with anyone who suggested there was.

His glance fell on the teddy bear wearing Fiona Hunter's tiny woolly jumper. The bear had arrived anonymously in the office one morning, although everyone knew who must have put him there. B Flight had immediately adopted him as their mascot and Rusty had dubbed him Rip Van Bruin. Maggie had dressed the bear in the jumper intended for Lydia's toy and Jeff had taken a photograph to send to the little girl on the clifftop waiting for a kidney transplant. B Flight appeared to have adopted her, too.

When a corporal ushered in Philip Spencer, Randal had a mild shock. He was uncannily like Maggie, which took a while to accept. His eyes were dark with pain and he was clearly very upset. Randal decided to cut the preliminaries and said right away that Maggie had told him about their bond of twinship.

"We can not only sense but experience each other's distress. It's as strong as that," he asserted. "And we're never wrong. At three this afternoon I had such an immense sensation of pain I knew Mags was suffering. I had no idea where she was or how to contact her, so I rang to ask and was put through to your commander. I was convinced she'd crashed, but he said something about it happening to a friend. When he told me she was flying back here, I had to come." His expression grew as determined as his sister's when she took a stand against any of them. "What I felt was so overwhelming I'm afraid I couldn't accept what your commander told me. I *know* she's suffering in some way."

"Not now. She's under sedation in our sick quarters. I'll take you over presently and you can see the MO." Still unsettled by this man's close resemblance to the girl he had come to know well, Randal hesitated before asking, "How much do you know about Mark Hascham?"

He looked puzzled. "Sorry?"

"He was killed when the Harrier he was flying exploded during an aerobatic display. Maggie and he were . . . well, they were deeply involved. At three this afternoon she watched him plunge to the ground in a ball of fire."

Philip Spencer paled further. "Oh, my God! I heard about the disaster on the car radio but I never linked . . . God, how terrible! Poor Mags!" He sat coming to terms with that for a moment or two, then he glanced across at Randal. "I knew nothing about this man. I thought she was dating an American financier."

"He was given his marching orders in January."

"I see." He frowned. "You seem to know a lot about her."

"If you fly with someone it's inevitable. When we're overseas the whole flight is billeted together. If we're on exercise Maggie's quite likely to sleep in a tent with three of us. We spend more time together than with our families. We *all* know each other pretty well."

Maggie's brother was not certain how to take that but apparently decided it was something of a rebuke. "In that case, you probably find it odd that I said my sister and I are so close and yet I hadn't any idea about who she's been seeing. There's a reason. Since Christmas it's been one thing after another. My wife—"

Randal got to his feet. "You don't owe me any explanation, Mr Spencer. You came when she needed you. That's the important thing. Shall we have a chat with the MO?"

Squadron Leader Prior was friendly and cheerful, reassuring them both that the effects of shock even as severe as Maggie had suffered subsided to containable levels within a day or two, when she would be granted leave. They glanced in at her but saw no more than a pale face on a pillow.

"She'll be drowsy until morning. I'll see how she is then. If she's anxious to get away someone should travel with her. I certainly couldn't let her drive herself anywhere. Are you staying overnight, Mr Spencer?" asked the MO.

He shook his head. "It's only a two-hour journey. Pointless to hang around when she's out for the count. I'll ring early

211

tomorrow, then come if you say she's recovered enough to be aware of me." He touched his sister gently on the forehead, and his voice was thick with emotion as he said," Tell her I knew and came right away. I want her to be told that as soon as she comes to. It'll help her." He glanced at the MO. "It really will."

"Yes, of course."

Randal was silent as Maggie's brother drove him back to the squadron offices. This twin business had always made him uncomfortable and dramatic evidence of it now added to the impact of today's tragedy. Seldom unequal to a situation, he found this one beyond him. Yet, when they pulled up alongside the hangars, he caught himself attempting to prolong it.

"I'm pretty well finished for today. How about a drink in the Mess before you leave? They'll rustle you up a sandwich if you're hungry."

"Thanks, but I'd prefer to get on my way. Left direct from the office and didn't call in at home on my way. Told my wife on the mobile where I was heading." He gave a nervous smile. "It'd be better to get back and fill in the details."

"Sure."

"Are you married?"

"Yes."

"Then you know how it is. They worry."

Randal ignored that. "Do you want me to get in touch with Maggie's . . . your parents?"

"No, I'll ring them tonight. And when she's fit enough I'll drive her up to their place outside York. That's if she'll let me."

"Don't give her any choice. It's the only way to handle her sometimes." Then he remembered who he was speaking to and changed direction. "She'll want to go with you. It'll be the best thing that can happen now. She . . . I had the impression that the bond between you was under strain lately."

Philip Spencer turned off the engine and twisted in his seat, faint embarrassment darkening his tanned cheeks. In that moment Randal saw Maggie so clearly in his features it unsettled him further. Her brother then spilled out a confession he plainly needed to make to someone. Randal had stopped him at his first attempt, but he now sat quietly listening to the full story of what Maggie had only hinted at under duress. There was no stopping this young man from revealing why she believed the ESP had ceased.

212

"It's been a hellish six months one way or another," he ended with a sigh. "Rob – he's our GP brother – wrote to Mags trying to mediate, but apart from brief telephone calls to our parents all any of us have had from her are birthday cards." He gave a rueful smile. "If the other woman in my life was a bimbo I'd deserve the grief from my wife and her."

With uncharacteristic insight Randal said, "I'm sure you'll find things easier on that score. You have Mark Hascham to thank for that."

"What kind of man was he?"

"You'll find out if you listen to the news but you should ask Maggie. She'll need to talk about him, particularly to you." He made to get out of the car.

With a heavy sigh Philip Spencer restarted the engine. "Poor Mags! What a terrible thing to see. I'll keep in touch with the MO and collect her as soon as she's ready." He leaned over to look up at Randal. "Sorry I've kept you so long. I expect you're anxious to get home. Goodbye and thanks."

Randal watched the car drive off, then stood irresolutely gazing at the dark clouds gathering to the west. The evening had grown sultry. There would be a storm later; he knew the signs. *I expect you're anxious to get home.* It was the obvious place to go to after a day like this but the atmosphere there was still cool after the row over the dinner dance. Fiona had been shaken by his walkout and pretended it had never happened. It came between them, all the same. They slept together; they had even made love. But the joy of their fresh start in a new luxury home had vanished. They were both simply going through the motions and making no real effort to tackle the problem.

Randal now saw the futility of what they were doing, the waste. At three this afternoon a gifted young pilot with an exciting future had had it snatched away. A lovely talented girl was lying here drugged because she had just lost the person who gave her existence the golden glow of loving. Life was so short, so unpredictable. He recalled the anguish of those hours while Neil lay unconscious. His son could well have been lost that night. That boy, his sweet little sister and their beautiful teasing mother all cast that golden glow over his own life. Why the hell was he allowing it to slip away from him through his own bloody-mindedness?

Turning swiftly, he took the stairs two at a time to his office where he snatched up the receiver and dialled.

"Fiona Price." Just hearing her helped.

"Hi! I'm coming home after all. It means having to leave again in the very early hours, but I've got this urge to be with you and that pair of little demons we've produced." He glanced at the clock. "I'm leaving right away. Should be there by nine. Earlier if I really put my foot down."

"Marianne, Charles, Pippa, Ben, Fran and Paul are coming for dinner. I asked them because you said you'd stay in the Mess."

"Oh Christ! I'd forgotten. Put them off, Fee. Please! I really need to be with you tonight."

"I can't put them off. They're already on their way. I told them eight for eight thirty." There was a short pause. "I suppose I could hold dinner until you get here, if it's that urgent, but you don't enjoy their company and I'll be furious if you start acting up."

"It's my bloody house!" He fought for control and eventually managed to ask, "Have you heard about the tragedy at the air show today?"

"I haven't had time to listen to any news. Mrs Barnes is OK with basics but she has no idea about *crudités* or *hors d'oeuvres*, and even less about mixing cocktails. I've had to do it all myself," she complained.

"A Harrier exploded in mid-air," he told her with some force. "The pilot didn't stand a chance, of course."

"How awful! That's why I keep asking you to give up flying. It's too dangerous."

He gripped the receiver tightly, wondering how she would feel if he identified the victim as the young South African she had attempted to use to make her point at the dinner dance.

"Well, are you coming or not?"

Taking a hold on himself he said quietly, "No. I have a feeling I'd start acting up."

He drove to the Mess and went straight to the bar with the intention of getting very drunk as quickly as possible. Along the road to oblivion he resolved to comfort Maggie with the fact that her lover had died doing what he was born to do and knowing she loved him. Better to go out on a high and never face the dark downward slide that follows.

214

September

D ave had been operating in the South Atlantic for five weeks and was due to return to Hampton in nine days' time. Two crews from B Flight were completing their normal stint on the Falklands, and Dave was the only man among them who had not been there before. The wild nature of these islands, surrounded by treacherous seas reaching to the frozen Antarctic and populated by unique wildlife, would have charmed a man dearly familiar with the Scottish Highlands and islands if only something remarkable had not happened to him on the day Mark Hascham was killed.

An orphan almost from birth with no brothers or sisters, Dave had never suffered the loss of a dear one. He had felt a certain amount of sadness and regret over Sir Hector's death, nothing more, but Maggie's grief had shocked him. He had never seen such naked emotion before nor had he felt such compassion. He continued to feel it, unable to banish the memory of that terrible day.

The one blessing was that her relationship with the lost pilot had not been made public and she had been spared media pestering. In cases such as this security was tightened and official reports were carefully worded. Within minutes of the tragedy the station at Wittering was security-sealed and all RAF personnel who had been involved in the air show were forbidden to speak to reporters.

Headlines speculated on every possibility and some described the crash as another event in the expanding cycle of violence. One prominent daily ran a series of editorials claiming that people no longer protested with placards but through deaths and injuries. They walked with home-made bombs in their pockets into large stores, rail stations and airports. They planted devices in laboratories, farms and along motorways. They set fires, released poison gas in underground systems, put shards of

215

glass in food on supermarket shelves. Was it no longer possible for civilised society to negotiate rather than slaughter?

With media interest fixed on how a saboteur had breached military security to tamper with a front-line aircraft, interest in the victim faded. Research into his career was disappointing. He had been a bright talented young pilot with no scandal in his life. The tabloids tried to find some in his South African links. Was his father involved in right-wing opposition to the black government? Hascham's mother had also died in an air crash. Was there a political vendetta against the family?

Reports of the funeral in South Africa were coloured by conjecture, with cameramen focusing on the father and male mourners, black and white. The gifted young man whose remains were being interred was forgotten in the search for sensation. When first reports from air accident investigators hinted at a fault in the complicated electrics of the Harrier, some tabloids still tried to link this with extremist action, until meatier news broke.

PUBLIC FURORE OVER
BEEB'S SOAP SHOCK

The BBC was last night swamped by phone calls, faxes and e-mail messages minutes after they killed off one of the nation's most loved characters. Viewers were either outraged or devastated by the graphic stabbing by his former mistress of Billie Freeman, hero of the long-running soap on motor racing, *Freeman's Way*. Was this shock move a ploy by the Beeb to dilute the effect of the first episode of new TV series *The Backpackers*, which threatened ratings? It was a dangerous gamble. How can *Freeman's Way* survive without the character created by Justin Thorpe, who had become TV's most popular sex symbol? Rumours suggest Thorpe has been offered a tempting Hollywood contract and wanted to leave the race-track soap. Fen Wilkins, producer of *Freeman's Way,* said this morning that a new heart-throb is lined up ready to appear on the 28th, the week after next Tuesday's episode which will feature Billy's funeral. This will guarantee that viewers will be glued to Channel One during the next two episodes of ITV's *The Backpackers*. The Beeb are keeping mum on who their new sex symbol in oily overalls and a sleek black racing car will be. But will viewers accept him? Wreaths are already arriving at the BBC bearing emotional messages to Billy. For comments of *Freeman's Way* addicts turn to page 4.

Glad that the heat had been taken from wild speculation about

Mark Hascham, Dave was amazed by this evidence of television influence on so many people's lives. He could not put from his mind that August afternoon when he had witnessed a real tragedy which had widened his vision and sharpened his understanding of human relationships.

He had not posted the letter to Ralph Finlayson, which had been written in the belief that it was the best solution to his own future. *I want nothing from you.* End of the matter! He now knew it could not be the end for him.

If that seventeen-year-old girl and a young married officer had been another Maggie and Mark what would it have cost Edwina to run from him with another man leaving no word of explanation? What pangs of jealousy and sense of betrayal would her lover have suffered? Lieutenant Finlayson had recovered and realised his professional ambitions. Maggie Spencer would recover, in time, and probably realise her professional ambitions: but Edwina Rowan had not lived long enough for *her* pain to ease, for *her* loss to become bearable. She had even been forced to forsake the child of the man she loved.

As he walked along the shoreline once more, Dave was painfully aware of that unknown girl eight years younger than he was, who had tried to compose a letter to a baby who could not belong to either of the people who had created him. He had now met Finlayson and had thought him a decent, perceptive, warm person. Dammit, he had *liked* the man. Would Edwina have made such a sacrifice if she had not truly loved Finlayson?

There was now no doubt in Dave's mind that he was the result of genuine passion, and that each of the lovers had suffered because of it. That certainty gave him a sense of belonging he had never known before. He was part of a family of three, one of whom had put in his hands the future of the two remaining. The haunting memory of Maggie sobbing so heart-breakingly that afternoon somehow merged into a vision of another girl bereft of the man she loved. Edwina Rowan and Maggie Spencer curiously became one and drove him to take steps to compensate in the only way open to him.

Finding shelter in a remote spot overlooking the cold grey ocean, Dave wrote a letter that expressed feelings he had denied all his life.

Dear Colonel Finlayson,

This copy of a letter from Edwina Rowan will be as big a shock to you as the original was to me, no doubt.

My first reaction was to let sleeping dogs lie. I then decided on a detached approach to you to fulfil a duty I felt she was asking of me between the lines of her letter but fate decided that I would not post that letter.

I share her wish not to harm your career or good name, so this will be between the two of us; not even the Rowan family will know. I hope her letter will help you to understand what she did, and that you will appreciate, as I now do, what that decision must have cost her. When we met at Sir Hector's funeral you mentioned that you had known my mother. I later sought you out hoping to learn more, but you were busy and my cousin then found an excuse to tell me never to darken his door again. Dougal can be very melodramatic, as I'm sure you know.

I'm writing this in surroundings not unlike those I grew up in, and I'm now fully aware of why my blood pounds and my heart sings in wild free places. I'm a Scot through and through.

I shall make no demands on you save one. The Rowans cut Edwina from their lives. Her name was never mentioned; pictures of her were destroyed or hidden. It was as though she had never lived. Could you write to me what you remember of her; make her real for me? I went to her grave just once and thought it enough. I now know it wasn't and I'm ashamed of my neglect. Will you help me to compensate for that?

He signed the letter David because anything else would be inappropriate, then he sat for a long time staring at the sea, lost in some other world. When it grew dark, he stood and returned to his quarters. He addressed an envelope, marking it PRIVATE AND CONFIDENTIAL, and slipped in it his letter and the copy of the other he had brought with him. Dave posted it, knowing Finlayson would receive it before he, himself, returned to England. The outcome was in the hands of Edwina Rowan's lover. If he declined to reply, Dave would accept that decision but he would have done what she had asked of him.

Knowing that would go a long way to easing his conscience over the fact that he had shrugged her from his life just as her family had.

The posting of the letter dealt with one of the ways in which the dramatic events of that day in August had affected him. He could think of no immediate way of dealing with the other, which was that he was halfway to being in love with Maggie.

It had been a perfect day for sailing. England was enjoying an Indian summer and everyone was making the most of those golden days with the scents of berries, chrysanthemums and garden bonfires, before the grey coldness of winter closed in. Maggie moved confidently about the streamlined vessel, working in partnership with Phil. They had sailed together from an early age, as they had done almost everything else. The sun was lowering as they headed for their mooring on a sea grown tranquil with approaching night.

Fay sat in the bows looking windblown and contented. "As you two have done all the work while I lazed, I'll go ahead and prepare the supper."

"What's to do?" asked Phil. "We made a huge salad this morning."

"And the potatoes are scraped ready for the pot," added Maggie.

"The steaks have to be grilled."

"Big deal," said Phil with a grin.

"So you don't want any supper?"

"There had better be some supper, woman, or you'll be out on your ear."

Their fond teasing hurt Maggie almost unbearably with its reminder of days with Mark, but she blamed the chill in the breeze for creating moisture in her eyes. She had been living in an unreal world for almost a month now and was longing to reach Hampton tomorrow; to be back with the team. She had wanted that for the past two weeks.

During those first days with her parents she had spent long periods sitting in the garden staring into space. Her father had been marvellous, listening to her talk about Mark whenever she needed to. Mrs Spencer was too emotional, too babying; Maggie could not have discussed the pain of it with her. It was her father who had listened while Maggie struggled to decide whether or not to fly to South Africa for Mark's funeral.

"I suppose I'd be out of place at a family ceremony. It's not as if we were engaged or even living together. I don't have anything of his to treasure. We met in hotel rooms – impersonal rooms occupied by others the rest of the time. But I loved him, Dad. I can't let him go without being there, can I?"

Mr Spencer let her speak without interruption. "I was probably going to lose him, anyway. I think we both accepted that his tour with the Red Arrows might change things. I wish . . . I wish he'd flown with them just once. He was so thrilled at being selected." She was silent for quite a while. "His mother's buried in South Africa so I suppose it's right to take him there, but he did all his flying in this country and I can't help feeling he'd rather stay here. Still, who am I to give an opinion?"

"You're the girl he loved very dearly, Maggie. Never forget that and be glad to have had his love, if only for a short time."

Although Mr Spencer let her argue with herself and reach her own decision, he did offer to accompany her to South Africa. She decided against it, however. Then, on the day of the funeral, she was swept by an overpowering need to take flowers to the crash site. Her father privately consulted Rob on the advisibility of this move, and his son told him to let her do it.

So Maggie had gone with her father to put red roses on the spot where Mark had departed from her life. On that great area of blackened earth which crash experts had only just cleared of debris, were a few wilting flowers from strangers who had either witnessed the crash or who had been moved by the tragedy. Clutching her red roses, Maggie had sobbed in her father's arms the way she had in Randal's.

From that day she had longed to be back with Jeff, Rusty, Dave and all the boys including the Boss. She wanted to gossip with Jill and Dandy; vie for a place in the queue for showers. Most of all she longed to be in the cockpit, hearing the familiar patter from crewmen and the rude banter on the airwaves. Instead, she had spent a week with Rob and family, then four days with Charles and his, and they all pointed out that she must let grief run its course. After two more days with her parents during which Mrs Spencer argued that her poor daughter should give up flying, Maggie moved down to her twin's house for the last three days of her leave. Phil would drive her to Hampton tomorrow after-noon.

As they made fast after Fay had left to grill the steaks, Phil said, "You'll be glad to get back to work."

"It'll be like going home. Mum and Dad's place doesn't seem to be that any more."

"Know what you mean. Once they got rid of us all they settled down and made it their own. So they should." He finished securing everything for the night, then held up a wine bottle. "There's enough here for a last glass each. Let's sit and watch the sun go down."

"What about Fay?"

"Her suggestion."

They settled on the padded seat, clinked glasses and drank in silent accord. As she gazed at the quiet estuary, Maggie said, "I'm so much calmer now they're leaving Mark in peace. I know it's happening all the time to someone, but when it's a person you love it's terrible, Phil. Newspapers and TV all speculating on which group of madmen blew him up; trying to link him and his family with all kinds of things."

Phil flung his arm around her shoulders. "Put that out of your mind, Mags, and remember the lovely man he really was."

"I keep thinking of a letter Randal sent. It chased me around from Chas to Rob, then back to York. It was very brief – he's straight to the point – but it said Mark had gone out on a high knowing he'd reached his aim of being chosen for the Red Arrows and knowing the woman he loved loved him in return. Which meant he had achieved more in his twenty-nine years than many manage in a normal lifespan." She glanced up at her twin. "He's right, isn't he?"

"Of course."

"But I'm selfish enough to wish someone else had flown that day."

He pulled her close against his side. "That's not selfish, it's normal. When Fay miscarried I wished it had been any-one's baby but ours. It's human nature to ask 'Why me?' We all do."

She wiped her face with the back of her hand. "Sorry about the grizzling, it just happens. I can't stop it."

"Grizzle away, Mags. You'll feel better for it."

After a short while she smiled through the rain. "By making

221

me love him, Mark showed me how to understand you and Fay. The bond we have is special, but the other kind of love is so powerful it swamps everything else, doesn't it?"

"Mmm." After a moment of uncertainty, Phil said, "You talked about how much Mark had achieved. I can add to that in an unusual way. Is it all right to tell you?"

She turned to him, their faces which were so alike now flushed by the rosy sunset. "Anything you tell me is all right. We're back as we used to be, aren't we?"

"Of course." He squeezed her shoulder but still hesitated before speaking. "Fay's been deeply affected by the tragedy. She read all the newspaper accounts, saw the TV pictures of Mark, and she knew what a difficult decision you had to make over the funeral. One evening she became very, very upset, and I eventually got from her the reason. She . . . well, she said she was ashamed of how she's wallowed in self-pity since the miscarriage. She said losing an unborn foetus was a small tragedy compared with the death of a happy healthy young man who was a bright star in the firmament. She now wants to try for another baby; to bring a new life into the world." Looking away at the shimmering pink water ahead, he added quietly, "I've been using the spare bedroom for the past five months. Last week we got back together and she's full of confidence." He turned back to her. "I thought you might like to know that."

After three weeks in Northern Ireland during a short emergency Randal was spending a long weekend at home. Fiona knew his movements only at short notice – he did not know them any earlier himself – so it was rare for them to be alone in the house. He sometimes wondered if this was an air force wife's revenge. *Darling, sorry we won't be able to do what you want. I have to do this, go there, see so-and-so. Can't get out of it, I'm afraid.*

On Friday there was a children's party-cum-barbecue to celebrate the start of Neil's days at Harford Lake Preparatory School. Twenty-five parents and about twice that number of children made free of the house, the swimming pool and the extensive garden. The adults nodded genially and said, "Hi!" each time Fiona waved a hand in Randal's direction. "My husband has three days' leave." But they all knew their way around so his presence made little difference.

It appeared to Randal that half a herd of cows, thickly sliced, was cooked and devoured during the late afternoon by people he had never before met, or if he had he had forgotten. There was a battalion of bowls of salad and enough crusty bread to feed the five thousand. Next came mounds of strawberries, cream, tubs of pink ice cream and sticky cakes in quantities enough to feed the pupils of Harford Lake twice over. All this was washed down with red wine, or Coke for the children.

Randal attempted to control the antics in the swimming pool until two little monsters vomited cake and ice cream into the sanitised water, putting the place out of bounds. He then tried in vain to prevent pint-sized demons from racing all over the house, bouncing on settees and beds, and exploring cupboards. Their parents were happily getting sloshed on the patio while a few enterprising couples in brief swimwear were indulging in wife-swapping experiments in the far corners of the garden. When they left, Randal supposed they were all correctly paired.

He said as much to Fiona as Mrs Barnes cleared away the food. "Thank God Neil can only start his schooldays once. We won't have to do this again. Who the hell were they all?"

"My friends. You told me to invite them while you're away, so I do."

He sighed. "The things we say on impulse."

"If you were here more often I wouldn't be lonely."

"Yes, OK. You've made your point."

"Don't snap! If I'd known you would be home I wouldn't—"

"I said you've made your point."

Neil appeared, holding Lydia by the hand. He had grown very protective since his sister had been dragged from the pool by Randal. "She was eating ice cream left in people's dishes. Ugh! I told her you'd be cross, Mummy."

"I am," she said severely. "Only dirty little girls do things like that, Lydia."

"Dad, what's going to happen to that yuk in the pool?"

"I'll have to clean it up, Tiger."

"Can't Mrs Barnes do it?"

"Certainly not. It's not her job, and it's the kind of thing men deal with, not ladies."

The boy screwed his face into an expression of disgust.

"You're always saying that, but why do we men get all the nasty things to do?"

Smothering a smile, Randal said, "Because we're the tough guys, aren't we?" At Neil's reluctant nod, he added, "Why don't we do it together while Mummy gives Lydia a shower and gets her ready for bed?"

"All right." It lacked enthusiasm, but the carrot of being a tough guy while his naughty sister faced bedtime was irresistible. Even so, he watched while his father did the unpleasant job. When it was finished and Randal suggested a shower and bed for him, Neil adopted an expression which invariably heralded an awkward question. Randal prepared himself.

"Dad, what's adultery?"

Suppressing his surprise, Randal perched on a lounger to be level with his son's face. "Where did you hear about that?"

Frank brown eyes gazed back. "Johnny Skinner's dad was down the garden with Mrs Goodall. They were *kissing*. Ugh! Sean Papworth said they were committing adultery. He said everyone does it, even you and Mummy."

"Then he's wrong, son. Adultery is when husbands and wives behave as if they're married to someone else. It isn't something everyone does. Sean Thingummy is a dope."

Neil looked immensely relieved. "I thought he was. I knew you wouldn't go around kissing other ladies."

"Of course not," declared Randal, hoping his nose was not growing longer.

"You're always too busy kissing Mummy whenever you're here, anyway." He sighed. "I don't really understand that. I mean, it's different with me and Lydia. We're children. But you should have grown out of that by now."

Randal gave a shout of laughter and ruffled his son's hair. "It'll be a sad day when we do. Come on, under the shower with you."

They walked around the pool and through the side door, which Randal locked after them. As they crossed to the bedroom area, Neil said matter-of-factly, "That horrid Mr Masters from the tennis club once kissed Mummy over there behind the bar, but she smacked his face so that wouldn't be adultery, would it?"

"Of course not." He aimed to call on Mr Masters at the first opportunity and aim a backhand drive at his balls.

When he was at home the children demanded their bed-time story from him. Fiona could invent endlessly, but Randal resorted to reading books about talking trains or buses that could fly. His mind was not fully on the job that evening, so he was glad when they fell asleep almost immediately. He went through to the main bedroom to announce that their children were snoring and found Fiona fresh from the shower and drying her hair.

Looking at him in the mirror, she said teasingly, "You read such dreary stories they fall asleep from boredom."

"I'll try one on you tonight and see what happens," he retaliated, pulling his damp shirt over his head.

"I'll tell you what'll happen." She switched off the hair dryer and crossed to him, her open bathrobe showing her long legs, slender body and taut breasts all evenly tanned from nude sunbathing. "While you're saying 'Once upon a time', I'll be doing this." Butterfly fingers moved over his bare chest. "When you read 'there was a little red bus that had grown so rusty it was left in the corner of the yard', I'll be doing this, and this."

His pulse quickened and the familiar undeniable desire flooded through him. "If you do, I'll start doing this."

Some of the old magic, missing since the night of the dinner dance, now returned. Fiona revelled in brute strength and Randal found plenty of that to give. Later, while Mrs Barnes dealt with the aftermath of the barbecue, they drank more wine and listened to CDs by candlelight. Circling Fiona with his arm as she snuggled against him and knowing their beautiful children slept peacefully nearby, Randal felt no man had a right to ask for more. Foolishly, he did.

"This is great," he murmured against her hair. "Let's just laze around tomorrow and have fun with the kids."

"Can't," she said. "I'm playing in the mixed doubles final at two, and it's the dinner dance in the evening."

Nerves that had relaxed began to tighten again. "What mixed doubles final? I haven't heard about this."

"You've been away for three weeks. The tournament's been played over the last fortnight."

"I didn't even know you'd joined a bloody tennis club."

"I'm sure I told you."

He was sure she had not. "OK, play your match, but we can surely give the evening a miss."

Turning her gorgeous eyes up to his, she said softly, "Of

course we can't, darling. It's the last social event of the season and they'll present the cups after dinner. If Perry and I win I'll have to be there with him."

Randal pulled his arm away, causing her to sit up. "Who the hell is Perry?"

"Perry Masters." She regarded him steadily. "You're not jealous, are you?"

"Should I be?"

"We-ell. I'd say any husband should worry if his wife showed interest in the club Romeo. Perry's blond, good-looking and very well endowed. Financially, I mean."

"And elsewhere, I take it?" he asked harshly.

"Oh, very," she said in silken tones. "He has a magnificent body with an all-over tan. He's a real macho knockout."

He reached out and switched off the music with unnecessary force. "Bully for him!"

"Trouble is, he knows it and I find him a crashing bore. I only put up with him because he's a good doubles player and I badly want to win the cup." She held out her glass with a provocative smile. "Really fell for that, didn't you? Is your hand steady enough to pour me some more wine?"

He drew in his breath. "It's steady enough to give you a damn good hiding."

"After you've poured the wine, darling."

On Sunday they did just laze around and have fun with their children. Fiona had been a popular winner with the tennis crowd, who had acknowledged her husband with a genial "Hi!" Randal had rated Perry Masters a Narcissus and he had resented the public embrace the man had given Fiona by way of congratulation – they made an attractive pair either in brief white shorts or in evening clothes.

During the course of Sunday, Randal caught himself watching his wife. She glowed with happiness; she was even more beautiful than when they married. She loved the house. She had settled there and made a good life for herself and the children. Neil was starting school on Monday; Lydia had been accepted for a nursery group three mornings a week. Fine for them, but what was their mother going to do while they were away?

With only half his mind on a giant jigsaw he was guiding Lydia to fit together, Randal felt a stirring of unease. His wife

226

was a tireless sex partner; it was always a wrench to untangle his limbs from hers at dawn to drive to Hampton, knowing he might not be back for perhaps five or six weeks. She would sleepily acknowledge his fierce kiss and drift back to sleep again before he had left the bedroom. Out of sight, out of mind?

Fiona was ten years younger than him and caused men's heads to turn wherever she went. She knew how to use her eyes, her slow smile and her exciting body to captivate him – he freely admitted he was a pushover when she pulled out all the stops – but what about when he was not around? He had seen the "adultery" going on at the end of the garden when everyone had been awash with red plonk. Fiona had looked sensational and Randal had wanted her badly. She had been the hostess on Friday and the host was for once at home, but if the party was given elsewhere and her husband was on duty would an opportunist have a shot at a bit of "adultery" with her at the end of someone's garden?

The thought of any man's hands cupping her tanned waist or stroking her bare shoulders put a pain in the pit of his stomach. He trusted her, yet as he presently studied the curve of her cheek, the line of her throat, the swell of her breast, he suddenly wondered how long he could hold her. She was twenty-four, desirable and highly sexed. There was no denying she craved the limelight wherever she went. He could only satisfy that craving spasmodically. Sooner or later, she was sure to encounter a man able to do it day in, day out.

"Daddy, wrong!" Lydia slapped his arm with a chubby hand and he looked down into eyes as blue and appealing as her mother's. "*Wrong*," the child repeated, pointing to the last but one piece of puzzle he had placed without really seeing it. "Doggie's head there."

He kissed the little hand. "Clever girl. I was testing to see if you'd notice. So where *is* the doggie's head?"

Lydia's triumphant smile smote him. "I *sitting* on it!"

"You little rascal." He made her shriek and wriggle with delight as he tickled her, scattering the puzzle over the floor.

"All right you two, calm down," said Fiona with a laugh.

Randal looked across at her. "I'll start on you in a minute."

"Says who?"

He got to his feet and she ran. The children loved it as they all chased around the huge garden, three against one, until Randal was pummelled into feigned submission by Fiona's two fierce defenders. As they went in for tea, he said in her ear, "I'll catch you tonight."

She flashed him a smile. "Who says I'll be running away?"

At bedtime Neil put on his school uniform because Daddy would be leaving too early to see him in the morning. Randal thought his son absurdly small to be wearing a striped blazer and long trousers but he said all the right things. Instead of reading a story he decided to tell them about a fat boy at his own first school who had demanded a pork pie from him every day or he would get a punch on the nose.

"What did you do, Dad?" asked Neil, wide-eyed.

"I took him a pork pie I'd tipped a lot of salt in. I told him it was one of my dad's best pies, and if he didn't like it my dad would be very upset and punch *him* on the nose. Then I made him eat it."

"What happened?"

"He was sick in the playground and stopped bothering me. Punching someone on the nose doesn't solve anything, Tiger, because he'll punch back and everyone ends up getting hurt. Better to solve things some other way."

"Horrid fat boy," said Lydia, patting his cheek as he kissed her. "I glad he sick."

Neil was serious, as usual. "Can I say *my* dad will punch them on the nose?"

"Only if you have to. Now work hard and behave the way Mummy and I have taught you. I know we're going to be very proud of you, son."

In the adjoining room Fiona put the uniform away again and Randal made the usual paternal grumbles about the price of it. "There's hardly more than a metre of stuff in any of them. And all this sports gear! When's he going to have time for lessons?"

"Darling, you went to view the school. They told us details of their curriculum. You agreed he should go there; I don't know what you're griping about."

"They never mentioned all the extras. Just look at the total cost for a single term."

"He'll get a first-class education."

"But he's not yet five, for God's sake. I could teach him the bloody basics for nothing."

"You're never here, so we have to pay someone else to do it."

The barb took him unawares. He looked up swiftly. "I thought you'd binned that line. You've just said I went to the school, I heard about the curriculum and I agreed he should attend. And I've been here for the last three days. So what are *you* griping about?"

"I wasn't griping; just stating a fact."

"I've just proved it isn't. I *am* here. Quite often."

"Sorry, sorry." She closed the doors of the wardrobe that would easily convert into something else when Neil was older, then turned her sexy smile on him. "Anyway, you'd never have time to teach our son anything. You're too intent on getting me flat on my back at every opportunity."

Already niggled, he took exception to a remark that was too close to one made at Farley Grange. "Today, I taught our son how to dive, how to mend Lydia's rocking horse and how to tell the difference between various dinosaurs. I stuck the hair back on the doll I gave Lydia for Christmas, I read two books on fairies and witches, and I put together the same ten-piece jigsaw six times over. I wrote to Lombards telling them to collect that faulty sunbed this week or else, and I fixed a short on the pool lights. I don't remember you being flat on your back since you got out of bed this morning."

She walked to him, still smiling. "Then it's high time I was."

She had drastically misjudged his mood. "Don't treat me like a stud, Fee. I do have an intelligence and a number of interests on a level higher than my flies."

She halted, her smile vanishing. "Yes, several thousand feet higher."

"Christ, you never give up, do you?" he cried. "If this place wasn't invariably full of your new friends when I come, maybe we'd have time to talk. Then you'd find out just who you married."

"You told me to invite my friends when you're away."

"They're still here when I get back."

"How do you expect me to know where the hell you're going to be from day to day?"

"You know just as soon as *I* know." They had been over this *ad nauseam*. The contentment of the day had been shattered and he knew it could not be recaptured. Yet he felt driven to calm the situation before it erupted into a full-scale row. "Look, I understand that some things have to be arranged in advance, but it seems to me your life is one round of parties that just can't be cancelled. We're never in this house alone."

"We were today," she pointed out coldly.

"And it was fantastic."

"Until now."

"Until you suggested I'm an insatiable lecher."

"Most men would be flattered."

"Perry Masters, for instance?"

Her eyes glittered brightly. "He got to you after all."

"Just so long as he doesn't get to you."

She turned away to wander to their bedroom. "Give me credit for more sense. Against you he's a wimp."

Randal followed, unsure what stage they had reached. "So we've established I'm not a bronzed poofter preening in front of susceptible women, but neither am I a flying penis, as you've twice suggested recently. What I am is a responsible husband and father who earns a living by flying. When Neil was thrown from that bloody pony I came and sorted it, didn't I? I supported and comforted you, I made peace with your parents and I got to the bottom of our problems. I bought this house so you and the kids would be happier than you ever managed to be at Hampton." He had said all this to her back as she unbuttoned her shirt. Now he took hold of her shoulders and turned her to face him. "I'm a husband and father as well as your lover. I enjoy being all those things. Trouble is, when I'm away for weeks at a time I get hungry and want you like crazy when I get here."

She stepped away and began unzipping her white shorts. "You get hungry when you're racketing around the world? A man with your appetite for it? Don't make me laugh."

"What's that supposed to mean?" he demanded.

She threw him a hot look. "You saw what was going on at the end of our garden on Friday. Men can't keep their hands off other women even when their wives are around, so we all know what they get up to when they're away."

"Oh, what's that?"

"They take all they're offered, of course. Do you think I don't know about Bosnian peasants giving the troops anything they want in return for food? And Irish widows exchanging sex for

230

a private bodyguard. Then there are women cut off by flood, snow or some other catastrophe who bed down with their brave rescuers."

A multitude of stark images raced through Randal's mind as he tried to equate such words with the beautiful creature wriggling out of stretch satin briefs with apparent unconcern. As she straightened up, it suddenly hit him that this was a ruthless kind of foreplay designed to get back at him for turning down her invitation a moment ago. Woman power? If it was it failed with him.

"Do you also have a theory on how we manage to rut on manoeuvres in the middle of nowhere?" he asked harshly.

"These days there are no end of women in the forces looking for a man." She headed for the bathroom and turned at the door, her golden skin highlighted by sunshine through the window. "You've got one in your squadron, haven't you? A blonde. Once she gets out of that ghastly uniform she's probably quite passable."

It was if the blood in his veins had come to the boil as Randal stared at the woman he had thought was the light of his life. "That blonde, as you put it, has recently lost the man she loved. He was the South African pilot you once invited to drive you to Farley Grange. His Harrier blew up last month and she watched him burn to death. It was on the day you held a dinner party you couldn't cancel, the day I rang and said I desperately wanted to see you all. I had the idea that being with you would help me through a difficult night. This is going to be another, but I'd rather be alone than with a woman I no longer know."

He left the house ten minutes later.

Rip Van Bruin was on the dressing table to welcome Maggie back. She guessed Jeff had put the mascot there. She cuddled the bear as she looked from her window at the Chinooks darkly outlined against the surrounding fields and knew a quietness of spirit: calm after the storm.

On her way to dinner she met Jill on the stairs and put her friend at ease with a smile. "How's the TV cameraman?"

"Filming the Amazon. Couldn't wait to go. Men love an excuse to get dirty, sweaty and dodge having to shave, don't they?"

"I don't know them as well as you do."

"Take my word," Jill said darkly. "Nice to see you, ducky. With Dandy up to her you-know-whats with wedding preparations it's been rather dull. No one to help me shred characters."

The bar was almost deserted this early, but they ordered and sat at their usual table as Maggie said, "Bring me up to date on who's been doing what and why they shouldn't have."

Jill nodded at the other three drinkers. "That blond hunk of muscle with Des and Ivor is Hal Phillips, A Flight's new engineer. Came last week. He looks really cute in greasy overalls with a smear of oil on his cheek – his facial cheek, ducky. Haven't had an opportunity to see the others, worse luck. So far, the only instinct he's aroused in me is my maternal one."

"You don't have one."

"We all have one. It just needs switching on. Tarzan of the Amazon didn't manage it but young Master Phillips is different."

"What's the latest on Rusty and Marsha?" Maggie asked.

"Finito! Very definitely. He's sleeping in the Mess and trying to decide if he's glad or sorry. As for her, I saw dreary Tom from the bookshop leaving her cottage late on Thursday night."

"Isn't he one of your standbys?"

"I can afford one less if he makes Marsha happy."

"Or Rusty jealous."

"Ha very ha! Our Rusty's as randy as they come if the tales you've told me are true. Girls all over Europe and beyond."

Maggie gazed into her glass. "They're all like that, given the chance, but sooner or later they find someone special."

Jill's hand closed over hers. "As we do, eh? I'm just along the corridor any night you need to talk."

She looked up. "Thanks. Now what about Pete?"

Jill raised her eyes heavenwards. "He bought 'Snootzie' a pedigree puppy for her birthday. Cost him a fortune. A week later she dumps Bonzo at his feet and goes off with the disc jockey again." Jill adopted a melodramatic simper. "It's *him* I really love."

"Poor Pete!"

"Poor Pete nothing! He's a dope. You've told him, I've told him, everyone's told him. Now he's left holding the canine baby."

Maggie chuckled. "What's he done with it?"

"Tried to sell it back to the breeder."

"And?"

Jill winked. "He went a bundle on the man's daughter, so he's keeping it as an excuse to visit, asking her advice as a vet."

"But what'll he do with it when he's away?"

"Well . . . I've agreed to keep my eye on Arnie for him."

"On who?"

Jill grinned mischieviously. "We thought Schwarzenegger was too long."

Maggie could not hold back her laughter. "And you called Pete a dope?"

"But Arnie's so sweet, Maggie."

"As sweet as Master Phillips with oil on his cheek?"

"I'm keeping my eye on him, too."

There was a slight catch in Maggie's voice as she said, "You have no idea how good it is to be home."

Randal signed in for the night and took his key. He had had quite a few beers at a pub along the way so he headed straight for his room. He was in no mood for company, especially that of his rowdy colleagues. Number 80 was at the far end of the corridor and he was passing the bathrooms when someone in a dressing gown, her blonde hair loose, came out carrying a towel and a sponge bag. She stopped in surprise. He also stopped, cursing the chance that had sent her across his path this particular night. *Once she gets out of that ghastly uniform she's probably quite passable.*

"It's good to see you, Maggie," he said quietly. "Ready for the fray tomorrow?"

"What've we got lined up?"

"Ten days in Poland. NATO exercise." He forced a smile. "No Captain Bloody Grierson, at least."

She smiled back. "Then you'll stay in a reasonable mood . . . unless he has a Polish equivalent."

"Don't worry, I learned long ago how to say 'Bugger Off' in the languages of all our NATO partners."

"That's all right, then." A short pause then she said, "It's good to be back with the team."

There are plenty of women in the forces looking for a man. "Glad to have you," he said, pushing away Fiona's words. "It's time the lads felt the length of your tongue again to keep them in line."

"Fat lot of notice they take! Anyway, that's your job."

"But you do it with more finesse." He nodded. "See you at briefing."

He was halfway to his room when she halted him again. "Boss!" When he turned she said," Thanks for your letter."

"Did it help?"

"I've thought about what you said, but the fact that you just took time out to write helped."

"I . . . good." He was not adept at situations like this at the best of times, and facing this girl with sadness deep in her eyes who was seeking reassurance that all was well, he had no idea whether to treat her as a colleague, a friend or whatever. Last month he had held her close and stroked her hair while she clung to him in desperation. Tomorrow she would again be one of his team, a pilot to place with a crew. Right now she was a vulnerable girl in a blue dressing gown and slippers, trying to handle the blow life had dealt her.

As he hesitated, she said, "There's something I'd like to get straight before tomorrow. Phil and I . . . well, I was wrong."

"About?"

"About the . . . the magic messages. We do still receive them. But that doesn't mean—"

"That you can't fly with a navigator," he finished for her.

She stood awkwardly in the corridor for a moment or two. "I don't remember too much about that day but Phil said you were very understanding. I just wanted to say I . . . well, thanks for coming in person."

He began walking away backwards. "All part of a boss's job."

"Like learning 'Bugger off' in umpteen languages?"

"Of course. Goodnight, Maggie."

"Sleep well, Boss."

He raised his hand in acknowledgement as he walked away. Once inside the room he stripped to his underpants and lay in darkness on the regulation bed to ride out the corrosive anger Fiona had aroused with her claim that he had only two interests, both beginning with F. If she believed that, she was harnessed to a stranger.

At the start of their marriage much of their time had naturally been spent in bed, on the floor, sprawled across the sofa and once in a collapsing hayrick when they had laughed so much nothing had been achieved. Later, when their nights had been disturbed by Neil, the desire for sleep had calmed their hectic lovemaking. Soon afterwards, defence cuts had put heavier demands on the squadron and reduced the number of days Randal spent at Hampton. When he did get home he was tired and stressed. That was when the rows had begun. Fiona had also been tired and stressed by life with a demanding infant among people she made no attempt to like. Sex had been their only common ground for a while. Then Fiona had begun going to Marylands when he was away, and things improved marginally.

The second pregnancy had been more difficult. Fiona had been irritable before he left and when he returned. Their relationship then gradually deteriorated to the point it had reached when he had been summoned from Bosnia to the hospital.

Randal left the bed to stand by the window. A full moon put a sheen across the open Dorset countryside. It was the kind of night that made flying the ultimate experience for him. Yes, he loved it. Yes, he loved hectic sessions with his sexy wife. He also loved his children; relished discovering their thought processes and their feelings. When Neil said "Da-ad," with the special inflection that heralded a knotty problem and looked up in trust and expectancy, Randal became Hercules. When Lydia teased or dissolved in tears and reached for him, something inside him melted.

The silver-washed fields beyond the tarmac became many things as he gazed into his life. He had seen war at first hand and at a distance. He had known fear and exultation while trying to help those in danger and he had surrendered to the pure thrill of swinging about the sky. For the past eight months he had led the Flight and he believed he had made a good job of it. He hoped one day to command a squadron.

He turned from the window in bitterness. Had Fiona truly no understanding of the man she had married? How could she believe he was as brutish as she had suggested tonight? What had happened to trust and faith?

He sat heavily on the bed and admitted the truth. By buying that house and giving Fiona access to the kind of life she loved, he had widened the gap between them. Yet if he had left things as they had been a year ago it would surely be wider still. She had settled happily enough in their luxury home and was rearing their children with love and care, but shadows had again appeared on the horizon.

Fiona's life was now so full of the people and activities she found essential for her contentment, she had little time to miss him. How long would it be before his presence actually became inconvenient; when her constant cry of "You're never here" changed to "Things were fine until you turned up"? He could not deny she was still full of fire and passion but was that all she needed from him now?

In five years of marriage they had probably spent not much more than half that time together. But between sex and games with the children, they had surely *talked*. Had she never listened? Had her mind been elsewhere when he aired his views or passed on items of special interest? He knew she loved fashion, swimming, ballet, Flamenco music, yellow roses, silk shirts, apricot mousse, Opium perfume and pink champagne. He knew she had never taken to riding – a great disappointment to Daddy – and hated pizza, French onion soup, the colour purple, hard rock, wearing aprons and sandals with thongs between the toes. She was afraid of spiders.

If he knew all that about her, surely she knew as much about him. Had she conveniently forgotten his interest in architecture, his passion for stained-glass windows, his fondness for jazz, his liking for bright colours, biographies of explorers, frosty mornings and paintings by abstract artists? Did she truly not know he followed the fortunes of Damon Hill with enthusiasm and drove a go-kart in squadron races that had DEMON HILL painted on the side? He had long ago accepted that she took no interest in his work but surely that did not extend to him as a person. Had she shut her ears whenever he had said anything other than sex talk?

Did Fiona believe he went whoring whenever he was away from her, as she had suggested? Did she doubt he had been faithful to a girl he had fallen for at first sight? Tonight, she had smashed that fidelity into small pieces with cynical words. The person he had walked out on was not the girl he had tried so hard to keep close. Something had died as suddenly as it had been born, and he was too tired and dispirited to care.

He finally fell asleep around three thirty, thinking about the coming days in Poland. Nothing and no one could snatch away his pleasure in flying, and he would be doing it for the next ten days with eleven of his team. He knew where he stood with them.

The telephone shrilled beside his ear. His watch showed that it was five a.m. Snatching up the receiver he growled his name.

"Did I wake you?"

He sat up slowly, unprepared for this. "Is something wrong?"

"Only between us," said Fiona quietly.

"The kids are OK?" He was still half asleep.

"Neil's already up and in his uniform." There was a long pause he made no attempt to break. "I wanted to catch you before you took off."

"Oh?"

"Are you still furious?"

"That's right."

Her voice broke. "Darling, I didn't know what I was saying. I had no idea that poor girl . . . that the dead pilot was the South African I met . . ."

"This call's going through a switchboard," he reminded her harshly.

"Could you . . . will you ring me back on your mobile?"

"No time."

Another long pause. "Please, Randal."

"I have to shower and dress, have breakfast and give a briefing all by eight thirty. This is a working day. I'll be fully occupied with the *other* of my two interests."

"Oh God, I must have been crazy last night," she said emotionally. "Can we talk when you get back? Really talk. I won't arrange anything. We'll spend the whole time on our own."

"I have to go." He replaced the receiver, unmoved by her olive branch and unwilling to bludgeon his brains further on the watershed their marriage had reached.

He swore heartily on discovering that he had left his shaver at home. It was the one he normally kept at the house but he had somehow failed to bring his travelling one back from Northern Ireland. After showering and dressing, Randal knocked on Rusty's door to beg the loan of his shaver. His friend was unhappy over the break-up with Marsha so their verbal exchange was made with the early morning gruffness and brevity of two moody men. Both ate breakfast silently half an hour later, then Randal went to his office carrying the bag he had packed and

237

knowing he would have to buy yet another shaver. The fact that he seemed consistently unable to bring them back whenever he left the country added to his bad temper. God help Jeffries if he began carping, God help B Flight if they were in too jovial a frame of mind, but even God would be of little help if they arrived to find a Polish Grierson taking part in the exercise.

On his desk a letter lay on the pile of forms and internal memos. He did not recognise the handwriting and knew no one in Plymouth. Frowning, he slit open the envelope and took out a single sheet covered in shaky childish writing.

> Deer skadron leeder I am in hostible. They gave me a kidnee wen I go home I can run and jump like you. I am pleezed but you wont cum again so I am sorry. I liked the pikchur of Teddy in my jumpur wot a funny name he has. Ted came to see me. He wont cum again too so I am sorry. But I want to run and jump. Now I can go to skool. Then I can rite you better.
> Luv and kisses Fiona Hunter

As Randal gazed at the letter, he thought of the little girl who had made a bond with the strangers who had appeared out of the sky. He thought of Lydia's triumphant smile as she revealed that she had been sitting on the vital piece of jigsaw. He thought of Neil asking if he could tell bullies that his dad would punch them on the nose. Children needed to trust and feel secure. They should never be deprived of that because of the pride and jealousies of adults.

For some moments he gazed at the telephone and almost lifted the receiver but too much had been said last night. When they flew in from Poland he might be able to think more dispassionately. He cut his meeting with Jeffries as short as possible then went to the briefing to break the news about Fiona Hunter. They all cheered and Randal noticed that Maggie's eyes were bright with moisture. Take a life; give a life!

October

W hen the crews returned from the Falklands they were due five days' leave. The rest of B Flight and all A Flight save the one standby aircraft and crew were dispersed overseas. Hampton was quiet; 646 Squadron offices all but deserted.

Dave and Sandy decided to tour Cornwall on the motorbike, staying in any place they took a fancy to. But standing in his room in the Sergeants' Mess soon after their arrival, Dave cast aside all thought of five days away from it all as he gazed at the sealed letter in his hand. It was surely a reply from Finlayson, and he delayed opening it for fear of reading a bold rejection accompanied by veiled threats of retribution if he tried to make his claim stick. After all, Edwina could have invented it all just to cause mischief, although if she had wanted that she would surely have written directly to her lover from her deathbed. All of his doubts returned, with an added new fear. He had no proof that Finlayson had ever been her lover, had he? Suppose he had made an almighty fool of himself? *I shall make no demands on you save one.* Oh God, he should have left the whole thing well alone.

These thoughts raced through his mind as he held the envelope addressed in thick black handwriting with a Scottish postmark. *I'm now fully aware of why my blood pounds and my heart sings in wild free places. I'm a Scot through and through.* How could he have written such tosh on the strength of a twenty-five-year-old letter from a young girl he knew nothing about? He had never played a piano to discover if his blood pounded and his heart sang to prove he was "Fingers" Ashmore's son. In the wild freedom of the Falklands what he had written to Finlayson had seemed so right but in his familiar room at Hampton the letter he remembered word for word now became unctuous and smug. *I share her wish not to harm your career or good name, so this will be between the two of us.* He burned with embarrassment. What a bloody nerve he had had to approach the man, much less promise not to tell the world he had a bastard son!

Dave sank on the bed with a groan. He was hopeless at relationships. Leanne had cost him professional excellence and had humiliated him by preferring a blue-blooded Rowan. He had now brought about his own humiliation with this claim. He was safer as a loner; he could handle that easily. Sighing, he ripped open the envelope hoping a written apology would placate the man and bring an end to something he should have had the sense to ignore.

Dear David,

I hold a rank requiring me to make swift decisions on which men's lives and safety might depend, yet this is my fourth attempt to reply to your letter. You wrote that you wished to make just one demand of me. I have one to make of you, which is that we meet as soon as convenient to us both. Perhaps you would be good enough to ring the above number to arrange this, as your schedule is more uncertain than mine.

With sincere good wishes,

Ralph Finlayson

Dave read the letter through three or four times, trying to gauge the man's mood. Had he demanded a meeting to avoid putting anything in writing that Dave might use against him? Yet he sent *sincere good wishes*. The letter was brief and to the point with no mention of Edwina's letter, but the first paragraph came over as warmly human, surely not the tone of an angry man. The ball was now firmly in his court and Dave was a sportsman who knew it should be played swiftly and with confidence. Seven p.m. A good time to catch him, perhaps. He dialled the number.

"Finlayson." There was a sweeping symphony playing in the background.

"Good evening, sir. It's David Ashmore," he said hesitantly through a dry throat.

"Ah! Hold a moment while I go to the other room." A faint murmur of voices and a woman's assuring him she would replace the receiver when he lifted the other one. Some moments elapsed. "Yes. Thank you, Mourna." A click cut off the music and Finlayson's voice lost its echoing quality. "I'm entertaining friends, David. Couldn't talk above Beethoven. When did you get back?"

"About two hours ago, sir."

"Then I must thank you for your prompt call."

"We have a five-day stand-down."

"I see." A long pause. "Well now . . . Do you mind coming halfway? One of my sisters lives at Windermere. Easily accessible from both directions. They're in Zimbabwe visiting their son. I have a key to the house, so why don't we meet there on Wednesday?"

"That would be fine," he managed rather hoarsely.

"Good. The house is beside the lake. Ask in the gift shop for Fernleigh Lodge. They'll give you directions. Twelve thirty? I'll have Mrs Babcock prepare some lunch then pop off home. You have your own transport, of course?"

"Aye. A Harley-Davidson."

"Oh, to be young and heedless again! Goodbye, David."

Dave replaced the receiver slowly. No threats. An invitation to lunch at his sister's house. He had sounded friendly, well, at least not aggressive. Dave's fears then took a new direction. Was Finlayson simply humouring him? Would it be a case of "There, there, silly boy, that letter was a load of nonsense from an infatuated teenager. You know what they're like. You must have set a few schoolgirl fantasies off yourself. But Edwina took it a stage further because she was afraid and far from home. Believing her fantasy maybe helped her through her last days. Poor kid!"

This reaction seemed increasingly likely the more Dave considered it. After all, Finlayson would hardly discuss his adulterous affair over meat and two veg. Of course not! Why, oh why, had he rushed headlong into ringing the man?

His thoughts were in turmoil while he showered and shaved. Then he went for dinner wondering how to tell Sandy the Cornish trip was off. They sat with three others to eat; the single men who had no one to rush home to after weeks overseas. They discussed their plans and it was later, when he and Sandy were drinking alone, that Dave made a sudden decision to suggest they both go to the Lake District.

Sandy's glass hovered just below his mouth as he asked, "So what's happening up there?"

"Had a letter from a relative." He rushed on. "Business to do with my great-uncle's will. He's going to be in Windermere on Wednesday and I have to meet him. God knows when I'll have another chance, and it'll only take up half a day. We can still have a great time walking and climbing."

Sandy thought about it. "OK, you're on. There'll be girls up there, too."

Back in his room, Dave admitted to himself that he needed Sandy along to stave off nervousness. The two days before his meeting would be fully occupied, leaving him little time to worry. Sandy was laid-back and good company. Maybe a bit too fond of picking up girls but that might be an advantage on this trip.

The weather held. Cumbria was in its autumnal glory and full of hikers, climbers, birdwatchers, honeymooners and senior citizens with picnics and folding chairs. Dave and Sandy encountered a small group of ramblers at their hotel and spent Tuesday walking with them, stopping only for beer and sandwiches at twelve thirty. After dinner, Dave decided that the only way to ensure he was not awake all night was to get drunk. Sandy approved the plan and they staggered back from the nearest pub under the guidance of two regulars, disturbing elderly guests in adjoining rooms by slamming their door, taking long noisy showers and flushing the toilet well into the night. Between visits to the bathroom they enjoyed log-like sleep, blissfully unaware that others did not.

They were both hung-over in the morning. Sandy stayed in bed but Dave braved hostile faces over the breakfast table to eat dry toast and drink large quantities of black coffee before going for a run to get his system working properly. His head thudded with every step and he told himself it would have been better to face Finlayson red-eyed through lack of sleep rather than dull-witted through an excess of beer. Back at the hotel he begged more black coffee from a susceptible waitress and was given a pot smuggled from the kitchen. Sandy was still in bed; the thick curtains remained across the window.

Dave stood beneath a cold shower until his body felt totally numb, then, wrapped in the full complement of towels, he sat on the closed toilet to drink the coffee. With the headache now dulled, he shaved and dressed in clothes appropriate for the occasion. He challenged his reflection. What *was* the occasion?

A son meeting his newly-discovered father; an upstart confronting a superior adversary; an idiot being shown his lack of sophistication by a man of the world? By this afternoon he would know and the ridiculous business would be over.

Zipping on his black leather jacket over dark-grey trousers, white shirt and a sober tie, he took up his helmet and left Sandy still snoring. Bearing in mind the disturbance they had made last night, Dave wheeled his bike from the courtyard where some elderly guests were now chatting over mid-morning coffee, and kick-started it on the road.

The middle-aged woman was clearly apprehensive when a large man in black leather and a helmet revealing little more than a pair of dark eyes entered the gift shop and approached her. If he pulled a gun she would hand over the money. If he wanted *her*, she would put up a fight and risk it. He wanted directions to Fernleigh Lodge. She gave them with a sense of guilt but it got rid of him. The moment he roared away, however, she telephoned Adele Babcock to warn her that a muscular tearaway in black on a huge motorcycle was heading for the lodge. Knowing the Cartwrights were in Africa, should she call the police? Adele was not at home. Fearful that she might actually be at the lodge, the woman rang to tell her friend to get out quick. A man answered, which threw her into greater panic until she recognised the voice of Felicity Cartwright's brother.

"Oh, Colonel Finlayson, I'm so relieved you're there," she breathed. "You'll know just what to do."

"Who is this?" he asked warily.

"Sarah Voke at the gift shop. I'm so sorry, but I wanted to be rid of him so I gave him directions to the lodge. He's on his way now. He may have an accomplice or there could be a gang of them."

"One moment, Mrs Voke," he interjected. "*Who* is on his way here?"

"One of those motorbike ruffians. All in black. I thought he was after the cash. We've been told not to risk our safety, but to hand over—"

"Madam, please calm yourself," he said with a touch of impatience. "Your villain has arrived and is presently divesting himself of the things that so alarmed you, before having lunch with me. I do appreciate your neighbourly warning. It's good

243

to know folk are keeping an eye on the place while my sister is away. Goodbye now, Mrs Voke."

Dave thought it wise to take off his gear before ringing the bell. He was unaware of being watched from a window as he tucked in his shirt more securely, straightened his tie, ran a comb through his thick hair, then squared his shoulders before approaching an attractive double-fronted house.

Finlayson opened the door almost immediately, and there was a moment of mutual hesitancy before he offered his hand. "Hello, David. You're a good timekeeper."

There was no smile, but the approach was friendly enough and his grip was firm. "My service training, I expect, sir," said Dave.

"Come in. I asked Mrs Babcock to give us time for a dram before we eat. You could do with one, I don't doubt."

Dave could well have done without it, but he followed Finlayson to a pleasant room with a view of the lake, saying, "Yes, sir."

As his host poured the drinks Dave studied him. A handsome man with crisp dark hair silvering at the temples; tall, tanned, not as muscular as Dave but sturdy enough to look good in well-cut fawn trousers, a cream silk shirt and a regimental tie. He had a definite air of self-assurance yet he remained standing – which obliged Dave to do the same – while he spoke with rather forced conventiality about the beauty of the area and how lucky they were to be seeing it on a day like this. When that subject was exhausted he asked Dave's opinion of the Falkland Islands.

"The Regiment had a spell there a few years back. A very bottom-of-the-world atmosphere about the more remote areas, I thought. You would have gained a different impression from the air."

"You certainly get an idea of how isolated they are, sir," Dave said stiltedly. "Looking down on small eruptions of land in an endless expanse of sea makes you very aware of that."

"Yes, indeed." He moved to the decanter. "Time for another dram, I think."

Oh, God, thought Dave, this is terrible. He had been far more approachable at Sir Hector's funeral. *But you hadn't then claimed he was your father,* an inner voice reminded him.

A thin cheery woman invited them to the table, and they

went through to a dining-room overlooking a large well-tended garden.

"My sister not only has green fingers, she has green toes, I suspect," said Finlayson heartily. "She only has to walk out there and something pops up to burst into bloom."

While they ate pale orange soup with a curious musky taste, he elaborated on his sister, brother-in-law and nephew in Zimbabwe, which led him to comment on the unstable state of some African countries. Dave tried his best to look and sound intelligent and interested in each subject, but his conviction that this was a ghastly mistake grew with every minute. Over trout with pan potatoes and *mange tout*, accompanied by a fine white wine that set Dave's head aching anew, they discussed the continuing tension in the Balkans and what might constitute a satisfactory solution to the problems in the Middle East.

Mrs Babcock cleared the plates, then brought cheese, biscuits and a large pot of coffee. "I'll be off now, Colonel, but I'll come tomorrow after you leave to put everything straight. You know where I am if you need me."

"Thank you. I'm most grateful. Good day to you."

After she had gone, Finlayson poured coffee into two Royal Albert cups, then glanced across at Dave. "Well now, I think it's time I stopped putting you through the mill. You asked me to tell you about your mother. I felt that should be done face to face, but I first had to get your measure. We had only a short chat at Sir Hector's funeral and I thought you a likeable young man, but that was not enough for me. My aim in asking you here was to sum you up, discover if you'd lied about wanting nothing more from me than a description of Edwina Rowan."

"I didn't," he said hastily.

"No, or you'd have raised the subject long ago instead of trying to give polite answers during my unforgivably long-winded impression of a colonel testing a new subaltern in the Mess. You see, David, I had to convince myself that you deserved to be told what you wanted to know." He stood. "Shall we take our coffee to more comfortable chairs in the sitting-room? You'd better bring the pot. I suspect you took a little too much Dutch courage before you came. Well, mebbe I'd have done the same in your place."

Dave followed him, his head thudding crazily and his feelings in rags. This man was canny. He had been playing it cool while he summed up the person claiming to be his son. Now he was reverting to the man encountered at the funeral. Settling carefully in a large chair beside the window framing a view of the lake, Dave assumed that he had passed the test, and they had progressed to the next stage. Gulping black coffee he began to relax in the more informal atmosphere, as Finlayson made himself comfortable in the other chair by the window and began speaking of the past.

"Edwina Rowan was very lovely, both to look at and to be with. There was a bubble within her that refused to burst, no matter what happened. When we met, I was twenty-four and ambitious to the point of obsession. I had married advantageously only to find my wife preferred to sleep alone. What do most men do to compensate for that?

"Edwina was brought along to her first regimental ball and I was instantly captivated by her warmth and passionate approach to life. I'm not proud of what happened, but at twenty-four one is very selfish and I unhesitatingly chased a dream. Very soon the dream became reality. I truly fell in love with her. We grabbed every opportunity to be together. It was like a fever within us both. I don't know if you can comprehend that."

Oh yes, Dave could.

"I was unable to sleep, unable to concentrate on my work as I struggled to figure out how we could be together. It was impossible without a divorce. I was certain my wife would refuse that, and to reveal my relationship with Edwina would be disastrous for us both, to say nothing of my career." He put down his cup, the coffee in it untouched. "Then I heard through the regimental grapevine that Edwina had run off to Paris with a jazz pianist she had known for a year or so." He sighed. "A very black period followed. I couldn't confide in anyone; I wasn't supposed to be that interested in the apparent scandal. I was shattered by her desertion but no one could be allowed to guess it."

He gazed from the window as if he were back in that time. "I grew very bitter, very aggressive. My wife began to spend long periods with her sister and it became public knowledge that our marriage was a sham." He paused so long Dave wondered if he should say something. "When I heard that Edwina had died after a complicated birth, I think my life dipped to its lowest point." He glanced back at Dave with a shadow in his eyes.

"If I had known then that I was ultimately responsible for her death I might very well have surrendered the career she had acted to save."

He leaned back in the chair and studied Dave with a frown. "Your letter, her letter, was a severe shock. Twenty-six years have passed and time heals all things, but you have partially reopened the wound by your very existence."

Dave asked carefully, "You believe her claim?"

"Aye, by the fact that she witheld the letter until Sir Hector could no longer be hurt. Or me." There was a long silence broken only by the chime of an antique clock and the song of a thrush in the garden. "But you've been hurt, David. She was very young and could not imagine the future life of the tiny boy left behind. For both our sakes I suggest DNA tests to confirm our relationship, then I'd like to do what I can to compensate you for the past twenty-five years as a supposed orphan." He smiled. "I'd like to get to know my son. I'd like to see you now and then, hear about your life, follow your career. I'd very much like to share with you my life and interests, my friends. How do you feel about that?"

"Fine," Dave mumbled, finding the situation running away with him.

"There are a few difficulties of which I'm sure you're already aware, so I think your suggestion to keep it just between ourselves is the best plan. For a while, anyway. We both have service careers and nothing would be gained by making it public. Agreed?"

"Yes, sir."

"You'd best get used to calling me Ralph. It's a bit late in the day for 'Father', and I can't have my son calling me sir." He grinned with sudden boyishness. "I've already had a complaint about you that deserves parental admonition. You must stop frightening matrons in gift shops by disguising yourself as a villainous biker with a gang waiting outside. Mrs Voke rang to warn me of a ruffian who had just demanded directions to this house."

It was so absurd, so light-hearted after the intensity, Dave laughed. "I asked very politely."

"Aye, I'm persuaded you did," came the amused reply, "but the puir wee creature was ready to hand over the takings rather than die defending them."

They laughed heartily. The ice was broken; the bond forged.

The Indian summer did not extend to Poland, where it had been raining relentlessly from the third day of the NATO exercise. While the rank and file moaned and swore, their commanders doggedly repeated that wars were fought whatever the weather and this was good practice. Then they moaned and swore out of earshot of their troops.

The days of hectic activity and difficult flying conditions helped Maggie to pick up her life again. She was warmly welcomed back and, although her colleagues did not mention Mark's death, Maggie sensed a change in them. It was as if the tragedy allowed them to take a more natural masculine attitude towards someone in need of sympathy and understanding. Maybe they had finally accepted that she could be a woman with strong emotions yet still be their professional equal. Whatever the case, the last frail barrier had come down. She was indisputably one of the team.

One sign of the change in approach was that the sleeping arrangements had been worked so that she shared a tent with only Jeff. They had clearly guessed it would be a mistake to isolate her and, as she and Jeff had a good friendly relationship and enjoyed flying together, teaming them up worked well. For Maggie, anyway. Jeff would have preferred to be with other men, but as they occupied the tent only for sleeping it could not be too great a sacrifice for him. Maggie suspected that their flight commander was behind the arrangement because Rusty was unusually sharing the "control" tent with him to prevent overcrowding in another.

She had had no real contact with Randal. For the first eight days she had flown with everyone, including the two navigators, but not with him. Initially seeing this as a deliberate signal that he was satisfied she was fully back on the ball, she then sensed a curious withdrawal in his manner towards her. During briefing or discussions on tasks and the progress of K Force, to whom they were attached, he treated her normally, as one of his pilots, but there was no chaffing or personal chat with her. If she had not had that encounter with him on the evening before their departure from Hampton she might have imagined that he could not handle direct contact with her after that day in August.

When she came to realise there was a marked change in his

whole demeanour she tackled Jeff about it as they settled in their sleeping bags one morning after two night-time tasks and a hearty breakfast.

"Did something happen to the Boss while I was away?"

Jeff was struggling with the heavy-duty zip which had caught on the thick inner padding. "He was in Northern Ireland for three weeks while I was on the biological warfare course and doing my stint in the desert, but no one's given me any scandal." He sucked his finger. "The damn thing's just bitten me. Why does mine always get snagged and not yours?"

"Because you yank at it willy-nilly. And you won't get anywhere doing what you're doing. Put your hand inside and gently ease the material free as you coax the zip up." She lay watching him do it all wrong and said, "If his wife has had another go at him, it's more serious this time. He's not just bad-tempered and snappy, he's . . . well, subdued. You've known him a while. Has he been like this before?"

"I don't know, do I!" he responded irritably. "I need to sleep. Wipe that clever look off your face and give me a hand with this."

Maggie rolled over, reached inside his sleeping-bag, touched his bare thigh and withdrew her hand. "I can't do anything with you inside it, idiot! Get out and give me room to manoeuvre."

Clad just in boxer shorts, Jeff scrambled out. "Good thing we don't fancy each other."

"Perish the thought!" She got busy on the zip. "Hasn't Rusty any ideas?"

"About what?"

"The Boss."

"Haven't asked. Rusty's bloody sour these days because Marsha's taken up with someone in the village. Pete's lusting in vain after the vivacious vet and Nobby's set on having a pistols-at-dawn showdown with a guy who's dating Renée when he's not around. They should play the field like me."

Maggie freed the zip and lay back. "Walked into any trees lately?"

"Oh yeah, excruciatingly funny!" he growled, sliding into the welcome warmth of padded cotton. "Matter of fact, that shapely lieutenant from Missouri we encountered in Sector Three yesterday would be worth another visit."

"Go to sleep, Casanova."

Maggie lay wide-eyed listening to the thunder of rain on canvas. She steered her mind away from thoughts of Mark and let it dwell on the renewed closeness with her twin. That led to a reminder of his confession of banishment to the spare bedroom for five months. Poor Phil! Surely a very cruel punishment for something that had also been painful for him. From experience Maggie knew a loss made one need others more than normally. How could Fay have rejected him so? How could he have let her?

Her thoughts moved on. She knew Randal as a naturally generous, intelligent, volatile personality. She had witnessed just one marital clash and seen the gaiety drain from him. He was presently restrained and pensive. How could his sensuous young wife play cat and mouse with him? How could he let her?

Jeff began snoring, so Maggie kicked out with her feet. He grunted, rolled over and fell silent. He was a breezy uncomplicated young man enjoying his sexual freedom, but he would fall into some girl's trap sooner or later. Maggie hoped the girl would not dampen his high spirits too much. She hoped he would not let her.

With a sigh Maggie told herself there would probably be someone else for her. A long time ahead, but one day. Whoever he turned out to be she vowed never to hold him to sexual ransom. They would relish love, like herself and Mark. Oh, God, here she was, having gone full circle, thinking of things she had tried to avoid at the outset.

"Jeff. Jeff!" she said with a touch of quiet desperation.

"Uh?"

"Are you awake?"

"No."

She reached out to pat the comforting sleepy hump. "Goodnight, then."

"S'morning."

She snuggled into her sleeping-bag glad she was not alone in the tent. Anyway, it was easier to cope with memories in daylight. It was darkness that brought problems.

On the ninth day of the exercise Maggie finally flew with Randal. It was another day of squally showers when visibility was poor and the men on the ground battled their way through mud and sodden undergrowth to counter an "enemy" doing the same. Tanks had turned the tracks into stretches of mire; jeeps and trucks soon became bogged down. Squadron Leader Price was not the only participant who was a multilingual blasphemer by that penultimate day.

Their task had been to deliver a tank and a light gun to the advance guard of K Force, and they were flying back through the murky dusk just above tree level, relishing the thought of a hot meal. In the cabin they carried a collection of ropes, chains, nets and lengths of strop which they were returning to base. Jimmy and Ray, who had got very wet on the job, had finally ceased grumbling and were quiet. Sitting beside a morose man whose only verbal exchange with her had been the minimum to fly the aircraft, Maggie found time dragging.

Spread below them were closely packed trees cut through by wide fire-breaks. It all looked as bleak as Randal's expression as he stared out in silence. Ten minutes later, they saw the boundary of the forest and gained height knowing there was a range of low hills ahead.

"It'll be dark before we get back," Maggie murmured, contemplating the gloom that would bring night too early.

The lack of response suggested Randal was lost in a moody reverie until he said sharply, "Someone's well and truly lost. Better check them out."

Maggie looked across his body as he banked and saw what his keen eyes had spotted in an area of scrubland scattered with broken blackened trunks indicating a past fire. A narrow earth track ran across the open space, and stationary on this was a canvas-roofed truck. On each side of the cab blue flags identified it as part of K Force.

"What the hell are they doing so far from the main advance?"

"That track leads into the hills and ends in a disused quarry. Flew over it yesterday," Maggie told him. "It's shown on the chart as a thin dotted line. Whatever made them turn on to it?"

"Lack of intelligence and no understanding of how to read a map. Oh . . . they're off. I suppose they think they'll meet a main road or a turning in the direction they want to go."

"Shouldn't we signal them to go back? It'll be dark before they hit the quarry."

"Nah, let them find out what bloody fools they are. Radio Control and tell them their position. If the buggers haven't turned up by the end of tomorrow, a search and rescue party can come out."

Maggie protested. "That's a bit hard, isn't it?"

"It's a hard life."

"But they're part of K Force – our own troops."

"God help us if the rest are like them."

"Oh, come on, it's a foul day. It'll be worse when it gets dark and they're miles off course. In a real war we'd give them all the help we could."

Randal watched the truck pursue its erratic way along the narrow slippery track. "This isn't a real war and all the help we can give is to notify Control – which I told you to do several minutes ago. Give their licence number and present position, with details of where they're heading. If they want to send some poor bastard out towing a large sign saying TURN AROUND, HOME'S THIS WAY, that's up to Control." He glanced at her. "If we weren't flying over at this moment they wouldn't have any help at all, would they? Go on, get on with it!"

Annoyed by his manner and attitude, Maggie got through to Control and gave the information, realising that Randal was basically right. The soldiers had a map and would also have a two-way radio on which they could contact Control if they got into serious trouble. The object of an exercise was to prepare for the real thing; to learn by experience. Her annoyance turned inward. Her reaction had been that of a woman, not a highly-trained military pilot. The loss of Mark had made her too vulnerable. Time she toughened up.

"Christ!" exclaimed the man beside her. "Emergency two o'clock, guys. Bloody bridge keeled over as they crossed it!"

He veered to the right, losing height, as Jimmy said, "OK, got it. Looks like the supports gave way on the far side."

Maggie took in the scene with dismay. To their right was a shallow gully containing a yellow-brown swirling surge of floodwater from the hills. A sturdy wooden bridge had broken away from one bank and twisted over to form a partial dam. The truck was beneath it, the cab just clear of the racing tide, apparently caught in the cross struts. The obstruction was causing a build-up of water that would surely flow over the vehicle soon.

Contacting Control again Maggie reported the new situation, adding that they would investigate and give aid if possible.

"Boss, the bridge supports on this side don't look too stable," said Ray. "Could go at any time."

"Not a hope of getting down on this side: all those burnt trees. It'll have to be across the water. Looks clearer."

"Still tricky," observed Jimmy from the side door. "Some of that scrub's pretty solid."

"We'll have to make it quick or there'll be no point landing anyway," Randal announced, circling to study the ground. "I'm going to go for that clear area about thirty yards from the bank. Keep your eyes on that clump of thorn, guys. Could be a problem."

While the three men concentrated on the landing, Maggie kept watch on the truck. The relentless flow had now divided around the obstruction to flood over both banks. This eased the threat of drowning for the men in the cab but it put further strain on the remaining supports which kept the bridge from being swept away altogether. If it went it would surely take the truck with it. It was a class A emergency and could have been dealt with far more easily if the Chinook had been fitted with a winch.

They touched down without trouble. Leaving Maggie at the controls, Randal scrambled through to the cabin and ran with his crewmen to the bank to study the situation. At that moment, Maggie saw a head wearing a tin hat emerge from the window of the cab. The men also spotted it and Randal signalled with his arms. There was no response; the trapped soldier was clinging to the cab door for dear life.

Back in the cabin, Randal told Maggie to inform Control there was one apparent survivor trapped in the vehicle and a rescue attempt would be made. "Get them to send out Casevac pronto," he added, "and keep in constant contact giving them up-to-date info."

Behind him, Jimmy and Ray were linking together some lengths of strop which they dropped through the front hatch and secured to the hook. The three men jumped out once more into the pelting rain and, while Randal tied two sturdy ropes to the harness he was now wearing, the crewmen ran out the strop to its full length. Maggie saw what they meant to do: Randal was going to scramble out across the wrecked bridge to the truck. Jimmy and Ray would hold the end of one rope as a safety line; the other rope would be tied to the strop. If the two men were unable to counter the drag on the first rope should Randal be knocked over by the force of water, the strop would prevent his being washed miles downstream. It was risky but it was the swiftest, most obvious solution.

As Maggie watched Randal take a running jump on to the cross stuts of the bridge and begin to edge his way forward, she recognised in him a humanity that overruled all else in moments of crisis.

Maintaining radio contact, Maggie watched the drama through windows rhythmically cleared by wipers. Every few seconds muddy water eddied over the legs of the man inching across the broken structure. Attached firmly to the Chinook he could not be swept miles downstream, but he could surely drown in that turbulence before they pulled him out.

Randal turned to shout to his crewmen. Against the thunder of water and circling rotors they could not hear, so he risked losing hold with one hand and held up two fingers. It was a signal that there were two survivors. Maggie could now see a second head at the cab window, which was no more than a foot or so clear of the cascading swell. Tense and anxious, she nevertheless calmly reported this to Control and was told a Casevac helicopter was on its way.

Randal was clearly being blinded by the rain, for he kept turning his head to one side and this slowed his progress. Knowing the water from the hills must be icy cold Maggie guessed he and the trapped soldiers would soon be suffering badly. She spoke to Control, and she was soon in contact with the American pilot of the medical rescue helicopter to ask their probable ETA. Fifteen minutes.

"Hurry it up," she urged.

"Will do."

It was a relief to see Randal reach the truck, but Maggie's tension immediately increased as she watched the first man climb free of the cab to a semi-secure perch on the framework of the bridge. His rescuer untied the rope held by the crewmen and fastened it around him. Randal then appeared to be having a conversation with the second man, bending into the cab which suggested there was a problem about getting him out. Maggie glanced again at the clock. The other aircraft was still ten minutes away.

Aching with a sense of helplessness Maggie watched the action unfolding in that desolate Polish landscape. It was grow-ing ever darker. The lights on the Chinook did little except illuminate the two soaked crewmen ready to brace themselves if the soldier fell. He certainly did not look too secure, although he clung like a koala grips the branch of a eucalyptus. Maggie shifted her gaze and was momentarily shocked to discover that Randal had disappeared. Then she realised he had moved down the far side of the bridge to reach inside the cab. It was impossible to see what he was doing; the light was too bad and the wooden spars hid his movements. Five minutes until help would arrive.

There was a sudden easing of the rain – surely only temporary – but it allowed Maggie a clearer view through the window as Randal resumed his original perch and bent to help the soldier from the cab. From the way he handled the man Maggie suspected he had been injured, and this seemed certain when the soldier flopped over the top spar in exhaustion while Randal struggled to loop his own rope twice around him in order to secure him also to the strop.

"We're approaching from the west and have you in sight," came the voice of the Casevac pilot. "What's the present situation?"

"Both soldiers have been brought from the vehicle and are clinging to the bridge. They are secured by ropes to us. One appears to be injured, and our pilot is roped to him. The other soldier can apparently move freely. Their situation is precarious. The bridge is shifting more dangerously every minute."

"OK, we'll lift them fast as we can."

For the first time Maggie understood the relief of those for whom the arrival of a helicopter meant an end to anxiety or suffering; the first time she was on the receiving end of airborne help instead of providing it. Casevac arrived in a blaze of light, and she overheard familiar instructions spoken in a transatlantic accent as the smaller medical aircraft closed on the scene fast.

"Jesus!" came the soft expletive. "We'll get the wounded guy up first. Then we'll go for the other casualty. Once he's safely with us, we'll get the last guy off before the goddam thing breaks apart. Let's go!"

The aircraft hovered at a safe height above the bridge, its light starkly emphasising the peril of the men at the mercy of the flood. Watching, Maggie's apprehension was doubled by being able to see everything more clearly but she contacted Control and gave a calm commentary on the rescue as it happened. The American winchman dropped down to alight on the bridge, then bent to help Randal unloop the rope tying the soldier to him. In the midst of this awkward operation a wall of water rose to wash right over them as the bridge shifted more violently than ever. Maggie drew in her breath but the three were still there.

"The injured man is safely up and the winchman is going down for the second," Maggie reported to Control.

The other soldier was successfully collected from his perch. As he was winched up, Maggie saw the rope drop away, but Ray and Jimmy made no attempt to return to the cabin. Until Randal was safe they were ready for the worst. As Maggie stared at the one remaining figure clinging to that uncertain support, a lump formed in her throat. He should get some kind of recognition for what he had done out there today.

"The winchman is going down for the last man – our pilot," she said thickly to Control. "He's locked on. They're being winched up. The rescue is complete. All three men are safe."

The other helicopter was already moving away from the river, and the pilot told Maggie he would land to let off their man before taking the casualties to the nearest aid post. "Could do with keeping him aboard. The soldiers are French and I can't speak it. None of us can, except your guy." A chuckle. "From the sound of it he's giving them a gutful for getting themselves in such a goddam mess."

Maggie laughed with relief. "That's our boss!"

They arrived back at Hampton to find the Indian summer continuing and the squadron offices manned by Simon, Vince, Nobby and Dave – the obligatory standby crew. Everyone else was out of the country or engaged in night flying, practice on the simulator or refresher courses in their own field of expertise. A Flight was dispersed overseas.

Randal took over from Simon who had been acting as squadron commander. Wing Commander Jeffries was on sick leave, having broken his wrist while playing squash. This news was greeted with howls of derisory laughter by those just back from Poland.

Randal wrote his usual report for the squadron commander and immediately countersigned it. Life was so much easier with Jeffries absent. He stayed in the office scanning a number of unimportant memos needing someone's signature. He wrote his own on them, then sat regarding the telephone on the desk instead of joining the others at the bar.

He had had ten days to think about going home, and in that time he had accepted the unpalatable truth that Fiona's love was merely love of his passion for her. She gloried in his response to her sexual challenge; delighted in his unbridled desire for her. It satisfied her need for attention and dominance. She had been reared by doting parents who had satisfied her every whim. A wealthy mature pilot fresh from war-torn Bosnia had offered the same slavish devotion with spicy sex added, and she had gone for it eagerly. Two children had clung to her as the most important person in their lives but the adoring husband had deserted her all too often, driving her back to parental cherishing. Now the husband had given her all she could wish for. She could be the star of the tennis club – of the whole damn precious scene – but woe betide him if he failed to succumb to her sexual invitations.

Randal swallowed hard as he faced the truth yet again. Where did they go from here? He was tired and strained after ten days of mock warfare; he could spend just four nights at home before flying out to support troops in a tense Balkan confrontation which might turn into active hostilities. He was in no state to salvage a relationship on the brink of failure. It had to be saved because he loved and wanted his children, but the fool who had mistaken lust for love now felt nothing for the woman waiting for him in the house he had believed would solve everything.

Sighing, he reached for the telephone and asked to be put through to his home number. It rang twice.

"Fiona Price."

"I'll be leaving in ten minutes."

"Welcome home, darling," she said breathlessly. "Drive fast. I can't wait."

For what, he wondered heavily. "Should be there by seven thirty."

"We'll have the place to ourselves, like I promised."

"See you."

By the time Randal reached the short stretch of motorway it was six thirty. The evening was a glory of pink and gold sky and chill clarity, the kind of conditions in which it was undiluted joy to fly. As soon as the sunset colours dimmed, bright stars would become visible and the atmosphere would

257

practically crackle with purity. It was too beautiful a night for the uncertainty ahead of him. He would rather be up there in that endless freedom with friends who understood and shared his great passion.

He slowed as he approached the bridge just beyond which he would take the junction leading north, then drove beneath it. As he emerged on the far side the sky crashed down on him. He hurtled into that fiery sunset, then onward to the blackest of nights.

Newspapers featured it on their inside pages the next morning.

PILOT FIGHTS FOR HIS
LIFE AFTER ANCHOR DROPS
FROM MOTORWAY BRIDGE

A helicopter pilot is dangerously ill in intensive care after boys dropped an old ship's anchor on his car as he drove beneath a motorway bridge last night. Squadron Leader Randal Price, 34, heir to the family food chain, was pulled from the wreckage of his Porsche and given emergency treatment at the scene of the accident. Eyewitnesses said some boys ran from the bridge after the crash, and police are following up a report from a woman walking her dog, who said four boys ran past her in a state of panic heading for Picton Chaney, a village half a mile from the motorway.

The victim's wife Fiona, 24, daughter of the well-known horse breeder, Gerald Holland, is under sedation at her parents' £6 million estate and stud. Mr Holland said the Prices' four-year-old son Neil had suffered a medical crisis in February, so this additional shock has hit his daughter hard. She was too upset to answer questions.

Rhona Price said last night at her £2 million mansion near Harrogate that her husband was in Jamaica on business and would return as soon as he could. She was in constant telephone contact with the hospital and would visit her son the moment doctors allowed her at his bedside.

November

The boys were traced, four of them between the ages of eight and eleven calling themselves the "Chaney Gang" and generally going through an apprenticeship for full-blown thuggery. They had found the old anchor on a council tip and racked their few brains for a place to hang it where it would cause a rumpus. Their first choice had been the cross on the church, then other sites which also proved inaccessible. One suggested dangling it from the bridge, but the chain had slipped through their hands before they had time to fix it in place. They had not meant to drop it on anyone. It was just a lark; a bit of fun.

Their parents all complained that they had never been able to control the little buggers. Do-gooders claimed it was high spirits not malice behind the deed; the police insisted it was a chargeable offence. The victim could not be asked the usual crass media question, "How do you feel about what has happened?" because he was hovering between life and death.

The next day reporters dug up what they could about the young Prices. No scandal, so they switched to questioning the vicar and leading residents of Picton Chaney, then the local social workers. The latter denied criminal intent by the boys and blamed lack of understanding by parents and teachers. The boys were offered counselling.

Two days later, dwindling interest in the affair was eclipsed by the sensational suicide attempt of Darcee, lead singer with the Sex Bandits, who had overdosed after his new single "If the world says no, I say yes" failed to reach number one in the charts after three weeks. His manager said Darcee had been under impossible strain during the group's tour of the US, and the stress of maintaining perfection had left him deeply depressed on his return to London. He had put his heart and soul into the lyrics of his song and saw its luke-warm reception, after a panning by the critics, as a personal rejection by all the oppressed people of the world he was championing.

While Darcee languished in hospital, vanloads of flowers and get-well messages arrived for him. Fans kept vigil outside the hospital and the song went to number one. It was destined to stay there for many weeks.

They had just told him, calmly and frankly, what had happened and what his present condition was. He was paralysed from the chest down, both arms were broken below the elbows and his neck was held rigid in a spinal brace. Machines monitored his heart, his blood pressure, his breathing and his brain activity. Tubes and bags dealt with his bodily functions.

Panic seized him. Four small boys had turned him into an inert lump of meat. It was crazy. It was a nightmare. It was just another attack of malaria. It could not be true. *Dear God, it could not have happened to him!* He lay as if in a transparent bubble, seeing himself in flying gear standing outside it and being unable to climb into his own body. His sense of panic increased and a machine began violently bleeping. A woman's voice spoke soothingly. A needle prick in his upper arm. The vision of himself grew smaller and smaller as it retreated into the distance.

Two men dressed as policemen were looking down at him. One had a notebook in his hand. What did he remember of the accident? Did he see any boys on the bridge? How fast was he travelling? They were part of the ongoing nightmare, as unreal as the bubble he was in. They went away unanswered. People he had known from a previous life loomed up. They mouthed things at him. "How are you?" "They can work miracles these days." "Chin up, son, things'll get better before long." "I'll pray you find strength in the coming weeks." Thankfully, they soon went away leaving him free to attempt escape from the bubble. There was none!

Time passed and he was forced to accept the nightmare as reality. He *was* an inert lump of meat; four boys had taken from him everything but his life. Why not that? He craved death. His eyes were not paralysed. By swivelling them he could see the switches of the life-support machines. If only he could reach out and turn them off!

Another day, he had no idea how much later. He did not

care. The machines and tubes were still with him. A man in a white coat said he was making great strides. Ha! Shoot the bugger for that tasteless pun. Shoot the one who decided to reduce the sedation. For an inert lump of meat everything hurt in inverse bloody ratio. Sleep was the only escape, except that he was terrified by visions of being hurtled into a fiery furnace. He still could not reach those switches.

Another day, he had no idea how much later. He did not care. The machines had been unplugged, the tubes and bags remained. He still could not move but he was to be sent to a special spinal unit where they could do a lot for him. Ha!

They did so much he had little time to sleep. X-rays, tests, more X-rays, more tests. Then surgery. He wondered why they were bothering. Surely they had more useful things to do? Apparently not. They came to him all smiles and cups of tea when he reluctantly emerged from the anaesthetic.

A man with a long horse face said breezily, "We've achieved a highly successful orthopaedic repair, Mr Price, which throws a more optimistic light on your future progress. The damage to your nervous system is far less than we had feared and it can be minimised with therapy sessions. Once the fractures of both ulnas have fused you'll have full use of your arms. We aim to get you in a wheelchair before long and start you on a course of physio to stimulate the circulation in your legs."

Randal glared. "Am I supposed to jump up and down with glee?"

"We don't expect you to be as gratified as we are right now," the specialist replied calmly, "but when you've mulled the facts over for a few days you'll probably see things in a different light. There's one aspect we should tackle right away, however. You've been steadfast in your refusal to see visitors, including your wife, since you arrived here. We've gone along with that for several reasons, and also because your father-in-law explained to us that your son suffered a crisis earlier in the year and your wife finds it difficult to cope with a second so soon after. It's understandable. An emergency call to a hospital to see no more than an unconscious hump beneath a criss-cross of cables, wires and tubes can be a considerable shock to close relatives. But you and Mrs Price do have to accept what has happened and talk about it together." He smiled. "Now your facial contusions have faded you look less villainous, so I'd like to arrange a visit from your wife as soon as possible." Without waiting for a comment from his patient, he stood. "I think Sister can ensure there's not a machine, drip stand or bedpan in sight when she comes."

When he left, the young woman with him stayed in her chair. Randal glared at her. "What are you hanging around for?"

"I thought we might have a chat."

"You thought wrong, chum."

"All right, we'll share a companionable silence."

He was too raw and weary to argue. His head ached and his eyes shot open again each time he tried to sleep. His body felt as if it had been pummelled, which was ridiculous because he had been robbed of feeling from his chest down. Both his arms were weighted with plaster; his neck was still in some kind of clamp. He was the living dead.

"When are you going to open this pile of letters?" she asked quietly. After a brief silence, she added, "He's really cute. I guess one of your children sent him in for you."

Randal rolled his eyes to see what she was holding. It was almost like a body blow to see Rip van Bruin in her hand. "How the bloody hell did that get here?"

He came with you from the emergency unit, along with these sealed letters. I believe you have two children, a boy and a girl. It's nice to have one of each."

"That's what kids should have," he said thickly. "A mother and a father."

"Yours have."

Her dogged reasonableness really got to him then and he poured out his rage. "A flaming lump of meat in a wheelchair? A pathetic bloody cripple who can do bugger-all for himself and has to piss into a bag? What the hell sodding use do you think I'd be to them?"

"You could teach them to swear better than the other kids in the street, for a start."

That jolted him with its warm sense of familiarity, and for long moments he held her calm challenging gaze while his rage evaporated. "You're beginning to sound like Maggie."

"Oh? In what way?"

"She also imagines she's got men sussed."

"Is Maggie your wife?"

"No. One of my . . ." He let the sentence trail off into the past.

"I've seen newspaper pictures of Mrs Price. She's strikingly lovely. All the men'll get a tremendous lift when she comes."

"She won't." He was banking on that. "She can't stand illness and hospitals."

"Most people feel the same, but they put it aside when someone they love needs them."

He swallowed his surge of dread. "All I need is that guy who was here just now to tell me I'll fly again."

"He can't do that."

"Yeah, I got the message on day one."

She approached and perched on the bed. "Things will get a lot better than on day one. Have faith. When we take the plaster from your arms you'll be surprised at how many things you can do. Once we've worked full power back to the muscles you'll be independently mobile. Some of the younger patients here are terrors in wheelchairs. At the first sight of a hypodermic they're off from nought to sixty in three seconds flat."

He studied her for a moment or two: dark cap of hair, smiling but shrewd brown eyes, slim figure, capable hands. "Are you some kind of shrink?"

She shook her head. "There's nothing wrong with your mind. Think of me as a liaison officer, if you like. Or an impartial friend. Any time you feel you want to talk, just—"

"You *are* a shrink."

Her smile was attractive. "I pity any psychiatrist who attempts to analyse you. If you change your mind about a chat ask for Millie. That's me." She stood, picking up the bear. "Has he a name?"

"Sure."

"Well, are you going to let me in on it?"

"It wouldn't mean anything to you."

"Does he belong to your little girl?"

"No, to my . . . a team. He's their mascot."

"For luck, eh? I guess that's why he found his way to you."

Two days later, Fiona was to visit him. They spruced him up, tucked the catheter and urine bag out of sight and put his mother's expensive flowers on his locker. The bouquets came regularly, but pork pies made heavy social and business demands on his parents so the flowers were probably organised by the company secretary. Still, the hospital staff were impressed and that was what really mattered.

Randal was propped against a mountain of pillows, plaster-encased arms resting on the pristine counterpane, his head held steady by an unyielding brace. He realised the full extent of his helplessness as he waited for the girl he had once loved so crazily to prove with one look what he already knew. He did not want this; she certainly would not. The break should have been made by letter, or by proxy. What had been crippled by the dropping of an anchor should be allowed to die with dignity. Like him.

As the afternoon crept by he grew more and more desperate, until he heard Millie's voice outside his open door. They had pulled the curtains across the windows facing the corridor so he could not see Fiona. The voices were hushed, but he recognised Gerald Holland's authoritative tones. Oh God! But he should have expected this. Fiona would need support, and from who else but Daddy?

He heard Millie say, "Just for the first five minutes, Mr Holland, then you must give them some time alone."

They came in. Fiona's eyes looked larger than ever in her pale face, so they transmitted her distress in double force. She wore a chocolate-brown fitted coat Randal had not seen before; the soft fur collar enhancing the vivid beauty of her features. Even under these conditions she looked stunning. Any lingering uncertainty fled as Randal remembered her generous response to his lovemaking. A gorgeous twenty-four-year-old vibrant with youth and energy would wilt and fade without passionate adoration to nourish her.

"Hallo, old chap," said Gerald with forced heartiness. "You look far better than the last time we came. Well, it was impossible to see anything of you, actually. Very alarming for my little girl. A terrible shock."

Fiona approached and quickly kissed Randal's forehead. "Hallo, darling. I brought some grapes. That woman is going to wash them for you." She retreated to her father's side, her haven.

It was Randal's turn to speak but he could think of nothing appropriate. It was as bad as he had known it would be.

Gerald filled the gap. "Mary sends her best."

"So do the children," Fiona said hastily. "I didn't bring them because it wouldn't do to let them see you like—"

He found words then. "Like what? Go on, Fee, say it in language we can all understand."

Gerald intervened. "Aggression won't solve anything, Randal. I'm sure it can't be easy for you, but have you given any thought to what Fiona has been going through?"

"Oh yes, and she'll go through a bloody sight more if she stays tied to me," he said, knowing it would all flood out now the dam had been breached. "I'll be in a wheelchair for the rest of my days. I'll have no control over my bladder and bowels, and sex will be impossible, even if she fancied it with a cripple. I'll be moody and bitter, which will lead to thundering rows. She'll have to deal with all the problems with the kids, the house and grounds. She'll have to chauffeur me if I ever have to go anywhere. She'll have to go to parties alone – go everywhere alone – and that'll lead to more thundering rows about who she's been with and what she's been up to." He turned on Fiona. "Your constant complaint has been that I'm never there. Well, I'll be there with a vengeance, hanging round your neck like a millstone, and I'll loathe and resent every single bloody helpless moment. You wanted me to give up flying. You've got your wish, pussycat."

Fiona began to sob. Gerald put his arm around her and led her away. At the door he looked over his shoulder. "You bastard!"

"Got it in one," Randal murmured unsteadily.

Millie came almost an hour later and perched on his bed. "I couldn't persuade her to come back. We'll have to leave it for a day or two. Why did you do it?"

"You're the shrink. Guess."

Her hand covered his as it lay on the counterpane. "It's too early to make that kind of decision. Far too early."

He said wearily, "You saw her. She couldn't possibly cope with this. She needs to be cossetted and admired."

"You can't judge her until she's been faced with it. Believe me, the most unlikely people often rise magnificently to challenges more daunting than you at your worst. I suppose you have the usual male attitude that if a woman is beautiful she must be generally useless. Give the poor girl a chance."

"They didn't teach you much at the shrinks' school. I've just given her the chance of her life – to opt out of a marriage that was on a downhill slide even before I drove under that bridge. I simply pushed it fast to the bottom. Better than struggling for weeks against overwhelming odds and suffering unnecessarily."

"What about your children?"

"They're used to my being away and they're very young. No doubt they'll soon get a new dad."

"How will the present dad feel about that?"

He glared. "You've done your stuff. I'd like to be left alone."

She went, pulling back the curtains that had shut him off from human activity in the corridor. It was her way of saying he could not be alone. But he was, utterly and irrevocably.

The big light on the corner of the building outside his room came on as it grew dark. It illuminated the washbasin facing his bed and highlighted the gold initials on his briefcase standing beside it. R.I.P. Oh God, if only he could!

Three crews had been in Egypt for eighteen days, flying troops and transporting cargo in desert conditions as part of their ongoing training. They attempted to occupy their free time with the usual things – beetle races, softball, sexy blockbusters, Trivial Pursuit, heated arguments on the topics of the day, and sand-kart racing – but they invariably fell to recalling the time when Rip . . .

Arguments tended to fizzle out without his provocative input. Games of softball were nowhere near as enjoyable when he was not making hilarious changes to the rules to suit his own performance, and kart racing was tame without his exuberant hell-for-leather participation. When the radio picked up a music station no one had the heart to suggest B Flight's Egyptian conga. The set was turned off. If their boss had been imitating Damon Hill – not unknown – and smashed himself up or even suffered a flying accident, they could more easily have accepted the outcome. It was the way in which his career and almost his life had been terminated that was so shocking. It overshadowed their spirits as they sweltered and thought about the odds on a white Christmas when they got home.

Dave had not been in the desert with them before but he knew enough of Randal's antics in other places to understand their mood. But despite that, and the fact that his work was very hot and sweaty out here, he appreciated the desert as he did most wild open country. He would like to see it under other circumstances; sense the immensity and silence of it. There was no get-away-from-it-all aspect to this visit. Their tents were pitched near an Army encampment where troops were on desert manoeuvres, and jets from a military airfield screamed overhead at all hours of the day and night.

Lying awake one hot afternoon while his tent-mates were snoring, Dave smiled to himself. As a person normally unwilling to discuss personal aspects of his life – unlike the rest who were prone to do so at the least encouragement – he had just written four pages of his thoughts, opinions and feelings about living and working in the challenging endless sands to a man he sensed would understand and share them. The DNA test had proved positive, and Dave now had someone who genuinely cared where he was and what he was doing. It was an experience akin to discovering religion, Dave supposed, because Ralph had become a focus for his life.

It was in this mellow mood that Dave spotted Maggie emerge from the next tent and wander across to sink down in the shade cast by one of their aircraft. In shorts, a loose top and a floppy khaki hat she looked very much like any ordinary young woman, rather than a pilot who had been making successful landings in rotor-induced sandstorms. She sat gazing into space, isolated in her reverie. Sad thoughts of Mark? A sense of loneliness in male company? She had been in Poland on his return from the Falklands, so Dave had had little chance to confirm his suspicion that he might be falling in love with her. The tragic fate of their boss had intervened, but he saw an opportunity now.

Pulling on a T-shirt over his shorts he crossed to her with a can of beer from the ice-box in the tent, to make his approach appear more casual. She seemed unaware of him until he dropped to the ground beside her, when she jumped nervously.

"Sorry. Wasn't creeping up on you." He waved a hand at three jets making a deafening approach prior to landing. "You'd not hear an avenging horde coming against that."

She tilted her head to watch them. "Mark said that brand of flying was like being in a world halfway between this one and the next."

"Any form of flying is halfway to heaven, I guess, so if you're travelling at jet speed it's probable you'd feel in a world apart."

Turning to study him from beneath the rim of her hat, she

said, "Something's come over you lately. What happened to the grouchy north-of-the-border misogynist?"

"Must be the heat." He adopted an exaggerated Scottish accent. "We've noo liking for warrrmth, lassie."

She studied him further. "Is there something you want or, saints preserve us, are you trying to be friendly?"

He probably deserved her attitude, but he pressed on. "I'd offer to share my beer if you liked it."

"I drink anything that's cold and wet out here."

He handed over the can. "Only half, mind. I want the rest."

She drank thirstily, then pulled a face. "A person has to be desperate to drink this stuff."

"It grows on you." He took back the can and they sat in silence for a while. Yet it was not awkward or uncomfortable.

Still gazing at the shimmering distance, Maggie said, "I can't get the Boss out of my mind. I took Rip van Bruin to the hospital before we came out here, as you know, but I feel I should do more. Write to him, perhaps. But what could I say?"

He shook his head. "What could any of us say, except that we'd like to tie the anchor to those boys and throw them in the sea. Wouldn't help, though, would it?"

"No." Another short silence. "He wrote to me when Mark was killed; said to remember he'd gone out on a high. It was comforting but it's a far greater comfort to know that Mark was spared what *he's* facing. I feel I should try to help him the way he helped me."

Unused to a girl offering confidences and a plea for advice, Dave was out of his depth. "His wife's the best person to help him."

Her head shot round. "She's a self-centred bitch! You didn't see that scene at the Mess dinner dance, but you've heard team gossip. She walked out on him, refusing to be a service wife. She demanded a mansion miles from Hampton before she'd live with him again, and she fills the place with her friends so that he feels like the lodger when he gets there. She won't help him. All she'll be concerned about is how this'll affect her cushioned life."

Taken aback by her vehemence, Dave murmured, "Mebbe a shock like this'll pull her together." Yet as he said it he thought of Leanne. Self-centred women never changed; they changed the circumstances to suit themselves.

His thoughts of Leanne at Sir Hector's funeral moved on to

Edwina's letter and the way his own life had changed. He said hesitantly, "You helped me once."

She gave a faint smile. "That cowbell business?"

The greater events of the past two months had driven the episode from his mind. "No, I was thinking of something quite different. I had to make an important decision – important for me, that is. I had to make it but I couldn't. Just couldn't."

She said quietly, "I just couldn't decide whether or not I should go to Mark's funeral. A major decision and it's so difficult, isn't it?"

He had been unaware of her dilemma; it had never occurred to him. Now he understood all too well. "If you'd gone, the media would have sussed out who you were and hounded you. Mark wouldn't have wanted that."

"I feel his spirit is England, anyway. What was your problem, Dave? You seemed tense and worried after your visit to Scotland. Anything to do with that?"

He chose his words carefully. "Aye. I was given a letter after my great-uncle's death. It revealed the truth about something in the distant past and put on me the onus of making it known or letting sleeping dogs lie."

"A skeleton in the cupboard? Gosh!" She hugged her knees, gazing at him with interest. "You said I helped you. How could I? How did I?"

Once he would have resented her words; clammed up and walked away. But the somnolent afternoon, the suggestion of being isolated with this girl in the burning emptiness all around them, the hot breeze which played over him instead led to further confession.

"I'd decided to take the easy way out and say nothing, but your feelings for Mark, and his for you, showed me that people can be extremely close to each other. I'd never had first-hand evidence of that and it helped me to see the situation more clearly. Put it right." As he gazed out across the empty sands he suddenly grew embarrassed. "I've never been too hot at explaining things."

When she spoke her voice was thick with emotion. "Thanks for telling me, anyway. It seems to be one more thing Mark achieved in his short life."

Dave did not understand that remark, but he took on board the fact that Hascham was still a powerful force in her mind. Would he, himself, ever be as important to a girl? To her?

She broke the short silence. "What you said just now; does that mean you've never been involved with anyone? I know men often play the field, like Jeff, and so long as they find like-minded playmates that's fine. But you don't seem to do that, which is why I've always thought someone must have hurt you. Or is that you just haven't met the right girl?"

He remembered holding her as they flew back from the air show; remembered wishing he could play God and bring Mark alive and unscathed from the ashes for her. Was it love or compassion he felt? Was he so caught up linking the Maggie-Mark tragedy with the long-ago one of Edwina and Ralph that he was unable to define his emotions? Studying the sun-browned girl beside him, Dave was uncertain whether it was she or Edwina Rowan he was trying to draw close to. The mystique of this ancient land must be affecting his judgement. That, or the burning heat.

"No one hurt me, I hurt myself," he confessed, knowing it to be true. "That's worse, because you can't shift the blame elsewhere."

She gave an audible sigh. "Life's a bastard, isn't it? You either love someone who hardly cares that you exist or you're crazy about each other and one dies."

Her words so closely reflected what Ralph had told him, Dave was deeply touched. "The other one recovers, Maggie. Eventually. I've recently had proof of that."

It was a minute or two before she said, "I've always admired your determination, although it meant you held out against me far longer than the rest of the team." A faint smile appeared. "You're still the enigmatic Highlander unwilling to give too much of himself away but I hope we're now friends."

"Aye. Friends," he agreed, still unsure if that was the only relationship he wanted with her. It was a step in the right direction, anyway.

The following morning Dave flew with Nobby and Pete, piloted by Maggie, on a task that involved locating and transporting an armoured truck. It was one of the Army's favourite tricks on practice manoeuvres to hide a piece of equipment then send a helicopter out to look for it, rather like ordering a gun-dog to fetch a dead grouse from somewhere in the undergrowth. It could be fun playing the game if it went smoothly, but Maggie was not in a fun mood after the lieutenant who had briefed them murmured to her in parting, "If you're not back by dusk I'll send a handsome sheik on a white horse to look for you." She spent the first few minutes in the air vowing to give the khaki bastard a taste of *Guju ryu* when she got back.

"A fat lot of backup you dozy lot gave me," she added.

"We didn't hear the guy," Pete said. "We keep telling you."

"He made certain of that," she raged inconsistently. "He didn't fancy overwhelming odds."

"If we had heard him," put in Nobby, stirring it, "we'd have asked him to send out a few harem girls as well, for us."

"Get stuffed, Nobby! That goes for the rest of you too. We're a team. We're supposed to support each other."

"Read my lips," said Pete forcefully. "We . . . did . . . not . . . hear . . . him!"

"If the Boss was here, he wouldn't have . . ." Her words tailed off. It was happening all the time. They could not get used to the notion that he was no longer with B Flight. Maggie stopped complaining and fell silent.

Dave was feeling light-hearted. Life was good; this game of hide-and-seek appealed to him and he was flying with Maggie. The comment of the army officer had probably been no more than a badly judged come-on, which Maggie would normally have countered with her biting wit. The man was not aware that she was trying to recover from a tragedy. Two, perhaps? She was clearly troubled by her inability to help Randal as he had helped her. Yet what could she do? What could any of them do? The team had conferred and decided to let enough time pass to allow the poor devil to come to terms with his fate. It was not as if they could send rude get-well messages, the normal practice when a team member was in hospital.

Pete was now rabbiting on about the dog he had bought for the girl who had then thrown him over the second time. The huge lumbering puppy had turned Pete into a huge lumbering idiot, in the team's opinion.

"Oh, pipe down about that bloody cur," put in Nobby, clearly in mischievious mood today. "Its breath's foul and it's full of fleas. Dogs are very unhygenic, you know. They can pass on awful diseases. I read about this guy who'd been fondling a dog, then went for a slash without washing his hands and—"

"Are you looking out for this truck or on a lads' outing?"

demanded Maggie. "We're approaching the area we were given and I want to pick this damn thing up and get back fast enough to shove it down that pathetic bastard's astonished open mouth."

Nobby and Dave exchanged looks as they moved to vantage points from where they could study the terrain. They had been given a large square area in which a sand-coloured vehicle was lurking beneath a camouflage net or alongside rocks. Desert terrain was not always mile upon undulating mile of untrodden golden sand; much of it was surface shale with rocky outcrops across which rough roads wound towards the horizon and isolated settlements. The area over which they now flew was like that.

It was hard on the eyes. Approaching mid morning the sun glared on the stony ground where their gliding shadow provided the only dark contrast. This exercise was twofold in that it trained them to look not only for lost equipment valuable enough to bring in, but also to spot enemy positions in time of war. The three men in the crew today regarded their task in the light of a boyhood treasure hunt rather than the earnest military operation Maggie had in mind, and they had even laid bets on who would spot the "treasure" first. That had been done behind their pilot's back. Wiser, knowing her mood!

"I'm not going to make the usual parallel runs," she announced. "It's too long-winded. We'll first make two diagonal flights over the area instead. Use your eyes. They won't have put it just inside the boundary. Much too easy. It's more likely to be nearer the far side or in the extreme corners."

Pete yawned. "Yeah, and while we're flying our guts out the handlers'll be drinking cold beer with their feet up, laughing at us."

"You won't be flying your guts out, I will," the tetchy pilot pointed out to her navigator.

"Ah, but I'm the one who'll guide you back in time to stop the khaki bastard sending out a sheik," Pete swiftly replied.

"Just shut up and start looking!"

Nobby and Dave exchanged more visual comments and started looking.

Maggie flew a diagonal from west to east, then followed the further boundary of the area to embark on a south to north course. Ten minutes later she cried, "There it is! Crafty devils. They covered it with canvas painted to resemble rocks but forgot that it wobbles when caught in our downdraught." As they circled what had initially appeared to be a rock formation, she added, "So I'll collect my winnings from you all when I've dropped our load on that sexist smoothie who thinks we're as brainless as he is."

"You weren't in on the bet," objected Dave, wondering how she knew about their deal. "So you can't collect anything."

"So you'd prefer me to land and sit around in the heat until you decide that I'm entitled to? Own up. I beat those Superman eyes of yours, Dave."

"They're only keen in mountains," he murmured, gazing from the door at the fake rocks moving in the force from their rotors as Maggie hovered above their objective.

The soldiers, who were also hiding, appeared reluctant to come out and acknowledge defeat, so Maggie began to descend saying she would frighten the living daylights out of them. Pete was not happy about that, and said so, but she was the boss today and her ploy worked. Laughing, she gained height when the men ran out. They untied the canvas and pulled it away to reveal an armoured truck and a desert jeep.

The airborne crewmen and the two army handlers cheerily exchanged vulgar gestures and then began the familiar business of attaching the heavy vehicle at the central hatch. While Nobby and he talked Maggie into position, Dave lay beside the hole to watch the soldiers secure the giant hook to the swivel linking the four chains together. The handlers wore goggles to protect their eyes from flying grit while the Chinook descended to within three feet of them as they crouched atop the truck. They were all highly experienced, so the task was done with speed and efficiency. The handlers then jumped to the ground to face a long hot drive back to camp knowing the helicopter crew would be there in a very short time.

Reciting the patter for Maggie as the aircraft rose up to take the full weight of the vehicle, Dave felt sorry for the two men left a very long way from their camp.

The chains began to take the strain and their load was soon swinging free of the ground. Then Pete set the course for home and they were on their way. The terrain was uniformly flat for the greater part of the journey so Maggie could stay low.

"Thanks, guys," she said jubilantly. "This'll teach them to

use their brains when thinking up camouflage in future. I sussed their pathetic ruse right away."

"Stop being so cocky," Pete chided. "It's only an exercise. You haven't just wiped out an enemy position."

"But I'll wipe out that insufferable bozo who offered to send out a search party. I can't wait to see his expression when we go in with this in record time."

They were all sensible enough to drop the subject. The subaltern's unwise joke had really got to her and her prime need was to rub his nose in his idiocy. Pete began relating an anecdote about a sheik who once wandered in to the wrong harem and soon became a eunuch, but Nobby said he had heard that old chestnut once too often and he would even prefer tales of flea-bitten Arnie to such tosh.

Dave was studying the load dangling beneath them. "It's one of those new Mark Four jobs, I reckon," he said to his companion. "They cost a bomb to produce."

"Nah, I heard they stopped production after the last defence cuts," Nobby said. "They only made two. Not likely to use one for this, are they? It must be some clapped-out job no use to anyone."

"Aye, but they had to drive it out there, didn't they? That thing doesn't look in the least clapped-out. Odd design. Can hardly tell front from back."

"Maybe it's a Mark Five," suggested Nobby with a chuckle. "Manufactured specially to hide from blokes like us."

Their interest in the subject waned and they went to their seats where they had bottles of water. It was stifling in the cabin, and the air coming through the open hatches was hot and gritty. They asked Maggie to gain a little more height so their rotors would not churn up so much dust. She climbed thirty feet. Pete was eulogising about Arnie once more. No one listened. There was only so much anyone could say about a dog, and he had already said it three times over.

Dave was taking another swig from his bottle of water when there was a tremendous thump beneath them. The Chinook began rocking and shuddering violently. He jumped up at the same time as Nobby. "Christ, what's that?"

"What the hell's going on back there?" cried Maggie as the helicopter continued to vibrate dangerously. "What's happened?"

274

Dave and Nobby gazed down to see the truck swinging on just three chains. Two links of the fourth remained attached to the hook, the rest hung down clanking rhythmically against the armour plating as the vehicle moved.

"One of the chains has busted. The load's now unstable," Dave announced tersely.

"Can you do anything?" she asked, cutting her speed to lessen the yawing of the aircraft. "I'm having a hard job holding us steady."

"Better jettison," Nobby reasoned.

"But we're almost there! Can't it be stabilised?"

The insecure load was creating a hazardous sideways pull on the fuselage and it had now started to swivel, twisting the chains, which increased the strain on the seating of the hook.

"Negative," said Dave. "It's all getting impossibly snagged up. If we don't jettison there'll be structural damage back here."

Although Maggie had slowed considerably, the Chinook was still juddering and yawing. Dave knew she must be finding it very difficult to fly the aircraft and he was about to insist that they released the load when there was a crack like gunfire and a second chain broke. As the Chinook lurched violently, he acted without hesitation and moved to the cabin button.

"Jettison! Jettison!" he cried. "Releasing the load now."

"*No, Hold it!*" yelled Maggie with such urgency that Dave's hand froze on the button. "There's a settlement below us. Can't jettison here."

"Have to," snapped Nobby. "It'll rip a hole in the floor."

As Maggie fought to keep the aircraft from careering all over the sky, she said, "We'll kill someone."

"You want to kill us instead?" he snarled back, making frantic signals to Dave to push the button as the metal around the centre hatch began to buckle ominously.

Dave hesitated. If their load tore free it would drop, regardless of what lay beneath them, and he could see people on the ground now. Then the Chinook jerked so suddenly he was thrown off his feet, the sound of staccato voices in the cockpit filling his ears through the intercom. The two officers were putting their utmost into staying in the air while heading for open desert. Dave met Nobby's furious gaze as the other man lay where he had been thrown by the bucking motion. The seating of the central cargo hook was being rent apart before their eyes as they clung to the nearest solid support.

"Load being jettisoned *now*," barked Pete, after a period of minutes that seemed to Dave like hours. The Chinook rose with a stomach-churning lurch as the spinning truck dropped away.

"That should have been done half a sodding hour ago," raged Nobby, releasing his tension by kicking at the fuselage. "Who'll get the blame for ripping up the bloody floor? You and me, Dave, that's who. I've been on this job for eight flaming years and never once gone back with a great—"

"Shut up, Nobby," snapped Maggie. "None of us has ever gone back in this state, but Pete and I would prefer a bollocking for slightly damaging the aircraft than for starting a new Middle East crisis by killing half a dozen Egyptians. Now, what about you, Dave? Anything to get off *your* chest?"

He said nothing. Maggie was clearly very shaken and was letting off steam by putting on a captain of the crew act. She had been faced with a critical decision and was lucky to have kept the Chinook in the air throughout. Lucky or very skilled? A bit of both, probably. Either way, they would all be facing an inquiry into the damage to their aircraft – something all aircrew dreaded – to say nothing of explaining why the truck had been dumped in the desert.

After a tense silence, Pete asked, "How come two of those effing chains broke, guys?"

"God knows," said Dave heavily. "They were either u.s. or the handlers misjudged the weight of the load and used the wrong ones."

"Looked all right to me," put in Nobby, back on his feet and calming down. "I reckon they'd been lying around a long time and no one tested them lately."

"So what do we tell Lawrence of Arabia?" demanded Maggie.

"Never mind him. What about this bloody chewed-up floor?" countered Nobby sourly.

"Better than chewed-up bodies," she said shortly. "Can I count on you two to back me on that, or can't I?"

"Of course."

Dave kicked Nobby's ankle pointedly, and the other man grunted, "Yeah, yeah."

"So what do we tell the Army about the truck?"

"The truth," said Dave. "When they go out to it they'll see the broken chains. They can't hold an inquest over it."

"Want a bet?" challenged Pete.

The army lieutenant was scathing and spoke about panic decisions. Dave and Nobby strenuously denied this and told him to wait until the vehicle was inspected before he laid blame. Unused to the freedom of speech allowed to aircrew sergeants, he took exception to being instructed on what to do by NCOs.

"I reach decisions based on facts," he snapped. "The fact is that you were sent out to locate and bring in an armoured vehicle. It now apparently lies arse-up some five miles from here. By the time someone gets out there it'll have been stripped of everything, leaving it bloody useless."

"Just like the chains attached to it," said Maggie swiftly. "If we hadn't jettisoned there'd also be an aircraft and crew arse-up five miles from here."

The smooth subaltern narrowed his eyes. "Tricky aerial situations should surely be handled by two pilots, one at least being a man."

Pete was furious. "I don't hold a licence to fly, but I know as much about the aircraft as any pilot. No one could have flown that load in."

"But the Chinook cockpit is designed for a pilot and co-pilot," the other man insisted coolly.

"Yes," agreed Maggie equally coolly. "But we're all so highly trained we're equally effective with a navigator. Don't you have the same versatility in the Army?"

"We've got more discipline," he told her savagely. "And we investigate very thoroughly any breakdown in it. However, I'm prepared to hold my fire until your claim has been checked."

"It's those chains that need checking," said Maggie, preparing to leave. "I'll submit my report through the usual channels. It won't deviate from what I've just told you. We might appear less disciplined in the Air Force, but we're professionally unbeatable. Tell that to the handsome sheik you have standing by, so he'll know why he wasn't needed."

Dave and the others followed her from the tent, smirking over the man's furious expression. Even so, Maggie looked pale and shaken as she walked with them to where their tents stood. She stopped by the first one and faced her crew.

"I take back all I said this morning about not supporting me.

277

Thanks for backing me just then. I hope that pig gets it in the neck over those bloody chains." She gave a strained smile. "I'll go and report the damage to the cabin. Nobby, Dave, I'll take full responsibility for it and report that you both wanted to jettison earlier. There'll be no comeback on you."

Pete spoke up immediately. "There were two of us in the cockpit. I share the responsibility, Maggie, and I'm coming with you to make that report." He turned to the crewmen. "All you guys'll have to say when questioned is that you took appropriate action according to your assessment of the situation, but that you were overruled from the cockpit."

Nobby grunted. "I'd have pushed the sodding button if I'd been Dave, no matter what you said. How we didn't all end arse-up under a pile of wreckage, God knows. Must've been due to some fancy flying. But I tell you now, I never want another fright like that. If that's going to be your style from now on, Maggie, I'll ask the Boss to put me with someone else."

"You can't ask him," she replied sadly. "He's no longer part of the team."

They all fell silent before the two officers walked off to make their report, then Dave turned on Nobby. "You miserable sod! She was in the aircraft, too. It was her life on the line as well as ours. She got us out of that with guts and skill."

Nobby grinned somewhat shakily. "I know that, but we don't want to make her cockier than she already is, do we?"

Dave was thoughtful as he watched the slim figure in the green flying suit. It seemed that Maggie Spencer was two different people. Yesterday she had been a caring young woman seeking friendship and reassurance from him. Today she was the captain of a crew, ready to defend her decisions with professional confidence. It would be a great mistake to allow himself to be too charmed by the first, and forget the second side of her personality.

December

They had been back at Hampton for twenty-four hours and Maggie had slept for twelve of them. Centrally heated stuffiness and the comfort of a real bed had caused her to fall asleep without the usual struggle against memories of a blazing aircraft plunging to the ground. It was gradually improving all round. Getting back to work had won half the battle; being fully embraced by the team had restored her self-confidence. Yet there was a new shadow over it all.

Mark had been uninhibited in all his passions, so she knew how he would have reacted to a situation like Randal's. She continued to be plagued by the urge to help but from what she knew of her boss he would fling sympathy back in her face. He could be prickly at the best of times, and this was the worst. Maggie was also certain that bra-less Fiona would soon dump him. There was really nothing any of his team – or rather his former team, because his career was at an end – could do. They reckoned seeing any of them would be more upsetting for him than their absence. She should accept their judgement. They had all known him longer than she had.

After a hearty breakfast Maggie decided to drive to the hospital. She had no plan and might well turn around and drive straight back, but she could not laze the day away knowing the man who had personally flown to fetch her on that terrible day now needed a friend, whether he liked it or not. She was fetching her car keys from her room when the telephone rang.

"Flight Lieutenant Spencer."

"Hallo, Maggie. They told me you'd be back today. It's Pete McGrath."

"Sorry, who?"

"Oh lord, am I that forgettable? Picture this: girl in taxi with plastered Scotsman. Ugly German driver demanding triple fare. Knight with shining stethoscope riding to the rescue."

She laughed. "That was months ago, and we only had one date. Lots of water under the bridge since then. Anyway, how are you?"

"Fine. I'm back in England, not all that far from Hampton. The hospital at Haslar."

"Pleased?"

"Yes, it's interesting work. Will you have dinner with me . . . or lunch . . . or breakfast?"

"Aren't there any women at Haslar?"

"Mmm, lots. None as nice as you."

"We had one date, in Munich, in April. We've had no contact since then," she protested.

"Munich was a case of ships that pass in the night. Now I'm back in England, and so near we have a chance of getting to know each other. How's the drunken Scot, by the way?"

"Reasonably sober. He's just flown with me on a difficult flight over the desert."

"Oh. Not sure I can compete with that. All I've done lately is brandish thermometers and puncture a few arms."

Maggie smiled. She had enjoyed her dinner date with him. He was easy, amusing and uncomplicated. "I'm sure you've done more than that."

"How about this date?"

"When were you thinking of?"

"Tomorrow? I've got a weekend off. There's a nice hotel near Hampton called Farley Grange. I could book a table and—"

"Not there! Look, I'm not sure this is a good idea."

"Oh." He sounded very disappointed. "Is there someone special standing in the way?"

Maggie was taken unawares by his telephone call. She had completely forgotten him. There was someone special. No, there had been someone special. For God's sake, this man was merely inviting her to dinner, not to jump into bed with him. One date did not mean total commitment, and she had to start somewhere.

"I know a very good pub in the New Forest near my brother's boatyard, Peter. It's reached very easily from here and from Gosport. I could stay the night with Phil and Fay. Catch up on all their news. Suit you?"

"*Jawohl, Fräulein!* Give me the name of this place. I've an orderly here who reckons he's drunk in every pub in the New

Forest, and has the red nose to prove it. He'll give me directions." Maggie told him the name of Phil's local. "Got it. Tomorrow at seven. See you, Maggie."

She sat for some minutes trying to accept what she had just done. Then she burst into tears. When that was over she went out to her car vowing to stop *en route* to the hospital for a gin and tonic. Or two. Maybe three!

The drinks probably led to Maggie's decision to go in when she reached the hospital. Dutch courage! Yet she had no idea what she would say or do when she faced him. At the door of the ward a nurse asked her to wait.

"One of our therapists is having a session with Mr Price, but she should be finished within a few minutes."

"How is he?"

"Physically much better. The psychological effects last longer, of course, and can badly hinder recovery. But he'll make it." She smiled. "If only to spite us."

Maggie smiled back. "That sounds like the man I know."

The therapist was an attractive brunette wearing a starched white coat over a pale blue blouse and grey skirt. She gave Maggie a quick all-over study. "Are you a relative, Miss . . . ?"

"Spencer. Flight Lieutenant. I'm one of Squadron Leader Price's pilots. Was one of them," she amended awkwardly.

"I see. Have you come far?"

"From beyond Dorchester."

"Oh dear. In that case . . ." She nodded at a day room leading off the ward. "It's deserted at the moment. We can talk."

Maggie went with the woman, wondering what could be wrong. The nurse had said he was better.

"Do you know Mr Price well?"

"I've flown with him for almost a year."

"Oh dear." She smiled faintly. "Sorry. You've come all this way and all I can say is oh dear. But I'm trying to decide if his seeing you right now would be a good idea."

"Rubbing salt in the wound? That's what the team thinks." She had to explain herself. "A few months ago I suffered a bereavement and he was the one who helped me bear the shock of it. I want to do what I can in return. We were both part of a close team and we've been through some tricky times together. I've come to understand him."

The therapist frowned. "You're not Maggie, by any chance?"

"Yes. Why?"

The frown changed to a smile. "Your name's come up once or twice. I'm accused of being the same breed: think we've got men sussed."

Warmth returned to Maggie's chilled senses. "That sounds just like him, and, of course, we have."

Dark eyes studied her momentarily. "It might be worth trying his reaction to you. He's gone through the initial rage against the world and he's now in the more difficult phase of utter depression. It's normal in these cases but it's a tricky period because patients can set back their recovery by simply refusing to get better. They see no point. They want to die and get shot of the problems. Mr Price is now in a wheelchair but he won't propel it himself. He sees using it as a means of getting around – as an acceptance that he's unable to walk. Once he accepts any of our therapeutic aids his dependence on them becomes fact, and he's fighting it all the way." She sighed. "He'll come around to it eventually. They all do. But he's presently refusing to communicate with any of us and he won't eat. I've just threatened him with forced feeding. It didn't bother him enough for him even to swear at me. He simply doesn't care."

"Can't his wife encourage him; persuade him to cooperate?"

"I'm afraid not." She was brisk and final as she led Maggie from the day room. "You'll find him in the end bay. Don't expect the man you knew. That one's gone for ever. All the same, patients with his type of personality invariably retain their immense drive to live, somewhere beneath their despair. Unfortunately, it's that same personality which keeps them fighting the inevitable for so long." She smiled again. "It's good of you to come. I'll say it because he certainly won't. I fear you'll get no reaction at all from him, but please believe it's a temporary phase. He will come out of it."

As Maggie walked through the deserted ward she was certain she should have taken the team's advice and left well alone. If a professional therapist and the wife he adored could not reach him, she was unlikely to.

He was hunched in a wheelchair staring at the floor – emaciated, pale and listless. Despite having been warned, Maggie was appalled by the destruction of an intelligent, virile, witty man in the prime of his life. Randal seemed unaware of her presence as she stood there. The bay had four beds and a central table holding a huge arrangement of chrysanthemums, holly sprays and shiny leaves. Three of the bedside lockers sported photographs, paperbacks, chocolates, grapes or other gifts from visitors. The only thing on Randal's locker was B Flight's mascot, and the bear had his back to the room.

This seemed so painfully symbolic that Maggie asked, "Is Rip van Bruin in disgrace, or is he studying the wailing wall?"

This brought a reaction, a violent one. Randal's head jerked up and his hollow eyes stared as if in shock. "What the hell are *you* doing here?"

Shaken, caught off guard, she responded instinctively. "What the hell do you think? I was volunteered by the team for this task. You know what they're like. Frank, Simon and Vince rushed home straight from the cockpit. Rusty grabbed the nearest phone to ring Marsha's sister for the present state of play with the guy in the bookshop. Pete took one look at Arnie, decided he should see the vet and drove off with the pooch in his MG. He's grown huge – the dog, not our lovesick navigator – and slobbers all over Pete while he's driving. Jeff had a date with another tree in a miniskirt, so as I had nothing fixed I was briefed and programmed for this. I should have brought grapes or something, but I had a few G and Ts on the way and forgot. D'you get beer in here? I can't imagine you going without."

His drawn white features and staring eyes so disturbed her she was driven to keep talking, hardly aware of what she was saying. "You'll never believe this. Dave's loosened up for no apparent reason and started chatting to everyone. He's even decided I'm his good friend, and you know how he's always shunned me. Oh yes, our revered squadron commander is gearing himself up for the Christmas cocktail parties and his revered lady wife is thumbing through her books on etiquette while her sensible, suitable black frock is cleaned. I think it's time someone . . ."

Her torrent of words petered out as Randal doubled up. His shoulders heaved with the force of his sobs. Growing cold, Maggie reached out to take his limp hands in hers. "Oh! I'm so sorry. Please don't. How cruel and thoughtless of me! I'm so sorry. So *sorry*."

She instinctively bent to him as her own tears began to flow, sliding her arms around him and stroking his hair the way he had comforted her in August. The wetness on her cheeks merged with the wetness on his as they clung together. Over his shoulder

Maggie saw the nurse arrive, stand irresolute for a moment or two, then go away. She was glad. This was a B Flight affair. Outsiders would not understand.

When the mutual distress ended. Randal looked exhausted but there was a flicker of life in his eyes that had not been there before. Maggie fell back on the female standby for unplanned emotional occasions and pushed her hair back with an unsteady hand.

"I must look a wreck."

"You're the best thing I've seen in weeks," he told her thickly. "Christ, you don't know how good it is to have you here."

Hugely relieved, Maggie gave him a wobbly smile. "I'd have come before but you know what it's like."

"Of course I bloody know what it's like," he blurted through returning emotion. "It's been my life for twelve years. It's . . . it's the only thing I want to do."

"Well, you won't at this rate."

"Oh, don't you give me that crap about counting my blessings."

"Who said anything about blessings?" she demanded. "I said you'd get nowhere *at this rate*, and that means letting your body go. Look at you! Skin and bone. How do you propose to get back in the game if you haven't enough strength to grip anything?"

"Back in what game? The wheelchair Olympics?"

Maggie shook her head. "You'd never get through the prelims. You're skin and bone."

"You're bloody repeating yourself!"

"And you're bloody cheating yourself," she retaliated. "If you want to do it put in more effort. My God, we had that drummed into us at Cranwell. From what I've seen here you're opting out."

"Sure I am," he flung at her. "I'd opt out altogether if they'd only leave the sodding pill trolley unguarded."

She grew genuinely angry. "If that's all you want I'll bring you a bottleful next time I come. Or would you prefer a knife to cut your throat? No, too messy. How about a revolver? No, still too messy. There's rat poison. Or you could do it without my help and chuck yourself from the window. Trouble is, you'd have to get the wheelchair across to it and you're too puny to do that, so you'd have to build up your strength first. It'd take a while, plenty of patience. That's not one of your virtues, Boss, so it'd better be the pills after all."

They exchanged lengthy glares, then he said heavily, "I'm not your boss any longer."

"You're not even your own boss," she pointed out more gently.

At that point, the nurse appeared with two cups of tea and a plate of biscuits. She smiled at Maggie. "I'm not supposed to give these to visitors, but as you had a long drive I've sneaked them from beneath Sister's nose. Keep it quiet."

Randal ignored the biscuits but drank the tea in steady gulps. Then he looked her in the eye. "I love to fly. It's the greatest thing in my life. If I can't do that what's the point of it all?"

"I honestly don't know," she confessed. "It's like a ballerina being denied her dancing, a skier being away from snow and mountains, Damon Hill getting a driving ban. Nothing could completely compensate. Nothing. What they usually do is the next best thing. Ballet dancers become teachers or choreographers. Skiers open sports shops and write books on the subject. Racing drivers . . ." She shrugged. "I can't think of anything for them, but I'm sure they do something."

His familiar grin on this present gaunt face was more like a grimace, but there was a momentary glimpse of the man she knew. "You're too clever for your own good. I've told you often enough."

"All right, how's this for a clever idea?" she said eagerly. "If people in wheelchairs can drive cars, why can't they fly? Cars can be specially adapted, so why can't light aircraft?"

"No reason, but who's going to give a crippled pilot a licence to take to the air?"

"Mmm, big snag." She came up with another bright idea. "How about becoming a balloonist? You're a wealthy man, and I can picture you in a leather helmet and goggles drifting over the countryside in an inflatable pork pie. You could go around the world."

It had been light-hearted chatter designed to perk up his spirits but she realised with surprise that he had taken it on board. "Forget the pork pie. That's gimmicky. To do it seriously the balloon has to be designed to exact specifications. Christ, what a challenge! No engine power, just the prevailing wind and your own skill."

"You'd need special nav charts and detailed Met info. You'd have to know the terrain pretty well. Couldn't gain height quickly if you came across an unexpected hill, like we do, and you'd have to have constant radio contact with your base."

They developed this theme for some minutes, but Maggie could see that he was tiring so she was not sorry when the nurse came to say her visiting time was over. She got to her feet feeling immensely tired herself. She had been there just half an hour, and yet energy appeared to have drained from her. She did not know how to say goodbye, so she told him about Peter McGrath's surprising call.

"He asked me to have dinner with him again." She forced a smile. "Two dates in eight months! Hot stuff!"

"Are you going?" he asked wearily.

"I've got to start getting back to normal." Reaching out she turned B Flight's mascot to face the room, saying, "I'm on a five-day stand-down. I'll come again, if you like."

"This is no place to spend your leave. Stick around the healthy."

"So you don't want the pills, the kitchen knife or the rat poison?"

He studied her for a long moment, a shadow of the man he had been but with a spark of life that had been missing on her arrival. "It was good to see you, Maggie. Tell McGrath from me he's a lucky guy."

The tiny tingle of hope, the pale glimmer of light in the dread darkness lasted long enough to spur Randal into eating some of the lunch they brought him, but when they settled him on the bed for an hour's rest before the usual massage session his spirits plunged again. Ballooning? Balls to that! It was not flying as he knew it: being in control of an engine-driven aircraft, making it do what he wanted with judgement and precision, feeling the power of it in his hands.

Bitterness returned. She had been joking, he saw that now. Hospital visitors' encouraging small talk. Bright smile, upbeat tone. There, there, let's think about *nice* things. The sugar-coated pill! He had ridiculously taken her seriously and blabbered on about specifications and rising to a challenge. Christ Almighty! What had she said? "I can picture you in a leather helmet and goggles in an inflatable pork pie." Yeah, he could do that. He could provide a comic turn at village fêtes and charity functions. Advertise the family business at air shows. For the final big laugh he could puncture the thing and bale out dressed as a clown and drift down to the waiting wheelchair – except that one day he would do it without a parachute.

He lay staring at the ceiling as the blackness of despair descended. It would be the best thing for everyone. He saw with great clarity the sequence of future events. Fiona was still at Marylands, "needing the comfort and support of her parents in this traumatic situation" as Holland had put it to Millie in response to a telephoned attempt to bring her patient and his wife together for counselling. Millie would not accept that the marriage was over although Randal had from the moment they told him what he had become. It was the one fact he could accept amid a clutch of others he could not.

As weeks passed, Fiona would settle to the life she had known before marriage. Their house in the country would stand empty – the socialities who had invaded it forgotten – no longer needed. Neil would go to a different school with a uniform just as bloody expensive and he would have his renowned Grandpa to threaten bullies with. Lydia would be given everything money could buy and grow to be as stunningly beautiful as her mother. The father who had appeared for short periods would soon be forgotten in the plethora of doting bounty. In any case, all Daddy had done was to get Mummy flat on her back at every opportunity . . . according to Mummy.

Randal closed his eyes in anguish. He would never get a woman – any woman – flat on her back again; and even if he could, it would be pointless. At that moment, impotence became in his fevered mind the worst of his punishments. He was only thirty-four and would never again know the intense pleasure of sex.

Fiona surely would – she could not exist without it – but she would not actually initiate divorce proceedings until she intended to marry again. The Hollands had their standards. It would not do for their daughter to display heartlessness by cutting her legal ties to a man in hospital with crippling injuries. Wait until he was out of medical care and established in a workshop for the disabled, making baskets. Then the Hollands' solicitor could discreetly untie the knot. No judge would stand in the way. One look at Mrs Price's appealing blue eyes, her sensuous mouth, her taut breasts, her sensational legs . . . Oh God, how easy it was to look no deeper than that! How easy it would be for him to slide from her world into the next if only he could get at the sodding pill trolley.

Two nurses woke him gently. "Fifteen minutes until your massage. Let's get you in the wheelchair." They looked small and delicate, but these women had been trained in the art of lifting lumps of meat easily. "Are you going to take yourself to the massage parlour?" joked one.

"Why should I? I don't want to go there," he grunted against her starched shoulder as they moved him off the bed and into the abominable chair.

His companions in the bay were able to make the transfer without help. They even joked as they did it. Randal knew what it was all about. Put him with men who were further advanced in their treatment, or less severely injured, so that he would be encouraged. Balls to their little trick! The only thing that would encourage him would be Christ appearing to say he could take up his bed and walk. The hospital minister had visited and been given Randal's frank opinion of God. He had first given it to the Padre from Hampton, who had misguidedly tried to offer comfort the day after he had regained consciousness in Intensive Care.

The Station Commander had arrived with the Padre to discuss emergency financial arrangements and to ask Randal if there were other things he would like handled on a temporary basis. He had not mentioned God, thank God! He wrote sensible to-the-point letters regarding Squadron Leader Price's RAF earnings and any other service matters – as if the lump of meat cared – and he had arranged for mail addressed to him at Hampton to be forwarded. This included letters collected from home by a neighbour with a key given to her by Gerald Hammond, who sent them on to the Officers' Mess.

Oh yes, unopened letters were a thing of the past. When he continued to show no interest in them, the nurses opened and read them to him. It was another of their tricks to keep him in touch with the outside world. He did not give a damn about the world. When would they accept that? Not yet, apparently, because he was no sooner in the wheelchair than the little blonde who had brought Maggie a cup of tea took from her pocket a fat envelope redirected from Hampton.

"This looks interesting. Who d'you know in a place called Pennmawgan?"

"You'll find out when you open it."

"Wouldn't you like to open it?"

"You never bloody give up, do you?"

"I wouldn't be much use here if I did, would I?"

Fixing her with a glare, he took the letter and made to rip it in two. Lack of strength in his hands resulted in no more than a tear across the thinner section of the envelope, and through it slid several colour photographs to rest in his lap. The pictures were of a child with dark plaits turning somersaults, riding a bicycle and sitting astride a goat. He did not know the child but, on the point of casting the pictures aside, something about the house and buildings in the background caught his attention. Tearing the envelope open he took out the thick sheet of paper folded four times, and spread it out on his knees.

Deer skadron leeder
I am home from hostible I did not like it much. It hert sum times but I didert cry, I want to be brayv like you wen you fly and bring things for peepul. My kidnee likes me. They sed if it didert like me I wud not feel well but I feel well. Thees pikchurs are for you so you can see I jump and run like you now. I go to skool after krissmus. I wish you wud cum like last yeer but I spec you are bissy taking things to other peepul. I am droring a krissmus card for you. Its speshul so I taking a long time. Plees send me one.
luv and kisses Fiona Hunter

A quiet voice interrupted his recollections of Dave tramping uphill through thick snow to check the state of the roofs, then the landing at dusk on a wild clifftop to take to a small girl the means of staying alive another month.

"Time for your massage, Mr Price."

He put the letter and photographs on his bed, hearing Jimmy saying, "My kids have everything they want, but none of them looks as happy as she does."

A nurse pushed him through the ward, but when they reached the long corridor he put his hands on the guiding wheels. "I'll take it from here."

289

She left him to it. He knew where to go, but it was bloody hard work. Dear God, where had all his strength gone?

The five-day stand-down was reduced to three for Jeff, Maggie, Dave and Sandy who were on station when a NATO bid for an additional Chinook came in. So, ten days before Christmas, they headed back to familiar quarters, where snow would be thick on the ground and flying could be a mixed joy. Dave was the only one comfortable with the low temperatures yet he was as glum as the others over this unexpected duty. They had needed a break, but the squadron was pledged to meet NATO demands and they were unfortunate enough to be the nearest aircrew to call in for the job.

Jeff was missing out on a hot date with a girl he had been pursuing in vain since meeting her at his sister's wedding. He complained throughout the flight that now she had succumbed he had had to stand her up.

Sandy, a member of the local model railway group, was helping with a massive project to reconstruct in miniature an early Tibetan line from old sepia photographs. The club hoped to complete it by March and recoup some of their expenses by charging for admission to view it. Sandy was "making mountains out of molehills" as he put it, to create a replica of the terrain and he hated leaving it.

When they contacted him Dave had had his motorbike in pieces, giving it a complete overhaul. His only consolation was that no one could borrow it in his absence because all the essential parts were in boxes in his room in the Sergeants' Mess, but he was very concerned that he might still be in Split at Christmas. He had banked on having at least seventy-two hours' leave for it.

Maggie was deeply unsettled. The desert seemed to have sapped her energy and she was still miffed over the armoured truck. It was the first time she had been forced to ditch a load – something that happened only rarely to any crew – and despite knowing it had been unavoidable she nevertheless felt she had failed in some way. Gerard Jeffries had made so much of it when he read the report she felt he thought so, too. Common sense prevailed, but she knew Randal would have put the matter straight with a few choice words.

This call to Bosnia meant she could not visit him again, and anyway he had told her to concentrate on the healthy. Would she have ignored that if she were still at Hampton? Seeing him had curiously drained her, and after her date with Peter McGrath the following evening she had felt depressed. It had been no more than an enjoyable meal eaten with an interesting light-hearted companion who made no demands on her, yet she had burst into tears later that night. If she were a man she would be getting drunk every night. It was their way of dealing with emotions, good or bad.

Split in mid-December was no place to drive away resentment or introspection, so the four flew in to leaden skies and biting winds in no mood for an emergency of any kind. Wing Commander Haslett gave them a general briefing when they arrived, and it was just the kind of news they did not want to hear.

A dangerous situation had developed in an area which had been fought over throughout the autumn months by Serb and Albanian forces, each side several times gaining then losing control of two villages. Little remained of them. The residents had either trekked to tenuous safety with their possessions on handcarts, or they had been slaughtered by crossfire. In the ongoing conflict between people whose hatred could never be appeased, the taking of lives was purely a means to an end. If the lives were those of their own people it was a necessary sacrifice for the greater cause.

A month ago, a UN peace-keeping unit had been installed in the ruins of what had once been a rural settlement in a beautiful valley bordered by wooded hills. The unit was meant to act as a buffer between the rival forces while diplomatic efforts to settle the dispute over the territory were undertaken. Like most diplomacy, it had dragged on without significant progress, and the British troops who had been given the unenviable duty held their positions while gunmen from both groups sneaked past them under cover of darkness to take pot-shots at each other. A British patrol had caught some in the act. All three were twelve years old.

There were regular patrols by Chinooks to keep an eye on the movements of the opposing fighters and daily supply runs to Army units including the one in the buffer zone village, but the hapless peace-keepers were now in possible danger.

Two nights ago the Albanian leader, hero of a last-man defence of his own village earlier in the year, was captured by Serbian infiltrators. The man's life and those of his family would only be spared in return for the surrender of weapons by his supporters. A British captain had taken an escort in two armoured vehicles bearing blue flags and attempted to negotiate with the Serbs. He had been confronted by men manning heavy artillery; men who looked wild enough to carry out their threat to blast his small force to kingdom come if he did not back off immediately. Seething with impotence the British had had no alternative but to turn back.

An attempt to calm the situation at a higher level also failed. The Albanians stood firm on their claim to the disputed area and their right to defend it with guns. They blamed the British unit for the kidnap of their hero, which had taken place under their noses. The presence of the British had caused the Albanians to relax in the belief that they would not be attacked and they had not been as alert as they would otherwise have been. They demanded that the UN unit be removed from the midst of a conflict that could not be settled by a small group of foreigners who had no interest in the rights of those fighting it. The Serbs made no response to the military approach other than to reiterate the demand for the peace-keepers to be immediately withdrawn because they were merely deepening the crisis.

The British troops were also keen to withdraw. They were living rough in freezing temperatures halfway along a snow-bound valley swept by icy winds, sandwiched between undisciplined irregulars who stopped at nothing. They had been there for four weeks, twenty-eight days too long as far as they were concerned, and tempers were growing short. So what if the Serbs had mounted an SAS-style operation and grabbed some bandit as a hostage? Their patrols could not possibly cover the area night and day; there were not enough of them, for a start. But their presence had stopped the fierce contest which had near enough flattened the area. There was supposed to be a ceasefire while talks were held, and their job was to keep things that way by maintaining a non-aggressive presence. That was what they had done. It was the worst duty in the book, and they wanted an end to it. Now they were being made scapegoats by the very people whose wholesale slaughter they had come to prevent. Standing in several feet of snow, frozen to the marrow, noses red and swollen, staring out over a scene bleak enough to sink anyone's spirits, the UN soldiers agreed with the warring sides. They should be withdrawn and sent home for Christmas.

Jeff and his crew were given this background information by Wing Commander Haslett, who then went on to reveal why they had been brought over from Hampton. "Last night, the Serbs made it known that they had executed their hostage because the guns had not been surrendered – murder portrayed as a legitimate act of war. We have it on good authority that they tortured their prisoner to death. The Albanians are well aware of this. They also know the man's mother, wife and three children have vanished. They are hell bent on vengeance. Our air patrols report evidence of reinforcements massing in the area. If they run true to form they'll give every male over the age of ten a rifle."

"What about the Serbs?" asked Jeff.

"They've done what they intended all along and put a match to the fuse. Their numbers are also increasing, so you can see why you're here."

"To evacuate our troops," said Maggie. "Presumably they're completely outnumbered in that valley."

Haslett nodded. "Although they have the right to fire in their own defence, this is seen only as a very last resort. Our masters are adamant that diplomacy is the only acceptable solution to the stalemate; we – the people on the spot – know that when one side or the other attacks our men will have to be brought out fast."

"Couldn't they be brought out now, sir?" asked Dave. "Surely they're superfluous at this stage."

Haslett pulled a face. "The pin-stripe-trouser boys are insisting that to remove the buffer will precipitate hostilities. When they *see* diplomacy has failed, we'll be expected to work our usual miracles." He gave them all his famous pep talk. "You've all been here before so you know the trials of winter. Roads are snowbound, mountain tracks get blocked, blizzards set in, yet troops need to be fed and kept warm. Who copes with all that?"

"We do," they chorused obediently.

"So we're doing it. But when – you note I say when not if – the lit fuse reaches the dynamite, two helicopters will be needed to airlift the poor sods from bang in the middle of the explosion. As from now, you're on twenty-four-hour standby along with Flight

293

Lieutenant Locke's crew." He managed a smile. "A Chinook of 646 Squadron's A Flight was called over from Italy this morning for this, but I thought you'd operate better with men of your own team so I've swapped things around, much to the chagrin of the new arrivals who fancied some heroics."

The door opened to admit Rusty. "Ah, right on cue, man," said Haslett. "I've given them the history. Fill them in on the small print." He gave them a parting nod.

When they heard their brief they realised they might need some heroics. Rusty said both aircraft would be armed. They would fly fast and low through the valley, below the range of possible crossfire from the hills. When they reached their target, Jeff's Chinook would land and take on board half the troops while Rusty and Simon would circle overhead with Jimmy and Ray manning the guns. They would reverse the tactic to pick up the remainder.

"Then we get out as fast as we went in," Rusty said. "The vehicles and stores will have to be left behind, of course."

"It's pure crazy not to bring them out now," Dave insisted. "Why risk two aircraft and the troops when they know a bloodbath's inevitable?"

"Orders, lad," Rusty told him, perching on the corner of the table. "This is not our war, and those guys have been told to act as a buffer until their position becomes untenable."

"It's that now," argued Maggie. "They've already been seen off at gunpoint trying to keep the peace. I agree with Dave. It's cock-eyed making them wait until it's practically too late."

Rusty nodded. "Can you imagine how the Army feels about it? These decisions are being made by civilians, If they were made here it'd be a different story. Haslett's been told both sides will be warned about our 'neutral' evacuation, should it become necessary, but we know how much bloody good that'll be to us." He turned to the wall chart. "OK, here's the nitty gritty."

They spent a while studying the chart and making notes so that all they'd need when the call came was Met information, advice of other flights in the area and the state of play between opposing forces.

Rusty wound up by saying, with a grin, "If you guys hadn't been kicking your heels around Hampton instead of being out on the rampage like sensible people, I'd have stayed on the 'coal and cabbages' run and missed out on the action. It should ensure my promotion."

"Oh yeah," said Sandy, suddenly coming to life. "We'll put it around you held off a savage horde with your bare teeth. That should shoot you straight through to Wing Commander."

"If Rip were here he'd have the perfect comeback to that," Rusty told him as he walked to the door.

"This'd be right up his street," said Jeff, following him.

Maggie walked behind them with Dave. "I went to see him when we got back from Egypt, Rusty."

The red-haired pilot looked back at her. "Never could take good advice, could you. So what kind of state's the poor sod in?"

"Much as you'd expect. All he wants is to get back in the air, or pack it in. He was pretty suicidal when I got there."

"What about when you left?"

"I'd talked him out of it . . . I hope."

Rusty shook his head. "I've known him a long time. There's no way he'd ever opt out. There's too much life in him." He walked on. "Dump your gear, guys, then meet us in the bar. We'll get nicely tanked up before the rest get back, cold and griping. I think we're in for trouble from Mike Leeds' crew. They flew in from Italy and were sent out on the task we should have taken. They weren't happy and promised reprisals."

"We have the perfect defence," said Dave with a grin. "We have orders to hold ourselves fit and ready for action at any time."

They did just that for two days and nights, swinging from excitement to apprehension to boredom, while yearning to get the order to go. Despite their frustration they did manage to spare a thought for the men in that bleak valley wanting some action even more than they did. Reports filtered through that the build-up was continuing.

Dennis Haslett continually pressed for an evacuation while conditions were favourable, but the RAF was told to hold its horses. Rusty and the two crews fumed, convinced the isolated unit was being unnecessarily endangered – as Haslett felt his crews would be when the top brass finally sent the signal to go in.

Maggie was solidly asleep when her door crashed open and Jeff yelled, "Go, go, go!"

She rolled from the bed, heart thudding, noting the time on her alarm clock. Five a.m. Jeff was already gone. She heard his "Go, go, go!" further along the corridor as she stripped off her pyjamas, swiftly washed, then pulled on warm underwear, flying suit and boots. Then she headed for the briefing room carrying her helmet and jacket, joined by Simon from the adjacent room.

"So this is it," he murmured superfluously. "Wonder what set things going?"

"Hope they actually tell us," said Maggie as they hurried along the dark corridor, their boots clattering in the sleeping silence. "If we're just told to go get them, without any info on what we'll be facing—"

"Haslett won't let them get away with that. He's nagged them non-stop these past three days; he'll needle them for the fullest facts now, you bet."

As they reached the top of the stairs, Jeff came from his room where he had collected the rest of his gear after rousing the others. "Rusty's with Haslett. Someone's yanking the crewmen out." He clattered down the stairs with them. "It's all systems go."

Maggie was now fully awake as she asked Jeff, "Any idea why?"

"Nope. Rusty tugged my bedclothes off and told me to get you two out. That's all I know. Something must have forced the issue."

They assembled in the room where an orderly had produced a supply of tea and bacon sandwiches. The men fell on these, but Maggie was too tense to enjoy more than the hot drink. They would take food with them. She could eat later.

Dennis Haslett looked heavy-eyed as he gave the facts. "Talks have clearly failed. The Albanian force has begun moving up on our troops in the village. At first light the Serbs will be aware of this and act. They have superior firepower so they'll most likely try to stop the advance with artillery and rockets. Or they could decide to advance and take the village first. Either way, the buffer unit is in trouble. We've been asked to effect an evacuation without delay." Not known as a particularly profane man, he then expressed his opinions in language that would have had Squadron Leader Price beaming with admiration. He went on, "Your aircraft are fuelled up; ground crews are giving them a final once-over. Rusty has the Met info. Not ideal conditions, but shouldn't give you any trouble. Other flights will be kept away from the area until you've done the job." His eyes narrowed. "Any data coming in will be relayed to you, but I guess it'll be a question of sizing up the state of play when you get there. It should be getting light by then. The snow will aid visibility and make movement on the ground easily discernible.

"I don't need to remind you that any task that can't be done has to be binned. Your first priority is the safety of your aircraft and crew. We are not at war with these people but you'll be dealing with a hostile situation. You will not fire unless deliberately fired upon. We don't want any video-game heroics to escalate hostilities. Any questions?" Silence. "Right, bring them out if you safely and sensibly can. If you can't, remember they're not defenceless civilians. They're fighting soldiers who know how to protect themselves."

"If they do that, won't that escalate hostilities?" asked Jeff.

Haslett ignored the pertinent comment. "Good luck, everyone."

Wearing night-vision goggles they took off and flew together on a course that would take them to the distant valley. The usual banter was missing as they gazed down at the snow-covered terrain they knew well.

Rusty said, "Rescue One to Rescue Two. Carry out guns test when ready."

Jeff acknowledged and instructed his crewmen. Maggie jumped when Dave and Sandy fired the guns mounted close behind the cockpit.

Jeff glanced at her. "Scared?" It was not derisive.

"Nervous. Aren't you?"

"Not half," he confessed. "But excited, too."

"That's what makes me nervous. In novels they're always steely-nerved and calmly confident facing something like this."

"I'm steely-nerved and calmly confident," boasted Sandy. "I've got a gun. You guys up front haven't."

"Watch what you do with it," warned Jeff. "We're not in *Top Gun Two*."

They kept low until they neared a range of hills, when they were forced to climb. The covering of snow certainly helped visibility. There was no moon, but the surface nevertheless glowed as they studied the stark black and white scene they crossed. It was cold in the aircraft, but it would be a great deal colder on the ground.

Maggie murmured, "Imagine being stuck down there with madmen on both sides and hills on the other two."

They were quiet for a minute or so, then Rusty spoke to them as if his thoughts had been running along the same lines. "Jeff, there's no way we can bin this. Those guys have been let down by everyone else, so we're not going to fly over them, decide it's a bit tricky and let the poor sods be blamed for escalating hostilities because they fired in self-defence. Unless they've already been overrun when we get there, we're going in."

Rusty might not be steely-nerved, but he did sound calmly confident about carrying off a successful evacuation. Maggie had a sudden memory of the man he was deputising for; a strong man sobbing in a wheelchair because all this had been so shockingly wrenched from him. Randal would certainly break every rule in the book, take any calculated risk to get these men out today. Was his long-term friend thinking along those lines as they approached their target?

It was considerably lighter when they neared the valley. Rusty was in radio contact with Split, and with the army captain commanding the 120-strong force waiting to be air-lifted from the village. Maggie overheard the captain say, "Defensive firing only, be buggered! We've been left here to freeze nearly to death. If anyone advances too close I'm not bloody waiting to find out if they're friendly. What's your probable ETA?"

Rusty told him thirty minutes, and the other said, "Speed it up, we want out of here."

"Have your guys ready to board. Stragglers will be left behind."

"We've been ready for five effing days," the voice said explosively. "I'm going to kick up one hell of a stink when we get back."

"Do that," said Rusty. "Our boss has for the entire three days we've been ready to come for you. Won't do any good but it might make you feel better."

Maggie detected the tension in the army man's voice and recalled her own impatience for the Casevac helicopter's arrival during Randal's rescue of the Frenchmen in the submerged truck. Was that only two months ago?

Rusty was still in contact with the man on the ground. "Is everything quiet there?"

"Too bloody quiet! It's light enough now for an advance from either force. We've lookouts watching both directions."

"OK, keep me posted." Rusty then spoke to Jeff and Maggie. "Rescue Two, we're advised zero hour's approaching, so I guess we could be in on the start of something. ETA twenty minutes. You know the flight plan. We'll stick to it until we see what's going on. When we get to the valley we'll drop to treetop height and go in fast."

Right on time they reached the head of the valley and descended, just as the voice of the army captain came over the airwaves. "They're on the move. The Albanians are about three miles away. Light armoured vehicles, a few small tanks. Not effective at their present range. What's your ETA?"

Rusty said calmly, "Eight minutes. We're approaching very low. Stand by!"

"Will do."

"Rescue One to Recue Two. We have a hostile situation. Repeat, a hostile situation. Let's get the job done and get out."

Maggie felt her stomach muscles tense as she strained her eyes, now free of the night-vision goggles, for the first sight of a small army on the move. "Get your Superman eyes on the job, Dave," she said. "They're good in snowy areas."

"There they are. Ruins, about half a mile ahead. Saw movement."

"Got it," Jeff confirmed. "The army guys are four miles beyond that at another flattened village. I'll stay low and frighten the Albanians as much as possible."

Jeff spoke to Maggie. "Soon as we spot our guys, look for a place to put down where there's unlikely to be anything hidden by the snow."

As he finished speaking they heard Rusty telling the captain he should soon see them on the horizon, and to get his men to an area which had nothing to impede their landing.

"Will do," came the more cheerful response. "God, you're a welcome sight."

Maggie said to Jeff as they flashed across dark figures struggling over the frozen ground, "Are they meant to be an army?"

"Poor buggers! Haven't a hope in hell," Jeff muttered.

Gazing down at the stumbling ragged ranks following the line of protective vehicles, Maggie saw the full tragedy of what was happening in this country. She had not flown here during the war, as Rusty and Jimmy had, but here was evidence that it was not yet over.

"There's the UN unit," said Dave sharply. "Some kind of buildings ahead. They're out on the far side."

"Rescue One to Rescue Two. Target in view. Descend and land immediately on arrival. We'll cover."

They were overflying the advancing Albanian vehicles when the Chinook rocked violently. "Christ," yelled Jeff, "the Serbs have started shelling! They *must* be able to see us from their positions. Haslett said they'd been warned of a neutral evacuation. What the hell are they playing at?"

Rusty sounded tense. "Rescue One to Rescue Two. Change of plan. The Serbs are targeting the tanks to halt the advance. The Brits are short of their range but as the tanks advance it'll close on them. We've got to speed this up, so we'll go down together, load up, then go out over the hills to the west. Too risky to beat back up the valley."

Jeff acknowledged. As they neared the second village where the soldiers were formed up with their kit, Rusty said, "Go for that stretch at three o'clock from the area where they're waiting. If we circle and come in behind them we can use the wreck of that church as our fixed point."

"Right with you." Jeff glanced swiftly at Maggie. "All set?" At her nod, he added to Dave and Sandy, "Forget the guns, guys. Stand ready to lower the ramp, then whip them aboard as fast as possible. Yell when they're on. I'm not hanging around."

The two Chinooks banked, gaining height ready to land on thick snow, and Maggie told herself she had come full circle from her introduction to operational flying during the January freeze. They slowly descended into the blizzard whipped up by the rotors, conscious of Serb shells exploding ever nearer to the British position.

As Maggie concentrated on the familiar routine she knew this was the greatest danger she had ever been in, yet she felt no panic. Randal had called her "bloody cool" during the mountain rescue. She was the same now. Mark would have approved.

In the cabin Dave was keyed up and on the ball. He had the confidence of youth that turns dangerous situations into challenges. He had hoped to exchange shots on this mission, but there was enough urgency to satisfy his penchant for taking risks. He listened to the pilots combining in a tricky dual landing in severe conditions, guided by their crewmen.

The moment he felt the familiar crunch on touchdown, Dave released the ramp. He and Sandy jumped down to hustle the troops across the frozen snow. The below-zero temperature reminded him of days in the Highlands. He gesticulated for the straggling troops to speed things up but the cold and inactivity had made them sluggish.

The thunder of the ground attack was slightly drowned by the overhead roar of the rotors, but Dave was very aware of shells exploding to send up showers of stones and earth not far away along the ice-gripped valley and he felt the ground shuddering from their impact. The ragged lines of Albanians advancing to take back what they believed to be rightfully theirs were dropping before his eyes. He was awed by this first sight of war.

Jeff yelled over the intercom. "Get the bastards aboard, for Christ's sake! The shells are getting too bloody close."

The two crewmen manhandled the weary troops to pack them in faster, knowing they could not risk being on the ground for much longer but determined no one would be left behind. As he thrust the last few men up the ramp, Dave said, "Seven extra bods aboard. OK?"

"I'm not arguing," Jeff told him with tension evident in his voice.

"Raise the ramp, Dave!" urged Maggie. "The Boss wants us off the ground *now*."

Jeff piled on the power as this was being done, and the Chinook unstuck from the snow somewhat wildly then immediately swung away towards the hills as Sandy gave staccato information on possible dangers ahead. Dave let out his breath with force. Jeff was a crazy flier at the best of times and he was pulling out all the stops today. As he looked down at the tragic scene they were leaving Dave appreciated the full scope of the work he did. Their own troops could not have been extricated from danger by any other means.

Glancing at the men crammed in the cabin he saw they were drawn and listless, too weary even to shrug off their packs. It then occurred to him that his cousin Dougal might well one day have to rely on a helicopter to lift him to safety. What sweet revenge if Sergeant Ashmore could hustle Lieutenant Rowan aboard with yells and thumps on the back, as he had with these soldiers. Maybe the day would come. He smiled at the prospect.

A sergeant sitting near Dave raised his voice to say, "You guys were a more welcome sight than bleeding Father Christmas."

Dave's smile broadened. "You can buy us all a few beers when we get you back to your base."

"You're on." The man frowned and inclined his head. "Is that a *girl* in the cockpit?"

Dave glanced at the back of Maggie's head with affection. "Aye, but she's one of the boys."

Headlines next day suggested it was time to stop talking and act to bring an end to the slaughter in troubled former Yugoslavia.

> After almost two months of dialogue the fresh outbreak of violence has brought further carnage with no victory to offset the loss of life. Is it possible for these people ever to live in peace together? With boys as young as ten being encouraged to take up arms what hope is there for reason and diplomacy to prevail? A show of force by NATO is surely the immediate if not the long-term solution.

At the foot of most articles was a brief reference to the successful airlift of a small British peace-keeping force that had been caught between the opposing armies for a month and had to be brought out when the fighting began.

> Their presence did not keep the peace. Even the most dyed-in-the-wool optimist must read the truth in that.

Christmas

The Chinook hovering above the green at Hampton Heyhoe winched down two Teletubby lookalikes, who scampered around the taped-off area behind which a crowd had gathered, to distribute brightly-wrapped parcels to excited children. RAF Hampton was making one of its annual appeasement gestures to local residents, who continued to complain about the proximity of the giant aircraft throughout the season of goodwill.

A few minutes later, in the cabin of the departing Chinook, there was a definite absence of goodwill when Sandy and Nobby removed their false heads then found they could not take off their huge inflated bodies because fellow crewmen had put superglue on the Velcro fastenings. The air was full of very un-Teletubby-like language while the crew came up with suggestions as to how to deal with the problem, the main one being an acetylene torch. It was as well Judge Jeffries had taken early leave, so did not see Laa Laa and Po being hotly pursued through the corridors of 646 Squadron Headquarters by personnel supposedly on duty. Well, it was Christmas!

B Flight's new commander, Squadron Leader Andy Forbes, had been welcomed in the Mess last night by his team's officers and had very properly sunk slowly and blissfully to the floor at the end of the evening, before being put to bed. The sergeants would provide a boozy welcome when they had the opportunity. Andy was already known to several of B Flight and promised to be easy enough to get along with. But he was not Rip Price.

Rusty's promotion had come through with a posting to Scotland as flight commander in a Search and Rescue squadron. He swiftly proposed to Marsha, but she turned him down; Scotland was too cold and too far from home. Rusty consoled himself with the thought that if he had married her when she had pestered him to, he would now be facing separation and eventual divorce. There were girls in Scotland who would welcome a sexy young pilot to warm them on cold nights . . . and he would keep his freedom!

The big surprise of the festive season was Pete's engagement to Jill. Arnie, the overgrown pup, had effected the sudden romance between the navigator needing to give his all to someone, and the vivacious girl looking for someone's all to take. Jeff declared it would be a *ménage à trois* "because that great slobbering tyke goes everywhere with them".

The only surprise about Jimmy's announcement that his fifth child would greet the world in June was that he had been at home long enough during the past year to influence the population of Hampton Heyhoe.

Jeff was in the station sick bay with colic and a persistent sore throat. The team, highly unsympathetic, told him with relish that the one would prevent his chatting up girls, and the other from doing anything about it even if he could. Maggie took him a santa-wrapped pair of boxer shorts with WHO'S BEEN TELLING PORKIES? printed across the appropriate area. It was a sign of affection which he failed to appreciate.

Dave flew to Scotland. He was nervous about this first Christmas with his father. In the air he once more scanned Ralph's letter.

> At Hogmanay I really go to town – you'll make it another year, I hope – but this will be a gathering of a few friends and family. Nothing formal, and there'll be others of your age – cousins, of course, and offspring of long-standing friends – so have no fear we'll all be old fogeys. I've told everyone that you're Sir Hector's kinsman. I think that's the best line to take for now. I look forward very much to seeing you again and in the place you have every right to be, just don't earn another wigging by arriving as a biker.
> Yours aye,
> Ralph

Dave gazed from the small window. He had cousins. Uncles and aunts, too. A family he had been unaware of until a few weeks ago yet he could not acknowledge them. He must continue to be Dave Ashmore. Smiling faintly as he looked down on the land of his fathers, he told himself that if these relatives were anything like the Rowans he might be better off without them.

He had been unsure what to do about gifts, and eventually decided on a case of fine old wine at the airport. It was now in the overhead locker with his heavy bag.

During the short train journey across terrain romanticised in the five paintings bequeathed to him by Sir Hector "in the hope that he would come to his senses and understand his heritage", Dave wondered if Edwina's spirit was rejoicing at this coming event. His thoughts then drifted to Maggie, who had unwittingly shown him what he must do about that letter. He wished he could tell her all about this great change in his life. It would surely forge an even stronger bond between them than the one brought about by those moments of danger. He would work on it when he returned to Hampton. Slowly, because she was not yet ready for another relationship.

He took a taxi from the station through streets where fine snow was beginning to drift. No one should mistake him for a villain this time, dressed as he was in fawn trousers, a chunky patterned sweater and a suede jacket. Then he was outside a house fronted by a short semicircular drive in which several expensive cars were parked, and he faced the moment of reckoning. Could he carry this off successfully?

A middle-aged woman opened the door, taking him by surprise. She smiled. "Saw you arriving. Come in. You must be David." Closing the door behind him, she said, "I'm Hilary Cartwright, Ralph's sister. Poor man has three of us, but he stands up to the strain pretty well."

Dave put down his bag and the wine, finding this secret aunt as friendly as Ralph. Before he could respond to her, however, a girl in a figure-hugging green minidress and black knee-high boots came from a room leading off the hall.

"Ralph wants to know if—" She broke off, gave Dave the optical once-over and smiled. "Hi, you must be David, the renegade who gave the regiment two fingers and took to the air. I've been dying to meet a fellow rebel. I'm Laura Croft. Daddy is Ralph's old school chum. They sometimes bore on about what they used to get up to, but they're both sweet old things really." She looked him over again. "We're just about to have tea and you look hungry. Take off your coat and come in."

Looking at her mane of glossy red hair, her misty green eyes and her exciting thighs, a devastating urge to take off all his clothes rushed through Dave and rational thought fled.

They sat around a dying fire in the waterside cottage trying to summon the energy to climb the stairs to bed. An early start was planned for the morning and they were enjoying the lull before the storm. Once they reached the Spencer house there would be the usual bedlam of a family gathering.

"Oh God," murmured Maggie, "the little brats'll be a year older and noisier."

"And hungrier," added Phil with a chuckle. "Are you all set for toast duty?"

"I did it last year; it's your turn, brother dear."

"I'll make the toast if you insist, Mags, but I'll feel driven to tell Mum the full unexpurgated account of your baptism of fire in Bosnia."

"You dare, Phil, and making toast will be the least of your worries," Maggie threatened.

He grinned. "Take your choice."

Fay glanced across the softly lit room to where Maggie sat with her feet curled beneath her in a white leather chair. "We have something to tell you, haven't we, Phil?"

He looked surprised. "It's your decision, sweetie."

Maggie guessed an instant before Fay spoke again, but she had enough sense to let her sister-in-law break the news.

"The 'bump' is twins. Or should that be *are* twins? It was confirmed yesterday. You're the first to be told."

It made Maggie very emotional. Things like that did, these days. She crossed to hug them both. "How wonderful! The best possible Christmas present." Sitting back on her heels, she then said, "That settles it! You *will* do the toast, Phil. Next year you'll be too busy changing nappies, powdering little pink bottoms and trying to get the monsters to sleep to deal with the complications of breakfast."

Her brother, looking immensely pleased with himself, said, "The nappy and bottom-powdering is Fay's responsibility. I'll be on the floor banging drums, blowing whistles and playing trains with them."

Maggie gave Fay a conspiratorial glance. "Hark at the boy with his head in the clouds! What a rude awakening he'll get."

Fay smiled happily. "Shh! I'm letting him enjoy himself while he can."

"In that case, I should be excused toast duty."

"Oh no," ruled Maggie, "that's nothing to the chores you'll be doing once your babes appear on the scene."

Phil got to his feet. "The odds are two to one here, so I'm going to bed. One of you wenches can bring me a cup of tea in the morning around seven. Two sugars. I need to keep up my strength with twins on the way."

Maggie grabbed a cushion and stood up. Phil ran for the stairs, but the missile caught him squarely on the back of his head causing him to trip over the first two. Laughing together, the two women collected coffee cups and glasses to stack in the dishwasher.

"Breakfast at seven thirty," said Fay. "I suppose the early hour won't bother you too much."

"We eat whenever it's convenient much of the time," Maggie said. "Night flying plays havoc with normal mealtimes. Once the two new Spencers arrive I dare say it'll be the same here. Thanks for telling me first. I'm so happy for you."

Fay said tentatively, "I think I've finally got the hang of how you two feel about each other. It's rather special."

"So's what you and Phil have. I've finally got the hang of that too."

Maggie made the morning tea and took it up to the sleeping couple who had forgotten to set their alarm. Phil carried down the luggage while Maggie and Fay made coffee and scrambled eggs on toast. The weather men promised sunshine and moderate temperatures over the holiday. An easy drive to York but no snowball fights this year!

The phone rang. Peter McGrath for Maggie.

"I know you're making an early start," he told her, "so I just wanted to say how much I enjoyed our lunch yesterday, and to wish you a merry Christmas."

"You've already wished me that."

"It's very sincere, Maggie."

"Pete, I—"

"Yes, I know. I said *sincere*, nothing else."

"Sorry. I sincerely wish you a peaceful time in the wards during the coming week."

"Not too peaceful. Got to have something to pass the time."

"How about snakes and ladders with the nurses?"

"Strip poker would be more interesting, except that most of them are men."

She chuckled. "You're an inveterate liar."

"I'll look forward to meeting up at New Year."

"If I'm not out of the country, and if I'm not flying."

"And if I'm not caught up in an outbreak of bubonic plague. The call of duty plays havoc with the call of youth."

"You should have been a Thespian."

"Then we'd never have met under those curious circumstances. I'll be in touch, and I'll hope for luck at New Year. Bye."

After replacing the receiver, Maggie stood for a few moments at the window watching the sky lightening over the sea. Peter knew someone she loved had been killed. No details, but she did not want him to think . . . She sighed. One life ended, two just beginning. The world continued to turn.

They were ready to set off by eight thirty. Phil's Range Rover was stacked with presents and travelling bags. He was grumbling about the amount of luggage women packed for a mere three-day visit when Maggie suddenly said, "I think I'll take my own car."

He looked up from closing the hatch. "I'm only joking."

"Yes . . . but I'll drive myself," she murmured, frowning. "It'll be better, more convenient."

Phil came up to her. "What's up? Are you all right?"

She looked at him without really seeing his face. "I'll . . . I'll meet you at Mum and Dad's." Taking the keys from her bag she got in her car and drove off without even a wave.

The ward was decorated with paper lanterns and plastic holly; in the day room stood a decorated tree with twinkling lights. The nurses drew the line at mistletoe, but some always mysteriously appeared each year. Father Christmas was due to tour the wards in the morning, but he had just come early to Randal, disguised as Philip Gross, the specialist who had been dealing with his case.

"I've been studying the results of your latest tests, Mr Price," he began in his usual grave manner. "It's very early days yet but you have been achieving a degree of response to physio which is quite encouraging. The human body needs time to cope with the physical injury and nervous trauma yours suffered. It goes into a state of paralysis to protect itself from further stress. We repaired the damage to your upper spine, but your nervous system has to recover at its own pace. You're well aware that therapists have been working on you in recent weeks to suggest to your body that it will be safe to try functioning normally. It appears to be responding, so I've decided to transfer you to the tri-services rehabilitation unit after this holiday break."

His thick brows met as he frowned at Randal propped up in bed. "At Headley Court there is the fullest range of equipment available to treat cases like yours and the staff are some of the most experienced in the country. It will be a long hard slog which will require determination and patience on your part. We all know you have an abundance of determination," he added caustically, "but you need to cultivate patience for any real chance of success. The staff at Headley Court will do their utmost for you, but you will have to knuckle down and give them your maximum effort."

Randal studied the man cautiously. "Maximum effort towards what?"

"Getting back on your feet."

It sounded like a bad joke; a badly misplaced metaphor. Yet this man was rarely jovial. "I'm not sure I'm taking this in."

"That's because your attitude has been negative from day one. It had to be all or nothing for you."

Randal's voice was slightly unsteady as he asked, "Are you telling me it's going to be *all*?"

"No, I'm saying that your present response to physio suggests there is a sixty per cent chance that you might eventually be able to walk with the aid of sticks. Much will depend on how long it takes to re-acquaint your body with the right responses to the signals it receives from your brain. And on your own willingness to work towards that end." As Randal made to speak he held up his hand. "Sixty per cent, Mr Price, and I emphasise the cultivation of patience. You're going to need it in the coming months."

Reeling from the impact of what had been said, Randal had some questions: "You're saying that this paralysis will go? To be able to walk it must, but how? I can't do a bloody thing now, however hard I try. This sixty per cent, does it cover my innards? Will I be rid of this damned catheter and the rest of the undercarriage? And what about sex? Will I get back to normal? What does the sixty per cent cover, for Christ's sake?"

"It's too early to give answers to any of those questions," said Gross in his familiar unexcitable manner. "All I can say is that as paralysis recedes internal organs often slowly begin to respond to controlled impulses. There's no guarantee I'm afraid, Mr Price, which is why patience is so essential. There will doubtless be temporary setbacks and you'll feel very frustrated at times. So much will depend on the success of the physiotherapy in the coming two to three months. Take a positive attitude from now on, but don't expect to run before you can walk."

"To hell with running," cried Randal, unable to smother his excitement. "If I walk again, I'll bloody well *fly*."

Philip Gross stood up. "I'll leave the RAF doctors to sort you out over that. It's their pigeon." He gave a rare smile. "Millie had better give you a bromide before you try to get airborne and come a cropper. Goodbye. I wish you well."

As the consultant departed, Randal's thoughts were performing aerobatics. If the man had said one per cent he would have had an all-out crack at it, but he had *sixty* per cent. That made it a dead cert as far as he was concerned. He would be an exemplary patient; do anything they said, swallow any muck they dished out. He would walk before the coming year was halfway through and be flying by autumn. He was going to be a normal man again. To hell with perhaps and maybe. Half measures would get him nowhere. He wanted the lot!

"Come down to earth, Mr Price," said a quiet voice.

Focusing on Millie, he said thickly, "I never dreamed . . . no one suggested . . ."

"I told you many times that it was too early to give up the ghost, but you wouldn't listen."

"No, I thought it was just shrink-talk. Jolly the patient along. I'm afraid I didn't believe a word you said to me."

"I know. Please believe this, though. Mr Gross's sixty per cent is the minimum assessment, but it could very well be no more than that."

"Not if I have anything to do with it." He was highly charged and needed some release. "You've been wonderful to put up with me. Come over here and get a kiss."

"We don't encourage that."

"I can kiss an attractive woman without any encouragement."

"I don't doubt it."

"Come on! If you're a shrink worth your salt you'll know I need to kiss someone after hearing that."

"Your wife?"

"Oh Millie, Millie, I'd never fly with you. You take far too long to grasp the basics. It's over."

"That decision was made when you were feeling suicidal. You have something to build on now."

He shook his head. "Last Christmas Eve I drove to her parents' place and begged her to come back with the kids and live with me again. I promised to sort our problems; put things right. I was whole, fit and eager, with a diamond brooch in my hand. She turned me down. What makes you think she'll want me now, sixty per cent or not? Anyway, you must be well aware that I no longer want her. My only regret is losing Neil and Lydia."

"You haven't lost them," she said gently.

"Oh, yes I have. Seeing me like this would upset them – Fiona was right about that. It's better if I make a complete break now. They have doting grandparents and a life of luxury to compensate. They'll soon forget."

"But you won't."

"No," he agreed. "It'll take me a lot longer. But *I* now have something to compensate, and I'll be too busy being a model patient to brood." He smiled. "How about that kiss?"

"I've told you the rules," she said, rising from her chair.

"Rules are made to be broken – especially at Christmas."

"You'd charm sweets from a babe, but I'm fully adult." Kissing her fingers she placed them lightly on his mouth as she prepared to leave. "I know you'll give it all you've got, but please don't lose sight of the odds. Good luck. I pity my successor," she finished with a smile.

Randal genuinely needed someone to be with; someone who fully understood what he had just been offered. He could join the others in the day room – some he could tell, others he could not – but this should be shared with someone special; shared, discussed, explored and rejoiced in. He gazed from the window at the grass and trees just visible between the jutting walls of adjacent wards. In his mind's eye he saw tarmac and a parked Chinook with a ground crew buzzing around it; the images of his life for the past twelve years. He could live with them again if he worked hard.

At Headley Court there would be other young servicemen like himself: air crew, pilots. Mixing with them would take him halfway back to the life he understood and loved. Once he got on his feet he would walk the rest of the way. It would take time; he could accept that. He would need to pass a medical board and take a flight refresher course, but he *would* get there. He was determined, this time next year, to be back where he most wanted to be. All at once, his euphoria became an ache of such incredible relief he shed tears over the intensity of it.

They were all in the day room for their elevenses. There were mince pies with the hot drinks because it was Christmas. Those paralysed from the neck down were being given their drinks by nurses, or by other patients who could use their arms. They were all in wheelchairs, and the younger ones planned to have a race around the spinal unit once the doctors went off duty. The prize was a bottle of whisky. Randal had agreed to take part, and he would now compete with his old gusto.

On the large TV screen Darcee and the Sex Bandits were performing "If the world says no, I say yes", which was this year's hit Christmas single. Appearing as another special guest was "Polly" Pollinger, fresh from the embraces of his team for scoring the winning goal against Brazil. He was surrounded by children of every race, who clutched toy parrots and smiled obediently at the cameras as they swayed to the music.

"Turn that bleedin' row off," growled an elderly painter and decorator who had fallen off a roof and would be permanently chairbound. "None of you's watching that load of long-haired ponces, are you? Pity the world don't say no to *them*. They'd have to get down to a proper job of work for once. We make heroes of the wrong bleedin' people these days!"

The patients looked up from their discussions, books, jigsaws or card games and were happy to have the TV switched off. The world they were living in here was totally divorced from the saccharine one on the screen.

Randal was trying to write a letter to John Baldwin, the station commander at Hampton, to inform him of his imminent move to Headley Court, but he was still on a high and needed to talk it all out with someone who would know what it meant to him, so concentration was difficult.

It was broken completely when a nurse approached and spoke

in his ear. "You have a visitor. We don't normally allow them out of the set hours, but she's on her way to York and we've made an exception as it's Christmas. Go to the ward where you can talk in private."

Randal was uneasy as he wheeled himself down the long ward. Surely Fiona had not taken it into her head to come. No, they would have said "your wife". Who the hell had come visiting *en route* to York? Not his mother. She would be too busy with the festivities and she had already sent him a huge arrangement of flowers and a Fortnum's hamper. She really had no idea! There was only one other person he knew with connections in York, and she would hardly come here after the way he had behaved last time. But she had, and he felt a sharp shaft of pleasure at the sight of her.

"I was on my way home for Christmas, so I thought I'd just look in to see how you are," Maggie said with unusual gravity.

"You're the answer to a bloody prayer," he told her fervently. "The one person who'll understand. Just listen to this!"

They sat together while Randal shared the news that had changed his despair to hopeful determination. Maggie's face glowed with excitement as they explored the long path that would surely lead to his complete rehabilitation, and she agreed that he could be back in the air by autumn.

"What a wonderful Christmas present! I can't wait to tell the team. They've been uncertain about getting in touch. You know. Maybe it would—"

"I know. It probably would have."

"But they'll get up to Headley Court when they can."

"When they're not in Bosnia, Northern Ireland, on a NATO exercise, on a course, out in the desert or keeping Judge Jeffries happy by prancing all over a squash court."

"Or propping up the bar."

"What's the news, Maggie?" he asked, already back in the familiar world. "What've the buggers been up to?"

Maggie gave him a complete rundown including the airlift under fire. Then she brought him up to date on station scandal, and Randal forgot the wheelchair and the significance of his surroundings as he laughed at anecdotes of the life they shared.

"You'll find Andy Forbes is OK," he said eventually. "Not a rule-book man, thank God. Used to be a terrible practical joker at Cranwell, but he's sure to have grown out of that if he's been made responsible for you lot."

In a swift change of mood, Maggie said softly, "A responsible bastard where your team's concerned."

He had said that to her on a balmy evening in Frau Spiegel's beer garden. She had worn red and had engaged him in provocative verbal combat. His mood quietened too. "Well, wasn't I?"

"You will be again, Boss."

Studying the girl in jeans and fluffy blue jumper, Randal slowly grew aware of something that must have been there, unrecognised, for quite a while. "Maggie, your nav's gone badly wrong today. This is way off course for York. What are you doing here?"

There was confusion in her eyes as she said hesitantly, "Just as I was setting out – about two hours ago – I got a . . . a magic message."

It startlingly confirmed what he had just realised, but it was completely the wrong bloody time. He had a long way to go, and she was nowhere near ready. Yet her infallible ESP could not be dismissed.

"You know what that means, don't you?" he asked softly.

"No. I . . . I'm not sure."

Forcing himself to be a responsible bastard, he smiled reassuringly. "You can't possibly fly with just a navigator."